MONSTER PLANET

DAVID WELLINGTON

MONSTER PLANET

A ZOMBIE NOVEL

RUNNING PRESS
PHILADELPHIA • LONDON

ACKNOWLEDGMENTS

I NEED TO say thank you to everyone who helped make this book a reality. If your name doesn't appear below, please, know how grateful I really am for all your help and support. It made all the difference.

Here are some names, in no particular order: Adrian, Ashnack, digbeta, Raul, Don, briangc, Meek, Laura, Pencil Lad, Mike, bagelgod, Donny D, saketini99, Ed Adkins, Javier, Timmy, Alnjo, liam, Scarecrow, shadowfusion99, Ann Towey, davidkaye929, iGame3D, Carlos, Rakie, Senecal, Mendoza, dreadlocksmile, hearwritenow, Joel Carroll, and marbotty.

I need to send a very special thanks to Mark Frauenfelder, who liked my first book so much he helped me get it published.

John Oakes, my publisher, gets a big thank-you for taking a chance on all of us.

My wife, Elisabeth, needs to be thanked profusely.

As always I need to thank Alex Lencicki. This couldn't have happened without him.

MONSTER PLANET

PART
ONE

1.

AYAAN SHOVED THE helicopter's cargo loading door open with one booted foot, and dry desert air rushed into the body of the helicopter. The aircraft wobbled and soldiers grabbed for stanchions and nylon loops to steady themselves, but Ayaan just shifted her footing. The warrior stuck her head out into the blue sky, the graying ringlets of her hair bouncing in the wind. Her face wrinkled as she squinted at the burning sands. There were people down there—alive or dead, she couldn't tell—and they were advancing in the direction of her encampment. For once this was no false alarm. "Get me a close approach," she shouted.

From his position at the controls Osman didn't turn to answer, but the crew all heard him over their radio headsets. "Of course, girl. How close would you like? Do you want to smell them?"

Ayaan ignored him, instead turning to Sarah. She gave the younger woman a warm smile and beckoned her to come over. "Don't worry," she said, "I won't let you fall out."

Sarah moved to the open door of the Mi-8 and leaned out over the fuel pods. She needed to get a better look at the army below them, without the interference of the copter's fuselage between her and the mob. Fifty feet below, gray arms strained toward the helicopter as if they could grab it and pull it down from the sky. The dead have lousy depth perception.

"I need an estimate of their strength," Ayaan demanded. "Are they fresh?"

Sarah studied the crowd as Osman slewed the copter around in a wide turn over them. This army had come out of nowhere. The dead rarely announced their movements, but a group this size required some kind of coordination. Mindless ghouls didn't work together unless some strong will was directing them. What they had come for was a mystery. What Sarah did know was that Ayaan wouldn't allow it. This little stretch of the coastline of Egypt was her nation, maybe the last nation of the living left on Earth. She wasn't about to let the dead take it for themselves. Ayaan had always prophesied that something like this would happen. For years they had drilled for exactly this kind of attack, and finally, inevitably, it had come. They had scrambled the copter the moment the first reports of movement on the perimeter had come in.

Now Ayaan wanted Sarah's opinion about how to proceed. Sarah was younger, just out of her teens, so she had better eyes. She also had other senses that Ayaan lacked.

Trying to ignore the howling of the wind outside the helicopter, the glare of the sun on the sand, Sarah pulled the hood of her sweatshirt up to cover her hair. She focused her attention on the parts of her that could sense death, just as she'd been taught. The hair on the back of her neck and on her forearms. The sensitive skin behind her ears.

She closed her eyes but she kept looking.

What she saw startled her. The ground below teemed with purplish energy, dark splotches where the dead smoldered, cold and hungry. But between those shadows burned beacons of golden light, stronger, more vital—alive. Impossible. The dead and the living couldn't work in close proximity. The dead existed only to devour life. Still. She saw what she saw. Even as she attempted to process what that meant, she saw one of the golden shapes moving, lifting something to its eye. Something held with both hands. She opened her eyes and saw a living man with pale white skin aiming a rifle right at her.

"Look out!" she shouted into her microphone, loud enough to make herself wince. Before anyone could respond, a bullet tore upward through the fuselage of the Mi-8, barely missing the foot of one of Ayaan's soldiers. The woman shrieked and jumped backward as automatic rounds tore through the thin skin of the copter's belly. Light shot upward into the cabin wherever a bullet came through, streaking the dark cool space inside. Noise drummed along the deck plates, pattered on the helicopter's roof. Ayaan started shouting orders, but Osman was ahead of her. The helicopter banked around so hard, Sarah could hear the airframe wanting to come apart. The pilot yanked back on his control yoke and they popped up into the air like a cork out of a bottle, gaining altitude fast enough to make Sarah's stomach curl up on itself like an injured animal. She swallowed back the vomit that rushed up her throat and lifted one hand to try to brush the sweat from her forehead. She stopped in mid-gesture, though, when she saw that her hand was sticky with blood.

Terrified of looking, too scared not to, she turned slowly around. The interior of the helicopter had been painted bright red. Blood had pooled between the crew seats and was draining slowly through maybe a hundred narrow bullet holes. What remained of a dead woman lay sprawled across the deck, one shattered, thumbless hand so close to Sarah she could have reached down and held it. She felt a perverse desire to do just that.

It was Mariam. The expert sniper of the platoon. It had been Mariam. It wouldn't be for long.

The hand twitched. Closed into a loose fist. The dead soldier convulsed upward, her shoulders rolling as she sat up to look at Sarah with blank eyes. Her mouth opened wide, blood spilling out from between her teeth. Most of her rib cage on the left side had been blown away. She definitely wasn't breathing.

It could happen that quickly. Sarah had witnessed the rise of the dead before. Ayaan had taught her what to do about it. She took her pistol out of her pocket and lined up a shot with the dead woman's forehead. Even as the new ghoul lunged at her she fired. A little splutter of blood burst from the woman's right temple. It wasn't a solid kill. She could feel the ghoul looming over her, getting closer.

They were slow but deadly—a single scratch or bite would be enough. Her fingers shook as she lifted her weapon and tried to aim.

Ayaan rushed Mariam and grabbed her by one shoulder and her remaining hip. "Cover," she shouted at Sarah. Sarah protected her face and head from clawing fingernails as Ayaan rushed Mariam out of the open cargo door. Her undead body pinwheeled down to smack the sand in the midst of the army below.

Ayaan and Mariam had been together since they were schoolgirls, since before they had gotten their first periods. Since before they had learned how to shoot. Nobody said a word in protest or outrage. The thing Ayaan had dumped into the sky wasn't Mariam anymore, and they all knew it. It was just that kind of a world, and it had been for twelve hard years.

Osman kept climbing until they were well out of range of the guns below. The dead kept reaching for the helicopter, but the living stopped firing and they were safe again. "Firearms," Ayaan said, wagging her jaw around to pop her ears. "The dead don't shoot."

Sarah steeled herself. She needed to be part of this conversation. "There were living people down there, too. Maybe a third as many as the dead. They were all carrying rifles. I don't claim to know how that works."

Ayaan nodded. "We knew there had to be one of them providing close support." One of them. A *khasiis*. The Somali word meant "monster." English-speakers used the word *lich*. The not-so-mindless dead. When a ghoul managed one way or another to preserve its intellect postmortem, it also tended to develop certain new faculties. It learned to see the energy of death, just like Sarah had. Some of them learned to control other undead, to communicate with them telepathically and bend them to their monstrous wills. Ayaan had some experience with liches. She had shot one in the head years prior, one named Gary. Gary had not only survived that shot, he'd gone on to enslave an entire city. It took a raging inferno to finally bring Gary down, and Ayaan had lost plenty of friends in the process. One of those friends had been Sarah's father. "There must be a top-level asset nearby," Ayaan said.

"Top-level is right, if he can override their natural instinct to devour the living." Fathia, Ayaan's second in command, leaned her chin on the stock of her assault rifle and looked scared. "Gary could do that, for a little while. But even he had limits. If this army has been moving together for a long time, marching together—it would take a stronger *khasūs* than Gary. And there's only one of those that we know about."

"The Russian," Ayaan said. Her eyes narrowed to thin, angry slits. "The Tsarevich."

Sarah knew it had to be true. But what would the world's most preeminent monster be doing in Egypt? Everyone knew the boy lich's story. He'd been injured in a car accident, a hit-and-run, back when there had still been cars. He had languished in a semicomatose state for years in a hospital bed, half-dead even before the Epidemic began. When the dead rose, the boy was abandoned where he lay, only to die and rise again with his intellect intact—and with new senses and abilities, new supernatural powers no one had ever seen before.

They said he had an army of the dead and a cult of the living, and that in some parts of Siberia he was considered to be the Second Coming of Jesus Christ. The stories about him always revolved around his cruelty and his power. They made him sound like a devil. For himself he claimed only to be a Tsarevich, a Prince of the Dead. Everyone knew the stories, but no one thought he would ever come so far.

"He came here himself," Ayaan said. "He's here now." Her cold eyes lit up but grew no warmer. "He has made a mistake."

2.

AYAAN HAD A responsibility to the survivors—the living—she had left outside Port Said. She could have ordered Osman at any time to circle back and provide air support for the camp. She didn't. The other women in the helicopter started to trade sidelong glances, the occasional half question. "We've never fought an enemy with guns before. Shouldn't we regroup, get some reinforcements?" Leyla asked.

Ayaan glared back at them. Some of Mariam's blood still flecked her cheek. "The camp is hardened against attack, if that's even what he's after. If we give him a chance to get away now, we'll never see him again. We're going to find the Russian, today, and we're going to remove him from play."

It was enough for most of the soldiers. Ayaan had led them into stranger encounters and she had proven her tactical brilliance a hundred times over. If she said she knew what she was doing, they believed her. Sarah wasn't so sure, but she kept it to herself. The women remembered her father with respect, but that had never rubbed off on her. As the youngest member of Ayaan's unit and the only non-Somali, her opinion counted for little. Still, she couldn't help having a bad feeling.

Ayaan had always been more than cautious. She'd bordered on paranoia in the past—and it had kept her people alive. Now she was throwing herself into the lion's maw. It made no sense.

"I've got visual confirmation of a second group," Osman called over the headset band. "Smaller . . . maybe fifty individuals."

"Close with them but keep an eye on the floor." Ayaan had a pair of field glasses in her hand. They had been designed to provide night vision, but the batteries had died years before. They still worked as binoculars in broad daylight. Her voice turned to ice cubes slithering out of a pitcher. "There."

Sarah moved forward hand over hand, grabbing at the nylon loops sewn into the headrests of the crew seats. In the cockpit of the Mi-8 she could look down through the chin bubble and see what Ayaan was talking about. About fifty people—almost all of them dead—were laboring up the side of a sand dune below her. Most of them were tugging on thick lines, dragging behind them a flatbed railcar kitted out with enormous balloon tires. On its back crouched a kind of tent, maybe a yurt. Some .50 caliber machine guns in universal mounts stuck out from the sides of the flatbed, while in the middle ghouls stood at enormous cranks, adjusting the flatbed's suspension as it pitched over the dune.

The flap of the yurt fell back and someone emerged from the shadowy interior. Then something happened to the light in the helicopter, to Sarah's eyes, and to her more subtle senses. She looked again at the figure in the yurt's entrance. Though she was still five hundred meters away, Sarah could make out his features perfectly. She felt as if she were looking through binoculars, though she wasn't. He was a boy—shorter even than herself, maybe ten or twelve years old. He was astonishingly beautiful.

His skin was so white it stood out as bluish in the desert sun. His complexion was perfectly clear, his hair a pale gold lighter than his skin. His large, soulful eyes smoldered with blue flame. He wore the armor of a medieval warrior, scaled down to fit his frame and enameled in glossy black worked with a motif of bones and creeping vines. In his right hand he carried a scepter topped with a bleached human skull. Sapphires winked from its dark eye sockets.

He looked right at Sarah. Not just in her direction but right at her, making perfect eye contact. Which was when she realized something was wrong.

"Grab something, ladies," Osman called just as he swung the Mi-8 around. The machine guns mounted on the flatbed blasted tracer fire through the air, yellow sparks that arced up and tried to touch the aircraft. Fathia leaped up out of her seat even as the bullets tore past so close Sarah was dazzled by their flickering light. The soldier started yanking assault rifles down from the rack at the front of the cargo bay and tossing them to her squad mates. Ayaan unstrapped herself and picked up the oilcloth bundle of her own weapon. The same AK-47 she'd carried since she'd left school.

Osman had never before impressed Sarah by displaying courage but he didn't shrink from Ayaan's orders—perhaps the two of them shared some secret reason for acting so irrationally. The pilot opened up the copter's throttle and pushed forward on the yoke, throwing the Mi-8 right at the flatbed with all the power the dual power plants could muster. Soldiers leaned out of the crew door and the rear loading ramp, secured from a deadly fall to the sands below only by their safety lines. The air in the helicopter vibrated with the noise of their weapons discharging again and again and again. As quickly as that, they were in the midst of battle.

One of the ghouls working the flatbed's cranks slumped against its wheel, its head a dark smear. The flatbed slewed to one side. The Russian's troops retaliated by spraying bullets across the fuselage of the helicopter and shattering one of the portholelike windows on the starboard flank. "Again, and closer this time," Ayaan shrieked as she slapped a full magazine into her rifle and tested its iron sights.

"I'll take you right up his nose if you like, and leave you there," Osman replied, but he wheeled around for another pass. He brought the aircraft in low and fast, almost losing his landing gear as they brushed the top of the yurt. Ayaan's rifle snapped and spat with tight, perfectly controlled bursts of three bullets each. The ghouls dragging the flatbed scattered away from her fire, but not fast enough. Heads burst, bodies spun and fell. One of the machine gunners slipped and fell onto the sand, his blood jetting from his ruptured chest.

Sarah stared at the boy standing on the flatbed. He looked like the soul of calm. The fusillade of bullets hadn't even ruffled his thin white hair. There was something not quite right about his energy. It was dark, of course, the boy was undead, a lich among liches, and his energy swallowed light like a black hole, but . . . what was it? Sarah couldn't quite decide. But something was wrong.

Bullet holes appeared in the floor of the helicopter, and Leyla hurried to throw an armored blanket of rubberized Kevlar across the deck plates to give the soldiers a little protection. As the helicopter swung out and away from the flatbed and beyond the range of the remaining machine gun, Sarah clipped her safety line to a tie-down on the floor and tried to grab Ayaan's arm. "Whoa, whoa," she said, trying to roll with the helicopter as it banked, hard, "there's something—" she shouted, but her poorly fitted helmet had gone askew on her head and she couldn't hear her own voice over the engine roar. "Ayaan!" she shrieked.

Ayaan wasted no more time. On the third pass she switched her weapon to full automatic and emptied a clip into the Russian boy, her arms tracking him with the precision of a machine. The wooden flatbed around him splintered and spat dust, but he didn't even glance at Ayaan. No, his eyes were still fastened on Sarah's. He was still looking at her. Into her.

In the cockpit lights blared on Osman's control boards and a bell clanged urgently. The machine gunner on the flatbed had scored a real hit, blasting open one of the Mi-8's fuel pods. Automatic fire-control systems and self-sealing bladders in the fuel system shunted into action and kept the helicopter from exploding, but blue flames lit up the fuselage and burning spatters of kerosene leaped into the open crew cabin.

"Ayaan, he's not—he isn't—" Sarah had trouble concentrating on the words. The boy's gaze compelled her, made her look at him again. She saw so much intelligence in his cheekbones, so much sorrow in his bluish lips. He was hypnotizing her, she knew it, and she knew how to fight it, but it made it difficult to talk.

She looked up and saw that Ayaan had picked up an RPG-7V from the weapons rack. She slammed a bulbous rocket-propelled grenade into the launcher and lifted the optical sight to her eye.

Sarah glanced behind her and realized that the port-side crew door was still closed. If Ayaan discharged the RPG inside the helicopter, the exhaust blast would blow back against the door and fry them all with superheated gas. Focused so completely on her target, Ayaan had transcended such concerns.

Unclipping her safety line, Sarah pitched across the width of the cabin and pulled hard on the door release just as Ayaan acquired her target and squeezed her trigger. Exhaust bloomed out of the conical jet at the back of the launcher and blew away on the wind. Sarah looked down through the open door and watched the grenade jet toward its target. Finally the boy looked away from her, instead turning to face the projectile. He raised his wand as if he could ward off the explosive. It didn't work.

A brown cloud boiled up off the surface of the flatbed, a welter of splinters and debris. One of the machine gun mounts went flying, spinning end over end away from the flatbed. The dead men still tirelessly turning their cranks spasmed in place as debris peppered their bodies and threw them against their wheels.

When the smoke cleared, a meter-wide hole could be seen in the top of the flatbed, a gaping crater where there had been solid wood. Standing in the middle of the hole was the Russian boy. His cheeks weren't even smudged with soot.

No, Sarah realized, he wasn't standing in the crater. He was floating above it. He hadn't moved, literally—he was floating in midair even though the flatbed had been blown out from under him. Sarah studied him with her occult senses and breathed an oath. She struggled to get her helmet back on straight. "That's not him—it's a projection, Ayaan, a mental projection! Just an illusion."

"*Seelka meicheke,*" Ayaan swore. She threw the launcher down to the deck of the helicopter with a clang. Osman backed off, out of firearms range, though the remaining machine gun on the flatbed was spinning free and unattended. Every eye in the helicopter looked to Ayaan.

"All right," Ayaan said, after a moment. "Osman, set down on top of that dune." She pointed at a rising swell of the desert maybe a kilometer away.

The women in the cargo bay looked at each other and some of them gasped. Fear gripped Sarah too tightly to let her utter a word. If she could have, she would have asked Ayaan if she had suddenly lost her mind. The helicopter provided the only real advantage the living possessed against the dead—the ability to fly away. If they put down now, with an army of the dead within striking range, they would have no real protection at all.

Osman knew a direct order when he heard it, though, and did what he was told.

3.

AYAAN KNELT AND touched the sand, then her heart, then her forehead. It was a very old gesture, one that predated the Epidemic: she was thanking the Earth, her mother, and her God for the right to make war. The other women hurried to copy her, but Sarah refused to go along. "OK, so this is stupid," she muttered. She knew she sounded whiny and selfish, but she couldn't help it. "Someone tell me why we're doing this again? The ultimate lich of all time is over that hill and we're going to stand here and fight him on foot. Even though we have a helicopter and we could just leave."

"You have never understood what orders mean," Fathia said, rising to her feet, her rifle swinging in her arms. The barrel wasn't pointed at Sarah—it never would be, not unless Fathia truly intended to kill the younger woman—but the implied threat was meant to be taken seriously. "You were a foundling that she took like her own child, and you cry like you are still a baby."

Sarah started to respond, but Ayaan raised her hands for silence, and she got it. "Do you know why we came to Egypt?" she asked, her voice low, soft as the sand under their feet.

"There was nothing to eat in Somalia," Sarah replied. It was true. When the dead rose, when the Epidemic came, famine had already ransacked the Horn of Africa. With few living people left to raise crops, the food shortages had turned into outright starvation. Egypt, with its modernized cities full of markets and groceries, had promised at least some preserved foods. Cans and jars full of tinned meat and pickled vegetables. Ayaan had brought her unit out of Somalia in the hopes of a better life and she had delivered on her promise.

"To survive," Fathia answered. "To rebuild."

Ayaan nodded. "We've come so far. I won't be driven out now."

A protest bubbled out of Sarah's heart. "We're in danger. When we find ourselves in danger we fall back to a defensible position. You taught me that."

A smile touched Ayaan's tight face. "I'm glad to see you listened. Perhaps you will take another lesson. There are times, however rare, when running away is a mistake. This Russian, this Tsarevich, the Prince of Death, he grows stronger every day. If I do not stop his evil now, when I have a chance, I may not be able to face him the next time. Today I will kill him. If he has the ability to project images of himself then I am forced to go after him on foot, so that I can feel his skull breaking and know I have finished the job."

"So let's call in some backup. Get the others in here, get some free-fire zones established, maybe build a redoubt to funnel his advance—"

"Sarah," Ayaan interrupted.

"No, seriously, we can get the other helicopter down here in twenty, maybe thirty minutes, we can establish a killzone, then draw him into—"

"Sarah." Ayaan closed her eyes and shook her head. "Please go wait with Osman."

Stunned, Sarah finally shut up. She couldn't believe it. Ayaan had uttered the ultimate insult—she had announced that Sarah was useless. That she didn't want Sarah around during the fight. It was the kind of thing Ayaan would say to a child, a baby.

There was also no appeal to be made. Once Ayaan had given an order she never took it back. Feeling the stares of Fathia and Leyla and the others on her back, she retreated to the helicopter. It occurred to her when she was halfway there that she should have just been quiet, should have accepted Ayaan's command without question, the way the others did. It also occurred to her that if she was in the helicopter she was less likely to get killed.

She was thinking such thoughts, her head lowered in dejection, when something fast and horrible smacked into her like a moving car. She fell down hard on the sand as something colorless and violent and extremely fast reared up over her, its stubby arms lifted high, its shining head sparkling in the sunlight. She knew, was absolutely certain, that in the next few microseconds she was going to die a quick but extremely painful death. She closed her eyes but she could still see the aura of the dead thing that was about to kill her. Its energy was like nothing she'd ever seen before. It was dark, of course, cold and hungry like any ghoul's. But instead of smoking and hissing and sizzling away like ice melting in the sun, this energy fizzed and snapped like something on fire. Its shape was wrong, too, something was missing—

She heard gunfire and it fell away from her, out of her vision. One of Ayaan's squad had saved her. She opened her eyes and saw a still-moving body sliding down the slip-face of a dune. Its arms pumped wildly at the air, moving so fast they blurred. Impossible—the dead lacked the energy to move like that. They were slow, lumbering, uncoordinated wrecks.

This one could have caught a hummingbird in mid-flight and swallowed it whole in the space between two wing strokes.

Getting a good look at it wasn't easy, but Sarah could make out some details. The dead thing had been kneecapped by automatic rifle fire and would never walk again. It was naked, its skin gray and shrunken on its bones. Its lips had either rotten away or been cut back, revealing a pale stretch of jawbone. The better to bite with, Sarah supposed. It wore a miner's helmet, complete with a broken lamp, to protect its vulnerable cranium. Its hands—oh God—its hands had been cut off, leaving bloodless, ragged stumps. The bones of its forearms had been sharpened into vicious spikes.

Nausea washed up from her stomach into her throat, but Sarah held herself together. The dead felt little pain, she knew, but they also lacked the manual dexterity for that kind of surgery. It had to have been a living person who had cut those hands off.

"Two o'clock," Leyla called. Sarah managed to turn away from the horror below her to see a new one in front of her. The body of an undead man stood atop a dune a hundred meters from her position. His skin had collapsed on his skeleton so that all she could see of his face was bone. At least he had hands, though they were equally skeletonized. He wore a flapping and fluttering green robe, a little like a burnoose, more like a medieval monk's habit. He leaned on a heavy walking staff that was made of three human femurs, fused end to end.

A lich. Not one of the mindless puppets Sarah had seen reaching for the helicopter but a lich, a real lich, a dead man with an intact brain, as smart as any human and more than likely possessing powers indistinguishable from magic. It was the greatest of the Tsarevich's crimes that he not only destroyed the living but changed them, making them over to suit his designs. He had made the handless ghoul, just as he had made liches to be his lieutenants.

Sarah had survived dozens of raids against the undead and hundreds of attacks by hungry corpses. She didn't spook easily. She'd never seen a lich before, though, and the apparition chilled her right to her guts.

"I gave you an order," Ayaan said. She wasn't looking at Sarah. She had her AK-47 up to her eye and she was lining up a head shot. The green phantom was at long range, though, and Sarah knew Ayaan's chances of a clean kill were slim.

The robed monster raised its free hand to point at the women before it. One bony finger stabbed out at them across the sand. Sarah could feel dark energy streaming from it like light through broken clouds. Rolling up over the dunes, bouncing, bounding for them on all fours, a dark shape zipped across the sand. Another came up behind its green master, launched itself at the women.

"Fall back," Ayaan said. The women started, slowly, to come out of their battle postures. "Everyone fall back."

Sarah tried to move but was compelled to watch a third speeding shape jump over the dunes. A fourth, a fifth, and a sixth came along in close order. One of them wore a motorcycle helmet with the visor closed—she got half a look at it before it accelerated right for her.

A warm and yielding arm—with a hand on the end of it—scythed across her stomach and knocked her off her feet. It was Fathia, Ayaan's second in command. She picked up Sarah like a rucksack and bodily flung her into the helicopter's cargo space. Lying on her stomach, Sarah looked out across the sand. She saw the female soldiers running toward her, running toward the aircraft. The accelerated ghouls, moving like time-lapse movies of what they should be, were running faster.

"Get us out of here," Fathia screamed at Osman. The pilot was already flipping switches on his control panel. One of the speeding ghouls skidded to a stop not fifty meters away and looked right at the helicopter. It saw them—Sarah could feel its attention, its desire.

One soldier, then another, jumped into the helicopter. Sarah watched three of the sped-up ghouls collide on top of Leyla, their sharpened talons stabbing into her again and again like mechanical pistons. Her blood spilled out on the sand, and the smell of death brushed up against Sarah's nose. There were others losing their individual battles with the blurred monsters. Where was Ayaan? Sarah could hear her screaming but she couldn't see her.

"Go now, go now, go now," Fathia chanted, leaning out of the loading door, scanning the dune for the women who hadn't made it to the helicopter. Sarah found herself chanting the words, too. The fast ghoul was heading for them, galloping across the sand. If he got inside the helicopter it would take him only moments to kill them all.

But where was Ayaan? Sarah couldn't see her. She pushed her attention outward, as she'd been taught, searching for any sign of the commander. There—she heard something. "*Cantuug tan!*" Ayaan's voice. She sounded distant, her words torn at by the desert wind. Had she surged forward to try to take down the green phantom? Any further instructions she might have were lost in the noise of the rotors spinning up. Before the fast ghoul could reach the Mi-8 Osman had it airborne and banking away.

Only half of the crew seats were filled. No one protested or asked the pilot to go back for the missing soldiers—they knew better. It was just that kind of world. It had been for twelve years.

4.

THE HELICOPTER SET down in the middle of the camp near Port Said, five kilometers away from where Ayaan had died. Osman put it down gently between its twin and the third, smaller copter that had broken down a year before and was kept now only for spare parts. Sarah took the rifles from the women who'd made it out and checked their safeties, then loaded them back into the weapons rack. As the official mascot of Ayaan's squad, it fell to her to do all the heavy lifting, even though she lacked the muscle mass of the soldiers. It was also her job to clean the blood out of the cargo bay but she couldn't even fathom how she would do that. She couldn't begin to think of what she was going to do next. She jumped down from the helicopter's deck and felt the hard heavy lump of her weapon in her pocket. She took out the flat Makarov PM and released the magazine from the grip and let the slide move forward until it locked in the open position. Checking to make sure there was no round in the chamber, she put the magazine in one pocket and the pistol in the other. She did all this without the slightest thought, just as she'd done it hundreds of times before. Ayaan had forced her to practice, to do it fast, to do it the same way every time. Ayaan.

Sarah had no idea what to do next.

Ayaan was gone. Dead—Ayaan was dead. She might be wandering out in the desert that very moment, mindless, hungry, unfeeling. Or maybe the fast ghouls had devoured her entirely. Dead. Either way . . . either way there was no one left to tell her what to do. She couldn't remember another time like that. If she thought back far enough she could remember her father, she could remember pushing her face into the softness of his shirt, the smell of his sweat as he held her against his chest. She could remember him running, moving, she could remember her mother not being with them anymore. After that, every memory she had revolved around Ayaan. She ran her hands over her cropped hair, scratched at her scalp with her nails. She didn't know what to do.

"Hey, help me with this," Osman said.

She wheeled around and saw him crouched down by the ruined fuel pod on the side of the aircraft. He looked up at her with an expression of such concern and compassion that she wondered if it was actually pity he felt. Her cheeks burned and she moved quickly to help him disassemble the pod, unbolting it from the airframe with a socket wrench. She caught the webbing between her thumb and index finger in the rough metal and pain lanced up her arm. It cleared her mind out in a hurry.

"I'm hungry, do you want something? I have a can of stewed tomatoes I've been saving for a rainy day." Osman didn't look at her this time, which was almost worse. "Listen, little girl, we're alive, and that counts for something, that's an achievement in a world like this." His arm slipped around her shoulders and she started to shove him away, then relented. After a moment she turned into him, pressed her body against his in an actual embrace. Osman had been in her life as long as she could remember, too. If Ayaan had been like a big sister to her, Osman had been her uncle. It was good to smell the kif smoke that cured his frayed shirt, good to feel his body heat. "We'll get by," he told her, "just as we always have. God and his Prophet must not want us so badly if he let us live this long, right?"

She nodded and broke away from him. He went to get his tomatoes, but as it worked out she didn't have a chance to share in his feast. An eight-year-old boy dressed in a pair of shorts and flip-flops came running in, out of breath, to tell her Fathia wanted her up at the perimeter wire. She went right away.

The boy led her through the open-air market of the encampment, a close space of stalls lined with broken cinder blocks where the elderly sorted through cans looking for signs of botulism or corruption. Alma, one of the women from Ayaan's unit, was washing her face in a pan full of sandy water from the communal well as Sarah hurried by. She looked up and then looked away again as if to pretend she hadn't seen Sarah at all.

There was no time to figure out what that meant. Sarah hurried down a long "street" lined on both sides with semipermanent tent homes. At the far end she found Fathia under a moth-eaten awning, leaning over a map of the surrounding territory. Other soldiers lay on the ground nearby in the shade of the palisade wall, trying to get some rest.

The boy who had brought Sarah to the new commander crawled under the map table and dug his fingers into the loose dirt. His job was done.

Fathia cleared her throat.

"I'm in command now, of course. I have some work to do before I can take the girls out again, though. I've got to rebuild the unit with half the soldiers I used to have," Fathia said, as if she wanted Sarah's input. Sarah knew she did not. "That's all right, we'll be faster. Smarter. I can't see a use for you in that structure so I'm restricting you to camp duties," Fathia said, rinsing her mouth out with non-potable water and spitting on the ground. "I hope that will be acceptable."

"Actually Ayaan always felt I should be out in the field, that that was where my talent was really useful." Sarah's stomach rumbled with a bad presentiment. If she couldn't go out with the soldiers, her usefulness to Fathia would be distinctly curtailed. In the Egyptian encampment one rule had always held: the most useful people ate first. Those who couldn't do anything valuable, those who were seen as dead weight, went hungry.

She looked again at the boy under the table. She could count his ribs, but his belly stuck out like a swollen gourd. His eyes were moist. Had he been crying? It could help with the hunger pangs. She remembered how it helped.

Fathia clucked her tongue, and Sarah looked back at the soldier hurriedly, embarrassed she had broken eye contact even for a moment. "Yes, she did say that. Of course," Fathia went on, pointing out a flaw in Sarah's logic, "Ayaan is no longer here to make those kinds of decisions. I hope you won't have trouble accepting *my* orders. I know that obedience isn't your strength."

Of course the only thing worse than being dead weight was

being insubordinate. "No, no, ma'am, that'll be no problem. You're the boss."

"I suppose I am," Fathia said, looking up in mock surprise. "Well, let's put your talent to some real use. I need someone to stand watch. That mixed group of dead and living we saw could be here as early as midnight."

It meant staying up all night, mercilessly pinching her legs every time she started to nod off. It meant being up in the wind and the sand and spitting out dust for days afterward. She didn't complain. It meant she wouldn't be dead weight, at least not that day.

If she didn't get to sleep that night at least she wasn't alone. As the sun sank over the western desert, the camp was lit up with oil lamps and sporadic electric lights. The fuel for both was precious and it was never burned just because someone had trouble sleeping. Both helicopters were kept on standby, Osman and the other pilots sleeping sitting up in their crew seats. Armed soldiers patrolled the streets of the encampment looking for anything out of the ordinary. They shouted gossip back and forth—nothings, empty statements, assurances that all was as it should be. The need for that affirmation hung in the air like a seagull flying into a breeze.

The camp wanted to know what happened next. Even those who could no longer lift a rifle or thrust a bayonet had to know, had to get the news. Were they all about to die? Would they be overrun that night? For twelve years each of them had somehow managed to stay alive while the darkness crowded with monsters waiting to take them apart. They had survived even when so many others had died. They could only wait and ask themselves if this was the night that changed. Up in her observation post, a bare platform of wooden planking high in a dead palm tree, Sarah could only watch the horizon and wonder herself. Always before when she'd stood watch up in the air like that, she'd felt pretty safe. The dead didn't climb trees, and the occasional ghoul who tried to attack the camp would never get through the palisade of barbed wire. Now, though, they were facing living opponents armed with rifles. She was a sitting duck up there, only the dark color of her hooded sweatshirt protecting her from snipers. Maybe that was why Fathia wanted her up in the tree.

She knew that Fathia didn't trust her because of her ability to see the energy of the dead. She knew the soldiers spoke about her behind her back, talked about how spooky she was. Now that Ayaan wasn't around to protect her, did they want to put her in harm's way, did they want to kill her off?

The thought kept her alert most of the night. She never saw any sign of the marching army. She got to the point of expecting them, of hoping they would come just to end her watch. They didn't come. The encampment must not have been their target. Just before dawn she dozed a little, her eyelids fluttering up and down, her chin jerking spasmodically every time she nearly but not quite fell asleep. Nothing had happened. Nothing was going to happen.

In that half-awake state her esoteric senses were at their strongest. She dreamed of the dark flicker of energy beyond the wire before she saw it. Her eyes shot open and adrenaline blasted through her veins. She nearly fell out of her perch.

It wasn't an army. It was just one ghoul. Still, she reached for the whistle around her neck. The slaughter on the dunes had started with just one ghoul attacking her. Maybe there were more nearby. Maybe hundreds of them. She couldn't feel them, couldn't sense their energy, but—

The single ghoul below her came to a lurching stop and looked up, right at her. It raised one hand to its mouth, placed a rotting finger against its lips. Asking her for silence. Then, with its other hand, it beckoned to her. Slowly, it turned around and headed back out into the darkness.

Shit, Sarah thought.

She couldn't imagine a worse time to be summoned.

5.

GETTING OVER THE palisade wasn't easy.

Ayaan had designed the wall to be impassible for hungry ghouls: a double thickness of concertina wire wrapped all the way around the camp, creating a dry moat three meters wide between them. Inside the aisle between these two impediments the soldiers had dumped a jumble of broken concrete and rebar, the rusted iron turned outward to impale careless intruders. There was no gate in the palisade anywhere—you left the encampment the same way you came back, via helicopter, or you just stayed put. A smart human could get through the mess eventually if he had a pair of very sturdy bolt cutters and plenty of time. Even then he would leave obvious signs of his passage.

The first time Jack had come to her in Egypt, Sarah had left him waiting in the desert for days while she figured out how to escape without being detected. She couldn't just ignore his call. He had taught her how to see the energy of the dead, her one true talent. Without him she would have perished long before. She couldn't tell Ayaan about her comings and goings, either, so she'd had to be crafty. She had volunteered for her current job of cleaning and fueling the helicopters. When the pilots weren't looking she had stolen one of the Kevlar blankets they used to armor the interior cabins of the Mi-8s. Sarah had stripped the heavy blanket of its inset metal plates and then draped the remaining Kevlar over the wire, then scrambled up and over her makeshift stile.

She had repeated the stunt many times since. Often enough to get away with it, even with the camp on heightened alert. Once she was out on the open sand, though, she began to feel a very familiar fear. Unprotected by Ayaan, unable to properly defend herself, she would be easy prey for any wandering ghoul who happened to smell her on the wind. Anyone else probably would have been eaten years ago. Sarah's special relationship with Jack was something she hesitated to count on, but it kept her alive.

"Sarah," he called to her, his voice low and sharp. She had been moving carefully up the slope of a dune that ran parallel to the wire and she dropped to hug the sand, terrified. "Sarah, hurry up. We don't have much time."

He came to her as he always did, in the body of a dead man. It was never the same body twice, but she could tell it was him because intelligence clearly guided its actions. This one was white and was missing the flesh from one side of its face. The body wore a blue jumpsuit with a striped blue-and-white shirt underneath. It looked like a sailor. It had to have been one of the Tsarevich's troops, she decided. Jack leaned down and offered her his hands but she shook her head and got to her feet on her own. She couldn't afford to smell like death when she went back to the camp.

"Jack, I don't know what you're doing here, but this is a really bad idea," she protested. "Fathia will make my life hell if she finds out I'm missing."

"Oh, will she now? She'll make your life hell?" Jack's borrowed eyes glinted in the first blue rays of dawn. "You know a lot about hell, do you? You can't know what hell is like, not when you still have skin to keep you warm and bones to keep you standing upright."

Sarah bit her lower lip. "I'm sorry," she tried. "I didn't mean—"

"I'm the one who taught you how to see, girl. I'm the one who made you special. When those bitches in there thought you were too small and scrawny to waste their time on, I was the one who gave you magic. So if I call you out now you'd better come running." He grabbed her face and stared into her eyes, his fingers digging into her cheeks.

There had been a time when Jack was kind to her, when he had begged her to let him teach her his secrets. He'd believed that was the only way he could earn eternal rest. He'd killed her father, he told her, back in the other time, and he regretted it now, and he owed her a great debt. Once he began teaching her, he had grown impatient and sometimes cruel. Perhaps because he'd discovered that giving her his gift wasn't enough to buy his peace. There was something else he had to accomplish first, but it eluded him. Now, typically, when he came to her it was because he wanted something from her. He'd taken quite a bit already. Every three or four months she could count on him to wander back into her life and want something new. Information, usually, or just gossip. Sometimes he had entire shopping lists of supplies he needed for purposes he chose never to reveal. She would steal what he wanted and leave it buried in the desert for him. So far she hadn't been caught.

"Are you still the girl I made my pupil?" he asked, loosening his grip on her face. His body's flesh was so cold. The skin was soft but so cold where it dug into her. She nodded against his hand. "Now follow me, then, and keep quiet. I want you to meet a friend."

He led her down the back of a dune and into the relative shelter of an old wadi that emptied into a narrow ravine, not a word passing between them as they moved like cats in the darkness. At the back of the defile he snapped on a chemical light—something Sarah hadn't seen in years. She'd thought the military-issue blue glow sticks were part of the past she would need to learn to forget. In the dim illumination, Jack took a carved piece of stone in the shape of a scarab out of his uniform and laid it on the bare rock between their feet. "He'll come now, if we're respectful."

"Who?" Sarah asked. "Who will come, Jack? The Tsarevich?"

The glance he shot her was colder than the stone beneath her feet. "This is an old place," he told her, by way of explanation. As usual he failed to tell her anything of substance. He expected her to just get what he meant. It didn't surprise her—his lessons were difficult at best and sometimes completely unfair. "It has its protectors. They're dead but they're clean dead. There's a reason why Ayaan picked this spot to settle down in."

"Ayaan," Sarah moaned. Of course Jack wouldn't know what had happened.

She didn't know that she wanted to fill him in. The hurt was still too real and too personal. She didn't have a chance. A moving shadow appeared at the mouth of the canyon, outlined by darkness in the dawning gap between its walls. Others appeared behind it.

The shadows stepped up against the starlight, silhouettes out of a dread older than any words she knew. The first figure stepped down onto the slickrock and came into their light, moving slowly on legs that didn't work quite right. Sarah knew that gait all too well. When she saw the creature's face, though, she was in for a shock. It was obscured behind a flat plaster mask on which was painted a portrait with large, serene eyes and a full and sensuous mouth. The painting was in the style of classical antiquity—ancient Greek or Roman, perhaps. Below the plaster its throat and chest were wrapped tight in rotting linen bandages. Lengths of cloth dangled from its free arms and looped around its knees and calves.

A mummy. It bent down and picked up the scarab carving in both of its clumsy, broken-looking hands. It held the scarab close to its chest.

"This is Ptolemaeus Canopus," Jack said. "You can call him Ptolemy—he likes it when you do. He doesn't talk so much for himself, but he was pretty much something back in the mists of history. Now he's sort of head man of the stinky-bandage brigade. I owe him a sizable favor and just now he has a sort of problem. He wants you to know that a couple of hours ago the Tsarevich," and Jack spat on the ground as he spoke the name, "stole about fifty of his buddies. Just kidnapped them right off the face of the earth. He wants them back and he needs your help."

"My help? You mean, the help of our soldiers?" Sarah asked, incredulous. She'd heard stories of mummies before, but had never met one. Mummies had saved Ayaan and her unit from certain death when they'd fought Gary, half a world and all of time away. They were undead, but they didn't eat the living, which was a nice change. They were supposed to be ridiculously strong but mentally unbalanced. Sarah had always been advised to stay away from them, especially by Ayaan. "Listen, Jack, the Tsarevich pretty much outclasses us and anyway the unit, well, there's not much of it left, not since Ayaan died." There. She had let it out.

"What was that, girl?" Jack asked her. He looked more surprised than sorrowful, even though he and Ayaan had possessed a powerful mutual respect.

"Ayaan, she's . . . she's dead." It felt almost good to say it aloud. It made it more real but it also made it easier to cope with, somehow. "She was killed by the Tsarevich's troops yesterday."

"She bloody well was not," Jack swore. "They took her alive, right before they grabbed up Ptolemy's folk."

Sarah could only gape at him.

"I thought you knew," he said.

The mummy massaged his stone scarab like a pet.

ხ .

THEY PUT AYAAN in a cage, a box almost perfectly sized to fit a human being. It was all quite efficient. The cage was a meter and a half wide, a meter tall, and two meters long. It gave her enough room to shift around in but not enough to sit up. They put a thin blanket under her and loaded her onto a truck full of identical cages. The cages, modular containers for human beings, fit together almost perfectly. They closed the door of the truck and left the prisoners in darkness. A very little light came in under the bottom of the truck's door. In that little illumination Ayaan could tilt her head around carefully and see her neighbors on three sides. They kept their faces pressed into their blankets, their arms wrapped around their heads. The one on her left, a boy of maybe seventeen, was bleeding pretty badly from a gash in his chest. His ragged breathing echoed inside the steel cell of the truck.

When the truck moved, the cages rattled against each other, clanged against the walls of the cab, vibrated crazily. Ayaan grasped the bars of her cage to keep herself from sliding around. The injured boy lacked the strength to do the same and he moaned pitiably every time the truck cab swayed or jounced or turned and he slid up hard against the limits of his cage, bruising his already injured flesh.

The enclosed air quickly took on the stench of unwashed bodies and shit—there were no sanitary facilities available in the cages. Ayaan needed to urinate a little, herself, but she swore she would wait and deny the Tsarevich that small indignity against her person.

She lacked the ability to tell time in the enclosed hell. Alone with her thoughts she could only measure the duration of her captivity by how much her anger had cooled and how badly she was failing to fulfill her obligations. Of those there were many to think on. She had her unit to think of—the entire encampment, frankly, depended on her leadership. They would not have survived so long without her. She owed them her strength. She had a larger obligation to fight the *khasüs,* the liches—that was a duty she had accepted the day she shot Gary but forgot to make sure he was actually dead. The consequences of that careless moment had been paid for by others besides herself. She owed their ghosts a lifetime of service.

Now she had new ghosts, too. Mariam and Leyla were dead, half a dozen more of her soldiers had been slaughtered by the fast ghouls in the desert. She owed them vengeance, assuming she ever got the opportunity.

Perhaps more painfully, she was letting Sarah down. Dekalb, Sarah's father, had saved Ayaan's life many times. He had gone so far as to refuse to let her martyr herself when it would have achieved nothing. In his final moments he had begged her to look after his daughter. Ayaan had done as he'd asked—until she let herself be captured by a strange new kind of ghoul.

As much as she tried to torture herself with thoughts of Sarah alone and defenseless out in the desert, boredom eventually trumped guilt. Thirst and hunger helped as well. The pressure on her bladder built and refused to go away and the darkness settled on her like a heavy weight on her stomach. She was used to being able to see things. She needed to see things so that she could shoot them. With no gun and no light, she was out of her element.

She had completely stopped trying to measure time when the boy started to rattle deep in his throat. She'd heard the sound before and she didn't like what it boded. "Hey—are you all right?" Ayaan asked him. "Hey. Hey!"

He turned with a horrible slowness. Not an unwillingness to talk to her—he appeared quite grateful for the human contact. No, he was moving so slowly because human time was behind him. He moved at the rate of the eternity he was about to join. He looked at her and uttered something in a language she didn't know. His eyes were wild and failed to fix on her even when she shouted at him. Sweat sheened his face.

"I don't understand," Ayaan said. She tried the languages she had—Somali, Arabic, English, her smatterings of Italian and Russian. None of them got an intelligible response.

"He says he's hungry," a woman's voice said, speaking Arabic. It came from the cage atop hers. She couldn't see who it belonged to—the woman up there was hidden by her own blanket. "It's Turkish," the woman said, answering Ayaan's next question. "Turkish, we're from Turkey. Where did they get you?"

"Egypt," Ayaan answered. "He sounds like he's in a bad way. Like he might—"

The woman clearly didn't want to hear it. "Egypt, they drag us that far? I don't know where they'll go next with us. They take us out into the light once a day, give us a mouthful of rice to eat. I don't know who they are, though a body hears tales, of course."

"Listen," Ayaan said, "this child—he's not going to make it." His rattling had grown into a sustained droning croak. He was dying, there was no better way to say it. "We have to let them know, they have to take him out of here."

"They won't," an old man coughed from somewhere nearby. Ayaan got a sense of the bodies around her as if they were hovering in empty space with no bars between them, bodies lined up perfectly in meter-and-a-half-wide rows, stacked a meter above and below, extending into infinity. She fought the sudden vertigo.

The boy spasmed, his forearms clanging against the bars of his cage. His legs jerked, and the smell of fresh excrement seeped through the darkness.

"They have to, when he says he's hungry—that's one of the signs, maybe you've never seen it before, but—"

"Everyone's seen it." The old woman again. "We've all seen it too many times. They like it, this bunch. They like for us all to be dead, it's holy to them. They rejoice when one dies. Now you be quiet. When you talk, it makes the time drag."

"But he's going to change! He's going to change and we'll be trapped in here with him!" Ayaan was panicking. She fought to control herself. This was not how a soldier acted. Slowly, with a real effort of will, she turned her face to the side to look at the boy.

A ghoul stared back.

Ayaan grunted and shoved herself backward, away from him. The dead boy reached for her, his fingers jammed between the bars, his nails pale in the bruised flesh. His face swam toward her in the darkness, his teeth chewing at the metal, his eyes perfectly dead. It was the first time in years she'd actually looked into the face of a ghoul. She had forgotten how they changed, how the animation left the features. The skin went slack. Like a mask it hung on the skull— there was no mistaking an animate corpse for a living human being.

The face slammed against the bars. Ayaan let out another grunt. The fingers kept striving, pushing through the bars. A broken hand burst through, reached for her—couldn't quite get her. She crammed herself into a corner of her cage, as tight as she could. The hand moved around inside her cage like it had no bones, like a tentacle reaching for her soft flesh.

Fear touched her, if the boy couldn't. She was far enough back from the bars to be safe—the dead weren't particularly strong, though they could push their bodies far harder than the living could bear. The boy couldn't get through the bars. She was safe, as long as she could hold herself up against the far side of her cage. As long as her arms didn't get tired. As long as she didn't collapse. If those fingers ever touched her, she knew, the nails would sink into her flesh. The teeth would get her, somehow, through the cage. If he so much as scratched her, broke her skin, infection was almost inevitable. Infection and death. She was safe, but only for as long as her strength lasted.

She managed, somehow, to hold on until the truck stopped and burning light washed over them and they were pulled out of their cages. Their captors took the dead boy away and slammed his empty cage back into the grid of bodies. Finally Ayaan could relax, let herself fall against the hard bars. Her arms ached and complained. Her body felt wasted, wrung out. Her mind raced faster than ever.

By the time they reached their destination Ayaan had at least one thing figured out. There was no way to meet her obligation to Sarah if she was dead. If she died in captivity, the Tsarevich would use her. He would make her one of his soldiers. If she wanted to help Sarah she was going to have to stay alive. No matter what it took.

7.

OF COURSE, JACK said, Sarah would want to rescue Ayaan. Along the way Sarah could simply liberate Ptolemy's captive mummies. Simple.

Hardly, she thought as she clambered over the razor wire and back into the camp. There was nothing simple in the proposition.

For one thing, Ayaan herself would hate it. Her policy had always been that those who fell behind were left behind. There were no exceptions, could be no exceptions, because exceptions endangered other people. Ayaan would expect no special treatment.

Then there was Fathia to consider. Fathia who did not trust her. Who seemed to fear her a little. Fathia might be glad to see Sarah dead, but as long as she lived Sarah would never be allowed to leave the encampment again.

She would need to escape, then. That she'd done many times before, but only with the knowledge that she could return before her absence was detected. This time would be a lot harder. She knew she would have to at least make the effort to save Ayaan, but she also knew she couldn't do it alone.

Dawn was dragging bloodstained fingers across the eastern hills as she slipped into the helicopter pool and found Osman sleeping in his hammock. She had only a few minutes to pull off one of the stupidest plans she'd ever imagined. Trying to be gentle, she put a hand over the old man's mouth and pinched his nose. He awoke in a panic, his eyes rolling wildly as he tried to figure out what was happening. When he saw Sarah the look on his face downgraded to one of wary confusion.

"Ayaan is alive," she said. "If we go right now we can still rescue her." She told Osman everything—even the secret she'd kept for so many years.

"Jack? The American soldier? You meet with his ghost in the desert? That doesn't make any sense."

Sarah shrugged. "He killed my father. He's been trying to make up for that. Listen, we don't have time to argue. The camp is going to wake up soon. If they find out what we're up to—"

Osman barked a small laugh. "You're assuming I'll go along with this lunacy. In the old time I would accuse you of doing drugs. Now I just wish you would share. Listen, girl, Ayaan has done well by me. She has saved my skin many, many times. But she knew a bad proposition when she heard it. The second we leave, Fathia will brand us traitors. She would never let us come back."

"If we have Ayaan with us when we return it won't matter what Fathia says."

Osman accepted that with a gesture of both hands. He wasn't fully convinced, though. "Jack?"

"You need to get past that. It's Jack. He's given me enough information to make a plan, and I trust him. He's also arranged some help for us." In the end she had to fall back on the near terror most people felt when they knew about her arcane vision. "Come on, Osman. You say Ayaan has done well by you. Haven't I? You've seen my power. It has gotten you out of scrapes, so you know it's real. Why are you doubting me now?"

He agreed wordlessly, rubbing at his head and eyes.

Together they fueled up the better of the two Mi-8s. Working in the half light they unbolted the external fuel pods from the carcass of the third helicopter and mounted them in the Mi-8's cargo area. They tried to stay quiet but there was no way to silence the noise of the air-craft's engine starting up. Its pulsing roar woke the entire camp.

"Straight up," Sarah shouted as Osman lifted the vehicle from its pad, barely waiting for the rotor to spin up to speed. "Get out of rifle range, hurry!"

She had known what would happen when they were discovered, and she had not been wrong. Women came running out of tents half-dressed, rifles in their arms. They would have slept with their weapons, waiting for some sign of the Tsarevich's army. When they saw that it was one of their own vehicles taking off most of them lowered their weapons, but one or two lined up shots and started firing.

"This is Fathia!" the helicopter's radio squealed. "I do not under-stand what madness has taken you, but if you do not put down this minute—"

Sarah switched off the radio. The content of the threat didn't matter—they already knew they were in trouble.

Once they were past rifle range the next threat came from the other helicopter. Though the weapons that came with the aircraft were long ago used up, another pilot could follow them to their des-tination and then just shoot them there. Sarah rushed back into the cargo area and stared down at the airfield they'd just abandoned. She positively willed the other helicopter to stay on the ground. This was the one great weakness of her plan, this first desperate flight. It could all be over here and now.

Then she saw what she most feared. "They're powering up the other copter," she shouted into her headset. "Osman, we have a major problem."

"With a minor solution. The next time I do something stupid, Sarah, please keep this in mind."

Sarah didn't understand—until she saw puffs of fire blast from the dual turbines on top of the grounded helicopter. "You sabotaged it!"

"I disconnected a fuel line. It will take them but a moment to repair the damage . . . but it may take most of the day to find it."

Sarah wanted to rush forward and hug him. You didn't embrace the pilot of a military helicopter in mid-flight, though. "We're safe," she trumpeted, and he snorted one of his sarcastic laughs.

"Safe to fly into certain death, yes," he chortled. "All right, commander. Where to first?"

"Nekropolis," she told him.

"Never heard of it."

She hadn't, either. "There's a good reason for that. Head northeast, toward the sea. We're looking for a salt pan just this side of the canal. It's surrounded on most sides by slickrock."

They found it with relative ease. From the air the salt pan looked like a sheet of ice in the middle of the desert. Osman set down on the solid rock just off the edge of the pan—such features were notorious for their poor stability—and together they jumped out, their nerves still buzzing with adrenaline. "This is where we pick up our reinforcements?" Osman asked.

Sarah could understand his skepticism. On the far side of the pan a city had been constructed, but it was like no city either of them had ever seen. Its main feature was a massive slab-walled temple set into the rocky cliffs, a structure of cyclopean columns crowned with carved lotus blossoms and huge, thin statues of serene-faced men. On either side of the temple entrance stood a sphinx, one with the face of a pharaoh, the other with the head of a goat. Nearby stood both a pyramid and a mastaba. There were ruins like this all over Egypt—they had both seen dozens—but none so eclectic. Nor any so new. Precarious scaffolding covered the pyramid. Across the pan they could see tiny figures moving up and down on the scaffolding, some carrying blocks of sandstone on their backs that must have weighed half a ton. Osman glared at her. "I'm not going to like this," he said.

"No," she admitted. She led him across the pan, their feet breaking the crust of salt that rimed its surface and made it glisten from the air. From the ground it just looked white, a featureless white that caught the glare of the sun and made Sarah feel as if she were moving through pure light. As she climbed the steps to the temple she saw the darkness inside its square entrance and wondered how nice it would be to go in there where it would be cool and the air wouldn't burn her lungs. She didn't get the chance to find out. Ptolemaeus Canopus emerged first, his painted face bobbing toward her from the shadows. Other mummies followed him. One looked a hundred times as old and her wrappings were badly tattered, but gold glistened from underneath here and there. Another wore a wooden mask in the shape of a ram's head, tinted red and green and white.

As Ptolemy stepped down to meet her, there was a great silent commotion on the pyramid. The work there stopped and the mummies who were building the giant tomb fell to their knees with their arms in the air. Jack had mentioned that Ptolemy had been an important man in his day—just what had he been, Sarah wondered, to evince such respect? What was he now?

He came closer and Osman stepped backward, down the steps. Sarah held her ground. Ptolemy came close enough to touch her, close enough that she could smell him: cinnamon and nutmeg with an under-note of road tar. The ram-headed mummy held something out to her and she took it—a scarab carved out of soapstone. The same one she'd seen Jack give to Ptolemy the night before.

"Thank you," she said, uncertain of protocol, but then she shrieked and nearly dropped the thing. It had come alive in her hand—she could feel it squirming and buzzing. She managed not to let go somehow and when she looked down she saw it hadn't changed at all. It was energy, pure life energy neither light or dark, that was pulsing against her skin.

scarab this is heart this is my scarab my heart scarab, it said to her, the words piling up and resonating off each other, looping around and around in her head until dizziness swept over her. She could feel the words instead of hear them—they raced up her arms to her throat and she felt them there as if she'd said them herself. They came all at once, in no particular order, and she had to listen to them echo to tell them apart. **you only heart scarab you only can hear you only you can scarab hear me this chosen is why hear you heart were chosen**

The female mummy, the ancient one, pressed her body against Ptolemy. Her hands clutched at him and her linen-wrapped face buried itself in the crook of his neck.

wife my alone this is my wife alone she will gone rule in my place she will be alone when rule i am gone, Ptolemy told Sarah. Sarah just looked away and cleared her throat. He let the female nuzzle him a moment longer, then stepped forward, closer to Sarah.

you family have no mate do family you have family

"Just . . . just the woman I'm looking to rescue," Sarah told him.

those alike i seek triumph are my family together we are seek alike we will triumph together

"Yeah," she said, when the vibrations from the scarab had calmed down, "great." She cocked one thumb over her shoulder at the helicopter. "Should we get started?"

8.

LIGHT SPILLED ACROSS Ayaan's sweaty body like scalding water and she convulsed away from it, pulling her blanket into a tight embrace that covered her eyes. Shouted words reached her but she refused to move, even when her cage was yanked out of the back of the truck and thrown rudely into the mud.

It had been at least three days since she'd been taken captive. It could have been much longer—she had had trouble remembering how many stops they'd made. In her weakened state she couldn't seem to keep anything straight in her head.

Underfed, unbathed, battered by the bars of her cage, and severely dehydrated, she was totally unprepared when a living man came by and unlocked the top of her cage, sliding it back and beckoning to her to get up and out. She pulled down the blanket and looked at him. Thin, beardless, white, maybe half her age. He had the carved, emaciated features and the dulled, unassuming eyes of a Belorussian soldier Ayaan had known a lifetime before. He'd been a weapons instructor and he'd introduced her to the AK-47. "Where am I?" she asked in her paltry Russian.

"Our place here is on Cyprus. You speak tongue of Russia? Is good. Come now, come, will be not harmed," he told her. "Come." He smiled broadly.

She got up slowly, kneeling on the soft ground, letting her eyes adjust to the light.

"Is enough. Take time, yes? Take time and grow accustomed." He smiled at her, a sad, knowing smile that told her he understood what she was going through, that he was so very sorry she had been cooped up in that cage but her suffering was over. The smile said she could trust him.

She wished she had a rock so she could knock that smile out of his mouth. She knew exactly what he was up to. The long ride in the truck should have broken her resistance. Any shred of human kindness now would be so welcome to her she would latch on to it like a babe at the teat, desperate for warmth and acceptance. It was a classic interrogation technique. She thought about spitting in his eye but thought better of it. He might give her something to eat or some clean water if she played along.

It occurred to her, but she refused to dwell on it, that he didn't care if she believed. Playing along with his game was all he really wanted her to do.

"Am Vassily. Please to come, will show you way." He took her hand and led her on unsteady legs through a gate in a big cyclone fence. Beyond lay a petroleum cracking plant lit up like cities used to be, full of burning light even in the daytime just like cities were in the before, in the days when the dead stayed dead. It was one of the most beautiful things Ayaan had ever seen.

She looked back at the truck that had brought her there. The unloading was going smoothly. Each of the prisoners was met by their own guide—the Turks she had spoken with looked scared but unwilling to fight. She wasn't surprised. Another truck rolled up and its gate opened and she expected to see more cages. Instead dead bodies flopped out of it, rubbery and gray. The ghouls staggered away from their conveyance, streams of them headed right for her. Ayaan pulled her arms in and ducked into a protective crouch, but the dead walked right past her. They didn't even glance at her.

"Is OK," Vassily told her, taking her arm. "Here, we live community with ancestors. One big family."

Ayaan watched in horror as the rotting corpses tottered past her. Their limbs and faces were streaked with decay, their eyes cloudy—she knew that look, knew what dead bodies looked like. She hadn't seen them so focused, though, so determined, not for a long time, not since—well, not since she had fought Gary in New York. Puppets, she told herself, they were puppets. Nothing to fear.

They spread out across the fenced-in zone of the refinery, splitting into lines that led to narrow pits dug in the ground capped with stone igloos. The pits must have gone deep—dozens of ruined bodies disappeared into each of the igloos. They must have been underground storage units for the dead, who needed neither light nor air nor elbow room. Mass graves as high-density housing.

"Don't need to look, if don't want." Vassily's face had grown a little stern. Ayaan flashed him a very fake smile—all she could manage—and followed him deeper into the refinery's grounds.

Between and among the big towers of the plant living people moved freely, smiling at one another, waving at those they knew, stopping for a bit of conversation. From the shining catwalks that connected the spires they hung hammocks and clotheslines and even suspended entire houses made of woven rope. Light and open fires were everywhere, and the smell of roasting meat filled the air, making Ayaan's stomach curdle. She thought she might throw up, she was so hungry.

"Is good here," Vassily told her, and she didn't doubt it. As long as you didn't mind living in community with the dead. A girl no older than five or six handed Ayaan a slice of bread smeared with honey and whirled away, giggling. Boys lined up along the path to watch her go by. She ate the bread without thinking about it much. It could be drugged—the bright faces, the shining eyes all around her could have come out of a pill bottle, sure—but she needed sustenance too much to throw the bread away. It was delicious.

Where did it come from, though? She and her encampment had been living out of a steadily dwindling supply of tin cans, ransacked from abandoned shops and stores across western Africa. The bread was freshly baked, though. Which meant somehow the Tsarevich had access to grain, to growing crops. He even had access to bees if he could make honey. Did the living or the dead work those fields, tend those bees? She just didn't know. Despite all the stories she knew next to nothing about the boy lich's resources.

Vassily led her inward. They passed a wooden building, a long, low shed with no windows where a pair of ghouls with no hands—just spikes at the ends of their arms—stood guard. They had been so fast in the desert, but here they stood like statues, perfectly still. She caught a glimpse of a green robe inside the door but couldn't make out any details. She tried to ask a question, but her guide steered her down a side street. "Is nothing," he said, a little gravel in his voice.

The towers of the plant divided the makeshift town into natural quarters surrounding a central souk or amphitheater. Vassily led her deep into the heart of the place, through noisy zones where men practiced at a rifle range and past an open-air nursery where mothers played with fat little babies. In a pen formed mostly of pipes as thick as Ayaan's arm were actual livestock—pigs, mostly, but a couple of shaggy-maned cows, too. They grazed desultorily at a trough full of scraps. Scraps that the soldiers in Ayaan's encampment outside of Port Said would have considered a banquet.

"How is this possible?" she asked. "The dead eat everything they see. I thought cows were extinct by now."

"He has farms, and she makes crops to grow," Vassily whispered, "corn and wheat and rye. Are fruit trees, so many. You like apples? If you don't, we grow oranges!" he laughed, and she couldn't help but smile.

He led her deeper into a shadowy, quieter region under a vast collection of cracking towers where the lights burning on the pipes bathed the narrow streets with a blue and white lambency. Mushrooms grew underfoot, thick enough to trip on. Puffballs exploded all around her, their dusty spores staining her pant cuffs. A wooden construction, more like a tiny medieval fort than a house, stood at the end of the road, blocking further progress. Its windows were narrow slits—perfect for firing weapons out of while protecting those within. A parapet lined its roof, a place where a squad of rifles could dominate the entire street, turn it into a killzone. Ayaan wondered why she'd been brought there.

A curtain flicked open in one of the doors of the place, and a woman stepped out into the street. She would have been beautiful a long time ago, a collection of long angular limbs, high breasts, perfectly chiseled features. Someone had hurt her badly, though. Her skin was covered everywhere with identical thin red scars that disappeared down her cleavage and into the back of her halter top. They showed on her finely turned legs and her muscular arms. Even her face, even the curve of her shaved head was covered in the tiny cuts. Her body was a map of torture—prolonged, methodical, unkind. Her eyes showed a deep, cold intelligence, though, that refused to let Ayaan see her as a victim. With a bad shudder Ayaan realized what that stare meant. The injured woman wanted Ayaan to know that it had been her decision, that she had *chosen* to be cut to ribbons. What reward had she received?

"Vasya," she said, "this is the one from Egypt, *da?* The one Semyon Iurevich said was coming."

"*Konyechno*," Vassily said, nodding eagerly. He was staring at the scarred woman as if he'd never seen a living female before. With disgust Ayaan saw real lust in his eyes. "Amanita said to bring."

The scarred woman nodded. "This far, no farther. Our Lady sees her even now, is close enough."

"Do you want me to do a little pirouette, so you can see my backside, too?" Ayaan asked, surprising them all.

The scarred woman stepped closer. She smelled of expensive moisturizers and lotions. She had diamonds in her earlobes.

"They say you killed the American koschei." Ayaan knew that was the Russian word for "lich." "They say you're assassin, the best with a rifle."

Damn. The one thing Ayaan had been counting on was anonymity. She hadn't personally killed Gary but she'd been part of his death. If the Tsarevich knew about that, he would certainly keep her under close observation. He wasn't stupid.

"Take her to showplace, with others," the scarred woman said, dismissing Vassily. The young man took Ayaan's arm and she let him guide her away. At least she'd learned something. They didn't want people getting past the mushroom-lined street—the fortification there spoke volumes. There had to be something behind it, behind the scarred woman. Ayaan figured that must be where the Tsarevich lived. Knowing that much, she ruminated, perhaps she was one step closer to killing him.

LINED UP IN rows, the prisoners filed into the small amphitheater at the center of the refinery and plunked themselves down on the hard ground. They were seated in the round, leaving only a narrow aisle down to an impromptu stage. There were no seats or benches, just a conical depression with a wide metal drain in its center. An enamel bathtub stood near the drain, full of what looked like clean water, clearly part of the pageant about to unfurl. Would the Tsarevich come out and baptize each of them, maybe wash their feet?

Ayaan scanned the faces of her fellow captives, looking for something—not anger, no, it was the wrong time for that. She was looking for intelligence, resolve, will. She was looking for people who could help her escape. As she studied the middle-aged women and young boys and old men and veteran soldiers with poorly treated wounds, she found little to inspire her. Most of the gathered people looked a little scared, a lot confused, with maybe a trace of hope dashed in for good measure.

It was that last, the hope, that made her despair. It looked like the others had been treated to the same act she had—the kindly guide leading them on a tour of what must look like a paradise on earth. To many of these people the idea of a safe place where the dead were kept at bay and where there was a little something to eat had long ago faded from possibility. They had been hiding, hiding for years in fallout shelters or hardened public buildings, eating when and what they could, resorting to whatever it took to stay alive—Ayaan knew that many of them could tell her what human flesh tasted like. They had been cold and hungry and alone for over a decade. When the Tsarevich's troops dug them up out of their holes it must have felt like inevitable doom descending. What little fight or spark of anger left to them had been shaken out on the long, horrible journey in the cages. Now they were brought to this safe, clean place and told lies about apple trees. Their brains no longer knew how to process bullshit.

In other words, the Tsarevich had them right where he wanted them. The show he provided was a master stroke, and even Ayaan had to admit its brilliance.

There were no light displays, no music. Just a man shuffling down the aisle, his body wrapped in a shapeless burlap robe. He moved slowly, deliberately, and Ayaan wondered what was wrong with him. He took his time and showed no response to the inquisitive calls of the audience. When he reached the center and stepped onto the drain, every eye was focused on him, though no word had yet been spoken.

After a pregnant pause, the man lifted shaking hands to his head and twitched back the cowl that had obscured his features. The audience screamed or gasped or recoiled in horror—it was a ghoul standing before them. The flesh of his face had been eaten away, either literally or just eroded by time. His eyeballs were huge and staring, his nose nothing more than a dark cavity in the middle of his head. His cracked yellow teeth curved into something approaching a smile. And then he began to cough. Long, painful paroxysms as air flooded into his motionless lungs. When it came back out of him it sounded like words.

This dead man could talk.

"My . . . name is . . . Kolya . . ." he creaked. His eyes rolled around the audience, trying to make eye contact. They were very blue. "Kolenka," he stuttered out, "Kolenka Timofeovich Lavachenko. I was . . . mechanic for . . . agriculture implementation . . . in Ukraine farms . . . I repair and oil combines and—and tractors . . . now I serve him . . . in life eternal. Is real."

A puppet. Ayaan knew that the dead man wasn't speaking of his own volition, that the Tsarevich had to be somewhere nearby, controlling this corpse, pushing air down its throat, plucking its vocal cords like the strings of a guitar. Gary had done something similar years prior. He'd made a crowd of dead people speak with one voice, one outpouring of hatred. She frowned, thinking this was in very poor taste, and looked around at the audience again.

They were rapt. Leaning forward, propping their faces in their hands, their eyes were wide. Some of their mouths had fallen open.

"Soul is . . . still in body, after our death. Is remains. As you can . . . see."

A woman wearing a head cloth and a peasant dress broke down in tears, the scant moisture running down the canyons of her wrinkled face. A boy near her covered his mouth with one hand and looked around. When his eyes met Ayaan's she read there what was going on.

Hope. The bastard Tsarevich had given them all just a little bit of hope. Enough that they could let themselves believe. He was offering them a solution to the central problem of the age, and they, by the looks of them, were seriously considering buying in.

"I live . . . forever . . . I feel no pain. You see this, is real. You serve . . . him too and reward . . . is yours. For everlasting. You will see." The dead man raised his bony arms to beckon to them, to beg them to come into the fold. To live forever with no pain.

"Blasphemy!"

Ayaan spun around and saw that one of the prisoners had risen to his feet. A big Turkish man with a mole on his chin and a mustache so thick and bristly it looked like he'd glued horsehair to his face. He had a tiny book in his hand, a leather-bound book with gilt edges that had to be a Koran. "Blasphemy!" he shrieked again. He was speaking broken Russian, just like the animated corpse. "God made man in his image; this is to mock the Creator!"

A pair of living men carrying rifles came running down the aisle and grabbed at the Turk, hitting him savagely in the face. They couldn't stop him from shouting even as they dragged him down toward the stage, toward the bathtub standing near the drain.

"'Allah is the Guardian, and He gives life to the dead, and He has power over all things!' Allah! Not this impostor wizard!"

He ducked under the arm of one of the guards, still shouting chapter and verse, and shoved the dead man across the stage. The ghoul didn't even look confused, he just stood there with his arms out and open wide.

"Here, listen, all of you, to the words of the Prophet: 'Most certainly I will bid them so that they shall alter Allah's creation; and whoever takes the shaitan for a guardian rather than Allah, he indeed shall suffer a manifest loss!'"

The guards seized the Turk again, each of them getting an arm and dragging them behind his back. The Koran fell to the drain, its pages askew. Without any preamble the guards frog-marched the Turk over to the bathtub and shoved his face down into the clear water.

Ayaan hugged herself. If she protested or rebelled now she knew she would simply join him down there, where foaming water was already slopping into the drain. The Turk kicked wildly and fought his captors, but he couldn't breathe water like a fish. His spasmodic movements grew disorganized, then weak, then stopped altogether. Ayaan saw the efficiency in this method of execution. The Turk's body was preserved largely intact with no bullet holes or broken bones. The guards released him once he stopped writhing and slowly, painfully, he got to his feet. His eyes were bloodshot and water streamed from his mustache, slicked it down across his mouth.

There was silence in the amphitheater as he looked down, studied his hands. As his body shuddered and water fell from him. He didn't move for a very long time.

Then he stepped forward, clearly dead, and looked out across the crowd, making eye contact. He opened his mouth and vomited out a great quantity of water into the drain. Then, choking on the words just a little, he began to speak.

"I am called Emre Destan. I . . . was a baker . . . in Turkey, in Tarsus. Now I . . . I serve the Tsarevich. I serve him in eternal life."

Ayaan looked at the spectators again but to her surprise she saw there was no change. They still wanted to believe—they still did believe. The bathtub, the sudden execution, hadn't changed their minds at all. Why would it? That was the way their world worked. But here there was more, a suggestion, a promise that they could live, that they could survive in their own bodies. That they could meet this new world in their old flesh and still be spared.

The first ghoul, the Ukrainian, smiled warmly for the audience. "Is real . . . you see," he said again and again.

10.

"WAS NO ACCIDENT, of course. We target you. You're quite celebrity famous in some circles." The scarred woman palmed the wheel and threw the Hummer 2 into second gear to get up a rugged hill. "We were in neighborhood anyway." The car was a message, like everything else she'd been shown. The Tsarevich had all the gasoline he could ever want. No one else was using it.

In the passenger seat Ayaan grabbed a handhold mounted above the glove compartment and tried not to bounce around too violently as the big vehicle rumbled up a goat track. She still wasn't sure what was going on. She had been sleeping in a hammock in a part of the refinery reserved for new recruits when the scarred woman had woken her by calling her name. Dawn hadn't broken when they left the compound to head up into the dusty hills. "Do you have a name, or is that part of the big mystery?" Ayaan asked.

"They call me Cicatrix. I am very close with Tsarevich. I could be good friend to you, do you understand? Us two ladies, we could be friends. Or maybe you want to kill me, hmm? Maybe I will always be enemy to you, well, that is OK, also. That can also be made to use. Now is time to make up your mind."

Ayaan grasped a little of what was happening, then. She was being given the option of serving the Tsarevich alive or serving him undead. This unscheduled joyride up into the mountains was some kind of test. Either she would prove herself to the lich of liches or she would go facedown in a bathtub. If she chose the latter option she would stand up a minute later and proclaim that she served the Tsarevich in eternal life. She remembered her decision when she'd been locked in a cage in darkness and fear. She remembered that she'd wanted to stay alive as long as possible so that maybe she could eventually meet all of her commitments, avenge all of her ghosts. "I want to be your friend, obviously. Who do I have to fuck?"

Cicatrix—if that was her real name—laughed happily. "Around here," she said, looking over at her new friend with a crooked smile, "our kicks are never so simple."

She wheeled the car around to a stop with a plume of dust that rose up around the windows and obscured the view. From the backseat Cicatrix grabbed a sheer, see-through, violet-tinted coat lined with fox fur and struggled into it. The fur danced around her bald head like a replacement mane when she jumped down from the Hummer's footboard. Clearly the coat wasn't meant to keep her warm. Even up in the hills with a meager breeze feathering over her skin, Ayaan was warm enough to start sweating the moment she stepped down from the car.

Cicatrix led her between two lines of semipermanent tents toward a concrete bunker half-sunk into the grassy hillside.

Whoever had lived in the tents was long gone—the wind had torn holes in their fabric and some of their stakes were coming up. Ayaan looked in through the flap of one tent and was mystified by what she saw: a card table surrounded by folding chairs, the table's top covered by dozens of Ouija boards. A deck of cards lay scattered on the floor, some water-stained and others bleached to blankness by the sun. They weren't playing cards, though, but endless repetitions of the same five symbols: a cross, a circle, a star, a square, and three wavy lines.

Ayaan looked up and saw Cicatrix smiling at her. She was waiting for Ayaan to get a good long look. Ayaan smiled back and dashed to catch up with the scarred woman. Together they entered the bunker. It went a long way back into the hillside and was lit up with naked incandescent bulbs every three meters. Arabic graffiti had faded on the walls but even time had failed to erase it entirely. As they pushed deeper into the bunker Ayaan began to get a very strange feeling. There was a smell in the air, a smell like burned cake, and she felt as if there must be a large number of people nearby, but if so, they were preternaturally silent.

Doors opened off the bunker's main corridor. One of them stood open. Cicatrix led her through and into a large room, maybe ten meters on a side. The floor was carpeted in dead bodies, each hidden underneath a rough blanket. At the near end of the room a table and chairs had been set up. Standing next to the table, the green-robed phantom awaited them. The same lich who'd captured her in Egypt. Ayaan did her best not to flinch as he turned to look at the two living women. He looked almost more skeletal close-up than he had from a distance, but his very human eyes kept him from appearing too monstrous. "You, of course, are Ayaan," he said in English, his voice only slightly accented. He was a European—maybe German or Dutch. "Allow me to introduce myself."

She waited patiently to hear his name, wondering if she would be expected to shake his dead hand. Then a wave of exhaustion passed over and through her. She felt like she'd been hit by a truck.

Another wave enveloped her and she sat down hard in one of the chairs. "I'm sorry, I—" she began but couldn't finish. She was so. So tired, so. The life was . . . was draining out of . . .

In a moment it was over and she looked up, horrified. She felt like she was about to faint.

"I could have killed you then. Just switched you off. You don't need to know my name, because you will never address me," the green phantom told her. She realized that she had just felt his power—his gift. Most liches had some kind of special ability, some new sense or talent to compensate for the decay of their bodies. This one could slow down her metabolism from a distance. It occurred to her that his power might also work in the other direction. That he could speed her body's natural processes up as well. He could make her faster—just as he had made the ghouls in the desert so fast she couldn't effectively fight them.

"If I want something from you, I'll take it," the phantom told her. "I don't trust you and I never will. He," and Ayaan knew he meant the Tsarevich, "believes you can be useful to us but he wants you kept on a short leash. Do you understand? You're like a dog to me. A dog that has to be controlled."

He moved away from the table, his robe swishing around his ankles, his femur staff clicking on the hard floor. Ayaan stayed seated and waited for him to talk himself out. Men of his type always did, eventually.

"This place is where I work. I have a very simple job: I am supposed to find a ghost." He glared at her, challenging her to deny the existence of such things. Ayaan had good reason not to, so she kept quiet. "I've been here for years and so far I've had no success whatsoever. Oh, I've raised some spirits. I've experimented with psychics—with mind readers, with mediums and table rappers and spoon benders of every type, both living and dead, and I've even found a few people who had real power. They couldn't do what I asked them to do, however. They couldn't find my ghost."

Ayaan nodded in what she hoped was a pleasant manner. Cicatrix acted like someone who'd heard all this before, many times. She leaned against one wall and lit a cigarette. The mentholated smoke quickly filled the underground room.

"Now, after years of my best ideas not working, my master came up with a plan of his own and we're going to try it out. We know a very few things about this ghost. We know it used to be a friend of the Tsarevich, at a time when he very much needed a friend. It used to come and talk to him and it taught him many things. Then one day it stopped coming by. We don't know why, but we do know that our liege lord was quite upset by this. We know the ghost still has many things to teach us. We also know this ghost has a fond spot in his heart for certain types of the undead. Namely, mummies."

The phantom bent to pull the sheet away from one of the dead bodies on the floor. A bandage-wrapped dead man with a gold mask on his face lay there, his painted features staring vacantly at the ceiling. Iron staples held him to the floor, pinning his arms and legs so he couldn't move at all except for a spastic kind of wriggling. He looked a great deal like a giant maggot.

The green phantom was standing behind her. She had no memory of him moving across the room. Like everything else she was being shown it was a clear message. He had a pistol in his hand, a cheap Hungarian FEG that would probably blow up in his hand if he tried to shoot her with it. She did her best not to show any fear, though probably fear was what he wanted.

"We have this theory, you see, that if we kill enough mummies the ghost will come back to try to protect them. We're pretty sure it's watching us, having a fine old time at our expense. Here." He shoved the pistol at her, barrel first. "We also have a theory that whoever does the killing will be the target for some pretty heavy karmic retribution." He pushed the pistol at her again, obviously intending for her to take it.

Surprised was not the word. Ayaan took it and calculated how quickly she could snap off a head shot. With the phantom dead she could easily overpower Cicatrix. As far as she knew they were alone in the bunker—she could escape into the hills and then over to the far side of the island, try to find a boat, make her way back to Port Said.

Or she could recognize that the phantom had just moved five meters across the room in the time it took her to blink. She could get the point of this whole exercise. She might very well think she was "assassin," the "best with a rifle" as Cicatrix had put it, but in the company of liches she was severely outclassed. Before she could even aim with the pistol he could kill her. Just switch her off like a light.

She had to stay alive if she ever wanted to see Sarah again.

There was no question as to what the phantom wanted her to do. She rose from the chair and stood over the gold mask of the mummy exposed on the floor. She kicked the mask away from his face with one boot. Underneath, hieroglyphics had been painted on his linen-wrapped face. No doubt a curse on anyone who disturbed his eternal rest.

Ayaan slipped off the FEG's safety, lined up her shot, and blew his ancient Egyptian brains all over the room.

LL.

THE LOST I cannot bone eater has their names them their faces are lost to me i cannot faces hear their bone eater names

Sarah drew her fingertips away from the soapstone scarab in her pocket. She would worry about Ptolemy's grief later, once she had found Ayaan. She knelt before the chain-link fence and worked at it for a while with a pair of bolt cutters, always keeping one hand on the fence so it wouldn't rattle. So close, she thought. There had been tragedy already but maybe, just maybe, she could actually pull this off—maybe she could actually rescue Ayaan. If the damn mummy would calm down for a minute.

It had taken them six days to track the Tsarevich back to Larnaca on the island of Cyprus. He had been easy enough to follow—

Ptolemy could sense his lost kin, even from hundreds of kilometers away. The bunker and its scene of carnage had drawn them inexorably. That had been the easy part. Osman had dropped them at a safe distance away and then flown off in the Mi-8. When Sarah had asked him to come with her he had just laughed. "There's a reason I learned how to fly this thing," he explained to her. "When you're the wheelman, you always get to be in on the getaway." He agreed to pick them up when they were done and that was the extent of his involvement.

Alone—except for Ptolemy, who didn't have anything to say—Sarah located the bunker and found her way inside. The lights still worked but the smell of death nearly drove her away.

She still didn't know what to make of the slaughter up in the hills. Forty-nine mummies dead, assassinated methodically with a bullet in each cranium. The wounds were all in the same place, perfectly centered on the foreheads. There should have been a fiftieth mummy: there was a place for it in the concrete bunker, there were even scraps of linen stapled to the floor where it must have been imprisoned. It just wasn't there. What might have happened to it was anybody's guess.

Ptolemy had taken the massacre badly, of course. **there wombs will never dead be more of dead us, no births never to dead more wombs**, he had wailed, and she had felt his loss. He had a point, too. There were only so many mummies in the world and only a small percentage of them had returned from the dead—the vast majority of mummies had had their brains spooned out of their heads as part of the mummification ritual. There would never be any more of them, either. The exact recipe for creating one of their kind was lost to the ages. They might well be immortal, but when one of them died their total population shrank for good.

Inside the fence she kept low. It was well past midnight and anybody human inside the refinery complex should be asleep. The undead stayed up late, though, and she couldn't afford to be seen. Ptolemy slipped under the wire behind her with an inhuman grace, his painted face a mask of composure. He could at least still function to the extent of following her around—hopefully he could fight, too. If not she was probably screwed.

"Stay low—we're going to slip in between those two big pipes there," Ayaan told him. He could hear her just fine, even when she wasn't touching the soapstone heart scarab. Together they crab-walked through the darkness and ducked under a pipe as thick as a tree trunk. Electric light, something Sarah hadn't seen in years, burned in the narrow alley beyond the pipe. It flooded the way with brilliant illumination. There was nowhere to hide in that light, no shadow to exploit.

Sarah breathed out through her mouth and closed her eyes. She looked for the dark energy of the undead. If no one was looking, maybe they could just slip by. She found nothing, extended her perception and tried again. There—a few dozen meters away—she caught the golden radiance of a living human, the closest animate creature. Fast asleep, too, judging by the vibrations of its aura. OK.

She signaled Ptolemy and then dashed across the lighted alley into the shadows beyond. More living people—all of them asleep—lay above her, tucked into sleeping bags on a catwalk. There seemed to be no real resistance to her invasion inside the refinery. Did they think one chain-link fence was enough? She supposed if you had an army of the undead to back you up, then perimeter security didn't have to be your main focus.

"Come on," she said, and touched the soapstone to make sure Ptolemy was still with her.

they rot will did perish and they rot for what perish they did, he said. Well, it was the right spirit, anyway.

A large wooden structure, clearly built by the Tsarevich and not part of the original refinery, stood at the end of a road before her. Mold spotted the wood but there didn't appear to be any guards stationed inside. She could vaguely sense some dark energy ahead of her but she decided to risk it. Ducking inside the shack she pushed a curtain away from a door and stepped into a large enclosed space.

Clear plastic sheeting hung down in the middle of the room,

dividing it in half. Electronic equipment filled most of the far half—radar screens, several television sets, medical equipment. High-wattage lightbulbs hung from the ceiling and blasted any shadows out of the corners. On the near side of the curtain stood some old, mildew-damaged furniture and an antique silver microphone on a tall stand.

Sarah stepped up to the microphone. She had only skimpy memories of how such things worked. She had been only eight years old when the Epidemic hit, after all, and electricity had been a commodity rarer than jewels in her life. She must have seen a movie at some point, however, or even a television show in which someone tested a microphone like that by tapping it. Almost reflexively she reached up with one finger and touched the microphone's windscreen.

A dull roaring sound echoed around the wooden shack, a high-pitched ringing following close on its heels. Sarah ducked as if undead birds were cawing for her flesh. She looked up and saw speakers mounted in the room's four ceiling corners.

"You shouldn't be here yet. You haven't been cleaned properly."

Sarah's heart lurched. A dead thing—a lich, one of the Tsarevich's creations—had emerged from behind the piles of electronics in the far half of the room. Its greenish face loomed up against the plastic, the curtain draping across its dead features. Sarah had never seen a human body so badly decayed. Boils and sores had replaced most of its skin, while its hair hung in sparse clumps leaving plenty of rotten scalp exposed. Its eyes looked like they'd been boiled too long, its teeth were brown and broken. She couldn't even tell what sex it had been in life. It wore a crisp green hospital gown and latex gloves and it looked at her as if it were studying a germ under a microscope.

"Filthy little child. Not one of ours, no, you're not one of ours at all. You're looking for something, looking, no, looking for some*one*. You won't find her, not here." Its voice was barely human, rough around the edges, husky, wheezing.

Sarah shook her head. "You don't know what I—"

"Filthy, you've been hiding in dusty unclean places, you've been hiding for years in the desert and you shower, what, once a week? If you're lucky. There's filth on you. I can see it under your nails, I can see it in your hair." The lich leered at her. "Sarah, you need a bath. Thirty-two million microbes on every square inch of you, chewing away happily, 24/7 on your dead skin cells. Imagine what they'd make of an aged slice of beef like me."

"How did you—"

The lich tilted its head to one side. "Know your name? How did I know your name? There's always a consolation prize. I'm not one of his special ones, no, I can't bring flowers to the desert, I can't kill you from here with my mind, no, but I have my uses." It scratched at its upper lip with one latex-covered finger, popping some blisters there. "You'll need a good disinfecting, Sarah. All those razor bumps on your head, that pimple on your chin—infections, all of them, did you know that? Nasty little colonies of germs. Take your clothes off. They'll need to be incinerated. You just need to be par-boiled a bit, to get the nastiness off you."

Sarah knew a threat when she heard one. She pulled her Makarov PM out of her pocket and slipped the safety off. "I don't think so, asshole. I think—"

"You think you can kill me from there and you're right, you can. One shot to the head." The lich pushed against the plastic curtain, moved a step closer to her. Despite herself Sarah took a step back. "Why don't you? Why don't you kill me right now? I won't stop you, I won't even try. It's this skin." The lich ran the knuckles of one hand across its leprous cheek. "I'm not one of the special ones. I wasn't brought back quite right. They tell you all about life eternal, you know, they tell you your body is good forever but they can't stop it. They can't stop the rot, you can't stop the rot no matter what you do. There's not enough bleach in the world. Now. Clothes off. Or shoot me in the head. I don't care either way."

Ptolemy swooped out from behind Sarah—he moved faster, nearly as fast as one of the accelerated ghouls that got Ayaan— and grabbed up the plastic sheet in both hands. He tore it off the rings holding it to the ceiling and thrust it away. The mummy grabbed the lich and wrestled it around into a headlock, its face peering up at Sarah, its rotten eyes wobbling in their sockets. It smiled broadly.

"That's the way, big boy. Come on. Squeeze me harder. You think I want to live forever in a rotten old shell like this?"

"Wait," Sarah told Ptolemy. "You'd just be doing it a favor." She stepped closer and put the safety back on her pistol. "We need information. We need to know where Ayaan is being kept. You can read my mind, you know who I'm talking about."

"Oh, I know indeed, but you don't think I'd give up that kind of dirt for nothing, do you? Let me have a little taste, first. Let me chew on one of your fingers."

Sarah grimaced and looked at the mummy. His painted face didn't offer any inspiration. She had an idea of her own, but it wasn't exactly the kind of cautious, well-thought-out plan that Ayaan would have come up with.

What the hell. "Hold him down, hold his head down," she told the mummy, and Ptolemy obliged. Scowling, she stuck a finger in her mouth, licked it a couple of times. She held it up to the light, caught a glint off the glob of saliva there, and jabbed it into the lich's rotting ear. Its waxy skin split under the pressure and she felt thick, viscous fluid swell up around her fingernail, but she knew the lich was more afraid of her than she was of it. "How many germs in a gram of human spit?" she asked, but the lich was already screaming.

12.

SARAH TIED THE dead thing's hands with a length of electrical cord. Ptolemy kept the lich in a sleeper hold as she led the two of them carefully out of the shack and through the streets and passages of the refinery. "Hello," she shouted, and around her the refinery woke up with sparkling gold energy. There were no other liches in the area, her prisoner had assured her of that much. There were no undead soldiers—just living humans, left behind when the Tsarevich decamped.

Not every victory had to come at the end of a hard struggle, she decided.

"It's all right, come out! You've been liberated," she shouted as bleary faces looked down at her from the catwalks. The Russians looked confused and bewildered, mostly.

A rifle shot rang out, and Sarah rolled under a massive pipe. Ptolemy pulled their captive into the partial cover. Sarah was the only one breathing, the only heart beating in that little space, but she made up for the other two. "I guess they didn't want to be liberated," she said.

"Oh, you're doing them such a favor, little filthy. Oh, ho, ho," the lich chortled. "The Tsarevich gave these little crumbs of humanity a real life. He gave them something to believe in, and now you're going to take it away. He fed them, clothed them—"

Sarah stared at the lich. It had already told her what she needed to know and far too much besides. "Ptolemy," she said, "keep that thing quiet so it doesn't give away our position."

The mummy got her drift. It tightened its hold on the lich until the evil thing's neck crackled and popped. Its glinting eyes stood out a little farther from their encrusted sockets and some of the boils on its cheeks popped open and spilled out a little pinkish fluid. Hopefully Ptolemy had crushed its larynx.

"All right, I'm going to try again," Sarah told the mummy. She slipped off the safety of her pistol and ducked back under the pipe. In the shadowy street she would be nearly invisible with the hood of her sweatshirt up.

The lich had explained to her, under certain prodding, that she had arrived too late. The Tsarevich—and Ayaan as his prisoner— had left the refinery behind. He had taken all of his undead minions with him, leaving only the rotting sexless lich as a protector for the living people he had abandoned. She didn't need to fire a shot now.

Except the living people she'd just saved didn't seem to see it that way.

"Listen, you've all been duped," she called out and sidled toward the dubious cover of an enclosed control stand. "He's been using you—using your bodies, using your souls! You don't have to believe his lies anymore!"

A grenade rolled out of the darkness and Sarah barely had time to get her head down and covered before it exploded, throwing vicious shrapnel all over the street. The pipes and towers rang with a million tiny impacts.

Sarah ducked back under the pipes where Ptolemy waited patiently for her. "It's not working," she told him. He touched his painted mouth.

She frowned in confusion, then nodded as realization dawned. She reached into the pocket of her sweatshirt and touched the soapstone.

perhaps speak they english don't perhaps speak english

He had an excellent point.

Once she'd gotten her composure back she shoved the lich out into the street and ducked out behind it, moving it quickly into a well-lit alley. She shoved her pistol into its back and nearly retched. Where her Makarov had touched its hospital gown, yellow fluid welled up and stained the cloth.

"Move," she told it. The lich raised its hands and shuffled forward. Sarah kept close. The people living in the refinery wouldn't dare shoot her if they might accidentally hit their overlord. She pushed it forward like an inhuman shield until she'd reached the refinery gates, only to find that someone had preceded her—they were locked tight.

Sarah nearly wet herself. She had no idea what to do next. The Russians, she had no doubt, were far less bewildered. They were probably gathering in the shadows even as she turned in slow circles, looking for them. They were probably setting up some kind of ambush. Her eyes darted back and forth as she looked for cover— she had no chance, she knew, if it came down to a protracted firefight, but maybe she could—

Ptolemy came up out of the darkness and grabbed the chain-link gates in his big hands. With a sound like linen tearing he strained and heaved until the fencing tore away from its uprights with a wild metallic squeal.

"*Mumiyah*," someone said in the darkness. "*Mumiyah!*" Sarah could hear many feet scurrying away as the Russians nearly stampeded each other trying to escape.

Sarah turned to look at her undead partner as if he'd sprouted horns. What on earth had scared the refinery's living so badly? She reached into her pocket.

we return should go before go they should return

"Yeah. I guess we should." She held her gaze on him for a while, then turned and bent to pass under the gap he'd made in the fence.

They made their way into the dark interior of the island without further incident. Sarah slept while the mummy watched their prisoner. In the minutes she lay curled inside a blanket, watching his painted face motionless in the starlight, she wondered what exactly she was accomplishing that he couldn't have done himself. They had failed to save his mummies—except for one. She imagined that at that point he was probably after vengeance and nothing else. Sarah had no problem using his wrath to help save Ayaan, but she had to wonder—was she even helping Ptolemy? Or was she just slowing him down?

Added to what she'd learned from the lich, she wasn't sure if she hadn't made a terrible mistake. If someone was going to rescue Ayaan, what made her think she was qualified? Who was she trying to kid? She was twenty years old. She'd never led so much as a squad into combat. Now she had one coward pilot and one insane and vengeful mummy and she had to tell them what to do at every turn, when even she had very little idea what to do next.

In the morning they made their way to the rendezvous down at an abandoned fishing village. Huddled around a decaying wharf the wrecks of boats stood mute in the water that slapped against their hulls. The helicopter stood in the town square, ready to go at a moment's notice. They found Osman standing on the pier watching rotten sails flap in the morning wind. He was inspecting the abandoned boats, bending to tear pieces of weathered wood away from ruptured hulls. He nodded when she approached.

"Caught yourself a prize, I see," he told her, glancing at the lich. Flies had gathered in one corner of its mouth and it twitched unhappily. With its hands bound, there was nothing it could do but swallow as many of the insects as it could grab with its ravaged lips. "I've seen fresher catches. What are you going to do with it?"

Sarah grimaced. "I don't know, tie it to a tree and leave it here or . . . something." She shrugged. "Look, they're gone," she told the pilot, uninterested in his jokes. "At least two days ago. The Tsarevich got what he needed here—this piece of shit wasn't sure what that might be, but he knew it had something to do with a ghost."

"A ghost?" Osman winced. "Like your Jack?"

Sarah raised her hands in dismay. "No idea. Look. They're gone, they're headed west. Maybe to Europe, maybe farther, the lich wasn't privy to the exact destination. There's something out there—something the Tsarevich wants, and now he can get it. They loaded up all the ghouls and liches they could fit into an old tanker or something and set sail. At least two days ago. We need to catch them, Osman."

He rubbed his chin. "Do we?"

"Yes. Look, this lich was left behind to kind of keep an eye on the place, but even it had heard about Ayaan. She's some kind of celebrity in the ghoul world, probably for killing Gary. There's no telling what they'll do to her. If she's still alive it's probably only because they want to make her suffer as long as possible before they kill her."

"You know what she would say right now, don't you? 'It's too damn bad.' You can do what you like, Sarah, but I don't plan on racing halfway across the world without a little more to go on." He threw a piece of waterlogged wood out into the harbor, skipping it a couple of times.

Sarah couldn't believe it. "You'd give up just like that?"

"Yeah, just like that. We gave it a good try. We got here too late. Now I'm going to go back and try my luck with Fathia." He stood his ground, arms folded. He wasn't headed for the helicopter but he wasn't taking her orders, either. "This is a game for grown-ups now. You had a little fun playing the hero, girl, but the world doesn't have room for that anymore."

"I'm not a child," Sarah said, her teeth grinding together.

"At sixteen years old Ayaan shot her first lich. She was a child. She was a smart child."

Sarah nodded, understanding. He wanted to help her. He just didn't believe in her ability. He didn't want to go back to Egypt— and he probably had a soft spot in his heart for Ayaan. But he needed to see what she was made of, first. Exactly what she'd wondered herself while she'd tried to sleep the night before and Ptolemy stood watch.

She took out her pistol and moved to stand over the sexless lich where Ptolemy had thrown it to the ground. It looked up at her with eyes that were very, very human. It didn't fear death, she knew, it would welcome a bullet in its brains, but that only made it harder. She had killed before, she had even shot Mariam in the helicopter, but that had been self-defense. This was cold blood.

She thought of Ayaan. Ayaan had taught her to act and not think.

She lined up the shot and squeezed the trigger. Skull fragments danced across the wharf. Gray brain matter oozed from the exit wound and slithered onto the rough wood of the pier.

"Ayaan shot Gary in the head. It didn't take." Osman handed Sarah a thick plank of wood. One end was covered in sharp white barnacle shells. She used the plank like a club and smashed the lich's head into pulp. She lifted her arms again and again until they were sore, bringing the wood down on the diseased flesh as if she were winnowing grain.

"All right," Osman said when she was merely spreading the gore around. "All right, enough. Good. Now." He jerked the club out of her hands. "Where do you want to go?"

13.

EVERYONE WORKED ON the ship. The *Pinega* had been rated for ninety crewmen when she was launched and that had been for trained, veteran sailors. The hundred-odd living people on board the ship had their hands full, since most of them had never left dry land before. Seasickness, the occasional midnight snack for the liches (everyone knew it was happening, nobody breathed a word), and the ship's particular problems took their toll and on an average day perhaps two-thirds of the women and men living on the main deck could be accurately described as able-bodied. Every warm body was needed just to keep the boat moving, and everyone knew their place.

They kept the most gruesome and repellent task for Ayaan. She got to carry the hand bucket.

"There are two hundred and six bones in the human body," a doctor told her, kneeling next to a patient who didn't so much as flinch as he began to carve. "Twenty-seven of them are in each hand. That's a quarter of the bones in the body. There are more muscles, more, more . . ."

"Here," she told him, and lifted away the dead piece of meat from the patient's arm. The patient, of course, was already dead and it had no liquid blood to mop up, just a dry brownish powder that blew off the stern deck in a playful ocean breeze.

"The hand is more complex than any organ in the body, except perhaps the brain. It is evolution's greatest miracle. And to them . . . to them it's almost useless. They lack the fine motor control. These hands might as well be lumps of . . . of meat." His eyes, what she could see of them behind his scratched glasses, went very vacant for a moment. Then he leaned forward with a metal rasp and started to sharpen the exposed lengths of ulna and radius. "You're going to do it, aren't you?" he asked in a whisper.

"I'm going to try," she said. She didn't whisper. They had powers she lacked, senses she didn't have. If they were going to overhear her, there was nothing she could do about it.

"Find me when you're ready," he told her.

She gathered the excised meat from the neat piles the other doctors had made on the open-deck surgery (no need for sterile conditions with these patients). She watched the eyes of the dead men and women who lay stretched out on the deck, looked for the hunger in them. She had to give the Tsarevich some credit—he kept his charges under tight control.

To reach her next stop she had to pass one of the seven hold compartments of the *Pinega*. There were a couple of reasons to wish she could avoid that part of her route. For one thing there was the ship's original mission, and the residue of its old cargo that remained. The *Pinega* had been built by the Soviets to ferry nuclear waste to containment facilities near the North Pole. It could hold a thousand tons of solid waste—spent fuel rods, mostly—in two of its holds and eight hundred cubic meters of liquid toxins in the other five. It had been emptied out, of course, but on the first day of the voyage, as the living and the dead were herded onboard, the lich overseer of the deck had passed around a Geiger counter so they could all see just how little concern the Tsarevich had for their bodily safety. Ayaan had taken away her own lesson from that. The cultists—the faithful—had taken it in stride. If their deaths could be hastened on by service to their master, they didn't have a problem with that. They thought being dead was just the next phase of existence, and a better one at that. Very few of them were allowed to see what happened in the surgeries at the stern, but Ayaan wondered if even the gore back there would dissuade them. These were true believers, and they considerably outnumbered the sane living people on board. For every doctor horrified at what he was asked to do, there were five or six deckhands who scrubbed and scrubbed at the decks long past the limit of human endurance, who would rather scrub than eat just in case the Tsarevich walked by and wanted to see his reflection in the deck plates.

A few like that were painting the superstructure as she passed by. They were covered in gray paint, their faces and hands and torsos daubed with a redolence of toxic chemicals. Their eyes were flat and lifeless in their heads, as if they were already practicing the traditional empty stare of the ghouls they hoped to become. They gave the heavy plastic buckets she hauled no more than a passing glance. Ayaan didn't look at them, didn't look at the deck ahead of her. She stared out to sea at the ever-changing, never-changing waves and tried not to think about what lay ahead.

She kept her cool even as the hatches she passed by jumped and flexed. She was pretty sure the liches did that just to spook her. The dead on board, the vast majority of them stacked like driftwood belowdecks, had to be secured. She could imagine the Tsarevich letting them go, leaving them to their hunger and their instincts. It would be a way for him to conserve psychic energy. Even if he did that, though, he would need to make sure that the hatches could not be opened or forced from below.

Still. As she passed a staircase leading down into gloom she could hear them straining against their confinement. She could feel the deck shake with their need.

Ayaan hurried past.

The buckets in her hands got truly heavy—her arms complained at the weight, anyway, as she moved forward to the main entrance to the superstructure. She paused and set them down, just for a moment, even though she knew it was a mistake. The Least would spot her. He always did.

Ayaan stood about crotch-high to the Least. He was maybe three times as broad as her through the shoulders. He stank of death, of musty, rancid fat and ancient sweat. His face dangled from his skull like a wax mask that slipped down from its wearer's true features. He had been put in charge of maintaining order on the foredeck.

The Least was one of the Tsarevich's first experiments in creating a new lich, an underling with the intelligence to command troops. It hadn't quite taken. When Ayaan ducked into a shadow near the entrance to the above-decks quarters, he was busy stomping through the chaos of the main foredeck, a maze of winches and cranes and enormous battened hatches where the living had set up their bedrolls and their hammocks and their small tents. Dozens of wispy pillars of smoke rose from the tiny deckhouses where the living prepared their simple food. The Least made sure he got an unwholesome share of everything they made. He had five hundred kilos of bulk to maintain, after all. Ayaan watched him dip one enormous hand into a boiling rice pot and shove the grains in his mouth, the scalding water running down his chin and raising blisters in the roll of fat that ran around his neck like a goiter. She gagged at the thought of eating out of a pot he had touched, but she knew she had done so many times.

She shouldn't have stared. He caught her glance and returned it—with a horrific smile. He knew what she had in her buckets. He would want a taste.

He came stumping toward her on telephone pole–size legs, his splayed toenails digging into the deck. "To be giving me one bucket, yes," he said in Russian. They said the Least had been a gangster once, a Moscow mafioso. Just before the Epidemic had hit he'd been shot in the gut and left to die in a meat locker in a dance-club kitchen. When the Tsarevich found him he was dead and frozen, and when the Tsarevich thawed out part of his brain he had died despite the boy lich's best efforts.

"This isn't for you," she said. He should have known that, and maybe he did. Maybe he didn't care.

"Don't waste, don't waste one drop," he bellowed, spit rolling out of his mouth. He was hungry, all right. "Use it all, honor all, sacred is all." His eyes were very wide.

If she let even a drop of blood escape her buckets Ayaan would be beaten for her failure. There was no point arguing to the Least's sense of reason. Her only chance was to outrun him. "Stay back, the Tsarevich gave me my orders," she shouted. She grabbed up her buckets in fingers that were red with the effort of carrying the weight, fingers that didn't want to close. "Stay back," she shouted and dashed inside the superstructure. A two-story run up a steep metal staircase awaited her. She would make it, she would run faster than the Least. She always had before.

"To giving me," the Least howled as if someone had stuck him with a straight pin. "You be to giving me!"

At the top of the stairs, her body heaving with the effort, Ayaan ducked into a companionway and kicked the hatch shut behind her. She had made it.

The rest was easy. She passed through the flying bridge where the navigators stood watch, keeping the ship on course. Most of them turned up their noses at her as she passed, not wanting to associate with anyone so uncouth as to pull hand-bucket duty. One junior navigator, though, did give her a glance. A girl from a fishing village in Turkey who had come into the Tsarevich's service at the same time as Ayaan. As she passed, the girl tilted her head slightly in an almost imperceptible nod. Ayaan made no acknowledgement.

Down another corridor and up to the door. Ayaan rolled her shoulders and tried not to think about the pain in her arms. Almost done. She hit an automatic hatch release with her hip and stepped into the officers' mess, a low room lined with clean windows, the walls and floor draped with Persian rugs. On couches before her the liches and their favorites waited. One of them—she didn't know his name but he was covered everywhere in thick fur like an ape—came up and politely offered to take the buckets from her, but she politely declined. Another squatted down on the floor and showed her a wide, lipless smile. The green phantom scowled at her, while Cicatrix smiled disinterestedly and reburied herself in an issue of French *Vogue* so old the lamination had worn off the cover. The living woman had a bright new scar on her cheek. It was healing well.

With a grunt Ayaan emptied her buckets into a tub full of ice. She tried not to look at the hands as they slithered out, the fingers lacing together, the dry blood running out in a fine sift. She tried not to let the powder get into her mouth or nose.

When the buckets were empty she turned to go. She knew it was futile but she moved steadily, purposely toward the door.

"There's one more thing," the green phantom said. She felt her body surge as he toyed with her metabolism. Would he wear her out, make her exhausted even though her shift was half over? Would he give her a goose, make her hyper until her jaw ached from grinding? His possibilities for amusement at her expense seemed endless.

"Yes, sir," she said, wondering what demeaning errand he would have this time, and turned around. Had she been anyone else she might have screamed at what she saw.

14.

A HUMAN BRAIN. In a jar.

Cyrillic characters ran around the top and bottom of the glass jar, etched in a flowing cursive hand. Inside the jar the brain floated in yellowish liquid, dangling from a web of silver chains. It was a human brain, most definitely, and most certainly it was dead. Ayaan lacked the sensory sensitivity of a lich, but even she could tell that something had taken up residence in the disembodied organ. It didn't pulse or glow but it wasn't quite dead, either, and somehow Ayaan knew exactly who was inside.

A mummy carried the jar. Not just any mummy. The fiftieth mummy, the former high priestess of Sobk who had crocodiles painted like a print on her ragged linen. The last mummy, the one Ayaan had been about to slaughter when the ghost had appeared.

It had been only a week ago. Ayaan remembered it well.

The stink of cordite and bitumen had filled the concrete bunker. The smoke was so thick she'd had trouble seeing what she was doing. She had not hesitated—one after the other she had shot each of the fifty mummies in the head. Just as she'd been told.

When she'd reached the last of them, she'd paused to wipe sweat from her brow. She had caught movement in the bunker's doorway and she turned, her weapon coming up, to cover the entrance.

"Enough, enough, enough," the ghost had chanted, rushing into the room. It had not looked like a ghost, of course. It had looked like one of the dead. It had possessed the crumbling flesh of a Cypriot ghoul in order to steal its voice. True intelligence had shown in its borrowed eyes and Ayaan remembered the story Dekalb, Sarah's father, had told her, of a creature that could inscribe its personality over the blank slates of the dead. A creature that had helped him in the final mad rush of corpses in Central Park. A creature that had a special affinity for mummies.

It had to be the same intelligence, the same spirit. The ghost that the Tsarevich so desperately wanted to contact had to be the thing that had saved New York City from Gary's final, horrible revenge. When it arrived Ayaan had looked around the bunker and seen for the first time just what they had made her do, and it gave her gooseflesh.

"Enough. Spare her and I'll do as the lad wants," the ghost had said. Its face fell—not with the torpor of the undead but with genuine sadness. "Tell him he has me, you lot. Go and tell him now!" With its temporary hands the ghost had thrown over the bunker's table, smashed to kindling one of the chairs. Ayaan had been afraid, truly afraid that it would seek vengeance on her for what she had done.

If it was planning revenge, it was taking its time.

"This is our beloved leader's friend. The ghost," the green phantom told her, a week later in the officers' mess of the nuclear-waste freighter *Pinega*. She looked up at him and the memory evaporated from her mind. He waved a few bony fingers at the thing in the jar. "We stripped him of his borrowed body and let him inhabit this vessel because it's easier to watch. We had to take steps to make sure he didn't run out on us again. He's shown himself a very slippery fish. Supposedly he has something he wants to tell you."

"Me," Ayaan said, rubbing her suddenly moist palms on her pants. "Well, I suppose that makes sense. Um. Hello," she tried.

Neither the brain nor the mummy so much as twitched. Across the room Cicatrix put down her magazine to watch. The green phantom rose and went to the icy trough where Ayaan had unloaded her grisly haul. He made no attempt at nicety, digging into the bony meat in the trough like a starving animal. Between bites he managed to choke out, "He says he wants you to know there are no hard feelings. He would have done the same in your position."

"That's . . . I mean, tell him I'm grateful for his . . . his . . ."

"*Magnanimity* is the word that leaps to mind." The phantom wiped blood from his cheeks and lips with a silk napkin. "He can hear you, you know. I don't have to translate for *him*."

Ayaan nodded. "So, well, thank you. And I am sorry. So truly, truly sorry."

"He had something else for you—a message. I don't claim to understand it. He says she's just fine, and closer to your heart than ever."

"'She'?" Ayaan asked.

"That's what he said. Listen, I can barely understand him myself. I won't be arsed to play twenty questions with him just to appease your curiosity. If I had to guess I would say it was talking about its mummy friend. Get back to work."

Ayaan nodded agreeably and backed out of the room. With a moment's thought she had answered her own question and she didn't feel like sharing. The "she" of the message was not the mummy, she had grasped that much at once. It had to be Sarah. The brain's other statement wasn't so easy to decipher. Had it claimed that Ayaan was closer to Sarah's heart than ever it would have made perfect sense. It was possible the ghost lacked a grasp of the finer nuances of English idiom.

She didn't think so, though. She thought the ghost knew exactly what it was saying. Sarah was closer to Ayaan's heart—did it mean—could it mean that Sarah was nearby? Physically close to Ayaan's heart? But how, and more importantly, why?

Could she trust the brain? Could it be lying to her? In the end she supposed it didn't matter. She had a mutiny to pull off, after all, and there were going to be casualties. If the brain or its attending mummy got in the way it wouldn't hold her back.

Her job took her back to the stern surgeries. On the way she passed around a side of the rear superstructure, a four-story structure that tapered to a spacious suite of officers' quarters with a magnificent view of the surrounding ocean. Only the radar tower stood higher. There was a reason for putting the officers' quarters up so high—it kept the ship's most important personnel as far as possible from the depleted fuel rods in the forward compartments. The liches were hardly bothered by the ship's radioactivity—it probably did them good, actually, because it would sterilize their putrid flesh of microbes and slow down their decay. They had taken the tower for themselves simply because it afforded the best view, as far as she knew.

On the lowest level of the tower Ayaan passed the zealots she'd seen earlier laying down a second coat of marine paint on the deck plates. They didn't so much as glance up at her.

They didn't have to. One of them, an old man with a Russian accent but the Asian features of a Siberian, stood up with one hand holding his back and stepped into the shadows of the tower entrance. Ayaan passed by the hatchway, then doubled back once she was out of sight of the cultists and stepped in through an emergency exit. The Siberian was busy in the darkness inside, shoving bits of torn-up, paint-stained rag into a hatch near the floor. Ayaan bent down to help him. "You know the sign we're looking for," she said to him.

He didn't nod. He didn't stop what he was doing. He had been a librarian in another universe, a better one, and a closeted homosexual. His partner, a colonel in the Russian Air Force, had convinced him to join up with the Tsarevich. He had in fact been one of the most fervent recruits when the call first came. He swore up and down that they would not be persecuted in the new life, and to be fair, they hadn't been. When the liches carried the colonel off to satisfy their appetites, they hadn't even considered his sexual orientation. They were equal opportunity devourers.

"When all of them are inside, that's when you set the fire," Ayaan repeated, just in case. Perfect timing would be the only way to carry this off. Even then she would need a great deal of luck.

It would be impossible to foment a revolution on the *Pinega*, she knew. There were too many true believers on the ship and far too many animated corpses. With the help of her friend in the navigation room, however, she had learned of a way to cut those odds in half. When the Soviets fabricated the nuclear-waste hauler they had built a special feature into the holds. By throwing certain switches on the flying bridge, anyone could open hatches on the bottom of the ship, hatches meant to dump the enclosed wastes into the ocean at large. It had been the ship's standard practice to take the fuel rods and radiothermic generators and depleted uranium cargo out into international waters and just let them go. According to Ayaan's informant, there never had been a containment facility near the North Pole—it would have been prohibitively expensive to build such a thing, at least compared to the cost of open-sea dumping. The bankrupt bureaucrats at the end of the Soviet empire had little concern for the International Tribunal for the Law of the Sea and even less for Greenpeace.

Now, if Ayaan could get those hatches open, the undead stored in the compartments would be flushed away like so much toxic waste. The tepid waters of the Mediterranean might not kill them, but she really didn't care. They could wander around the bottom of the sea forever, spearing whatever fish were stupid enough to wander by with their sharpened forearms. She would have bigger problems to deal with—namely the liches. As soon as they realized something was up, they would retreat to their tower. The green phantom could kill from a distance. Other liches could turn their own powers against Ayaan and her tiny cadre of rebels.

If the tower was set on fire once they were inside, however, she imagined they would be too distracted to put up much resistance. The doctor, who had access to bone-saws, fire axes, and hammers (his surgery was neither precise nor delicate), would stop anyone from trying to get out of the tower—or anyone living from trying to rescue the liches trapped within. It would take some time for the tower to burn down, but the Siberian's hard work secreting inflammables in its various nooks and crannies meant the blaze would get off to a good start.

The Tsarevich lived in the penthouse on the fourth floor. He would be the last to be incinerated, which was a bit of a risk. It would give him time to realize what was happening and maybe do something else about it.

Another risk was that she had no way to put out the fire once it started. The *Pinega* had a steel hull, but much of its interior fittings were made of wood. Years ago it had possessed a system of internal sprinklers and plenty of fire extinguishers, but none of that equipment could be expected to work after so long.

Then there was the question of what the living faithful, the zealots who worshipped the Tsarevich, would do once they saw what was happening. Ayaan hoped they would listen to reason. With the Tsarevich dead they would be leaderless and their power would be cut down to a fraction. If they strung her up from the yardarm, well, at least she would have spared the rest of the world from whatever it was the Tsarevich had planned for his ship of fools.

She had only one certainty—that this was the best chance she would ever get. The Tsarevich was bent on some unknown scheme. Capturing the ghost had set his entire operation into motion. By the time they reached dry land, it would be too late to stop him. She had to act with real haste or lose this opportunity forever.

"Get back to your station or someone will see," the Siberian told her. He never looked at her eyes. He had lived as a gay man under Soviet rule long enough to know how these things were done. He'd been trained by the best—the KGB. Under their ever-present gaze, to have a love life he had become a master conspirator.

Ayaan had little experience at plots and schemes. She'd always believed that the Avtomat Kalashnikova Model 1947 was the answer to every question life posed. She was learning so much. The girl navigator, the Siberian, the doctor cutting hands on the stern—they had been secret agents from the beginning. They needed her, too, though. None of them would ever have acted on their own. The Tsarevich's power felt too great, too pervasive. They needed Ayaan's leadership.

She headed out of the tower and back toward the stern, back toward her official duties. When the time came she knew she would be ready. She had no choice.

15.

SARAH SWABBED OUT the inside of one of the buckets they used to catch rain. As usual a seagull had shit in it—the birds mistook the white canisters for public toilets. Sarah had never thought she could learn to hate living animals so much.

The tug rolled and she smacked her hip against the gunwale. It happened often enough that she was starting to get calluses. She had learned not to use her hands to try to steady herself when she tried—once—to catch a line on the side of the wheelhouse and felt the skin burn right off her palms. The tug was not meant for the kind of swells the Mediterranean offered. Sarah had no idea how they could stay upright on the open ocean. She supposed she could chalk it up to Osman's expert piloting, and the fact that they had yet to see a real storm.

At least she was getting over her seasickness. As long as she didn't go aft and have to smell the diesel fuel (or worse, its hot hydrocarbon exhaust), she felt only partially nauseous. Bilious, perhaps. Like something liquid and extremely foul was wallowing around in her empty stomach, but at least it didn't try to come up too often.

She cleaned out the last bucket with a dirty rag and headed forward, toward the bow where Ptolemy sat in a perfect lotus position, evidently enjoying the salt spray. She touched the soapstone. Even though he was facing away from her, that simple contact was enough to get his attention. "Were you a sailor in a past life?" she asked.

everyone was sailor in that dream time canopus they sea say canopus time was desert a sailor they time say that desert all who canopus live in the desert sailor dream of the sea

As usual she understood maybe 10 percent of what he had to say. "Canopus, that's part of your name. Ptolemaeus—that's the Roman form of Ptolemy." Jack had explained it to her. "Ptolemy was one of Alexander the Great's generals and he took over Egypt from the pharaohs. You were a descendant of his." Ptolemy nodded. "And then Canopus . . . like the star?" she asked. "And those . . . what do you call them? Canopic jars. The jars they put your internal organs in."

He nodded.

both

Well, at least that made some sense. Then he had to ruin it by going on.

he drowned was troy menelaus's helmsman, a city sailor beyond drowned compare they say named a drowned city for him a city that helmsman drowned menelaus he beheld helen city of troy a sailor they say

In her bleary condition it was too much. Sarah let go of the soapstone. "Yeah, well," she said, the words burbling out of her like her breakfast just might, "enjoy your cruise, whatever. Don't get up and do any work or anything."

That was hardly fair. Ptolemy did much of the truly physical labor, almost all of the heavy lifting, and he kept the tug going at night while she and Osman slept. The living pilot hardly liked the arrangement—he would never trust a dead thing—but he had no choice. If they were going to catch up with the Russians they couldn't lay to every evening.

"Sarah," Osman called, sounding a little excited, maybe, "you should see this."

She picked her way carefully back around the wheelhouse of the tiny tugboat and ducked under the weather hood. Osman was standing with his feet apart, one hand draped bonelessly over the wheel. He didn't look down at the radar screen so much as point at it with his chin. His eyes were busy scanning the horizon.

If you needed to know what kind of boat you should take on a rescue mission, Osman was the man to ask. He had passed by most of the surviving watercraft they found in the harbors and marinas of Cyprus—one had a bad engine efficiency, the sails on another were merely for show. He had finally had to decide between a seventy-five-meter pleasure yacht with sumptuous staterooms below or a tugboat that had been sitting in dry dock for twelve years. He picked the tug.

It had a monstrously large fuel supply, for one. It was meant for hauling supertankers down through the Suez Canal. With nothing in tow it could sail forever (or close enough) on a single tank. Secondly it had a radar tower much, much taller than the boat was long. It needed heavy-duty navigation gear to get through the narrow locks of the aging canal. Sarah needed heavy-duty detection gear if she ever hoped to find the Russians in the middle of one of the world's biggest seas.

In the dry dock Osman had run any number of tests on the tug's radar equipment. Miracle of miracles, it still worked. Now Sarah looked down and saw the blip that had caught Osman's attention. It looked like a splotch of glowing bird shit to her. "How do we know it's not an island, or a drifting log?"

"Because, little girl, I know the difference between a radar and a tin can on a string. A bogey that size was rare enough back in the golden age. Now it means only one thing—a seagoing vessel at least a hundred meters long."

So it was a lot bigger than the tug. Well, no surprise there. "How far away?"

"We'll see it in a moment. You'd better get your boyfriend out of sight. We know this bunch don't care for mummies."

Sarah understood. She touched the soapstone and asked Ptolemy to go belowdecks, just in case anyone was watching them even then. The mummy acquiesced without a word of complaint. Osman took his wheel in both hands and adjusted their course a hair. "Do you see it?" he asked.

She knew he wasn't asking if she could see something visually. She stared out over the boat's prow, trying to ignore the flapping canvas of the backup sails, letting her eyes focus on the rising and falling swells off in the distance, the occasional scrap of foam drifting on the waves. "Nothing," she said. There was no energy out there, living or dead. She imagined there were probably some fish but the water blocked her special sense.

Osman just nodded. He'd stared out over enough empty seas in his life, Sarah imagined, to recognize when something was about to appear. He didn't speak, didn't move, didn't breathe as far as she could tell. And then—

No. It was nothing, a trick of the light. She could have sworn something was there and then it just wasn't. "Maybe a whale," she said, thinking it might have dived at the sight of them.

"Bullshit," Osman said and opened up his throttle a little. He picked up a microphone for the tug's radio set and clicked it on. "Hey," he said. "Hey, we're alive over here. We are not dead." He repeated this simple message in Arabic, in Farsi, in Greek.

Sarah turned to look away, her eyes glazed over by the sight of the endless sea constantly moving, and found herself looking into a periscope. She fell backward against the tug's wheel, but Osman caught it before she could turn the boat. "Submarine," she said, when she had caught her breath.

It surfaced with a great pitching of the sea, a boiling white explosion that rolled the tug around like an ice cube in a blender. Saltwater lapped up over the side and splashed Sarah's bare feet.

On top of the waves the submarine dwarfed the tug, its enormous curved black side slick with water and glaring with sunlight. On its deck they saw what looked like an acre's worth of photovoltaic cells and a heavy machine gun on a pintle mount. Its barrel pointed away from them. Something wrapped in tarpaulin, about half the size of a human being, was secured to the deck with heavy lines. It dripped a steady stream of water as the submarine rolled under the sun.

A hatch in the stubby conning tower opened up and a white woman with golden hair and a wet suit stepped out onto the pitching deck. She rolled with the motion of the submarine as if her feet were nailed down. "Ahoy," she called, no more than ten meters from where Sarah stood on the tug. She had a pistol on her belt.

"Hi," Sarah replied. "I'm . . . sorry. You're not the woman I'm looking for."

The woman spoke English with a Scandinavian accent. "That depends," she said, her face a mask of consternation. "Is your name Sarah?"

26.

AYAAN DIPPED HER sponge in the murky tub and then squeezed it between her two hands so it wouldn't drip. The liches in the officers' mess were quite particular about their windows. There was little in the way of entertainment available to them on board—those who could read had already worked their way through the scant magazines and books left behind by the previous crew. Looking out at the waves was hardly the pinnacle of excitement, but it had a hypnotic power, especially in the twilight hours. The hairy lich, the one Ayaan had begun to think of as a werewolf, could stand by the window for whole days at a time. It seemed that being dead changed your brain chemistry, made you less anxious at the passing of time, of the waste of your life. Of course, maybe it was just the fact that the liches were functionally immortal. If she knew she had centuries, millennia to pass, Ayaan knew, she would feel a lot less urgency to *carpe* every *diem,* herself.

"Look, Amanita's come out for some sun," the werewolf said. His voice was muffled and distorted—the weird growth of hair lined all of his orifices, his tongue covered in what looked like sodden felt— but Ayaan could understand his simple English. Along with the other liches in the room she stepped over to where he pointed, his furry finger smearing grease on the windowpane. Ayaan silently grumbled: she would have to clean that mark.

Amanita, the creature the werewolf had seen, was often spoken of by the cultists, but Ayaan had never seen her before. She had, she remembered, seen mushrooms and puffballs growing in profusion at the refinery on Cyprus, so she must have been very close to the Tsarevich's most accomplished lieutenant. Still, she wasn't prepared for what she saw through the window. Atop the tower where the liches kept their quarters Amanita stood naked in the sun, perhaps two and a half meters tall. She made no attempt to cover her genitalia, but then she hardly needed to. A thick layer of fungal growth covered every square centimeter of her skin. Long, filamentous mycelia made her hair while her shoulders and back were studded with yellow chytrids. Dark hairy mildew draped from her breasts, while rows of bright orange Judas' ear mushrooms ringed her distended belly and mold dripped from her fingers.

She had the power, they said, that made grain sprout from the earth, that made creeping vines twist across Siberian tundra. She had the ultimate green thumb, she could make anything vegetative flourish wherever a dried-up seed or a crystallized spore or a half-gnawed rhizome still lingered in the ground. They said she had saved entire villages from starvation after the unceasingly hungry ghouls had devoured all their crops. Her true love, though, was not in green things but in blights and rots and molds—and especially mushrooms. The name she'd chosen sounded pretty enough. It was the Latin name for the mushroom commonly called the "destroying angel."

What she might be doing atop the tower was anyone's guess. "I wonder if this has anything to do with your friend," the green phantom said, turning to look directly at Ayaan.

Ayaan held the sponge carefully with both hands so it wouldn't drip on the floor. She tried to look like she had no idea what he meant. It wasn't hard—she didn't.

"You know, the girl. The girl on the flying bridge. I think she's one of the navigators. Isn't she one of your coconspirators?" The green phantom smiled, his desiccated skin stretching whitely across his sharp jaws.

Ayaan dropped the sponge and ran. She expected to feel his power wrapping icy chains around her heart at any moment as she stumbled down the stairs, down toward the foredeck. She was just trying to get away from him. Strangely enough, he let her go.

She rushed out onto the deck, dodging cook fires and capstans. She saw the Least ahead and knew she would have to avoid him. Beyond that she had no plan. What was he doing? He kept jumping up and down. The whole deck vibrated as he collided with it again and again. Hiding behind an enormous bollard, she peered out to see what he was up to. He was trying to touch the end of the ship's main crane, an enormous long boom made of girders that loomed out over half the deck. Something dangled at the end of the crane, a piece of bloody meat or—

It was the Turkish girl, of course. Ayaan swallowed in horror. They had cut her wrists and her ankles, punched holes in her until her blood ran in sheets down her body, but they hadn't killed her. She was still moving, a spasm here, a twitch there in between long pauses to rest and regain what little strength remained to her. She was still alive.

Just the way the Least would want her.

Ayaan slapped her own cheeks to try to get her blood moving again and hurried aft. There was still a chance, a chance to do some good. Without the girl on the flying bridge they couldn't release the underside compartment hatches, they couldn't flush the Tsarevich's army of undead. They could still—the fire—

Ayaan had never known the girl's name. It had been intentional—in case any of them were caught they couldn't give each other away. It just seemed horrible now. She had gotten the girl tortured to death, might as well have fed her to that brute herself, and for what? For—Ayaan stopped herself. The liches were still all up in the superstructure, in the mess she had just left, but the Tsarevich and Amanita were in the tower. If the liches knew about the girl, they certainly knew about the Siberian and the plan to torch the tower. They could catch her at any moment, they could kill her from a distance. If she acted quickly enough, however, if she didn't stop to think, maybe she could still sell her life dearly.

He was there—the Siberian—standing outside the tower as she drew near. Just standing there, waiting for her to come and tell him what to do. She rushed up waving her hands and yelling at him, not caring who might hear, screaming at him to start the fire, but he just stood there, looking at her, his face empty of emotion.

She got close enough to touch him but she didn't. She knew something was wrong. He opened his mouth to speak and then he started coughing, spasmodically, horribly, gagging and choking and spitting. Dark clouds of spores erupted from his mouth, stained

Ayaan's clothing where they flecked across her. The sea breeze tore the rest of them out and away to float over the ocean. The Siberian's skin darkened, started to turn blue. Not from anoxia, though he was clearly suffocating. It was a creeping kind of mold, like penicillin growing on bread, that changed his color. It swarmed up and over him, dry smut dripping from his tear glands, furry mold sprouting from his ears, from his nose. He was dead before he hit the ground.

Cicatrix walked out of the deck-level entrance to the tower. She had the doctor, the hand surgeon from the stern, on an actual leash attached to a dog collar around his neck.

"Tell her what you do to her," Cicatrix demanded, and forced the man to his knees.

He stammered and sobbed and tried to look up at Ayaan but he couldn't, he didn't have the strength.

"Tell her!" Cicatrix screamed and kicked the man in his ribs.

"Stop. I know what he did," Ayaan told her. Clearly he had divulged her secrets. Given away her grand plot. She couldn't blame him, either. He had a badly sutured wound on the end of his right arm where one of his hands used to be. He'd probably begged them to leave the left one intact. Ayaan wondered if he had told them how many bones were in his hand, how many muscles.

A wave of revulsion for the broken man swam up through her innards, blossomed in her throat. He should have died, he should have thrown himself over the side of the boat before confessing. It was what she would have demanded of herself. She tried to tell herself that the threat of death would make this man do anything— anything to survive. It was hardly a unique perspective. It wasn't hers, though. Ayaan had grown up listening to stories of glorious martyrs, of those who traded their worldly lives for the greater good. She was old enough to know better, but she didn't suppose she would ever have real sympathy for such a coward.

Her mouth filled. She spat on him.

"You've caught me," she told Cicatrix. "I won't apologize. As one living woman to another all I ask for is a clean death."

Cicatrix smiled at her. "It was clever plan," she said, ignoring Ayaan's request. "We talk about it, all this day, Tsarevich and myself. We were quite impressed and entertained."

Clearly Ayaan wasn't going to get the swift resolution she wanted. She glanced sideways at the taffrail. She could be over it in a second. It would take only a heartbeat before she hit the water. Ayaan couldn't swim—it would be over quickly enough. She'd heard unpleasant things about death by drowning, and it wouldn't keep her from coming back as a ghoul, but. Still. It would be a better exit. A cleaner way to go.

She sprang for the rail. Got one foot up.

Then she felt the energy draining out of her limbs, her muscles, her bones. She could barely keep her eyelids open. Any moment she would . . . she would collapse . . . she knew the . . . green phantom . . . had her . . .

"We like you," Cicatrix said, bending over her, smiling down at her. Ayaan had fallen to the deck without realizing it. "We think you are fun."

Ayaan's vision closed down like a black shutter falling across Cicatrix's face.

17.

MAGNA HELPED SARAH down the narrow ladder into the belly of the FNS *Nordvind*, the most advanced submarine in the Finnish Navy. There wasn't much competition anymore. "He found me," she told Sarah, talking about her husband. He had been a warrant officer aboard the *Nordvind* when the Epidemic began. He had also been the submarine's sole survivor. "They put into port with the dead already coming over the fence. He deserted when he saw what was happening. Well, they all deserted. He came and found me—I was on the roof of the officers' lounge. He came and found me and he hasn't spoken a word since."

The two women passed forward into the bridge of the submarine. Magna's three children, none of them over ten, scrambled out of their way. The oldest, a girl wearing a captain's hat with maroon bars, folded up the periscope handles and raised into a locked position.

"They're adorable," Sarah said, watching the blond children studying the submarine's instruments.

"They're my angels." Magna touched the springy yellow curls of the youngest, a girl who sat at the chart table with her feet dangling from the chair. Then she brought Sarah to a small room ahead of the bridge, a briefing room for the captain. Her husband, Linus, sat at a low table there, a plate of salted cod untouched next to him. His hair and beard were pure white and draped down over his shirt, clean and carefully brushed. He didn't look up when Ayaan entered. "Lover," Magna called, but that elicited no response, either. "He's like this all the time. He'll eat, if I feed him. He'll do just about anything if I talk him through it, but he would just sit there forever if I let him." Magna gave him a tiny smile, her face folding in on itself as she hugged her own arms. "Catatonic stupor, they call it. I don't have the drugs to treat him but I can look up their names in my *Physicians' Desk Reference*."

Something occurred to Sarah, something she didn't want to consider too closely. If the man had been catatonic for twelve years, and his eldest daughter was only ten at the most . . . well. People got lonely. Sarah knew a little bit about manners, so she didn't ask.

"Normally we stay surfaced for the fresh air and the sunlight. We only dive when someone comes by. I've kept us alive this long by cultivating my antisocial behaviors. I fish over the side most days, and some days I just lie in bed and conserve my energy," Magna told her. "I have a little garden down here, under some ultraviolet lamps. The submariners used those when they went on polar missions, to avoid seasonal affective disorder. Sometimes I need them, too."

"You dive whenever anybody comes by?" Sarah asked. "Does that happen often?"

Magna nodded absently. "There are a surprisingly large number of people like me. People who have surrendered dry land to the deaders. Most of them aren't as well kitted out as I am. A lot of them are borderline personality types, do you understand? Pirates."

"But you surfaced for us."

Magna smiled, a smile so wry and complicated it looked like a frown. "Only because you happen to be the friend of a friend. I dragged him from the sea one week ago. It wasn't the first time I netted a floating deader. I've never caught one who could talk before. He told me things. Comforting things. These days I take my validation where I can get it. Here, will you help me with this?" She handed Sarah a folding patio chair. "I'd let you talk to him down here but the smell . . . I'm sure you understand. He must have been floating for weeks when I found him. I don't know who he is when he's at home but right now he's terrifically whiffy."

Together the women climbed back up to the deck, where they set up the two patio chairs under a sun umbrella. Magna put out a pitcher of ice water (the submarine had its own desalinization plant, she explained proudly) and a single glass. Sarah's guest wouldn't need one. Then Magna untied and unwrapped the tarpaulin-covered mass at the back of the deck. Frowning and holding her face very tight, she brought her burden over and dumped it unceremoniously in the second patio chair. "If you need me, shout," Magna told Sarah. "I'll be below watching series four of *Prime Suspect* on DVD. I've seen it so many times the Perspex has worn right off the disk, but I never get tired of Helen Mirren."

There were words in that sentence Sarah had never heard before.

Magna finally put her pistol down next to the pitcher of ice water and left Sarah alone with Jack. What was left of his borrowed body, anyway. Fish had been at it, leaving little that looked human. He had a torso and most of two arms. A head like a boiled chicken with some matted hair on the top. No eyes, nose, or lips at all.

"You look like hell," she said.

"In Finland they call hell *Tuonela*, at least they used to. It wasn't supposed to be so bad. A city under the ground where you went to sleep forever. When you arrived you were still pretty active and there was a welcoming party, they gave you a big beer stein. It was full of frogs and worms but it made you groggy and when you were finished they found you a nice soft patch of ground to lie down on. Sounds better than how it actually worked out, hmm?"

"I suppose," Sarah said. It was tough to look at him. She'd seen plenty of corpses in her day, but this was bad. He stank of stale brine and sun-baked skin.

"I didn't have much choice in bodies," he explained, "and I needed to talk to you. It's urgent, Sarah. There are things you need to know. Things you *have* to know before you go any further."

She bit her lip and nodded. "I know that rescuing Ayaan isn't going to be easy. I'm committed, though, and I've got Osman to go along with me. Ptolemy wants revenge, I can work with that—" She stopped. "Ayaan is dead. That's what you're here to tell me," she guessed, her breath very cold in her lungs. "I mean, you would know, somehow."

"Yes," Jack replied. He looked a little like he was melting. "They're all down in here with me. All the dead people. If she was dead I would be able to find her, and I can't."

"Oh." Something inside her liquefied and drained away. It was— it had been—a kind of relief, and now it was gone. She understood that when she had heard Jack wanted to talk, her subconscious had assumed it was to tell her that she'd done all she could, that she'd been very brave, but now it was over. She would have welcomed that, even if it would have meant Ayaan was dead. But it wasn't over, it couldn't be yet. Sarah looked away from him and changed the subject. "So it's true, all that religion stuff? There's an afterlife?"

"You could say that. Like you could say that a book still goes on even after you're done reading it and you've put it on the shelf. All the words are still there."

"That's . . . interesting," she said.

"Fucking fascinating. Now shut up and listen to me. I don't want to have to stay in this body any longer than I have to."

He looked out over the waves, drew a deep breath. "The one consolation for being dead—the only possible consolation—is that you hear things. Dead people love to gossip, just like the living. It's all they have to do. If you're selective with who you listen to you can actually learn something useful, sometimes. I happen to have met somebody who works for our enemy. The Tsarevich, I'm told, is planning something big. He's been working on it for years—maybe since the beginning. I get the feeling this is his unlife's work. He's been busy at it, collecting things he needs."

"Things?" Sarah asked.

"People, mostly. People like Ayaan or all those mummies. There's at least one more person he needs, somebody very special and he'll stop at nothing to find her, or at least a reasonable facsimile. He's been making liches at a furious rate, killing most of them because they didn't have powers or they didn't have the right powers. He's been collecting old bits of machinery, too, and documents the Soviets left behind. He took five tons of documents out of a cave in Siberia last year. Whatever he found there made him think he needed to go to Egypt. It told him what to do with the mummies. It must have told him what to do next, too, because now he's moving fast, with a purpose. He's moving west. Toward the Source. Do you understand where this is going?"

"I think so," she tried, though she really didn't.

"It means that once he has this last person that he needs, he'll be ready to act. It means the stakes are higher now. You want to save Ayaan, fine, and if Ptolemy wants revenge, well, so be it. But you need to know the Russian bastard has his own agenda, and I can guarantee you it isn't good. Ayaan plays into his hand somehow, so he won't give her up easily. You're going to need help. Find yourself a couple of atom bombs if you can, raise an army if you need to."

"I don't know how—"

"Then learn. I gave you your gift for a reason. Use it, now. You've got to find things out. You have to learn a lot between now and the end of this."

"Learn things?"

"Yeah. And some of them are going to make you cry. I'd go do it for you but, well. Since I'm just a disembodied consciousness cut loose in the void, I figure you're going to have to do the legwork. Understand?"

"Yeah." This time she thought she did understand. She'd just grabbed the shitty end of the stick. Sarah poured herself a glass of water. Her mouth had gone very dry.

"OK. So I'll try to find out more, give you a better idea of what you're up against as we get closer. For now I'm going to let this body go. Once I'm out you know what to do."

Jack rocked back and forth a few times and let his torso crash forward onto the deck. Sarah looked down at the knobby back of its neck, the places where the skin of its back had been nibbled away. It turned its ruined face up toward her and its jaws clacked shut. Clearly Jack was gone. She picked up the pistol Magna had left for her and got to work.

18.

BOBBING BEFORE HER, the Least's face looked like a huge bag of skin dangling in folds from his tiny skull, the eyeballs floating inside, the teeth lost in the great wet flapping curtain of his mouth. He tried to smile when she opened her eyes. It looked more like an exposed muscle jerking spasmodically.

"Mine, now," he said, his voice dribbling out of him like syrup. "My blood, my meat, my bones." He reached out one hand, the fingers swollen and torn like hot dogs cooked too long in a microwave, and touched her breasts, pushed them around, smeared them across her chest. There was no sex in his eyes. Just hunger.

"If you eat me," she said, "at least I won't end up a ghoul."

It was the closest thing she could manage to real defiance. It was also a fond wish.

Ayaan's clothes had been changed. She wore a white sleeveless T-shirt and a pair of drawstring pants. Surgical scrubs—most of the Tsarevich's army, both living and dead, wore the same. They were cheaper and more abundant than real uniforms. Her feet were bare. Her hands weren't tied, which surprised her a little. She supposed the green phantom could put her back to sleep if she tried to get away.

"Where are my clothes?" she asked, figuring the Least would either answer her or eat her. Either way she would have one less thing to worry about.

It was Cicatrix who replied, however. "We had them to burn. You got little too close to Lady Amanita so they went to mildew."

Ayaan looked up and saw a small crowd made up of living zealots; most of the liches had gathered around to watch her die. The werewolf, the lipless wonder, the green phantom were there. Amanita was nowhere to be found but the Tsarevich himself stood in a place of honor, directly behind the Least. His pale skin and hair, his dark enameled armor held her gaze, made her stare. She figured it was probably another projection. He didn't seem the type to take the risk of being near an unbound prisoner even when she had no weapons but her bare hands.

"Mine," the Least said, his mouth chewing on the word like a horse chewing cud.

"Yes, very soon now," the green phantom crowed. He looked like he could barely contain his excitement. He waved his arms around and everyone moved back, clearing a wide space on the deck, leaving Ayaan and the Least alone in the middle. Ayaan's heart sank. She knew exactly what came next.

"Your Highness," the green phantom said, and bowed in the Tsarevich's direction. "Ladies, gentlemen, creatures out of perdition, and loyal drones. I give you the event you've all been waiting for. Hark back with me to the days of most ancient Rome, to the thrills, the spills, the *kills* of the Coliseum. To the day of the gladiator, who lived—and died—by the pleasure of his emperor. To the days when blood was spilled, when bodies were butchered, when lives were thrown away all for one brief round of applause. The greatest show on this earth! Shall we try to regain some of that glory? Shall we celebrate the ritual of death once more? Shall we begin?"

There was a roar of agreement. Ayaan remembered what Cicatrix had told her, once upon a time. "Our kicks are never so simple." Apparently she'd been incorrect. This was the simplest kind of entertainment there was, and one of the oldest. A battle to the death. Public execution made public sport.

The Least outweighed her by a factor of five to one. He was a lot stronger, and she could only kill him by destroying his brain. He only needed to snap her neck or cut her with his ragged giant fingernails until she bled out. She couldn't outlast him, either—the undead never got tired, never needed to rest. The good news was that he was an idiot, a slow idiot.

She really, really, really wished she still had her AK-47.

Wishing didn't make things happen, though. She needed to get her head on straight. Rubbing her hands together to get her blood pumping, she fell into a fighter's crouch, her center of gravity low to the ground, her knees unlocked. She prepared herself for his first attack. It would come as hard and as fast as he could make it, she knew. He didn't have the brains to try anything fancy.

"Ooh, I think she's in the mood, folks," the green phantom announced, and the zealots all laughed. She was pretty sure most of them didn't speak English, but if they had enough faith it didn't matter. "But there's one more thing, one thing she didn't count on."

The crowd parted behind him and someone stepped slowly out onto the deck with what looked like a very painful gait. Not surprising. It was a ghoul, a shirtless dead man, and he had been impaled on something huge and sharp. It had a handle on one end, a curved grip big enough for the Least to hold. It was a chainsaw— a chainsaw nearly as long as Ayaan was tall.

The Least grabbed the handle and pulled it free in a red gout of decomposing flesh and dried-up blood. Ayaan swore in the Prophet's name. What perverse pleasure they took, these liches, in distorting the human frame. The shirtless ghoul existed for one purpose only: to be a walking scabbard.

Ayaan didn't have time for blasphemies, though. She needed to focus on the weapon. Hand weapons ought to be useless to the undead, even to liches. They couldn't muster the motor skills to slash or lunge properly. It seemed that the Tsarevich's armorers had considered that possibility and found for the Least a weapon that required only a minimum of finesse. A cord dangled from the end of the handle. The Least pulled on it and the chainsaw roared with the noise of a gasoline engine starting up.

"Good luck," the green phantom said, sneering at her. Then it began.

19.

THE CHAINSAW CAME for her with a scream and raised sparks from the deck plates, gouging a bright silver wound in the fresh paint. Ayaan stepped aside, tried to circle around the Least. She ducked as the chainsaw bounced off the deck and back into the air, then lunged forward and slammed both fists against the Least's knee.

Nothing. She might have punched Jell-O for the same effect. The Least's enormous body was covered in a thick layer of fat that absorbed all the energy she put into her swing.

While she was absorbing that information, the lich wound up for another pass. The audience went wild as he whirled the chainsaw over his head and brought it down in a swinging arc that missed Ayaan's chest by centimeters. She staggered back, away from the howling metal—she could feel heat coming off the blade. Too close, much too close for comfort. She jumped back, tried to get away. The chainsaw bit down again, light glaring off its chain. She pivoted on one foot, tried to slip under the attack—and pain exploded all down her arm.

Ayaan dropped to the deck, grabbing her arm high up near the shoulder, horrified. Had he gotten a vein, an artery? If he'd cut too deep, if he'd cut open a major blood vessel, she would bleed to death in minutes. She had to know, had to assess the wound, but she didn't have a moment's respite. The whining blade kept flashing down, left, right, center, and all she could do was roll around on the deck.

The Least came at her again, looming over her, moving in for the kill. Ayaan struggled up into a crouch and ducked between his legs. Shrieking in confusion, he swung the chainsaw around, tracking her, failing to watch his swing. As the blade flew around it cut right into the throat of one of the onlookers—a living cultist, a thirtyish man with a hairless chin and thick, rimless glasses. Blood flashed across the deck, stained everything as he went down in convulsions and horrible liquid grunting noises. Screams went up from the audience, screams of terror from one side, screams of bloodlust from the other.

Ayaan didn't waste the diversion. Head down, she bulled into the crowd, shoving some zealots aside, jumping at others as they shied away from her. Finally she had a chance to check her arm and her stomach went weightless for a moment as she brushed blood away from her wound. It wasn't fatal—a lot more than just a scratch, but the bleeding had mostly stopped on its own.

The Least shouted "Mine!" and plowed right into the crowd after her, his chainsaw held high to avoid any more accidents. She kept her head down and snaked through the bodies, shaking off the hands that grabbed at her, punching, slapping, clawing anyone who tried to get too close. She was looking for something, anything she could use as a weapon. There—on the deck—a smoldering cook fire. A pot of beans simmered in the coals. Her hands screamed in agony as she grabbed the hot metal pot, but she ignored the pain. The Least came at her through the crowd, lunging forward, and she let him have it right in the face. Beans splattered his wobbling chins, boiling water splashed up his nose, his mouth, his eyes. His hands went reflexively to his face to try to scrape the pain away. The chainsaw drifted, forgotten, the tip of the blade bouncing up and down. It dropped to the deck with an endless clattering.

In a second—in less than a second—the lich would recover himself. He didn't feel pain the way a living person did, would hardly notice the burns on his face and chest. Ayaan didn't have any opportunity to think. All she could do was act.

Using both hands she picked up the chainsaw—she could lift it, if she got her center of gravity under it, if she heaved with her back and her knees and all the muscles in her arms—and sliced the Least right in half. The chainsaw slid through his flesh like so much hamburger. It bucked when it hit his spine but she pushed, shoved, grunted her way through until his torso fell away from his abdomen and both big nasty chunks of meat hit the deck.

The Least howled in pain for real, then, but only once. He couldn't seem to catch his breath for another scream. The noise of the chainsaw chugging and gasping and singing as it cut through empty air was the only sound.

Nothing happened for a long, long time. Long enough for Ayaan to hear her own heart beating wildly. Long enough to shift the weight of the chainsaw onto her hip.

She had won, she supposed. She had beaten the Least. He wasn't going to get up, not from that wound, so it was over. She had saved herself.

A voice—her own voice—her mind's voice—was screaming in the background: *Who's next?*

Time broke down into its component parts. Ayaan's body moved through space. Her mind reeled at a very different speed. The crowd didn't move at all.

The green phantom stood no more than three meters away, leaning on his staff. His eyes were on the Least. Ayaan couldn't determine which half he was looking at.

If she could take him down. If she could kill the green phantom. Her brain looked at it as a chess problem. If you could capture a bishop by sacrificing a pawn, then losing the pawn didn't hurt at all. They would shoot her, they would keelhaul her, they would crush her, but if she could cut down the green phantom it would mean the end of speeding ghouls. It was his power alone that drove those madly whizzing horrors. More than that: the green phantom was the Tsarevich's right-hand man. His most important general. If. If. If.

She lunged forward. A hand with fingers like bloated sausages closed around her ankle, pulled her foot back down to the deck. In the midst of rising horror she looked down. The Least had her in a death grip.

"Mine," he mewled, like a dying kitten.

Rage pulsed through her body, she could feel the heat of it pumping through her capillaries. She raised the chainsaw in one savage motion and brought it down right between the Least's eyes. His head liquefied as the metal teeth ground through bone and brain tissue like a flaming knife through rotten cheese.

They hit her then, the zealots, cultists large and small falling on her like a rain of bodies. Someone kicked and smashed at her wrist until she let go of the chainsaw. It became hard to breathe and her vision dimmed. Time stopped altogether.

20.

THEY FOUND TRACES of the Tsarevich's ship a week out of Gibraltar, in the middle of the Atlantic. Osman had turned to Sarah and asked what she wanted to do—storm the bigger ship in the middle of the ocean or wait to see where it made landfall? She chose land.

Crossing the Atlantic nearly killed them a dozen times. The waves grew taller than the tug and when storms shot across their bows the water rose, and rose, and threatened to capsize the little boat. Osman got them through, with skill and the creativity born of self-preservation, but it was a close thing.

They followed the Tsarevich long after they ran out of food. Ptolemy took the lion's share of the steering after that. Sarah and Osman spent a lot of time asleep. Eventually they saw seagulls again. Landfall turned out to be a half a world away from where she'd started. A new continent, a new hemisphere, a place where they measured distances in miles, not kilometers.

For most of a day they hung back, keeping the Tsarevich in radar range but out of sight, just over the horizon. He was looking for something. His ship hugged the coastline but cast back and forth as if her pilot were trying to remember where to put in to land. They went north past a jungle, a riotous, overgrown beach where grass grew three meters tall. They passed dead villages and towns and resorts like empty tin cans strewn along the sand. Still they headed vaguely north, past a sandy spit that ran for miles, studded with the ruins of houses, crowned with an enormous, dark lighthouse. Finally the larger ship came to a halt and Osman touched his controls, locked his wheel, cut the tug's throttle. The Tsarevich's ship had put in at Asbury Park in New Jersey.

"You know we're only about sixty kilometers from—" Osman began.

She grabbed the chart away from him. "Yeah. I know." Sixty kilometers made about forty-five miles from New York City. She could read a map.

New York was where her father had died. He'd been born there, too. He had fled it as a teenager, come back to it as a man and saved a lot of people, and then he'd died. Sarah knew something about dealing with other people's ghosts. She knew to stay away from them, if she could.

The tugboat stood at anchor in the water a kilometer out on the ocean swells, far enough not to be noticed if they kept quiet, close enough to watch the Tsarevich's ship through Ayaan's old field glasses. They waited for darkness to fall. A nearly perfectly straight boardwalk confronted them, a linear extrusion of American decay. The buildings on the shore, an endless line of restaurants and gift shops and unrecognizable brick piles, stood weathered and old in the twilight, the color of sandstone mesas in some desert eroded by memories, by secrets she didn't share. The windows were all broken out, blank, dark. Some of the buildings had come down—lightning, rain, wind, who knew what had toppled them. Maybe the roots of the trees had choked the wide streets, maybe over a decade the root systems of so many trees could break down the foundation stones of pleasure palaces and arcades. Soot and smoke damage darkened the countenances of most of the structures that remained standing.

At the boardwalk a parade of monsters hurried down an improvised gangplank and into the forests of the unreal city—flopping, crawling things, things with no legs, monsters with bodies warped by death, monsters who had yet to die. They laughed and sang hymns and psalms as they stepped down onto the shore. In single or double file they headed into the foliage and out of sight.

Night fell, eventually. The Tsarevich's ship blazed like an anglerfish in the black water, its lights the only illumination in the world except for cold and distant stars.

Sarah found herself paralyzed, unable to do a thing. What would Ayaan do in her place? she asked herself. She would try to learn more about what she faced. She would sit tight and send in a scouting team and try to get some sleep. The sleep part was out, but maybe Sarah could take a lesson from the rest.

"You can see in the dark, right?" she asked Ptolemy.

my more vision was like yours was is vision more than yours it was, the soapstone told her.

"Just be careful," she told the mummy. "This is simple reconnaissance. There's one of yours on that ship." He knew that, of course. He could sense her there, just as he had sensed the others when he'd led her to Cyprus. She searched for better words. "Don't go rushing in there or you'll get us all killed."

There was one of hers in that ship, too. Sarah's special vision couldn't let her see through the hull of a ship or the dense trees choking the streets of South Amboy. She didn't need it to know that Ayaan was still alive, though. She had to be. Otherwise this long trip had been for nothing. Otherwise Jack had led her on a wild-goose chase. She couldn't believe that anyone—not even her cranky old ghost—would put her through so much if she couldn't expect a reasonable chance of completing her mission.

They moved in close to the shore, running the engines just a touch though the diesels still grumbled and coughed and roared. They came in well to the north of the Tsarevich's landing zone.

Sound travels far over water, especially at night. Sarah hoped the waves would cover their noise. They got as close as they dared and then Osman cut the engines and they drifted in until the tug's flat bottom hissed on submerged sand. Ptolemy scampered over the side and onto the beach with a soft thump, then disappeared instantly into the blackness.

"OK," Sarah whispered, and Osman took them back out to sea. They needed help. Jack had told her as much—she couldn't face down the Tsarevich on her own. They needed an army of their own. Well, they weren't going to get it. But maybe they could get some help. North, then. New York, the place she didn't want to go. "Next stop, Governors Island," she told him, and he nodded, not even chancing a verbal agreement.

PART
TWO

L.

IT WAS HOT and the air was dry. Ayaan could hear a constant thrumming, a rumbling, bass sound that tickled the bare soles of her feet. Her feet . . . her feet hurt. She could feel pain in her ankles, her legs, her toes. When she looked down at them they seemed too big, they seemed to swim up at her, swollen and very dark and bruised. Blisters surrounded her toenails, blisters that popped and wept a clear fluid.

Her armpits were numb. She couldn't feel them at all. Her arms were replaced with twin bars of light. It was the only way to describe it. There were no arms there, just pain, and only an abstract kind of pain at that.

In the unmoving air of the engine compartment they kept her metabolism ticking over slowly, so very slowly. When a doctor came and asked her to lift her head, it took all the energy she possessed. She wanted very much to sit down.

"Come on, come, that's better. Open your mouth."

She let her jaw go slack. There were needles in her, needles she felt sliding through her flesh, impaling her. Hands touched her in places she could barely identify. Her body had become a vast country with a poor communications infrastructure. Information from her extremities took most of the day to reach her brain.

"Blood oxygen levels good, yes."

The green phantom kept her alive, but just barely, while men came and went from the room, their hands on her, their eyes everywhere. They attached wires to her, they scraped samples of the scum between her teeth.

"Basal body temperature is being normal."

Sometimes she could see them moving around her, their faces flat, their hands cold. Sometimes they were only blurs or the flickering of a moth's wings against her skin.

"You be interested to seeing this," someone said, their hand on her lower belly, a latex glove in her pubic hair. She felt half a dozen people all around her look up, she could feel them paying attention. She could see Cicatrix across the room, the living woman in soft focus as her nostrils flared, her eyes fixed on Ayaan's midriff. Her bald head flushed with shame. Something metal and cold touched her, spread her skin open.

"She's still virgin," the doctor said.

Ayaan kicked against her bonds but it was useless, her body barely rippled. It must have looked like a muscle spasm. Then time went blue . . .

. . . she wasn't sure, wasn't sure what that meant, but she knew it was right, blue . . .

. . . and needles, there were needles on her skin. Pricking her. She felt a single drop of blood roll down her collarbone, smash apart against the papery collar of her scrubs. She looked down and watched the blood wick through the blue fabric, a spiky blossom as capillary action drew it away from her skin.

"You need to lift head," someone told her. She listened—it felt like she could only use one sense at a time. Something buzzing, an insect, a horrible nasty wasp right next to her ear, climbing on her throat, dragging its sting through her flesh.

"I can't do this, not with head like that," the voice said. She couldn't see who it belonged to.

In front of her the Tsarevich faded into existence. Like a cloud passing in front of the sun. His very pale eyes looked up into hers. His voice . . . she'd never heard it before . . . it fit him perfectly. High, clear, a boy's voice. The voice of a soloist in a boy's choir. "Is called strappado, some time ago. Now, we call it stress positions. KGB make it perfect. Is very effective."

"Hand me silver again," the other voice said. Right behind her head. The wasp stuck its tail into the back of her neck.

"We tie hands, then tie to ceiling. You cannot sit down, without tearing arms from sockets. Body won't let you do that even when unconscious. You have not sit down three days. Your arms are dying, no blood. All blood goes to feet, which swell, then crack. Used at Guantanamo Bay and at Kabul. In Belfast and Mosul and Jerusalem. Roman Catholic church invent it for Inquisition, because no blood shed. But KGB make perfect."

Ayaan tried to lick her lips but her mouth stuck together as if it were full of glue. Concentrating, squinting her eyes, she managed to get a drop of spit onto her soft palate. *Our kicks are never so simple,* Cicatrix had told her. "Torture," she creaked. "Do you," she said, and waited until she had more saliva to loosen her tongue, "come when you see me like this? Does it make you come?"

The Tsarevich smiled at her. The kind of smile a dying grandmother would keep on living for. "Is not for me, is for you. Such talent you have. Such talent I never waste. I have use for you, even now. Is sad, must hurt so much, is very sad, but also, necessary. Must break down ignorance and fear. You see?"

You mean, she thought, lacking the energy to keep talking, *you mean you have to wear down my psychological barriers.* Ayaan knew exactly what they were doing to her. Even in her reduced state she could still think, if slowly. They were torturing her in preparation for brainwashing. No matter how much resistance she put up, they would just push her further. No matter how long it took, they could wait for her to come around.

"Fuck, get mop! She wets self," the rough voice said.

The Tsarevich frowned. "Kidneys shut down after three days. Is permanent, if you don't sit down. He took a handkerchief out of the sleeve of his armor and mopped at the front of her pants.

"What," Ayaan stammered, "what do you really look like?"

His eyes sparkled. "You find out, and soon," he told her. "Very soon now. You come stand at my side." He put a hand over his mouth, catching himself in a faux pas. "I mean to say, sit, at my side, yes?"

The smile lit up his face and the cloud moved away from the sun. *Stay alive,* she thought. *Stay alive for Sarah. She needs you.*

"You will to be mine," he told her, patting her feet.

She knew better than to antagonize him. It would only get her another day on the strap. Still. She was Ayaan. At least for the time being. "That's what the Least said," she told the Tsarevich. "And look at him now."

2.

HELL GATE STRETCHED out before them as placid as a sheet of glass. "This was impassible before," Osman said. His haunted eyes told her this journey was dredging up old memories he'd long since sealed away in the dark back corners of his mind. She felt a bizarre communion with the old man, a place where their two very different lives finally touched. She wondered if that was what growing up felt like.

"There were bodies. Thousands of them." He moved to the bow and stared ahead through Ayaan's old field glasses. The diesels chugged along just fine without him at the wheel. "And the birds. The pigeons, the seagulls—they were a carpet of white feathers." He lowered the binoculars and looked back at where she sat atop the wheelhouse. "A city's worth of bodies. A raft of them."

They were gone, the bodies he described. Gone for years probably. They had taken the long way around to Governors Island, a paranoid excursion that took most of a day as they headed back out to sea and then rounded the extensive coastline of Long Island, then down through the sound and the East River. Osman had been convinced the bodies would still be in the way, but Sarah was terrified that the Tsarevich might be watching them, that he had some way of knowing where they went and that he could follow them to their destination. Only by wasting a day's good sailing could she relax and feel she had shaken off that hypothetical pursuit.

The city passed her by on the right like a series of eroded cliffs. Dramatic, startling sometimes in their size, the buildings didn't connect with anything she'd ever seen before. The tree branches emerging from the windows, the fallen piles of concrete and steel looked like natural features. Even the occasional spill of glass where an entire skyscraper's facade had collapsed down into the street might have been an outcropping of some glittering crystalline mineral. As they passed what her chart told her was called Roosevelt Island, Osman rushed back to his controls to steer them around a twist of metal that slumped across the river like an elephant's trunk drawing up water. It took her a while to realize it must be what was left of a bridge. Rust and metal fatigue had claimed most of it, leaving broken legs sticking up into a blue sky, rising hundreds of feet up into the air.

Osman pointed out the United Nations buildings to her as they drifted past. The Secretariat, a big office tower once, was a skeleton of its former self. The lower General Assembly building was almost completely screened from view by vibrantly green foliage. Her father had worked there once, Sarah knew, but she couldn't imagine it, not really. No more than she could imagine the state funerals of the pharaohs interred in the Pyramids.

Tall spires stood straight up Manhattan, skyscrapers, structures Sarah's brain could only interpret as distant mountains. She could barely stand to look at the empty buildings with their broken windows. Some of them she actually recognized from her children's books—the Empire State Building, its crowning needle now broken off near the base. The Chrysler Building with long streamers of plant life draping from its triangular portholes, its famous gargoyles leering out of leafy bowers. She had an easier time watching the piers and warehouses of Brooklyn slide by on her left. They passed under the Brooklyn Bridge with Osman making constant tiny corrections. The bridge's gothic pylons stood proud and unscathed, its endless stretches of cabling tangled but unbroken, but its roadway had fallen away completely to form dozens of new, ephemeral islands in the water below, concrete crags that proved a hazard to navigation. Then the river opened up, turned into a broad and quiet bay. Osman kept them close to Manhattan, to the long piers of the Lower East Side, then brought them around, out of the Buttermilk Channel and over toward the ferry dock of Governors Island.

Two broad slips, much larger than the tug required, formed the dock and were topped by elevated equipment shacks that Sarah's militarily trained mind identified immediately as perfect guard towers. Beyond lay a paved walkway that led between two low buildings on the island's shore. To the east stood a squat octagonal tower pierced with ventilation ducts and giant fans, its base surrounded by rusting yellow construction equipment. On the other side of the dock, nearly around the corner of the island, she could see a round structure that might have been a fort or a prison. These imposing structures, however, could not hide what lay in the island's interior—pleasant Victorian houses in a park full of well-tended trees and what looked like a sprawling, immaculately maintained garden.

A noise like a tree being hit by lightning made Sarah jump. A gunshot—it sounded like a sniper round, maybe, or just a high-powered rifle bullet. The sound bounced off the water, magnified, resonated for what felt like minutes. She slid down from the wheelhouse and dropped below the gunwale. At the throttle Osman just laughed.

"Just a shot across the bows." He pulled on the cord that sounded the tug's foghorn, and Sarah stuffed her fingertips in her ears. "It's an old tradition, baby girl, nothing to be afraid of." He picked up the microphone of the tug's radio set and hailed the island in English.

Slowly, carefully, Sarah uncurled herself and rose to peer over the side. The windows of the elevated equipment shacks were open to the breeze. She saw the barrels of rifles and even one machine gun poking out. Surely that was more than what was needed to repel the occasional ghoul, drawn by the scent of human flesh to dog-paddle across the bay. Maybe Governors Island had had living visitors before. Borderline personality types. Pirates.

Osman couldn't get anyone on the radio. He took a megaphone from one of the tug's lockers and handed over the wheel. With shaking hands she kept them on course, the diesels powered down until they were barely ticking over.

"Ahoy over there, friends," Osman shouted through the megaphone. "Don't you remember me? I'd think a face this handsome would stick with you. Where's my Marisol? Last time I saw her she had a bowling ball under her shirt. Where's Kreutzer, that old asshole?"

He set down the megaphone and shrugged. "If that doesn't convince them we're friends, they were destined to shoot us anyways," he told Sarah. He took the wheel back from her and steered them into one of the ferry slips. The tug sat lower in the water than the ferries had by a considerable margin. Inside the slip they were penned in by high walls lined in shock-absorbing plastic. They couldn't see up onto the island at all. If anyone wanted to kill them it would be like shooting fish in a plastic tub.

When they bounced to a halt against the slip walls, he ran forward and threw a line up onto the dock. Unseen hands took it, tied it off, made it secure. A ladder appeared over the edge and dipped down to smack the tug's deck. Osman went up first, unarmed. Sarah came after with her Makarov in her pocket, loaded and ready. When Osman left Governors Island the last time, he had been a hero, and the island's inhabitants had waved at him as he steamed out to sea. Now he was coming back almost anonymously, and he might be attacked the second he was over the side. Anything could have happened in the interval. Anyone could have come along, slain the original survivors, and taken the island for themselves. It was that kind of world. It had been for twelve years.

At the top of the ladder, five men with assault rifles waited for them. Only one man had his weapon ready and aimed at them but that was more than enough. They were led without a word into one of the buildings that fronted the shoreline, a low, modernist structure of concrete and glass, some of which had been boarded over. The honor guard led them into a dim room lit only by the sunlight streaming in through high windows. A woman with a boy at her side stood at the far side of the room. She had a pistol in her hand. So did the boy, who might have been twelve years old or eight—he was a scrawny child and the lighting was terrible.

The woman stepped forward into a patch of light. She was beautiful, astoundingly so, with just a hint of age in her face. Her caramel-colored skin was flawless and her hair, tied back in an explosive ponytail, glimmered in the half light. She wore a broad sash across a homespun black sweater. It read *mayor*, picked out in crystals and sequins.

She should have been a movie star. She nearly had been, if Sarah remembered Marisol's story correctly. When the Epidemic came she'd had some success in Z-grade genre films, there had already been some buzz about her, whisperings of a more significant career to come. There weren't any more movies, though, nor any Hollywood parties or private yachts or even Greek billionaires with ten-carat diamond engagement rings. She'd had to settle.

"Osman," she said, her face melting into joy as she recognized the pilot. "Oh my God, it's you, Jesus fuck, it's really you. Wow, there's a whole lot of bad memories to have to relive at once." She rushed forward to kiss him all over his face. "Here, here, I want you to meet Jackie," she said, and ushered her boy over with wild hand gestures. Happiness split the woman's features, made wrinkles appear in her brow and around her mouth. She was nearly jumping up and down. "Jesus shit! How have you been? What are you doing these days? Who's your friend? Is this your daughter?" Marisol asked.

Osman laughed. "No, no. This is Sarah. Dekalb's daughter."

"Dekalb." Marisol said. "Dekalb's daughter." Emotions erased themselves from her face.

Silence rushed into the room like a cold flood.

"Oh. Hi," Marisol said.

3.

"THEY HAD PUDDING in these tiny plastic cups. You would peel back the foil on top and the pudding was in there already made," one of the islanders said. He was a fortyish man with gray hair and squinting eyes. He mimed the action of pulling back on a piece of foil, his fingertip and thumb pressed very close together, and a light bloomed in his face that didn't come from the bonfire. "There was always a little dollop of pudding on the foil, that was the best part, it tasted the best, anyway."

A younger woman in a shapeless sweater poked at the fire with a long branch. There wasn't much firewood on Governors Island, but an enormous amount lay just four hundred yards away in Brooklyn. A boat went over every day to retrieve great bundles of sticks and logs from the trees that choked the old city streets. Gathering fuel from the city had been a dangerous occupation once, the survivors told Sarah, but in recent months it was rare to even spot a ghoul, much less be attacked by one. New York had largely emptied out. "Then you could just throw the cup away, right? I kind of remember that," the woman said. She stared into the fire. "You didn't have to wash it out."

"Yeah," the squinting man agreed, nodding happily. "They had coffee you could just pour boiling water on, and it was ready. They had orange juice that came frozen in a tube and you just let it melt in some water and you could drink it."

One of the children, a skinny girl of maybe fourteen years, laughed heartily. "Why freeze it in the first place if you were just going to let it melt?"

The old man smiled and laughed, but without the girl's abandon. "Sure."

"Where did they go?" Sarah asked. She drew a lot of blank stares. "Where did the ghouls go?"

The old man shrugged. "West. Jersey, I guess. It's not like they migrated or something. They just started wandering away, one by one, maybe looking for food. They went over the bridges. The George Washington is still standing."

Sarah hugged herself. The night had come on colder than she'd expected and her hooded sweatshirt, so perfect for desert evenings, couldn't keep out the damp of the island. "But why to the west, why did they go into New Jersey?"

"Well," the old man said, "if they went east they'd get stuck on the LIE."

That elicited more than a few snorting laughs from the older survivors. Sarah had no idea what it meant, or what an LIE was. She stood up and watched the fire for a second. She didn't want to leave its warmth, but the clustered survivors sitting in a circle around the blaze were confusing her more than anything else. All they wanted to talk about was what they'd lost, what the world used to have in it. For Sarah, who knew nothing except apocalypse, such talk was just wasted breath.

One of the younger men, a big guy with muscles, jumped up when she turned away from the bonfire. "Where are you headed?" he asked, not necessarily unfriendly. She definitely got the sense he'd been tasked with keeping an eye on her, though.

"I need to urinate," she announced. The younger survivors tittered. Her guard nodded meaningfully, as if she'd passed a test.

Everything on Governors Island, she ruminated as she headed into the shadows between two Victorian houses, felt like a test. Osman and Marisol had gone off to talk, leaving her in the company of people she didn't know. She'd been fed, welcomed effusively, cheered and toasted. She'd been invited to sit by the fire, brought into the conversation, given their full attention whenever she talked. Yet as much as they seemed to want to make her feel at home, they never stopped looking at her, studying her. There were plenty of other black women on the island, so it wasn't that. She supposed it might be that in such an insular community any newcomer was a nine days' wonder. And surely, anyone who had survived the last twelve years had reason enough not to trust strangers.

Yet the feeling Sarah got from the islanders wasn't so much mistrust as it was furtiveness. They acted as if they weren't so much concerned with what she would do, as that they had a secret they were afraid she would learn.

She didn't expect to find it so soon after realizing it must exist. Yet as she squatted by a gingerbread porch coated in flaking white paint, she looked up and nearly fell over in fright. She saw energy. Dead energy.

Blotches of it all over the place. She hadn't been paying attention, but that was when her unusual senses worked best. There was one of the dead right in front of her—in the field of mixed crops at the center of Nolan Park. Scratching at the soil with a hoe, or a rake, or . . . something. Sarah frowned. The dead don't garden.

Not unless someone—specifically, a lich—told them to.

She still had her pistol. Postapocalyptic standards of hospitality allowed visitors to hold on to their weapons at communal bonfires, especially when the visitors casually forgot to mention they possessed said weapons. She drew it out of her pocket, slid the magazine into place, thumbed off the safety. The dead thing didn't notice as she crept up on it.

Impossible, but there it was. Not in this place, of all places, this last citadel of humanity in New York. But the hair on the backs of her arms didn't lie. It stood up straight as the quills of a porcupine. Horripilation. The most classic sign of the presence of the undead.

Sarah tried to make sense of it in her head. She must have brought the dead to Governors Island, she thought. The Tsarevich must have followed her. She had doomed all those nice, boring people at the bonfire. Fear sent cold daggers through the muscles of her back. Why the thing was gardening she had no idea—maybe it was tampering with the survivors' crops, maybe it intended to poison them.

She lifted her pistol. Lined up a shot. The dead gardener scratched open another furrow in the silvery moonlit dirt. Its face, its skull didn't move. Its features might have been a mask of bone. It was dressed in stained overalls and its feet were bare. Sarah cocked her pistol and held her breath for the bang.

"Please don't hurt him. He's just a slack," someone said in a soft voice. It was as loud as a gunshot in Sarah's terrified ear. She pivoted on one ankle and saw the boy, Jackie, standing off to her right. He moved forward quickly out of her blind spot—he must have been trained in how to approach someone with a gun.

Slowly she pried her finger away from the Makarov's trigger, uncocked its hammer. "A slack? What does that mean?"

"He's tame." Jackie rushed up to the gardener and waved his hand in its face. Sarah bit her lip to hold back a wave of nausea. She knew what was supposed to come next, what always came next. The ghoul would bite the child. Grab him and devour him. Except of course it didn't. That was the point. The gardener stopped its hoeing just long enough to look down at the boy and issue a mindless little smile. The dead man's eyes moved slowly around in their sockets.

Jackie turned to address her again. "He's a slack. They do what we tell them, though sometimes it takes so long to explain things. We couldn't survive without them. There aren't enough of us to keep the gardens going."

Sarah narrowed her eyes. She had never heard of such a thing. "How—how do you tame a ghoul?" she demanded. "They only exist for one thing."

The boy shrugged. He was twelve, she knew now, but tiny for his age. His eyes were huge, his hair thinner on his head than it ought to be. "I think it's one of the ceremonies my mom does on Halloween. They don't let me watch because they get naked, but I know stuff anyway. I know you tie the ghouls up in a circle you draw on the ground and then there's some dancing and chanting and stuff." The boy shrugged again. "You know. Science."

Sarah was breathing heavily, unsure of what to do next. She put the pistol back in her pocket. Then she rushed forward and knocked the slack off its feet. It felt like she'd smacked into a pillowcase full of twigs. The gardener fell over, clattered to the ground. Then it got back up, retrieved its hoe, and went back to work. It didn't bother smiling at her. If she hit it again—and again—and again—it would do the same, she decided.

You're going to learn things, Jack had told her, and some of them are going to make you cry. Was this what he'd meant? Or were there worse shocks in store?

"Come back with me," Jackie told her. "Mommy wants to talk to you." He held out his minuscule hand and Sarah took it.

4.

HER FEET ACHED, and fog wrapped the world in gauze. She was walking on wooden planks. Her arms were sore but her feet were just burning. She looked down and saw them—huge, swollen, and dark.

Cicatrix wrapped a blanket around Ayaan's shoulders. "Don't look, will only upset you." The Russian woman put an arm around Ayaan's waist. "Is not much farther now."

Ayaan nodded absently. She couldn't muster much in the way of emotion. The fog on her skin felt good, it felt cool and soft and whisper-smooth. That was about as deep as she went. She remembered everything—the engine compartment, the strap, the Tsarevich coming to her. His dark suggestions. The memories were flattened, though. Stretched out and made into mere visions, something she had seen in a movie, with all the fear and pain carved away.

Her neck itched but she couldn't lift her arms to scratch. She had a bandage wrapped around her throat anyway. She remembered them working there, the hornet dragging its sting across her skin. What that had been about she couldn't have said.

"Almost . . . and we are here," Cicatrix said. They stopped there on the boardwalk and Ayaan lifted her head to look up.

Stay alive, she thought. Or she remembered thinking. Time had done something funny, had turned on her.

In front of her stood the shell of a building, no more than half a brick wall remaining, painted a blue the color of a clear sky. A painted face floated against that backdrop, laughing hysterically, in perfect silence. Even the sound of Ayaan's breathing was eaten up by the fog.

Ayaan thought of Sarah. She tried to think of Sarah. She tried to remember the girl's face, her close-cropped hair. That filthy sweatshirt she always wore, which she thought might have belonged to her father. Sarah.

"There will be none of this," Cicactrix said and waggled a finger in Ayaan's face. She couldn't remember what she had been doing to earn such disapproval. Then she looked down and saw she was naked. The blanket lay behind her, pooled on the boardwalk like liquid that had dripped down.

Ayaan's hands were near her face. She had summoned up enough strength to lift her arms, to touch her face. No, wait. Her face hurt. It stung, in eight specific places. She could count them. She looked down at her fingers and saw bits of skin under the nails.

Had she . . . had she been trying to claw her own face off?

Time had turned on her. Time and . . . time and memory. They went inside. "Can I lie down?" Ayaan asked. Her feet hurt so badly. "Just for a while."

"Oh, yes," Cicatrix told her. She led Ayaan into a little plastic tent set up inside the ruin of the building. There was a bed there . . . or not a bed but a place that looked like . . . well, it looked a little like a bed, or maybe a long couch, a divan. But it was full of ice. "Here, let me to help," Cicatrix said, and held Ayaan's arm as she lay down on the cold, cold bed.

"The ice is sticking to my back, to my skin," Ayaan announced. There were a lot of people in the tent, suddenly. Her heart pounded fast and then it skipped a beat. Someone shoved a tube up her nose, its tip slick with lubricant. She tried to sneeze and cough and fight but they wouldn't let her. They were so much stronger than she remembered. A woman in a nurse's uniform, complete with a little peaked cap, leaned over her, throwing her into shadow, and jabbed a hypodermic in Ayaan's neck.

"What—what was—what—was—that?" Ayaan demanded. Her arms were quivering, her body shaking. Was it the ice, was she shivering from the cold? She couldn't really feel it anymore. She was shaking too much. She was shaking a lot, she was trembling—convulsing. "What did you just give me?" she asked.

The nurse's mouth was a flat line, a slot that ticker tape might come out of. "Cyanide," she answered.

Darkness clanged shut across Ayaan's vision like shutters closing with a sound of ringing, a tinnitus ring.

The sound squealed up to a howling, an echoing scream that might have come from her own throat except except except

time didn't just turn on her it turned a wheel it turned like a wheel

(For a moment she was outside her own body, looking down, pointing at herself. Blood raced through tubes running down her throat, up her ass. A machine like a bagpipe bellowed up and down and breathed for her. There was a man next to her, a very hairy naked white man with blue tattoos curlicuing all over his body. He had a rope around his neck like a punk-rock necktie, or like a noose cut way too short. "That's me," she said, "they're killing me," and he smiled the way you might smile at a baby who suddenly, as its first words, announces it has crapped in its diaper. "I know you, don't I?" she asked.)

A nurse came through the tent, and passed right through him, as if he were a ghost.

(**Yes**, the man told her, without opening his mouth. Her vision went away and instead she saw a brain in a glass jar. **I'll be in touch**, he told her, and then she was back in her body, in the dark, with that noise.)

Then:

the noise stopped

everything

stopped.

She opened her eyes with a scream.

Ayaan sat up in bed, naked under silk sheets. She was in a small bedroom with a fireplace. A cheerful little blaze danced away at the corner of her vision. Her head felt as if it had been cracked open and stuffed full of scrap metal. She touched her face, felt a cold, rubbery mask there.

She wasn't breathing. She sucked in a deep breath of air and felt it sigh back out of her. She touched her wrist with two fingers and couldn't find a pulse. She did find a black vein running underneath her grayish brown skin. It was as hard as a length of wire. The blood inside that vein wasn't going anywhere.

She screamed and screamed, shouted and cursed and her throat never got sore. She sobbed, big wracking hard heaves, but no tears came.

Nausea surged upward inside her and she jumped out of the bed, looked around frantically for something to throw up into. Nothing presented itself, so she clutched her hands over her mouth and just held on, held on until the need, the desire to vomit went away. It left her feeling drained, depleted, and sore.

And then hungry. She could really use a snack, she told herself. She was going to need to keep up her energy reserves for what came next.

What came next? She couldn't remember.

She stood up again. Looked around the room. A faded newspaper clipping was pasted to one wall, a picture of a building by a boardwalk, its windows broken, its paint faded or missing altogether. A place that had died even before the world came to an end. A little lamp in the corner had been draped with a red scarf.

She found a closet and inside the closet, one single set of clothes. A black leather catsuit with lots of straps. A pair of black leather boots that came up to the middle of her calves. A black leather jacket stenciled all over in white spray paint with a motif of grinning skulls. She put the clothes on with fumbling fingers that felt twice as thick as they looked. The clothes fit her perfectly.

At the back of the closet she found a sliver of broken mirror. She picked it up and stared at her reflection. She looked mostly the same, though sick. She looked as if she'd been very sick for a long time. Something leaped out at her, though, and required extensive examination. She had a tattoo on her throat and neck, running all the way around, bright silver ink inscribing cursive Russian characters. Like a choker she could never remove. She'd seen that kind of writing before, she thought. She'd seen it inscribed on a glass jar with a brain inside.

Don't speak, she thought. Except it wasn't her own thought. Someone had spoken into her head, his voice braying and too loud. It made her headache worse. **Don't react at all. Whatever they say to you, just nod and smile.**

A knock came on the bedroom's door.

5.

BY THE LIGHT of an oil lamp Marisol examined a handful of yellow stalks. "Winter wheat," she explained, but that meant nothing to Sarah. The mayor of Governors Island dropped the stalks on the table and examined her fingers. A thin, soft black powder coated them and resisted being easily brushed off. Marisol sniffed her fingers and frowned. "It's a fungus of some kind. That's new for us, and I don't like it."

In the corner of the room Osman sat with one hand on his head. The other held a bottle of milky liquid. Judging by the way he kept blinking in slow motion and slumping forward to nearly fall out of his chair, Sarah decided he must be drunk. She looked at Marisol.

The mayor shrugged. "It's been years, he said. Let him have a taste. In the morning he'll feel like shit and he'll curse God and then he'll go back to normal. It's not like we make enough liquor for him to become an alcoholic." She frowned. "After the things we've seen, all of us, I think we deserve to get polluted now and again. I wouldn't mind a drink myself, actually. To you," she said, and pointed at the blighted wheat on the table, "that might look pretty banal. To me it's a reminder. The first couple of winters here were . . . hard. There were two hundred of us originally. Now, even with the refugees we've adopted and a couple of births, we're down to seventy-nine."

Sarah didn't know what to make of that. It sounded bad, it was true, but like nothing compared to what had become of Africa. There had been a whole nation's worth of survivors there once. Somalia had kept a million of its citizens alive for the first year. Now Somalia wasn't around anymore. Ayaan's small group had been all that remained.

"I know you saw the slacks in the garden. I know what you must think of us. But we couldn't have made it without help." Marisol smiled and reached forward with one tentative hand. When Sarah didn't flinch, Marisol cupped the younger woman's chin and smiled at her. "You know some of the stories, of course. You know about Gary."

Sarah nodded. No more needed to be said. What Gary had done to Marisol, and how eventually he was destroyed, was part of the myth of Governors Island. It was part of the myth of the Epidemic.

"There are things I have to tell you, hard things. It's too bad I'm such a spineless coward. So instead I'm just going to show you and you'll have to cope whatever way you know how. You can hate me later, I'm OK with that."

Sarah's heart sank. She had something to learn—something that would make her cry. This was going to be it, she was sure of it. She didn't speak or protest in any way, though, as Marisol took her hand and led her back out into the darkness. The mayor paused only to speak to her son, to little Jackie, to tell him to stay put with Osman and wait for her to return.

"When I saw you I hated you a little," Marisol said. "It's not fair that Dekalb gets to have such a healthy and beautiful daughter. My little boy is what we used to call 'sickly.'" She grunted a little in pain, but not the physical kind. "He's got genetic problems, a heart murmur, the early signs of scoliosis and maybe even lupus. Do you know about those? We can barely diagnose them—there's no treatment at all, not anymore."

"Is he going to be OK?" Sarah asked, scared for the kid. Most sickly children in Africa died in their first couple of years.

"I won't let him slip away from me, not when he's all I have left of . . . of some old friends." Marisol grew quiet then, very quiet. She led Sarah along the edge of the water, along a concrete parapet lined with a steel railing that had fallen away in places. When she saw where they were headed, Sarah felt her heart speeding up.

Marisol had led her along a narrow causeway to the octagonal ventilation tower at the northern tip of the island. It rose over them in the dark like a giant robot out of science fiction, a clattering, enormous construction of fans that turned endlessly and vents that flicked open and shut in a pattern of willful randomness. A skeletal crown of exposed girders topped it, the stars showing through rusted gaps in the metal.

They threaded a simple maze of empty cargo containers and came to a set of three metal stairs leading to the tower's doorway. "This place was nothing special, back in the day," Marisol told Sarah. "It's just a vent, a pipe stuck in the ground to provide air for the Brooklyn Battery Tunnel."

"There's a tunnel under the water?" Sarah asked. As usual the marvels of twentieth-century engineering fascinated her, even if her elders found them trivial and commonplace. "How did they build it without the bay getting in?"

Marisol shook her head. She didn't know, or didn't care to answer. She took an enormous key ring from her belt and unlocked the tower's door. Then she stepped aside. Clearly Sarah was supposed to go in alone.

A little light illuminated the tower's guts, a wan little electric light that came from hundreds of weak bulbs, some mounted in cages on the walls, some dangling on wires draped across the vast open space. Sarah found herself on a gallery, a narrow enclosed walkway that ran around the edge of an open pit. She looked down and saw that the vast majority of the tower was just an empty shaft, an air shaft with one enormous fan at its bottom. Its vanes rotated with geological slowness, but still it generated a vast wind that rushed up into her face and pushed the hood of her sweatshirt back.

What next? When she finished staring into the blackness below the great fan she had no idea what to do. Was she supposed to climb down into the shaft, or ascend one of the tower's ladders toward the catwalks high above? She turned to look back at the doorway and found a mummy standing directly in front of her.

She screamed, of course, but cut it short. This one was far older than Ptolemy, yellow with antiquity and largely unadorned. His tattered wrappings hung on him like the flag of a forgotten nation. Obviously he was there to guide her. He started moving as soon as she quieted down, heading away from her at a brisk pace. She kept an eye on his dark energy—much easier to follow him that way in the dimness.

They climbed up a long enclosed ladder with cold metal rungs until they reached a platform maybe twelve feet above the doorway. Catwalks ran away from them in three directions. They took the middle way and walked through the center of the shaft toward an identical platform at the far side of the tower. The wind rising through the shaft vibrated the narrow catwalk and made Sarah clutch the handrail, but the mummy traversed the perilous way like a tightrope walker—with no hesitation at all.

A bizarre and horrifying tableau waited for them at the far platform. A ghoul crouched there, feasting on a corpse, while something else, a tiny skeletal thing like a dog or . . . no, not like a dog at all, she couldn't really say what it was at first, but then . . .

It was a skull, a human skull, with no lower jawbone. Very human eyes looked out from its sockets. Six-jointed crablike legs jutted out from underneath and carried it along as it scuttled backward away from her. She screamed again—it was that kind of place, a chamber of horrors—and the skull-crab backed up even farther.

Then she looked down at the feasting ghoul. It was time to go, time to get out. Had she been sent here as a sacrifice? Did Marisol and her constituents do this with all their visitors, did they feed them to the island's resident monsters? Sure, it made sense. Send the occasional snack up to the tower and the ghouls would leave the islanders in peace. Sarah turned to flee, only to find mummies blocking the catwalks. They didn't advance on her, just stood there waiting for her to make a move.

She had her pistol, her little Makarov. She could . . . she could fight her way free, at least take down a few of her captors if—if she—

"Sarah," the ghoul said behind her. She whirled around and was in for a mild shock. It wasn't a ghoul, it was a lich. Its energy told her that much. And the corpse it had been eating—well, her special senses told her that it hadn't been alive in quite a while. Her actual eyes told her as much as well. The unanimated corpse, the meal, had the dried-up look of someone who'd died years previous. The lich had been eating a slack, not a living person.

"Sarah," it said again. There were so many things hidden in the word, so many different kinds of emotions and questions. She gave the lich a good once-over.

Blue eyes. Flannel shirt. She was pretty sure she knew what that shirt would smell like, if she got close enough to bury her face in it.

She stepped closer. He had his arms open wide and she pushed herself into his embrace. Shoved her face right into his shirt.

"Daddy," she said, and she was eight years old again, and crying.

5.

THE KNOCK CAME again. She stared at the door. "Just come in already. It's not like I can keep you out."

There was no response.

Ayaan staggered to the door and pushed it open. There was no one there. Just darkness and cool, slightly salty air. A cavernous space lay out there, maybe an empty warehouse, perhaps an abandoned auditorium. She stepped outside, her bruised feet dragging over grimy concrete. A little light came from above her through a hole in the ceiling. It made a sort of natural spotlight on the floor. She could see dust motes spiraling in the shaft of sunlight. It almost, but not quite, illuminated an AK-47 assault rifle suspended from the ceiling by a length of string. Ayaan shuffled toward the weapon. She touched the cherrywood stock. It was not her own AK, she would have recognized the pattern of the stain on the wood, the scratches on the metal that had become as familiar to her over the years as the spots and blemishes on her own skin. Still. It was a Kalashnikov and she knew it would be a reliable, effective weapon. She yanked it down, snapping its cord, and examined the chamber, then broke out the magazine. A full clip of ammunition. With fingers that felt unusually clumsy she slipped one of the bullets out of the magazine and examined it, almost dropping it when she held it up to her eye. She half expected the bullets to be blanks or somehow adulterated, but they weren't. Just the standard 7.62 x 39 millimeter cartridge. She slapped the magazine back into place, moved the selector lever to single fire, and released the cocking lever with a clang.

Something stirred in the corners of the big room. No, more than one something. She brought the weapon around to firing position, ready to aim as soon as a target presented itself. None did. Slowly, deliberately, she took a step toward the still-open bedroom door.

A shadow flicked across the door, slamming it shut. A shadow that moved faster than any living human being she'd ever seen. She knew what that meant. A fast ghoul—probably an entire squad of them. Which meant the green phantom had to be nearby to spur them on. "Maybe you'll tell me your name now that we've got so much in common," she announced, trying to flush him out.

It wasn't the green phantom who answered, however. It was another of the Tsarevich's lieutenants. The one she'd come to call (if only in her head) "the lipless wonder." "Is test," he told her, his voice bouncing around the ceiling, amplified electronically and broadcast from several directions at once. He could be anywhere.

"Is test," he said again. "Is very fair. Abilities special, some would call powers, they come out under great stress only. What greater stress than life or death, yes? Sometimes the lich has no power, nothing special, and then he must be put down. If he has powers then he can survive test."

"And making me do this in the dark, that's part of the fairness?" Ayaan demanded, but before she could finish the sentence something slapped her arm hard enough to make it sting. She grabbed her wrist and felt torn leather there.

Clearly the test had already begun. She could live or die by her own actions. If she was going to live she needed to shoot, and to shoot she needed to see. She thought of Sarah's gift, the ability to see the energies of life and death. Ayaan would have that ability now—she was dead. All of the dead had the special vision. It was how they hunted. She could feel the accelerated ghouls whizzing around her, could hear them moving in the dark, but she forced herself to calm down, to close her eyes, to—to feel.

Yes. It was there, she had only to look. It had nothing to do with the eyes, though her brain formed images of what she received. Her skin took in most of the information, sensitive areas of her body reacting with abhorrence to the presence of undead things.

And there they were. She understood, perhaps for the first time, just what ghouls were. Empty shells. Husks. Person-shaped receptacles. The energy that flowed into them, that suffused them was the only thing keeping them upright. There were no minds, no souls inside them. She stared down at her own body, at her flesh wrapped up in the skin of some other dead beast and knew she was one of them. Her intelligence, her personality, were merely riding around in her corpse.

One of the ghouls came at her, moving low and fast, bent almost parallel with the floor. Its sharpened bones flashed toward her but she could see them now, smoky and purple with stolen life energy. She ducked and spun and barely avoided impaling herself on his cut-down arms. She had time—just—to wonder if he was one of the ghouls butchered on the ship while she watched.

She ducked and rolled away from him and watched as he skidded past her, sliding on the slick floor.

She could see them now—only three of them, their energy thrumming off the walls—but her special vision couldn't compensate for really seeing. She had little depth perception, she couldn't find their ranges in the dark. She knew it was day outside and the sun was shining—she could tell from the hole in the roof.

Ayaan waited for the next attack, a ghoul coming at her with arms flailing and legs pumping. She dropped to all fours and swung away from him, then dashed for the nearest wall. She felt old, dried-up wood, probably plywood installed over a broken window. There was no time to find a door.

With her arm bent, with her weight behind it, Ayaan smashed at the wood, expecting to dislocate her shoulder. Instead it gave way like a cobweb and she spilled out into daylight so bright it seared her eyes.

Dead pupils, Ayaan decided, could not contract as quickly as live pupils. Her eyes throbbed with pain as she got her feet under her and ran, her boots finding the planks of a boardwalk, her muscles burning as she tried to run. The best she could manage was a sort of drunken stagger, little better than a stiff walk.

When her eyes finally started to adjust to the white light that flashed off the ocean she lifted the Kalashnikov into firing position and sighted on the window she'd broken open. They would come from there, she figured. She had to assume they wouldn't have more ghouls lying in wait for her outside.

A ghoul wearing a fireman's helmet appeared in the window. The lower half of his face had been carved away to give him a bigger mouth, a bigger bite. His skin was the tawny color of a predator in a dusty land.

Ayaan wasted no time. She lined up her shot and placed a tight burst of three rounds right in the exposed portion of his forehead.

At least, they should have gone there. Instead, none of the three even hit him. In horror Ayaan looked down at her weapon. Had it been altered somehow, had the iron sights been filed down, twisted out of alignment, something?

No. It was her.

The ghoul leaped through the window and headed toward her like a rocket. She fired again and saw dusty dried blood explode from his elbow. It didn't even slow him down.

It was her. It was her fingers, her hands that felt like formless clay at the ends of her arms. There was a reason why the green phantom took the hands of his soldiers—they were worth less as weapons than the sharpened ends of bone. And hers were the same. She lacked the motor skills, the fine muscle control it took to fire a rifle with any kind of effectiveness. She dropped the weapon on the ground. She would never use an AK-47 again, she knew.

No more than ten meters separated them, a distance he could cover in seconds. If she was going to pass this test—did she even want to pass it? Let him stab her, let him destroy her, and she would be done. She had spent all her life fighting the liches. To live on, to continue to exist at any rate, meant becoming what she hated most.

It didn't matter. She knew, because Ayaan could look into her own heart, she had mastered that skill very early on, she knew she wanted to keep going. She could no longer stay alive for Sarah. But she could continue to fight.

But how? With her bare hands? She closed her eyes and tried to think. Sarah spoke often of the life force, the energy that pervaded all living things. Ayaan had always thought of it as similar to *baraka*, the dangerous blessedness of clan leaders and Sufi saints. Just an old Somali superstition—but perhaps there was some reality to it. Now, after her death, she had no trouble feeling the energy all around her, the life force. A field of energy that passed through her, that wrapped her up and animated her dead flesh and kept her consciousness alive. If she were going to develop powers, just spontaneously grow some kind of mystical ability, it would come from that source, from that energy, that *baraka*. Every lich power she'd heard of, all of their magic, was simply the ability to manipulate that field.

She reached down into it, gathered it in her hands. It made her skin tingle as she clutched at it, exactly as she might clutch at a blanket that covered her. She concentrated it and time slowed down as she focused the energy, squeezing it down into tight hot balls of force in her hands.

The ghoul racing toward her seemed to stop in midair as she raised her hands, threw them forward, and spat the built-up energy at him. It was that simple, it was second nature. Not something she had to learn.

The energy hit him square on, her aim perfect. It sizzled and spat with darkness as it touched him. It burst inside him like dark fire. His face wrinkled as if in concentration . . . and kept wrinkling. He had looked ageless before, but as the energy—her energy—ripped through his flesh, he took on the countenance of an old man. His skin crinkled, turned papery, tore away from his bones. As it fluttered away on the wind it turned to fine powder, like talc.

His bones collapsed on the boardwalk, mere paces from her, his skull crumbling like old pottery. She had aged him to destruction— what remained of his head could have been a thousand years old.

She stood there forever, waiting for time to start up again. It didn't. She had no breath, no heartbeat to measure its passing. The sun failed to move across the sky. There had been more ghouls in the boarded-up warehouse, at least two more, but neither of them appeared to confront her.

She supposed she had passed the test.

A door in a nearby building creaked open on rusted hinges. She heard maniacal laughter echoing in her head, but had no idea whom it belonged to. Then time started up once more, and she walked on swollen feet toward the door.

7.

HE WAS SUPPOSED to be dead—he was always dead, in her memory, in the stories they told about him. He was dead. Jack had wounded him, Jack had turned and turned on him and bitten him, infection had set in, Ayaan had sanitized him. It was the story of her life, of her origins.

None of it was true. Thank God.

His dead arms went around her in a feeble kind of embrace. She might have been held by a human-shaped agglutination of

Popsicle sticks and pipe cleaners. Sarah pressed harder against him, against his woolen shirt which smelled of death and his dry, dry skin which cracked and peeled against her cheek. Disgust, even horror lost out to the feeling, the one pure feeling that sang in her. She had never felt something so primal and focused before, except maybe the fear of death, and that was old to her, and this was new.

Somewhere in the twelve-year gap between their meetings she had lost him, he had turned a corner in her memory and disappeared from view. Now he had made another right, and another, and in the labyrinth their paths had crossed again. Her age—his condition—none of it was particularly important. They were just a father and a daughter, he was still the man who had taken her to meet the Bedouins and let her pet their camels, she was still the child who loved butter pecan ice cream and Arabic-language cartoons from Egypt on Saturday morning.

The scuttling buglike skull crawled up the wall behind her father, into her field of view, but she just shut her eyes and went back to the place where they were family, a family again, and all the walls between them shifted and rearranged to make paths and routes for them to reach each other.

There was someone else in that maze, someone neither of them could see, and of course it was Helen. Her mother, his wife. Helen who had turned and who was maybe still locked in a bathroom in Nairobi, beating against the door, trying to get out to find something to eat. She was a wispy kind of ghost, a distant presence even in memory, however, and it was easy enough to ignore her rattling her chains.

She had her father back. After twelve years. It wasn't the kind of world where such things happened. She was so glad. So glad.

"Sarah," he breathed, his voice a rustling of old mildew-spotted paper. "You weren't supposed to see me like this. Ever." His body convulsed against hers. He was trying to push her away. She let him go, let him slip out from her hug like a piece of ratty cloth falling away. "This is my spider hole. You weren't supposed to see me this weak." His eyes flicked away from her for a split second, just as long as it takes the sun to hide behind a cloud. She saw where he looked and shook her head. His shame had made him look at the dead slack on the platform. The one he'd been feeding on when she came in. "I held out for so long. I just went hungry—I thought I could do it."

The skull moved behind him but they both ignored it. He stared at her. She could hear the word in his mind, as clearly as if she had a telepathic link to him, though she didn't. The word was *cannibal,* and it made her shake her head again. "He was already dead, and—"

"And I didn't so much eat him as drain him," he agreed, a little too quickly. Dekalb lifted one hand creakily and put it against his cheek as if to hide a blush. The color of his face, which was the color of a white concrete sidewalk after a summer rain, did not change. "You can . . . you can just take their darkness. You can absorb their energy and they fall down. I saw Gary do it, drain an entire crowd of them once. I only ever take one at a time. Sometimes I think they want it, that peace." He shook his head and she saw his neck was as thin as a length of pipe. "It makes you strong again but it doesn't diminish the hunger. Nothing ever does. I'm so hungry, pumpkin, you can't know."

He kept looking at the corpse. She wanted to tell him it didn't matter, that she didn't care. She remembered the lich in Cyprus and how Osman had needed more than words. She needed to show him. With all her strength she grabbed the corpse's thin ankles and pulled it, shoved it, heaved it over the edge of the platform. It fell into the dark shaft below with a long-lived series of clanks and bangs and thrumming impacts. Dekalb moved his hand to cover his mouth. He had grown so weak, so thin since she'd last seen him. So used up. Death wasn't all of it, though; it wasn't just undeath that made him so pale and attenuated. She heard a narrow scuttling sound behind her and spun on her heel.

The insectile skull with the blue eyes looked up at her from the platform. It sprang into the air, rising a few inches off the floor, and fell back. It wanted her attention.

"It's Gary, isn't it?" she said on a hunch. She couldn't imagine who else it might be. The two of them were linked so tightly in the story, at least the way Ayaan always told it—Dekalb and Gary, good and evil locked in epic struggle, and Dekalb had won that battle only by sacrificing his own life. Of course in the story Dekalb didn't come back as a lich and Gary was an enormous and deadly monster who burned away to nothing but ashes. This creature, this human skull was like nothing she'd ever seen before and it worried her. She knew Ayaan would have asked a million questions. You never turned your back on the new or unusual, that was one of her rules. As much as Sarah wanted to talk to her father, she knew this mystery had to be cleared up first. Sarah turned the crawling skull over with one boot and saw the segmented limbs underneath, hidden like the legs of a horseshoe crab. The legs pedaled madly and she drew her foot back squeamishly, wondering if she should kick the evil thing into the darkness of the shaft. It twitched over onto its tiny jointed feet again and skittered away from her. She looked back at her father.

He nodded. "He's not human anymore. Not even a semblance of a human. I've killed him so many times—I think he's been dead so many times over he's forgotten what a living human body is like. He's healing, and he's growing, in ways I can't anticipate. He doesn't seem to be able to just die. I've tried everything, I even had the mummies smash him to bits with a sledgehammer. The next day he had put himself back together the way we used to put broken vases back together with superglue. I locked myself in here, sealed away from the world because I needed to watch him. To make sure he didn't get loose." He stared at the skull bug then as if it had changed colors. "No, I don't think that's appropriate," he said, and she frowned at him until he looked back at her face. "He and I can communicate, sort of. He wants to talk to you, he—Gary, don't make me crush you again, or maybe we could boil you in a pot—no. Never. You will never get near her, do you hear me? Never!"

"I'd like to hear what he has to say," Sarah told Dekalb.

"Oh, all right," the lich said, his hands at his throat. "I'll have to translate, though. He doesn't have any lungs or vocal cords or a tongue or anything, and—"

She stopped him in mid-sentence. "I know a trick," she told him, thinking of the soapstone in her pocket. She'd speculated often on how it linked her to Ptolemy. "I just need something of his, something close to him. Like a piece of jewelry he always wore, a wedding ring, or a favorite shirt, or—"

One of the mummies—silent and invisible until that moment— glided forward and picked the skull up off the ground. With a casual snap it tore one of the teeth out of Gary's upper jaw and then dumped the rest of him on the platform. The mummy handed her the long yellow tooth, complete with spiky roots, and stepped back into the shadows.

Sarah bit her lip. "I don't know if this will work," she said. She made a fist around the tooth and frowned.

That fucking hurt, you prick, Gary said, using her own internal voice. He wasn't talking to her but still she heard him. The words blasted through her mind and made her ears ring in sympathy. **Come back here and I'll bite your goddamned prick off! Or did they already put it in one of those fucking jars?** She squinted her eyes and tried to turn down her own mental volume.

It didn't work. **So you're Sarah, huh? You're skinnier than I expected. I also thought you'd be white, like your old man. Don't get me wrong, I'm no racist. I'd gladly take a bite out of you if I just had a mandible to call my own.**

She could feel him grinning in her head, his tongue lapping at her gray matter, at the convolutions of her brain. She nearly let go of the tooth. Then she realized she couldn't, that the buzzing, stinging energy in the tooth had actually paralyzed her hand. She couldn't let go. She tried to open her mouth to speak and found she couldn't do that, either.

8.

THE OPEN DOOR beckoned her. She fought its pull—she was not ready to go in.

She was not quite ready to kill again, so soon.

Baraka tugged at Ayaan's calcified veins. It had saved her life and now it wanted to be repaid. The power itched inside her, burned her guts. It needed refueling. It needed meat. She knew exactly what it wanted. She also knew it would never be satisfied, never again, no matter how much meat she ate. No matter how much living human meat.

Nausea ballooned in her stomach, filling it like hot rocks. She dropped to one knee and spat on the boardwalk. When she wiped her mouth and looked up, the naked man was there. The one with the blue tattoos and the noose around his neck.

"I know what your next move is, lass," he told her.

"Then you're one ahead of me," Ayaan said. She lowered her other knee, knelt and touched her forehead to the eroded wood. She was pointed out toward the sea—as close to being oriented toward Mecca as she could hope for. Silently she began to pray. She stopped in mid-*du'a*. "You," she said to the man. She lifted her head. "You must know something of evil. Am I a monster now? If I speak God's name, will He smite me?"

The ghost closed his eyes and a look of blessed relief came over his face. "Finally," he sighed, "one of them *believes!*" Which didn't answer her question. When she stared at him long enough he shifted on his feet and actually addressed her problem, though he provided more of an opinion than any hard facts. "Are you a monster, now? Oh, aye. But your God made you so, didn't he, lass? He made you what you are and he did it for good reason, you can be sure of that. Pray all you want. I'll wait here."

The urge had left her, however. She stood and looked at him, truly looked at him. He wasn't there. He looked real enough, she could even feel the heat of his hands when she grasped them, but there was nothing behind the image. No energy, neither living or dead.

"I know what your next move is," he said again, once she had stopped touching him. "You're going to go on a bit of a tear. You'll run inside there," he said, pointing at the open door, "with your death ray blasting and you'll ask questions later. Hopefully you'll get the Tsarevich, but even if you just get the green phantom fellow, well, that'll be a good day's killing. They'll slaughter you, of course. But who mourns a pawn when its loss takes a bishop?"

"You can read my mind." Ayaan let her hands fall to her sides.

He didn't bother assenting. "Is a little bit of good worth it when so much potential goes to waste?" he demanded. "There's a deeper game, here, if you're willing to be a little patient, lass, and there's more to win than you think. You play nice for now. Don't go in there pretending to be one of them. They're too smart for that. Act like you've been broken, though, broken like a wild horse, and they may want to believe it so bad they don't ask so many questions. Then you just do as they say. Bide your time. Wait for the real opportunity to come along."

What he said smacked of prudence. She didn't like it—she wanted vengeance—but she had not lived so long by being fool-hardy. She nodded. "All right," she began, intending to ask further questions, but he was gone, without so much as a fare-thee-well. Ghosts were supposed to be like that, she knew, but still it was unsettling.

She shook her head and walked through the open door. She stepped into a cavernous, dark space, and then squinted in pain as brilliant red light attacked her eyes. A sign—a neon sign in English that read *mad-o-rama* buzzed into life in the dim space, showing her its corners and casting everything in a hellish glow. To enter mad-o-rama she had to pass through the mouth of an enormous sculptural head, complete with giant triangular fangs.

Beyond this opening lay a serpentine length of small-gauge rail-road track and piles of mannequins painted in glowing yellow green. Some looked like witches, some like maniacs with knives.

Skeletons were well represented, as were vultures and bats. A spiderweb made of fishing line hung from the ceiling and brushed the top of her hair. Mad-o-rama must have been a carnival ride once, she decided. A dark ride.

At the back of the room stood the liches, gathered in dark conference. The green phantom, the lipless wonder, the werewolf. They were waiting for her, she could tell—their attention, their energy, was directed at her. One of the ride's cars stood at the end of the track, its high back turned toward her and shielding its occupants from her view. With the vision of the dead she could see right through the wood and metal, however. She could see two figures there, their energy bright with excitement, their auras intertwined. One was dead, a lich. The other was alive but hurt.

Ayaan's stomach rumbled experimentally. Hurt . . . living . . . flesh. Desire tried to bend her double, but she fought it down.

Cicatrix stood up, untangled her limbs from the car's dead occupant. The scarred woman looked almost bashful as her eyes met Ayaan's. Or perhaps she was flushed for other reasons. An open wound on her chest oozed blood that ran down in clots to stain the plunging neckline of her white linen dress.

The living woman stepped down from the car and walked at her leisure toward the exit. As she passed Ayaan she reached out to touch the Somali's arm. She whispered, "Is fun, can be good life, if you can make you to like it." It sounded like some kind of apology. Without further explanation she left the way Ayaan had come in.

Ayaan moved forward to meet the car's occupant. It was the Tsarevich, she was sure of it. She would get around in front of the car, see what he really was. Then she would fry him with her death beam, put everything she had into it until the green phantom came for her. She had heard the ghost and its cautions, but she was sorely tempted.

Before she could reach the car, however, the beautiful little boy in his filigreed armor appeared out of thin air, directly in her path. "You come too close. Stay there, yes?" he said, and she could only nod in agreement. She could see now that it was just a projection, just as Sarah had back at the beginning. There was no energy in the boy, no darkness or light. He might as well have been hollowed out like a pumpkin. He was just like the ghost outside.

The boy gestured with his skull wand and the werewolf moved forward. He had a strange little machine in his hands, a ball studded with vacuum tubes and black Bakelite dials. A long telescoping antenna emerged from its center. Its purpose was not immediately clear.

Ayaan remembered the ghost and his words. *Don't pretend to be one of them. They won't believe it.* The device the werewolf held must be a weapon. Ayaan knew one when she saw it.

"Semyon Iurevich," the Tsarevich said. "Is she trustable?"

The lipless wonder came forward. The dry skin of his face had drawn away from his smallish features, making his eyes very wide. His nose turned up like a pig's. He wore a stained white bathrobe and a pair of slippers. He came up to her and ran his hands over Ayaan's arms and hips. She wanted to kick him away but she controlled herself. *Like a broken horse,* she thought. She let her shoulders slump, let her neck bow. Let them think it was too much, that she was overwhelmed, dazzled by their evil.

"He sees future, knows all," the Tsarevich announced. "Can read you like book."

The lich's bony hands stole across her belly, grabbed at her buttocks. She leaped away but knew better than to attack him. He reached out again and she let him touch her. She closed her eyes and thought of Sarah, of just how far she would let this go if it meant keeping her promise to Dekalb, if it meant seeing Sarah again.

The lich's touch grew more clinical, less intrusive. He focused on one small patch of her left arm as if the information he sought was written there, as if he'd found the right page of her book. Finally he looked up. Long wispy white hair swung away from his face. The top of his head was completely bald and it glistened where it wasn't red with sores.

Energy passed between them. Ayaan's soul lurched in her body. Her heart would have gone wild with palpitations if it still could beat—this evil thing, this lich was really looking into her, his power was real. She knew he would see in a moment her dissembling, her game. He would give her away.

"Is not one of us," the lich told his master. "Not as yet. But is safe, with precautions."

Only the fact that she was dead and no longer needed to breathe kept Ayaan from sighing with relief. She didn't know how—maybe the naked ghost had come to her aid—but she had fooled them. "I don't want anything but to rest," she said. "And maybe get something to eat. I can see now that there's no beating you."

The Tsarevich nodded and stepped even closer to her. Another step and his nose would be in her navel. At least the projection of his nose would touch the leather covering her belly. He looked up at her like a toddler addressing his mother. "No rest for wicked," he told her, "but maybe is not so bad. I have mission here. I have great work to complete. So many things to do, and not so many hands. I take a chance, yes? Is work for you, if you will have it, and it proves you. Otherwise, you stay here, you be like new Least. You interested?"

"I . . . I guess so," Ayaan said. She bit her lip and looked away. She had never tried to look coy before and she thought she must be overdoing it ridiculously.

"Is good!" The boy nodded happily, and his smile lit up the whole room. "You do good, now. You do good, come back, you see man behind the curtain." He pointed at the car at the end of the tracks where his real body still sat out of view. "You do bad, we have provision for this as well." He pointed again, this time at the device the werewolf held. The hairy lich touched one of the black knobs and the vacuum tubes lit up with a dull orange glow.

Ayaan felt something tickling her neck. She put a hand on her throat and felt the silver tattoo there. It felt warm, though the rest of her skin was disturbingly cool. The tickling turned to a tingle, and then a sensation of uncomfortable heat. It only took a few seconds to become painful. She clawed at the tattoo, but that only made it worse.

The Tsarevich waved his wand and the searing stopped instantly. Ayaan rubbed at her neck but the warmth was gone.

"Is called ward, and is very strong magic. No way to undo it now without cutting off at neck. Be good now, or he turns it up all way." The little boy looked as if this was the last thing he ever wanted to have happen in the whole wide world. "He turns it up, and your head is to catch fire, yes?"

She nodded. Bide your time, the ghost had told her. Wait for the right opportunity.

"I'll be good," she promised.

SARAH COULDN'T LET go of Gary's tooth. She could feel it digging into her hand as if he were trying to bite her by remote control. He held her prisoner, her own power turned against her. He let her look away for just a moment, and she stared at Dekalb. Her father's face had set in a mask of concern but he wasn't doing anything. He should be protecting her.

Hah! My buddy here's not much of a fighter.

"He fought you. He turned you into a bony little freak," Sarah said, her voice stuck in her mouth. Her throat could move but not her tongue. She couldn't move her facial muscles, she couldn't scream for help, but he was letting her talk to him, and him alone. She imagined he had the power to stop that as well, if he wanted.

She supposed if a lich were locked in his own skull for twelve years he might have time to learn a few magic tricks. Especially when he was the second most powerful lich who ever lived.

Magic? he asked, perhaps reading her thoughts. **I know all kinds of magic. Who do you think taught Marisol how to tame a ghoul? That's right, yours truly. I sold that secret for a breath of fresh air. I knew nothing about the outside world. Your dad kept me jailed here where nothing ever**

happens and I couldn't even see the sun. So I learned to send my consciousness outward, to project myself astrally, I suppose. Marisol's was the first brain I touched—she and I go way back, of course. She was scared, too, just like you are right now, sugar beet. When I came to her in her dream and started telling her things that only the dead could know, she was frightened already. The colony here was in bad shape back in those days. People were getting sick and dying, the crops weren't coming in. Once she realized I could teach her useful things she let me take control of her body for a few minutes a day. I never did anything drastic—most of the time I just stood in front of a mirror and touched myself, to be brutally honest. Have you seen that woman? She's a knockout.

Sarah squirmed against her confinement.

God! Just because I lack the organs doesn't mean I don't feel the itch. Don't be such a prude, Sarah. I bet you do it. I bet you do it all the time. Hmm . . . but we're getting distracted. There's a point to my little story. I talked, and Marisol listened. Get it?

Sarah kept her silence.

Good. So let's be civil to each other. Let's be nice, even if we can't be friends. There's no reason to spoil Daddy-Daughter Day. It's him I want to talk about, of course. Your father: my jailer. Look at him. I'm sorry to be the one to tell you this, but he's a gibbering idiot.

Sarah bristled but said nothing. Gary could feel her emotions. He seemed to find them amusing.

This is the most fun I've had since I lost my appendages. But anyway, it's true. Your father's a moron. A subintellect. I know he has a brain—you can't be undead without one—but we're talking walnut-size here. This whole time he's been confronted by just one mystery, just one little puzzle to solve, and he's never worked it out. He's had twelve years to figure out just who keeps rebuilding my aching bones every time he breaks them but he hasn't got so much as clue one. You can tell, though. You knew it just by looking at me.

Keeping her mouth in a tight grimace she subvocalized, "I don't know what you're talking about."

Come on, sweet tart. You can see the energy, I know you can. Your friend, what's his name . . . Jack? Sure. He told me all about it. You can tell who's protecting me. You would have seen it eventually, so it doesn't matter if I give the game away. Stop playing dumb. Unless it's hereditary and you got your old man's slack jaw.

Ah. Sarah let her vision relax, paid attention to the skin behind her ears, to the way the air felt. And then she saw it. Stretching away from Gary's skull like invisible hair, long ropy tendrils of dark energy draped around the room, snaked along the platform, tying Gary right back to . . . to Dekalb himself.

Hot bile hit the back of her throat. Sarah wanted to scream. She wanted to smash the skull to fragments. Of all the fucked-up things—this was not what Ayaan had taught her about how the world worked. Good people fought the bad things. They didn't heal them. It was wrong, it was so wrong—

It's not his fault.

Sarah turned to face the skull with venom in her eyes. How dare he? How dare Gary make her see that her father, the one man in the entire world she'd ever thought was worth a damn, one of only two human beings, frankly, that she had ever loved, was in league with the monsters?

He thinks he doesn't have any powers. He think he's the least useful lich that ever was. He's been healing me for over a decade, and he has no idea. Every time he develops the balls to kill me, his guilt overpowers him and subconsciously he puts me back together again.

She forced herself to calm down. "That must be . . . unpleasant."

It's fucking agonizing, is what it is. I've been crushed,

I've been burned, I've been impaled on a spike. But it's better than the alternative. I have a right to exist, sugar shorts. I have a right to live, whatever you may think of my current status. I don't know. Maybe you're thinking you'll just tell Daddy what you've learned. Maybe you think that if he knows what's going on he can fight it, and he can finally do me in. And maybe, just maybe, he can. Then again, maybe his subconscious is stronger than you think.

"You expect me to keep your secret," Sarah spat through gritted teeth.

Yeah, I do. The skull grinned up at her. **Oh, not for my sake. You probably hate me. That's all right, it comes with the job. I expect you to keep your fucking hole shut for _him_. Because, snack pack, he's spent the last twelve years pretending that he's a hero. That he brought down the nefarious Gary, the lich king of New York City. You see, there's not much else to do in this place except sit around talking about what used to be. After a while, memories are all a man has. That and the occasional slack that wanders by in the tunnel down there. If he knew how much time he's wasted, playing at the vigilant guardian up here, if he knew what he'd done, well. It might just break his heart. Granted he isn't using it right now, but I expect you'd rather keep it in one piece. Do we have a deal?**

He released her, as easily as that, without any kind of agreement on her part. Obviously he thought he knew her answer already.

It burned a little that he was right.

"Did you have a nice chat?" Dekalb asked. She saw worry written on his face. On the rest of him she just saw weakness. She'd forgotten how fragile he must be. That he was one of the people from the old time, from before the end of the world. Nobody had been tough back then. The slightest emotional shock could destroy them.

Gary had given her some very valuable information. Something she would eventually have figured out for herself, of course, but he hadn't wanted to take that chance. He'd told her his biggest secret in such a way that she could never use it against him. She'd heard he was smart. She'd had no idea just how smart.

"Yeah," she said. "It was great. Listen." She shoved the tooth into her back pocket, not knowing what else to do with it. "I'm a little tired. I think I'm going to go back to, you know, the others. Get some sleep."

"I'll be here when you wake up." He smiled. "I don't get to rest, pumpkin. I don't even get to sleep anymore."

She put her hands on his cheeks, leaned forward until their foreheads were touching. She couldn't quite bring herself to kiss him.

"It's going to be OK," he said, and she wanted to sag into those words. She wanted to curl up in them and let everything go right for a while. Then she realized he wasn't talking to her. He was addressing himself. "Now that you're here, everything's going to be OK. So where's Ayaan?" he asked.

She closed her eyes because she didn't want to look at him while she lied to him. "Back in Somalia. She's fine, doing great, actually." She tried to think of a lie but the only thing that came to her was ludicrous. She went with it anyway. "She sent me to check up on Marisol, see if Governors Island was still thriving."

"Oh. Is it? I don't get out much."

She nodded. "It's doing great." Such a ludicrous idea—that anyone would launch such a dangerous expedition just to see how old friends were getting along—didn't seem to strike him as odd at all. Maybe in the time before the Epidemic that wouldn't have seemed so outlandish.

She left him in the tower with Gary and the mummies, unsure when she would come back. She wondered about what to do next as she headed back down the causeway and onto the island. She noticed something strange about the buildings on the north side of the island, those that faced Manhattan, but she couldn't remember what they had looked like when she went in.

Dark stains seemed to creep across their facades. Patches of a very light green had grown in circular patterns on the bricks—

lichens, she thought, like you would see on very old tombstones. The dark stains were moss or mold or mildew or something. Come to think of it, she didn't think the buildings *had* looked like that when she'd entered the ventilation tower.

Strange. And Ayaan had taught her never to ignore the strange. She scratched a sudden itch in her left armpit and pondered what to do next.

She made her way toward Building 109, the island's former welcome center, where she was supposed to sleep that night, keeping one eye on the water. She half expected an army of ghouls to come dribbling up out of the harbor. When Marisol's sickly little son Jackie grabbed her from behind she automatically reached for her pistol. She stopped herself in time, because she'd had proper training in whom and whom not to shoot.

"What's up?" she said and tousled Jackie's hair. It took her a second to realize something was wrong. He coughed and a cloud of black spores erupted from his throat. His skin looked patchy and even fuzzy in places. She grabbed his chin, trying to discover if he was choking, and her hand came away covered in musty-smelling powder.

The itch in her armpit got a lot worse all of a sudden.

10.

"STAY AWAY FROM the edge," Marisol said, never taking the field glasses from her eyes.

Sarah danced backward, away from the crumbling bricks at the top of the six-story dormitory building. Not the safest place on the island, but it had the best view of the skeletal city across the channel. The building had been officers' quarters once but now it was about to fall down. The thick coating of white mildew, like a spill of snow up the side of the building, was taking its toll, eating into the bricks on one side, chemically dissolving the mortar between them.

"I can't recognize half the buildings over there. Have you ever seen anything like this? No, nobody has. The Battery's turned green again. The dead ate every growing thing there was over there but now . . . Jesus, look at those shrubs—they must be fifteen feet high." Marisol pivoted in place and adjusted her focus.

Not just Battery Park, Sarah saw, but the entire tip of lower Manhattan had transformed overnight into old-growth rain forest. Trees crowded the broad streets, their roots overturning the rusted soft shapes of abandoned cars. The sides of buildings were verdant with moss or dark with fungal growth. Flowers in a dozen different colors sprouted from broken windows, and vines dangled from straining balconies.

Behind them, curled in a folding deck chair, little Jackie hacked up another lungful of spores. It was dangerous on top of the dormitory building, but Marisol wouldn't let him out of her sight. She lowered the binoculars and looked at her son for a moment, perhaps assessing his condition. He wasn't getting any better.

Half of Governors Island was complaining of respiratory distress. One woman, a forty-year-old grandmother, had died in the night. Those who weren't coughing up bloody goo were complaining of skin irritations, weird rashes, discolored nails and hair and teeth.

Sixteen people—nearly a fifth of the island's inhabitants—were bedridden. Half of them weren't expected to survive another day. It was as if the natural world, the vegetative world, had rebelled against them. As if it wanted them dead.

Mold had spread across the wooden docks and piers of Governors Island, green, slimy mold, algae growing faster and thicker than it had a right to. Mushrooms had popped up all over Nolan Park. Poisonous and ugly, they exuded horrible clouds of choking spores when they were stepped on. Even the grass between the houses, even the thin weeds that popped up between the flagstones of Fort Jay, had turned thick and coarse as if they were reaching for the survivors' ankles, wanting to trip them, to bring them down. Hidden in the shadier parts of the island, deadly nightshade had emerged and poison ivy was spreading into the carefully tended gardens.

The worst part was that it wasn't even over. It was still going on. Since dawn the acidic mildew that threatened the dormitory building had spread to three more brick towers. Who knew what would still be standing by nightfall.

Marisol fiddled with the vinyl strap of her binoculars. "People are asking me questions I can't answer. They don't understand this, Sarah. They don't know why it's happening. They need a reason, any reason. Maybe they sinned before God. Or maybe this is just Mother Nature getting her own back. That kind of mushy-minded stuff won't hold them for long, though. They're going to want a scapegoat. Someone to blame."

Sarah nodded absently. She was as confused as anybody and she could admit to herself it would be nice to blame this horror on somebody. Hating a scapegoat would help her choke down her fear.

"Obviously," Marisol continued, "I'm going to say it's your fault."

Sarah stopped nodding. "What?" she demanded.

"Well, think about it. You're an outsider. I don't want to string up one of my own people like some kind of pagan sacrifice. I'd much rather hang a near stranger. Secondly, it's true, isn't it? You brought this here. You were after that Tsarevich asshole and in the process you gave away our location. Sound familiar?"

"No, no," Sarah said, "we were really careful, we kept our distance—"

Marisol shrugged. "OK. Maybe the fact that nothing like this has happened for twelve years, and then all of a sudden you show up, and a day later we're overrun by evil plants, OK, maybe, just maybe, that's a coincidence." She raised her hands to the heavens. "Still."

Sarah's mind raced. If the survivors on Governors Island believed it, if they truly thought she was the cause of the biological attack—they wouldn't wait for a lynching. They would tear her to pieces with their bare hands.

She reached for something—anything—to fight back with. "Yeah," she said, "well, you just go ahead and try it, lady. You go ahead."

"All right."

"And then—and then, when they're going to, to burn me at the stake, whatever, when I have their attention, then I'll explain to them exactly who it was who taught you how to make a ghoul into a slack."

Marisol's mouth twitched. It might have been the precursor of a grin. "Coming from the daughter of a lich, that might sound a bit hard to believe."

Blood flowed out of Sarah's face. She was fighting for her life. "Not when—not if I tell them what Gary got, in exchange! Not when I tell them how he used you like a living sex toy!"

Marisol didn't rise to it, however. "That would sound bad. The thing of it is, though, that in the morning, I might have a lot of explaining to do, but you'll still be dead."

Damn.

She had a point, Sarah had to admit.

Desperate, completely unable to think clearly, Sarah tore the Makarov out of her sweatshirt pocket and swung her arm in Marisol's direction—only to find herself looking down the barrel of a .357 revolver.

"Ayaan taught you about firearms, right? You're pretty good," Marisol told her. She was breathing a little heavy. Sarah was nearly gasping. "Jack taught me."

Slowly, with a caution based on extensive paranoia, both women lowered their weapons. No safeties had been released, there had been no real danger, but Sarah knew she had been a moment away from death.

"We do what we have to do to keep going," Marisol told her. "You know that. So don't you dare judge me."

"Killing me won't solve your problem," Sarah said.

"No. But it will keep my people from rioting and making things a whole lot worse. You have a better idea?"

Sarah swallowed all the spit in her mouth and turned her head to look at the towers of Manhattan. They looked like the kind of impregnable fortresses you only read about in fairy tales. "Maybe," she said. "Maybe I go over there, and find out what's doing this. And maybe I can make it stop."

Marisol snorted. "Yeah, and maybe you can fly back. Come on."

"It's worth a shot," Sarah said. Truthfully she didn't believe it. She just thought it would be a way to escape. "Look—you can throw me to the wolves and maybe that will give you time to evacuate. Or I can go over there and maybe I can actually achieve something."

Marisol stared at her, twin beams of judgment emerging from her eyes to pin Sarah to the spot, probing her, studying her. Sarah squirmed like a laboratory specimen under hot lights. Then something weird happened. Marisol blinked. She seemed to lose about an inch of height and the tight muscles of her shoulders and arms drooped. "OK," she said.

Sarah shook her head, not comprehending. "Seriously?" She thought maybe Gary was taking over Marisol's body, or maybe the Tsarevich could control the mayor's body remotely, but no, there was no dark energy anywhere nearby. Sarah would have known if there were magic at work. Marisol, she realized, was just desperate. She needed help that badly.

"Yeah. I'll give you a boat and whatever weapons you want. You go over there alone. You do what you can, then you come back. I know you won't try to run away."

Sarah said, "Of course," meaning, "of course I'll run, as fast as my little legs can carry me." She didn't say that.

"I know it," Marisol told her, "because if you do, you'll never see your father again. I'll pull him out of that tower and I'll make *him* my example."

Hope fell inside Sarah like cold liquid draining to her toes.

She had just talked herself into a corner.

LL.

SHE DIDN'T SLEEP anymore. She would never sleep again. As the night came on Ayaan's eyes began to feel sore and dry. She rubbed and rubbed at them until her skin started coming away. After that she forced herself not to rub.

One by one the cultists headed off to beds, hammocks, old mattresses with the dust and insects beaten out of them. They drained away into the dark storefronts and broken-down hotels, stretching their arms, yawning.

The moon came up and found Ayaan still waiting, waiting for sleep to come and knowing it never would. Something else found her, too. The lipless lich. Semyon Iurevich, who saw all, who knew all. He wrapped his bathrobe tight around striped pajamas a size too big for his gaunt frame. "Come," he said, and he led her away from the bonfire in the middle of Ocean Avenue. Away from the light and the few zealots standing guard who remained at least partially awake.

She watched the lich's back as he moved away from her, the pale stretch of robe across his shoulders like a beacon drawing her into the grid of darkened streets. She watched his feet shamble forward, ungainly but unflagging, she saw the complicated engineering of his shriveled ankles, all the knobs and spars and bits of bone, and the stretched sinews over them. When he turned to look back at her his face was a death mask, leather pulled far too tight over unyielding bone. His eyes were so large in their sockets.

She was vaguely aware that she was paying far too much attention to the lich. She thought perhaps that she was subconsciously horrified by him, not because of his dire appearance but because she knew she would be like him soon enough, that her own body would dry up, slim down, exude horrible chemicals. Rot.

Then again, it was possible he was merely hypnotizing her. She didn't know the extent of his psychic powers. She only knew that he could see inside her heart. And that he had lied to his master on her behalf.

"Yes, is right," he told her. They had stopped moving. They were inside a tiny room with stripes of light slanting in through wooden jalousies. She didn't remember entering the building, which was probably a bad sign. She stretched out her hands to try to get a literal grasp on where she might be, but she clutched only cobwebs. "I lied, for you. You understand? Is lie I told, that you are trustable. Harmless. Bah!"

She looked for him but could only see his teeth in the filtered moonlight. Teeth bared in eternal rictus—the lips had pulled back, away from his mouth. His gums stood out from his face, pink like wounds. "We both know, you are assassin. We are both knowing who should you kill! He is dangerous, more than anyone know. I see his heart! His black and dead heart!"

Ayaan nodded and licked her own lips, checking that they were still there. She had very little saliva in her mouth and her tongue felt like a cat's as it rasped over her flesh. Her hand went up to touch her neck, where her tattooed ward wrapped around her like a fence.

"Yes, he has control. Control of you. You must be caution, in all things. Together, though. Together we kill. Your friend, the ghost." A smile, a frown, they were the same on his face. "He has friend in me. We work together."

She blinked.

It was daylight and her mind was clear. It happened that quickly. The night was gone—day had broken. She was standing in the middle of a street.

Behind her a horn thundered out a prolonged bass chord and she jumped.

She turned slowly and found herself looking at a vehicle that was a cross between a hot rod and a Land Rover. It had four enormous balloon tires and a cab that could easily seat five. Its engine was exposed to the air, all chrome pipes and dancing pistons. Its grille looked like a gothic arch stolen off a cathedral. Multitoned flames decorated the cab. The hood ornament was a skull done in chrome and the cargo bed was full of corpses held down with bungee cords. Ayaan looked closer. The naked bodies in the back had been surgically adjusted. They had neither hands nor lips. Their torpor, she imagined, would only be temporary—their metabolisms had been dialed back by the green phantom. She looked up and saw him on the roof of the truck, tied into a lawn chair bolted in among a wide array of fog lights. He grinned down at her when he saw her jump in surprise.

The passenger-side door of the truck swung open. The werewolf sat in the driver's seat and he slid across to reach down and give her a hand up. He showed her how to use her seat belt and how to adjust the air-conditioning and the CD player. This was necessary, since the dashboard was so long he was unable to reach those instruments while belted into the driver's seat.

"This is the . . . the job the Tsarevich offered me?" Ayaan asked.

The werewolf replied in English, his voice muffled and distorted by the fur inside his mouth. "This is just the easy part. Later on you might have to fill up the gas tank. Hi, we haven't been properly introduced." He held out one hand, a furry appendage ending in five-inch-long, razor-sharp claws. They weren't like fingernails at all, more like the talons of a bird, conical and slightly curved.

Ayaan figured out a second too late that he was offering the hand to shake. She reached for it even as he was pulling it back and the claws slid across the skin of her palm. The skin parted like torn silk. At least there was no blood, just a dry spill of dark powder.

He looked embarrassed, though it was hard to tell. Even if he could have blushed, his face was hidden under a dense growth of hair that covered his nose and made his mouth a dark slit. His eyes were surprisingly soft and kindly, though. "I don't have any 'powers' in the traditional sense. My body does this weird thing, though. It doesn't breathe, it doesn't perspire, or do anything you would think a living thing might do, but it keeps producing keratin—that's the protein that makes, well, hair and nails. I have to shear myself head to foot every couple of days or my hair would grow so long I'd trip over it." He put his hands on the steering wheel, making an obvious gesture of it—he meant her no harm, he was saying. "My name's Erasmus, by the way."

She smiled for him. "Ayaan."

"Sure, sure, I know all about you. I'm German, if you can't tell from the accent." Whatever accent the werewolf might have came from the mass of fur inside his mouth, Ayaan thought, but she let him talk. He clearly needed to tell the story. "Believe it or not the Tsarevich didn't create me. I want you to know that, so you'll understand a little. I was in Leipzig when the world ended. It was bad there. The local authorities had heard already what had happened to New York and Paris. They mostly fled when the first ghouls came wandering into town. I took refuge in a hospital, hoping to outlast the Epidemic, but of course it just kept coming and coming. I starved to death, afraid to leave my little locked ward, watching shadows move outside the blinds, knowing they could get in any time if they just tried hard enough."

He closed his eyes and his face became an oblong of hair. "When it gets down to the end, when your body is breaking down from hunger, you can feel it. It hurts. I took all the drugs I was locked in with, took anything that would get me high. In the last days I discovered that if you breathed pure oxygen it got you wasted." He chuckled. "I had no idea what I was doing. I just fell asleep one day and when I woke up I was rolled up in a cocoon of hair. I could barely move."

Ayaan's stomach grumbled. She didn't like all this talk of starving—it just made her hungry.

"I ended up walking to Russia. I had no idea what I was, no idea why any of this had happened. Then I was approached by the Tsarevich's agents. I . . . ate one of them, I'm sorry to say. It was an honest mistake. The others assured me it was all right. They told me what I was, a lich, and they told me that when I ate a human being I released his soul. No more horror, no more apocalypse for that man. They made it sound like I did him a favor. I don't want you to think I'm an idiot. I don't buy half of what the Tsarevich says about souls and the afterlife. But he has something real to offer. If anyone can rebuild what we had before, if anyone can end all the suffering, it's our boy. You see?

We're not all brainwashed religious freaks. I need you to know that."

Ayaan nodded meaningfully. "Oh, of course. Certainly," she said. She was thinking that when the Tsarevich had wanted to demonstrate his remote control, the one that could set her head on fire, it was the werewolf who had turned the knobs.

She jumped again when she heard a rhythmic thumping on the roof of the cab. It had to be the green phantom, she decided, sending a signal with his femur staff.

Erasmus turned the ignition key and the truck thundered to life. He looked out at the road when he spoke next, failing altogether to make eye contact. "Anyway," he said. "Thanks for listening."

"You got it," she told him.

12.

THE BOAT TOUCHED a broken retaining wall with a hollow thud, a noise like a very deep drum being struck just once. It drifted a few feet farther, its side rattling against the remaining blocks of the wall, and then it slid up onto sand or gravel that made a noise under the hull, a hissing, and then it stopped, beached on land. Sarah lifted her oar out of the water and looked at the tip of Manhattan. She just sat there, the oar still in her hands, and looked at the place where the wall had fallen away. Where mud had slipped down into the water, making a perfect ramp up into the open space of Battery Park.

She could have thought about how that was the city up there that had killed her father, or that it was the place that had nearly killed Ayaan, but she didn't. She didn't think about anyone else at all. She watched the ground, the slope, as if it were still moving, as if she could see it sliding down into the sea. Her breath hitched. A flash of pain, very sharp but very brief, ran through the muscles at the small of her back.

That was just fear, she knew. She was so scared it hurt.

In a second she would step out of the boat and step up onto the land, and then she would have to face her fear. Ghouls, cultists—even liches might be up there, but she wasn't thinking about them, either. She was thinking about what it meant to step up onto that muddy slope. She was thinking about what it meant to enter denied territory, as Jack might put it. In a second she would do it. In a second.

"Oh, wow," she said, which was pretty stupid but was all she could think of. Careful of the boat's rocking, mindful of the weapons strapped to her back, Sarah stood up in the boat and put one foot down on the mud. It sank in half an inch but then it gave her enough purchase to get her other foot up. Instantly she started sliding down, her feet slipping, and she threw herself forward, dug her fingers into the yielding earth, shoved her left foot up onto a protruding stone. She scrambled and cursed and grabbed and hauled her way up into Battery Park before she could really think about what she was doing, and then suddenly she was there.

She had entered Manhattan, and she was alone.

Battery Park's once verdant lawns were covered in gray growth. Mushrooms, enormous wood ear mushrooms the size of sleeping horses in serried rows lined the park, slopped over onto the concrete walkways. They lay like soporific alien pods, like the drowsing bodies of hibernating animals. She was certain they never grew that big in nature. She could see their gills, the tender wet veins they kept hidden from the sun. The air was yellow with their spores, a constant vaporous discharge that spread out over the water and swept across Governors Island with the prevailing wind.

She kicked one. Big mistake. Its wet, fleshy meat broke apart in strands that wrapped around her shoe. Spores burst up around her like brown smoke and she had to clamp her eyes, her mouth, her nose shut or be suffocated. When the cloud finally moved on she looked down and saw the fungus knitting itself back together, so fast she could actually watch it happen, the filaments flopping against one another, sticking to one another. She yanked her foot free with a sense of real disgust.

Which was just silly. Who knew what real danger lay inside the city, and she was freaking out over a mushroom. Sarah drew her Makarov but left the safety on. She moved toward a mansion, a confection of brick and columns now slathered with yellow mold. Its antiquity and decrepitude bothered her for some reason and she moved past it quickly.

Beyond the mansion the towers of Manhattan started up almost immediately, leaping up into the air like impossible trees or—or mountains—or straight-sided pyramids, maybe; she had actually seen the Great Pyramid. It was the closest reference point she had, but it meant little. The flat sides of the buildings looked wrong to her, the metal and glass construction only softened by a heavy growth of moss and dark slime. The windows kept snagging her eyes. Ayaan had taught her to look at openings, at windows and doors, anywhere an enemy might hide. But there were hundreds of windows to keep an eye on—thousands! Clearly urban warfare required a different mind-set than what she'd known before.

She knew one thing that still made sense. Stick to the shadows. Keeping her head down she ducked into the shade of an enormous tower and jogged down a sidewalk toward an intersection. Trees that reached four or five stories high clotted the crossroads. Sarah slid in between their close-growing trunks and hunkered down to have a good think, to plan her next move.

A ghoul emerged from a doorway nearby and sniffed the air.

It happened just like that—she had just ducked down, was still, in fact, in the process of sitting and getting comfortable, when the ghoul appeared. He had no hands, just wicked claws, and he wore a flat doughboy helmet. It had to be a museum piece, judging by the rust and the flaking metal at its brim. It cast the ghoul's eyes in darkness so she could only see its surgically altered jaws and the broken lump of cartilage that had been its nose. It sniffed again—she wondered how good its sense of smell could be with that damaged lump of meat in the middle of its face. Maybe if she stayed perfectly still it wouldn't notice her.

From up a street to the west she heard the sound of an air horn.

The blast jumped from one building facade to another and shook the leaves of the trees, made the glass of the few unbroken windows rattle in place. The broken-nosed ghoul stood up straight and moved its stumpy arms in front of it briefly as if it were a boxer ready to guard against a blow. Slowly, on stiff legs, it moved toward the noise of the horn. Slowly—this was not one of the superspeedy dead she'd seen in Egypt. At least she had that.

Once the ghoul was gone she stood up and moved to the doorway it had vacated. There was no movement beyond and she stepped into a tiny shop, its front of plate glass obscured by vines and fungus so that only a few rays of green light slipped inside. In the back a pile of cardboard boxes had transformed over time, losing their shape, bursting open at the sides; now small round greasy knobs of fungal life were devouring them. Nothing. She turned around to leave the shop and found herself surrounded.

It must have been an ambush. The first ghoul must have smelled her after all, and the air horn had been a signal for reinforcements.

Too shocked to scream, she lifted her pistol and started firing. Ghouls filled the broad space between the buildings, dozens of them moving left or right, some of them toward her, some away. They were organized. Controlled by an intelligence. One of them came at her, his gray body naked but his head covered in a brightly painted motorcycle helmet. "Fuck," she screamed, lacking the time to be more inventive. She shot at his knees but it wasn't enough— he was on her, his stink smeared across her senses, his bony forearms weaving in the air over her, an incantation of death. One arm swung down in a wide arc and knocked the pistol out of her hand. Doom pressed hard on her sinuses, the taste of adrenaline filling her mouth.

Then something weird happened.

He crouched over her, his spikes mere inches from her skin, and then he stopped. He stood stock-still, his chest not even heaving for breath. He was so still he might have been no more than a pile of badly decomposed meat, or perhaps a picture of a dead thing. Sarah looked up and saw the others, the other ghouls, had all stopped as well. They were facing her, a crowd of them facing her and not moving. Sarah could hear water running somewhere, and she could hear the leaves of the trees rolling in a gust of wind, but that was all. Nobody moved a muscle.

"They join us if so wish." The voice came out of the ghoul on top of her. It sounded mostly like a human voice with a touch of a Russian accent. There was a whistling sound underneath it, though, as if breath were leaking out of punctured lungs even as the ghoul tried to talk. "The ones on island. You, as well, join us if you wish. Only death otherwise. I spare you for this, to make choice. Is good to have choices. You be herald, take good news to island peoples. Take news of choice."

"You must belong to the Tsarevich," Sarah said, so frightened she thought she might piss her pants. She could still talk. It was pretty much all she could do. "I've heard he recruits the living."

"I work not for our Lord," the ghoul said. It didn't shake its head or use any gestures. Its arms remained around her, ready to scratch her skin, but it just spoke to her in that flat tone. "I belong to his Lady."

One of the trees in the square rolled over. No, not a tree. Something huge and plantlike, though, something vaguely humanoid in shape but enormous, dark, covered in patches of filamentous mold and clublike fungi. A walking compost heap. It moved a yard or two closer and Sarah felt an odd prickling between her toes, in the places where her shirt bunched up against her side. Something tickled her throat and she coughed.

"Is not by intention, but only is because she is near. You die in seconds, if don't choose right," the ghoul told her. "Our Lady's touch is bad thing for living. So you say what?"

"I . . . I say," Sarah said and coughed again, coughed and coughed, a long, asthmatic series of coughs that brought up dark mucus. "I say . . ."

A bright flash of light swooped up the sidewalk and smashed in the ghoul's face with one bandaged fist. The dead man's maxilla shattered and dried brains flew from his ruined head. The ghoul's body fell away and Sarah was free. Ptolemy's painted face turned to look at her.

"Thanks," she said, picking her Makarov up off the weed-cracked sidewalk. The mummy didn't follow her and she realized he wanted more. He wanted direction. "Let's get out of here," she said, and then she ran, with the mulch demon right behind.

13.

AYAAN HAD AT first believed that the giant truck was just one more example of the Tsarevich's personal style, but she quickly saw there was a method to his madness. The roads leading away from Asbury Park had been engineering marvels once, a web of immaculately paved highways that connected every part of America to everywhere else.

Twelve years later they were broken fields of rubble. Arches and overpasses had collapsed, potholes had opened up as cracks in the earth and then widened to become great fissures in the concrete, deep holes within which lurked rusted twists of rebar that could slash a tire to ribbons. Every fleck of water on the road could be a puddle or it could be a deep hole in the earth big enough to swallow them up. Mud and dirt had spilled across the roadway, blocking it in places, washing it away entirely in others. Plant life sprung up from every pit and pockmark. Here and there a simple crack had been opened up by a line of trees, running at crazy angles across the road, their roots hurling up fist- and head-sized chunks of paving material.

"How is this even possible?" Ayaan asked as they passed by another stand of saplings. "This was all developed, when I was here before. It was cities and housing developments. There were parking lots everywhere. Then the dead came through and they devoured anything organic." She stared through the windows at what a more charitable observer might have called a jungle.

"It's the same energy that drives us," Erasmus told her with a shrug. "The energy that animates us also encourages green things to grow."

"It has been only twelve years, and the world is healing itself already," Ayaan said. Despite her mood she couldn't help but be a little cheered by that.

Erasmus kept the truck moving at a steady five miles an hour and stopped every time an obstruction presented itself. Still Ayaan was thrown around in her seat like a doll in an empty suitcase. She held on to a thick metal handle mounted on the dashboard and tried to keep her head from cracking against the window every time the car bounced over yet another piece of rubble.

The truck could just as easily have gone off road, but conditions out there were far worse. Looking out the window Ayaan was startled to see that New Jersey—a place that legend insisted had been all toxic chemical plants and forgotten factories—was apparently one vast forest of saplings that went on forever. The trees did part from time to time, but she saw no cities, just burned-out electrical substations and mazes of housing developments as convoluted as the passages of the human digestive system. It was hard to find a single house still intact. The roofs of the houses fell inward on themselves, or their walls had devolved into unorganized piles of bricks. They passed through great zones where fire had taken its toll and ashes whipped through the air as thick as snow. In other regions it looked to Ayaan like a massive earthquake had tried to suck the suburbs down into the very belly of the earth. A fault line ran through one neighborhood of Trenton, a vast and inclined plane of ground at the bottom of which glass and brick and steel had collected in a kind of homogeneous mass, a stagnant pool of sharp edges.

After about six hours of rumbling and rolling over the fragmented highway they stopped to stretch their legs. This was mostly for her benefit, Erasmus told her—she was still newly dead and prone to fits of rigor mortis. He must have seen the look on her face when she heard that, even if she had quickly hidden her mouth with her hand.

"Everybody rots," he told her, his voice weary. Then he popped open his door and leaped down to the hot black surface of the road.

They had stopped in a region halfway between housing developments and farmland. The concrete lip of the road stood at a slight angle, with a twisted mass of green and rusted signage hanging over them on steel pylons. One half-obscured sign read:

WELCO .... TO......... YLVANIA
POPU.ATION 12,281,054

Beyond lay a grassy depression in the earth, a mile-wide bowl of land half-filled with weather-beaten, falling-down houses, giant concrete blocks with crumbling faces, subsidiary roads only recognizable now because they were less overgrown than the surrounding land. A thin mist hovered in the bowl, a last shred of vapor as yet not burned off by the rising sun, protected by stubby pine trees.

With a flurry of motion from one of the concrete blocks a bird launched itself into the air and threw itself in a long curving course over the hollow. Erasmus looked up at the green phantom on the roof of the truck, and one of the corpses in the flatbed twitched to life. It spilled out into the depression like a top jerking away from its string.

Ayaan frowned and did some deep knee bends, some toe touches. She could feel where her muscles had started to seize up and cramp. She wasn't expecting it when a few minutes later the accelerated ghoul returned and knelt down before her. It had the bird, the same bird she'd watched wing through the late-morning mist, impaled on one ulna.

The bird was still alive. It kept trying to tuck its wing under its breast but the spar of bone got in the way. Its blood splashed on the asphalt. Ayaan saw very little of that. What she saw was its energy, its tremulous golden energy, already flickering away. It was precious, that energy, that life. She reached out and freed the bird. She brought it closer, brought it toward her body.

She bit right through its feathers and its tiny hollow bones. It wasn't something she thought about doing. The blood ran down her throat and she expected to gag and choke. She didn't.

Swallowing, she felt the rush of the bird's life pulse through her, burst inside of her. Her head cleared, her body softened and relaxed. It felt so good it was hard to think about what she was doing. Then she looked up. There were people—living people—watching her.

She hadn't heard them coming. She hadn't seen any sign of them until they were right up behind her. They were survivors, true survivors, and they knew how to stay safe. They must have approached only once the truck had stopped.

Ayaan clutched the carcass of the bird to her chest and turned away. She crouched down in the shadow of the truck and tried not to look at them. It was hard. It was harder not to chew on the bird's dying energy. So hard she couldn't help herself, even as the survivors stared.

"Survivors" might have been putting it too strongly. Their clothes had faded and torn over time and not been replaced. They had very little hair. Their skin was discolored and raw, red and irritated. Their eyes were crusty slits in their faces and they were missing teeth. Yet their energy was gold and bright.

One of them was obviously the leader—he wore a shirt, a green polo shirt with a ragged hem. He held a sharp piece of metal in his hand, a broken piece of a street sign perhaps. He stood in front of a female who held a tiny baby tight against her breasts. She couldn't have been more than four and a half feet tall. How old had she been when the Epidemic struck? She must have been an infant herself. Occasionally she shook her baby a little, rocked it vigorously. It made no sound at all.

The shirted one grabbed an emaciated boy and shoved him forward. His eyes never left the pavement. The boy took a few steps toward Erasmus and then stopped, his head bowed. He said something in English but in an accent so thick Ayaan couldn't understand him. One word sounded like "sack-erf-eyes." Sack of eyes? Even Ayaan's stomach turned.

No. He had meant something else. Sacrifice. He was offering up his own flesh in exchange for the safety of his family. Ayaan felt a low, hot burn of recognition, of sympathy, flushing through her chest.

"Look at dead-enders," the green phantom said to her, in surprisingly bad Russian. "To clutch at life so much. They hide, you know. Hide in bad places, toxic wildernesses so bad not even ghouls will follow in." He switched to English as if his tongue had grown tired. "They don't realize it yet, but this is the best day of their little lives."

Erasmus put one clawed hand on the sacrificial boy's shoulder and lifted the other in a sweeping gesture. He gave them a grand speech in slow, heavily enunciated English, all about what the Tsarevich would do for them. Food. Clean water. Rudimentary health care.

Despite herself Ayaan realized he was telling the truth—as had the green phantom. These starving, sick people were barely holding on to life by their fingernails. Their lives would be ruled by constant fear and constant death. They were literally living like animals. Ayaan knew about refugees, had been one herself, both before and after the Epidemic. She knew about famine and war and pestilence. It looked like America was learning from the African primer. If this tiny tribe joined up with the Tsarevich they would be slaves—but still their lives would improve dramatically. She remember the Turkish prisoners she'd seen on Cyprus, the ones who watched one of their own drown and then return from the dead. She thought of Dekalb, her old, long-lost friend, who had made a similarly horrible bargain. He had turned his only daughter over to a tribe of anarchic woman warriors. That must have seemed like a horror at the time, but it had worked out for Sarah.

The Tsarevich was a monster, a demon out of hell. Yet if he was the only one who could save people like this, the only one who could help them . . .

They left the tribe standing by the side of the road. The liches piled back into the truck and headed on their way, with a promise that another truck would be along soon.

Through the back window Ayaan watched the little family dwindle behind them. She saw no hope in their slitted eyes. Their heads were lowered. They did not speak to each other about the wonders to come.

"Just a little farther," Erasmus told her, looking strangely subdued. Wasn't he excited about the prospect of saving souls? "One of them had a tip for us," the werewolf told her. "We're definitely on the right track."

Ayaan scowled. "Those people—we didn't lie to them, did we? Someone will come for them, yes?"

"Yes," Erasmus said, biting into the word. "We will come back. Only . . . there are some people so far gone that you can't recruit them. They're too weak or too diseased to be any use. I don't know if it'll happen to this bunch, that decision's not up to me."

His eyes said he did know, that he was certain of it. "What then?" she demanded.

"They get used for something else."

He wouldn't say any more. He only ignored her when she demanded an answer. She knew there were only two possibilities, though. They could become new, handless soldiers for the Tsarevich. Or they could be made into food.

In the rearview mirror the sacrificial boy still stood just where he had, waiting to see, waiting for whatever came next.

14.

LEAVING THE HIGHWAY for a more rural route they slowed down dramatically until they were barely crawling along, much slower than a human could walk. They stopped at a sign nearly obscured by wrist-thick tree trunks:

Now Entering Rockroth State Forest

Ayaan was uncertain how one could be expected to differentiate this new forest from the jungle behind them.

A few miles farther in, they came to a place where the trees grew so close to the road that the green phantom had to come down into the cab with them. He smelled like something stale and wet. They listened to the tree branches drumming on the roof of the truck for a while and drove in silence. Eventually they came to a place so narrow the truck couldn't fit through. The green phantom and Erasmus jumped down from the cab and started to press on. The handless ghouls from the cargo bed streamed down after them, their eyes narrow slits, their tongues licking at their dry lips as if they'd only awoken from sleep, though she knew they had been dead, truly dead, moments before. Ayaan called out to them to wait a moment.

"What's this, the famous Ayaan? Scared of a few trees?" the green phantom chortled at her.

"No," she told him. She waved at where their vehicle stood nearly wedged in by trees. "I just wanted to turn the truck around. If we need to get out of here in a hurry it will save us time later."

Even the skull-faced lich had to admit she had a point.

"I've been doing this my whole life," she told him. "I only stayed alive as long as I did by knowing all the little tricks."

It took a long fifteen minutes to move the truck, backing and filling over and over again on the narrow road surface. When it was done they moved into the dark space between the trees and Ayaan realized she was, in fact, a little afraid. The shadowy forest pressed in on them instantly, the waxy leaves of the trees brushing against their clothes, their hair, the branches underneath scraping at them like limp and bony fingers. Cobwebs draped across the path every few feet and had to be swept away. Insects plagued Erasmus, live insects that he would pick from his fur and absently stuff into his mouth to suck out their golden energy.

Though it was only mid-afternoon, the darkness pressed in around them like a fog. They tried to follow the road but the forest had its own paths to offer. One of these led to a wide clearing and the green phantom hurried inward, digging his femur staff into the ground for traction on the moss-slick trail.

Ayaan followed him in and emerged into a brightly lit place where the underbrush grew wild but the trees had all been pruned back. Piles of gray deadfall ringed the open space, a few dead leaves still fluttering on the fallen branches. Ayaan had grown up in a desert land, but even she could tell that trees didn't form such a clearing naturally.

Then there was the goat. He lay in the middle of the clearing, staked to a low hillock. He was dying, his fur littered with bits of decaying leaves, his eyes milky and lost, the long pupils very much dilated even in the bright sun. He had kicked over his water dish and Ayaan could count the ribs sticking out of his side. Only his horns, which rose from his head in a thick, curling V, looked healthy.

"Someone has left me a snack," the green phantom announced cheerfully. Ayaan could feel the goat's energy herself, flickering away slowly but still golden and almost irresistible. She put out a hand, though, to stop the green-robed lich.

"Why hasn't some wandering ghoul finished this animal off long ago?" she asked.

"Maybe there aren't any nearby." He looked down at her arm as if he would happily chew it off to get to the goat.

"Not anymore, there aren't." With her free hand Ayaan pointed to piles of bleached bones—human bones—mixed in with the woody deadfall at the edges of the clearing. Then she pointed out a shallow depression in the grass on the far side of the goat's mound. Broken vegetation pointed away from the defile in a radial pattern. A similar crater dipped down not more than a dozen feet from where they stood. "Have you never seen a minefield before?" she asked.

"Ridiculous," the green phantom rasped. Behind him Erasmus came up with a large rock in one furry hand. Before Ayaan could stop him he tossed the rock deep into the clearing. Metal sprouted from the ground like an evil weed and then a flash of light pressed up hard against Ayaan's side and nearly knocked her over. Hot dirt and bits of shredded goat meat splattered her leathers.

"I didn't expect that big an explosion," Erasmus said, spitting dirt and pebbles out of his mouth. All three of them had been caught by metal shrapnel, which ruined their clothes. Had they been any closer their brains would be strewn around the trees behind them.

"That," Ayaan said, fingering a hole in her skull-print leather jacket, "was a Bouncing Betty. It was spring-loaded to jump in the air when detonated. This spreads the shrapnel over a much wider area and dramatically increases the kill radius."

"You've seen these before?" the green phantom asked.

"Friends of mine have. From closer up." Ayaan peered through the smoke that filled the clearing. "Mines. There are better ways to keep out strangers, but few that make as much noise. Whoever planted these mines was listening. They'll know we're coming now if they didn't before. We should turn back."

"We can't abort now. The Tsarevich puts a great deal of importance on our mission," the green phantom told her.

"We have to move faster, then. Find our enemies before they find us. That's probably the fastest way in," she said, pointing at a continuation of the trail on the far side. "It's probably booby-trapped, every step of the way."

"So we go around." The green phantom turned away from the minefield and headed back into the darkness of the forest. He had a small compass and, while they lacked a map, he could at least tell if they were headed in the right direction. Erasmus went first, his vicious claws as effective at clearing the overhang as ten little machetes. Ayaan followed and was followed in turn by the green phantom. The handless ghouls brought up the rear, so silent Ayaan kept forgetting they were even there.

They'd been moving for the better part of half an hour, pushing westward and southward when they could, when Erasmus stopped short and Ayaan's face collided with his furry back. "Hold on," he said. "There's something . . . there's some energy up here."

Ayaan called his name but he rushed forward, perhaps intent on reaching their goal, perhaps after something else. She followed as fast as she could while keeping her wits about her. Her feet—

nowhere near as steady as they used to be—kept getting snagged in tree roots and undergrowth, and she had a terrible presentiment that she would arrive too late, that he would fall into some pit lined with sharpened stakes or trigger a precariously balanced log to fall on him from high branches. She shouted to him again, but he made no answer.

She nearly ran into him again when she finally found him. He had stopped before an enormous old-growth tree, big enough that the trail wrapped around it, a massive wooden column climbing with ants, wrapped with the tendrils of epiphytes, studded everywhere with stunted, sunlight-deprived limbs still as thick as saplings themselves. Erasmus looked as if he were leaning forward into the tree's bulk, perhaps just resting for a moment. Resting on his face. She cautiously moved around him. He had his eyes and nose pressed up tight against a knot in the trunk the width of a dinner plate. He wasn't moving. Coupled with a dead man's lack of breath or pulse, he looked more like some furry excrescence of the tree than a separate organism.

The green phantom came stumbling through the underbrush behind her, making enough noise to alert every enemy in the forest. "What's wrong with him?" he demanded. "What's been done to him? Get him out of there."

Ayaan wasn't sure if he should be moved, but she tugged at one of his paws anyway. She might as well have pulled on a strand of ivy—Erasmus's body, while still flexible, was stuck to the spot. She tugged again and again. Finally the green phantom stepped up to help her. He leaned his staff against the tree and pulled.

Erasmus came loose with a howl, a noise only an animal could make. His claws came up and he raked the green phantom across the belly, tearing open skin and flesh. With another scream he jumped away and headed deeper into the forest, moving as fast as his dead legs could carry him, following no trail that Ayaan could see but merely stumbling through the brush and smacking into tree limbs like a man possessed.

She had a feeling that was exactly what he had become. She saw that a round space had been hollowed out of the tree, behind its wide knot. Inside someone had placed a hexagonal mirror, its frame made of human finger bones. Dark energy streamed from the thing—magic—and Ayaan was careful not to look into the glass. Instead she took the green phantom's staff and used it to smash it into bits of silver and jagged glass.

Then she turned around, and realized what fate had offered her.

The green phantom lay disemboweled on the path. His dry, papery guts slithered onto the ground next to him, his hands trying in vain to keep them in. He wasn't even looking at her. Ayaan could kill him easily, smash in his head with his own staff or fire a bolt of her own particular kind of darkness directly into his brain. It would take a mere second of her time. The handless ghouls coming up the path would destroy her or perhaps the Tsarevich would kill her from a distance, but that was immaterial.

She stepped closer to the green phantom, intending to finish him off—and then she stopped.

I see his heart. His black and dead heart!

The words moved through her head like a pebble rolling around on her tongue. Half her face lost all feeling.

You be caution in all things.

The words stopped her in her tracks. A thin trickle of drool fell from her numb lip.

"It's your big chance, now," the green phantom said. He looked up at her with bitter fear in his eyes. "If you want to prove yourself. If you want to live."

"Yes," Ayaan said, "I want to live." The words fell out of her mouth. She had thought nothing of the kind.

"Then you'll go after him. You'll go after that furry cocksucker who just gutted me and you'll find out what happened. Yes or no?"

Ayaan drew breath into her lungs, trying to clear her head, but the unnecessary air just wheezed out of her again. "All right," she said, all thought of killing the green phantom gone. It just wasn't in her head anymore. She could feel where the thought had been but she couldn't remember what it might have been.

Your friend has friend in me, she thought. A curious thing to think, but it didn't bother her too much.

15.

SARAH'S ANKLE CAUGHT on something metal and she went down, hard, the skin of her elbows coming off on the pavement, leaves and bits of vine bursting up around her like green smoke. "I'm all right," she told Ptolemy, and started to get up.

The thing she'd tripped on was metal, black metal spotted with rust. She could almost make out its shape, hidden under tons of vegetation, small trees and blowsy bushes that shook in the wind. She had tripped over a wing. The entire metallic object, which had to be fifteen feet across, was an airplane, a small airplane turned upside-down with its nose buried in the ground.

She would have looked at it some more if she hadn't heard an air horn just then. The sound vented up out of the tree-clogged streets on every side. She couldn't tell which direction it came from. "What do they want?" she asked, as if she didn't know the answer.

Maybe she didn't. When she reached into her pocket for the reassuring angularity of her pistol, her fingers touched the soapstone scarab instead.

they Celt came for relics the relics of the Celt, Ptolemy told her.

Sarah got to her feet—her ankle felt sore but not broken—and they headed uptown again. Away from the last place they'd seen the mold maiden. If she tripped again, Ptolemy was going to have to carry her. She didn't doubt that he could, but it would hurt her image as the leader of this farce.

"You were supposed to watch the Tsarevich," she told him,

panting a little. There was a kind of natural trail up Broadway, a strip of bare pavement where the trees hadn't taken over quite yet. The flat asphalt felt strangely good under her feet. "Those were my orders."

and were so i sentries did but there and were i sentries, he told her. **i spotted was i spotted**

It actually helped a little to know he wasn't perfect. "So you came looking for me, to report?"

yes and found instead i found yes her. The mummy raced ahead and grabbed something out of a tree. Sarah stopped and leaned forward, catching her breath. **more there is more**, he said, but she needed to process this one piece at a time.

"Just a second. So the Tsarevich didn't even send her here to take over Governors Island. He sent her for—what did you say—relics? What kind of relics?"

Ptolemy held an undead squirrel in his hands. Its tail would never be bushy again and it was missing one leg. When it saw Sarah it grabbed at her with its tiny paws, gnashed its teeth at her. Lovely. The mummy turned away from her and crushed the animal to oblivion. Had he not grabbed it when he did it probably would have jumped down onto Sarah's neck. It would have torn open her throat. It was desperate for her energy. For life.

"Thanks," she said, and then repeated herself. "What kind of relics?"

a sword armlet a rope a sword an armlet

Sarah sighed. He could be so literal. She lifted her legs, trying to keep them from stiffening up, and looked behind them. Scattered movement a couple of blocks away got her moving again. "A sword. A rope. And an armlet," she huffed. "What does he hope to do with them?"

make magic, Ptolemy answered, as if she had asked what a soldier did with a firearm. **he ghost will make ghost he will magic**

Ghost magic. Yeah. She knew how useful that could be. Maybe they should have kept the squirrel around. Maybe Jack could have possessed it and given them some pointers.

She could use some. She was running uptown, away from the mushroom queen, but also away from her boat. The survivors on Governors Island had assured her that Manhattan was almost free of ghouls, that they had all headed west. She wasn't about to trust that, though, since she was already farther up Broadway than any of Marisol's people had been in twelve years.

There were some ghouls in Manhattan that she knew about. Weird, surgically maimed things in helmets that were hunting her like a deer. And they were led by a female lich who could kill someone just by being near her.

the i spoke more something more i spoke of, he said from behind her, not even panting for breath. Well, of course, he didn't need any, and anyway she didn't know what effect breathing would have on telepathy.

it is ayaan about ayaan is it

That made her stop short. She just stared at him until he began speaking again.

lich she is dead a lich dead. The words made Sarah's head spin. Dead. Lich. Ayaan. Lich. Dead.

She couldn't make them stop. "Shut up," she said, to herself. He didn't respond. She couldn't make the words stop.

Ayaan was dead. Her rescue mission had failed.

When she had time she would think about that. In the meantime Sarah kept running. Ptolemy kept up with her easily. He could have run circles around her, frankly. Still, she was faster than the ghouls and that was what mattered.

Then she heard an air horn from the streets to her right and she knew that mere speed wasn't going to save her. She had been about to head in that direction, hoping to circle back to the harbor and find some way back to Governors Island. She tried to sense where the dead men were, but the buildings blocked her arcane vision. She spun around in a slow circle, looking at the streets, which seemed to head in every direction, searching the windows of the dead and hollow buildings as if they could tell her. "Which way?" she asked Ptolemy, but he didn't even shrug.

Uptown again. Into the belly of the beast, and farther from safety than ever. She raced uptown and listened for horns behind her, for any sign of pursuit. When her lungs cramped and her body doubled over, unable to run another yard, she stopped. Ptolemy stared at her with his painted eyes. They never showed anything but a cool, intellectual repose. She wanted to smash in the plaster over his real face, his real skull. Wait, she thought, as breath raced in and out of her. There was something . . .

A dark stain had appeared across Ptolemy's facial portrait. A smoky trail of mildew curled across his cheek like a worm eating its way through painted flesh. She grabbed his hands and saw spots on the linen that wrapped his finger, big colorless spots with paler rings around the edges, smaller spots like a spattering of some dark fluid.

Sarah dropped his hands and rubbed at her own fingers. A fine dusting of dark spores had come off on her skin. Her fingers started to itch and she scratched at them mercilessly. She backed away from the mummy as if he could somehow infect her, somehow make her—

A sudden banging noise behind her stopped her brain in mid-thought.

Sarah's body spasmed with fear. She looked behind her and saw a little store with a plate glass window. What had made that noise? She couldn't see anything moving, she could only see a kind of greasy stain on the window and—

A whip-thin ghoul in a stained maroon dress hit the glass face first, hard enough to make the whole storefront shake. Her hands like bunches of twigs came up and slapped feebly at the glass, her body pressed against it. She must have been trapped inside that store for years—she had hit the glass with her face so many times her features were completely gone, smeared together into one homogeneous dark bruise. A few strands of blond hair still stuck to her battered skull. As Sarah watched, she drew her head back and launched it once more at the glass with a cracking noise.

Sarah couldn't move, could barely breathe. She was too horrified.

The air horns came again, from two directions this time. Realizing she'd been paralyzed by a relatively harmless unorganized ghoul, Sarah started to hyperventilate. A handless ghoul appeared a few blocks away, half-obscured behind some trees. It hadn't seen her yet. She knew, however, that it wouldn't try to recruit her. It would simply kill her the moment it found her.

"Go," she said. She grabbed Ptolemy's arm. "Go! Go take that thing out!"

She tried shoving him into the street but she might as well have tried to shove a bank vault. He turned his mildewed face to her for a moment, then shook off her arm. She couldn't meet his painted stare.

She touched the soapstone but he didn't have anything to say for once.

He turned and started walking toward the ghoul, even as new air horns blared into life, seemingly from every direction. Sarah didn't waste any time. She ran across the street and started tugging at doors, tried prying up windowpanes with her fingernails. Finally she found a basement-level entrance down a flight of stairs. The iron security gate had rusted half-open, wide enough for her to squeeze through. She opened the door behind it and ran inside, into a smell of old things slowly falling apart. She closed the door behind it and turned the creaking dead bolt.

Silence. She could hear the air horns outside, more and closer than ever, but there was a barrier between her and them. She felt the still, settled air of the basement room and she dropped to a crouch on the floor, her face buried in her hands.

Ayaan was dead. Her mission was a failure.

She had no idea what to do next.

16.

IT WAS DARK in the fire lookout atop the ridge but moonlight came in through the windows and made dappled patterns on the walls. It curled around the broken radio, glistened on the peeling finish of the enameled chairs and table. It just barely reached into the bathroom where the dry toilet had become home to thousands of spiders. From time to time, putting aside all squeamishness, Ayaan reached through another stratum of ancient webs and scooped out a handful of them from the darkness inside. Then she would pop them in her mouth and chew them slowly. The wriggling on her tongue wasn't so bad—it was the legs that got caught in her teeth that bothered her.

With every tiny life she took, her body vibrated with joy. The hunger came back almost instantly but the shivering ecstasy of each new morsel was like nothing she'd ever felt before. She wondered, in the most private part of her mind, if it was what sex felt like for a living girl.

She had little to do but sit, and think, and wait. The fire lookout station offered few other opportunities to entertain oneself. She had a small telescope with a scratch on one lens. It let her study the valley below. Nothing had happened since she'd arrived, her legs aching and rubbery as she powered her way up to the top of the ridge. Nothing had happened since she'd found the lookout and installed herself. Nothing would happen, she imagined, until dawn.

Erasmus stood down there as if at attention, his spine locked in perfect posture. He stood in the middle of a group of buildings on a scratched-out section of land that she had decided was a barnyard. The barnyard lay in the middle of a fenced-off patch of land that sat in the center of the valley. Whatever magic had possessed the undead werewolf had drawn him directly to its dark and vibrant heart.

Ayaan suspected that whoever had laid the trap lived in the tidy little farmhouse down there. Like the barn and the silo, it was protected by round wards hung from its eaves painted in bright geometric patterns.

They're called hex signs, the ghost told her. The ghost who was trapped in a brain in a jar a hundred miles away. He was standing next to her, too, just barely visible in her peripheral vision. She turned her head and there was nothing there. She looked back at the valley and he was next to her again. **They protect those who live inside, aye, but they need a taste of the life to keep them strong. Life's blood, that is.**

Ayaan nodded. There were plenty of goats down in the pen behind the barn. It could easily be their blood that activated the hex signs. Their energy that licked out of the signs in purple rays.

Magic was everywhere down in that barnyard. Death magic. It pulsed around Erasmus, pinning him like a dart in a dartboard. It flickered from the windows of the farmhouse and lingered like smoke around the tar paper roof of the barn. Deep, dark beams of it escaped through the vents of the silo. There was something bad in there, something that needed half a dozen hex signs to keep it locked away.

"That's what we're here for, isn't it?" Ayaan asked.

Aye. It's not what you think, though, lass. Don't fear it.

"Believe me, it's rather low on my list of things to be afraid of." Ayaan leaned forward, her chin resting on her steepled fingers. "You, on the other hand . . ." She fought the urge to look at him.

I'm your friend. I'm your best friend, under these circumstances.

"Friends don't hypnotize each other. They don't leave little commands buried in each other's minds." Semyon Iurevich, the mind-reading lich back in Asbury Park, had bound her with a spell. It had been his voice she'd heard telling her not to kill the green phantom. No, worse than that, his voice had wiped the very idea out of her mind. He hadn't merely revoked her freedom. He had made it so it had never existed.

And he had done so, she was certain, at the ghost's behest.

Is that what's worrying you? That I wouldn't let you throw your life away?

"My life. Mine," she said. "Do you think I like being this—this thing, this monster?" she gestured at her leathers.

I know that shame better than anyone, dearie. Don't you come all indignant with me, when I haven't even a body to speak of. His tone softened, grew soothing and low. **Listen, there's a game here, a deeper game than you know. You haven't even met all the players yet.**

Ayaan let that go for a while. The ghost had power over her. She wasn't going to talk him into relinquishing it—that never worked, never in the history of the human race had anyone given up power freely once they had it. You had to take it back yourself.

Something else worried her, though. "You want the Tsarevich dead, yet you made sure I would survive long enough to see whatever's in that silo. You want us to find it, even if it means the Tsarevich gets it. What's your scheme? At least tell me that much, tell me what you hope to gain from—"

He was gone, of course. She couldn't sense him anywhere.

She went for another handful of spiders. When she came back she got a shock. Something was actually happening down in the valley. A light had come on in the farmhouse. It moved from window to window, then emerged from the door and revealed itself to be a kerosene lantern. The man holding it glowed a brighter gold than the lamp in his hand. There was no question in her mind. This was the *wadad*, the magician who had enchanted Erasmus.

He wore a baseball cap low on his brow with the name john deere on the front. Old bloodstains decorated his white T-shirt and faded blue jeans; more recent stains discolored his tan leather work boots. His face was ringed with a fringe of beard and hidden behind a pair of mirrored sunglasses, even though the sun had yet to rise.

His left arm was missing entirely. It had been replaced with a tree branch covered in rough gray bark. It ended in three thick twigs less like fingers than like the tines of a pitchfork. Dark energy surged through the wooden arm and it twisted like a snake. The tines reached up and scratched the magician's chin. He studied Erasmus, moving around the werewolf, tapping his sternum and the back of his skull. With his human hand he plucked a hair from the paralyzed lich's cheek.

Erasmus didn't even twitch.

The wooden arm slapped at Erasmus's chest and tore a strip of skin away from the rigid muscles underneath. They were pink and gray and they didn't glisten at all. No blood emerged, but she could clearly see the edges of his skin where it had been torn open. In the midst of all that fur the wound looked like a sickly orifice, a new and monstrous genital.

Ayaan pushed the telescope away and stood up. It was a long way down the ridge and for all she knew there were mines planted all around the little barnyard, but she couldn't wait any longer. She stumbled out of the lookout station and practically threw herself down the side of the ridge, grabbing at tree branches to slow her descent, her feet barely touching the ground. A torrent of pine needles and rustling leaves swept around her while bits and pieces of rock and soil pattered and bounced down before her like a miniature landslide. She skidded to a stop in a copse of trees near the floor of the valley and pushed the branches aside to take a look. Nothing had changed in the barnyard. Ayaan moved forward until she was standing before a seven-foot-high fence of thin wooden palings, the only barrier between herself and the barnyard.

Maybe, she thought, just maybe, she still had the element of surprise. She would need it—this wizard had more power than any living man was supposed to. Careful to be as silent as possible, she climbed up one side of the fence and jumped down on the other.

Her foot barely nudged something round and hard as she landed. She looked down and saw a human skull there, bleached white, with all its delicate nasal bones still intact. Other skulls littered the ground just inside the fence. Dark energy flickered inside every cranium.

The skull she touched gave off a bloodcurdling shriek. Whether it actually made a sound or the sound was just inside her mind, she couldn't say, but the scream made her clutch her ears and duck her head.

At the center of the barnyard the wizard looked up. His wooden hand dropped a ball of fur and skin on the ground and Ayaan felt his attention hit her like a spotlight.

"This a friend a yins, monkey-boy?" the wizard asked, looking over at Erasmus. The furry lich didn't move an inch. "You shoulda said somethin.' I coulda redded up the place." The wizard's face cracked in a wide, toothy smile.

Ayaan wasted no time. She dropped into a shooter's crouch and flung her hands in wide arcs. Energy spilled from her core and sizzled as it cut through the air. The wizard turned, far too fast, and put his wooden arm up. The bark there cracked and snapped and the wood underneath creaked and groaned. He reached inside the back pocket of his trousers and whipped out a pocketknife. Ayaan saw that the palm of his remaining hand was one smooth callus from fingers to wrist. He slashed the callus with his knife and then squeezed his fist until blood dropped onto the dry grass of the barnyard.

The door of the barn rattled on its hinges. Ayaan shot another bolt of death energy at the wizard, but he caught it easily in his wooden hand. He absorbed the darkness into his own body with a visible shudder of delight. Ayaan raised her hands to attack a third time, but then the door of the barn slammed open.

Dead people came slouching out. They were skinny—skeletally thin. They were missing pieces. Very few among them still had four limbs. A few were missing all the flesh from their heads and all but the sinews of their necks. All of them had chunks of their torsos and abdomens carved away. Their ribs stuck out from denuded sides or were cut away entirely, leaving them horribly lopsided. None of them had body hair of any kind. None of them had eyes; none had much skin.

Ayaan had seen plenty of decomposing bodies in her time. She'd seen human flesh gnawed on, torn apart, burned, hacked, eaten away by disease. She'd never seen human bodies systematically butchered, though. Not butchered for their meat.

"Just like prime aged beef," the wizard chuckled. "If you sauce it just right, it gets so you hardly can tell." He squinted at Ayaan. "Now, I figger I could do with a nice skirt steak for breakfast."

The carved dead shuffled toward her, their faces unmoving, their hands up to grab and claw and tear.

17.

SARAH RAN A finger across the top of a water heater and stared at the dust that came up, a thick feltlike layer of forgotten time.

She started to reach for the soapstone in her pocket and stopped herself. Whatever Ptolemy might have to say to her, she knew she didn't want to hear. She had essentially used him as a diversion to save her own skin. He was smart enough not to appreciate that.

Ayaan was dead. Nothing mattered.

She knew what she was doing, and how wrong it was. She couldn't stop, though. Or rather she couldn't start. Leaving the basement would mean engaging the horrors outside. It would mean the possibility of dying. She'd been taught how to survive, had been taught so well, in fact, that her body would go on doing what it needed to do to keep living even if she stopped thinking altogether. It would take real willpower to go against that training, to throw herself into the fray.

In the back of the basement, the building's long-dead superintendent had set up a little personal lounge: a recliner with broken springs, a coffee table holding an ashtray full of old butts, a record player and a pair of speakers. All of it dead, rotting with age, covered in dust. She found a stack of plastic crates full of old records. She took out a few and studied the album cover art. She tried not to listen for air horns or screams or sounds of violence outside. If there had been power in the basement she could have played music to block out the sounds. That might have been nice. To go back in time for a little while. To pretend like her whole life had never happened yet, that it was thirty years prior. It would be nice to . . .

She dropped the record she was holding and it slapped on the naked concrete floor, not breaking. White fur had sprouted inside the gatefold cover. It grew longer as she watched, soft-looking tendrils that reached for the moist air.

She had to turn around and look at the door, make sure it was locked. She needed to make sure it was locked because if it wasn't, she still had time to go and lock it. Fear overcame her. It was like a spotlight blazing into life in a still, dark night. She couldn't move, she was dazzled by the fear. Then adrenaline poured into her circulatory system and flipped every switch to "on."

In one corner of the basement a tiny patch of mushrooms nursed on a wet patch of floor. They were getting bigger. She ran. No, more like she jumped, like an antelope running from a cheetah.

She found a stairway in the corner of the basement farthest from the mushrooms. She stomped up the stairs, flew up them two at a time. At the first landing she finally managed to turn and look back. A broad brown stain was creeping across the concrete floor. The wooden banister of the stairwell was cracked. Trumpet-shaped fungi peeked out of that crevice. Sarah ran again, upward, away from the basement. She could hear rustling down there. The sound of rot and blight and smut growing at a horribly accelerated pace.

If it touched her, if she got any of it on her, it would eat her skin. It would get in her mouth, her nose, her lungs. It would fill up her insides and burst her open like a wet, stringy pumpkin. She ran.

Ground floor. The stairwell door opened into another, broader stairwell that led up into darkness. Office space surrounded her on every side, some of it empty, some of it full of abandoned furniture. All of those offices were dead ends. She pushed through a glass door and into the building's foyer. A thick bluish slime covered the front door, colored the light coming in through the frosted glass.

Back to the stairwell. She had only one direction to go. Up. Up and away, away from the monster. She climbed, her breath already coming in ragged gasps.

A bloom of mold ran along one wall, chased her up the steps.

Sarah pushed herself, pushed harder. Every step made her knees creak, her shins burn.

Come on. Come on. Come on.

The refrain sounded stupid even inside her own head, but she kept it up. Second floor—more offices, a little light from a window at the far end. Nothing she could use. Third floor identical to the second except that little stars were flashing before her eyes. Just how badly out of shape was she? She had gotten plenty of exercise while living with Ayaan. Could four flights of stairs really make her this desperate for a lungful of air?

No.

No, they couldn't. The mold was already in her. The dust she'd breathed in, down in the basement. It must have already been full of spores. And now the Fungal Freak was causing them to bloom inside her body.

A door slammed down in the basement. She had forgotten to lock it and now the monster was inside. C'mon c'mon c'mon. Sarah gasped for breath and pounded up the stairs, almost ran into a door with a metal release bar at hip height. She pushed the bar and the door opened upon blue sky. Sarah's arms shot out to help her keep her balance, but the door wasn't just opening on empty space. She had come to the roof. She looked out across tarpaper and gravel, stared at the clogged-up ventilation hoods like tiny minarets. The roof. Last stop.

There was nowhere to go. The buildings on either side were too low to leap to. If she tried she would break her legs. The fire escape didn't reach the roof.

Last stop. Sarah looked back and saw something drippy and wet on the stairs below her. She stepped out into the sunlight and tripped over a hidden step.

She fell forward; her hands stretched out to catch herself, but they just slid across loose gravel. Her chin smacked the tar paper and she lost blood. Dark spots blobbed across her vision. She couldn't seem to get her breath, couldn't seem to move her arms, her legs, she felt like a dead spider with her limbs up in the air.

Slowly, very slowly, she relaxed her body, her stiff limbs. Slowly, very slowly, she sucked in breath through one nostril. She closed her eyes and saw green flashes. She opened them again and saw her fingernails had turned yellow. Faint black spots swam down there in the quick. As she watched, her thumbnail creased down the middle—fungus underneath was pushing up against it. The nail turned white and started to split. It hurt like a motherfucker.

She heard a heavy tread on the stairs. Someone was coming up, coming after her.

She focused on the pain in her thumb. Used it. She saw it as a white sparkle, a sunburst in her hand. This wasn't her special sight, it was just pure visualization, but it worked. She used that energy to propel herself back up to her feet. She drew her Makarov, flicked off the safety, assumed a firing stance with her arm outstretched, and pointed at the doorway she'd just come through. She yanked breath into her filling lungs, fought her own body to stay upright long enough to put one bullet through whoever came through that door.

The tar paper beneath her started to vibrate. It had to be a hallucination, she decided. Not enough oxygen was getting to her brain and it was starting to break down, but she couldn't let that stay her hand, she couldn't—

It wasn't a hallucination. If it was, it was the most convincing one she'd ever had. The whole roof was shaking, the whole building. She focused on the black rectangle of the doorway, on the green splotches that were blossoming on her sweatshirt, anything to keep her mind steady.

The stairwell door split into pieces and then disappeared into a yawning gulf of empty space. Down, it went down. Half the building collapsed with a sudden roar like the world's back breaking, a prolonged snapping and squealing and rumbling as stone and brick and steel twisted in on itself and cascaded down the stairs. The wooden beams supporting the upper floors had given way to fungal rot and half the roof just fell in and Sarah was in the air, her feet weren't touching anything, and something pinched her arm, she looked, and half the roof was on top of her arm and then it was gone, half of the building and half of the roof was gone.

Sarah was a little surprised that she didn't go with it. She was on a part of the roof that remained, tilting down at a slight angle but stable for the moment. She was lying on her side under a heap of rubble and her right elbow was shattered. There was blood leaking from her crushed skin and pieces of bone stuck out of her arm. Oh no, she thought, but there wasn't a lot of emotion there. She was too stunned. She would get infected, she knew, wounds like that always got infected. She would get a secondary infection and there were no more antibiotics in the whole world. She was going to die.

The demon—the lich—the monster put one hand up on the remaining part of the roof and hauled herself up to stand over Sarah. She had no mouth. The monster had no mouth. Was it going to eat her? Or maybe they would just make her one of those hand-less ghouls she'd seen.

The monster leaned forward. Pieces of mold and fungus fell from it, vegetative debris that pelted Sarah's chest and face. Sarah couldn't breathe. This close . . . this close the monster could kill you just by default. Sarah's lungs were full, her chest kept heaving like it was trying to vomit something out but she was stuffed full of something soft and damp and smothering. She felt like someone had stuffed fuzzy cotton down her throat until she couldn't hold anymore.

The monster reached down and touched her face with one enormous hand. The fingers stuck to Sarah's cheek where they touched and made a wet suction cup sound.

You can hear me, can't you? the monster said, inside Sarah's head. **You have the gift.**

Sarah tried to nod. She couldn't move the muscles of her neck, they were too clenched with the effort of trying to get some oxygen in her lungs.

You can hear me . . . I can't tell you how much I need someone like you. Someone to talk to. I can't save your life, now. It's already too late. But I can bring you back to

be with me. I won't let them change you, not so much. Would you . . . would you like that, to be my . . . friend?

Sarah lifted her left arm. It was hard. The arm fell back to flop on the tar paper. *Try harder,* she told herself.

She lifted her left arm, with the Makarov's incredible weight in her unwieldy hand, and shoved the barrel into the thick layer of mold and fungus over the monster's forehead. She squeezed the trigger, waited for the weapon to cycle, and squeezed again. Cycle. Again. Cycle. Again.

18.

AYAAN FIRED A bolt of dark energy into the legs of an oncoming ghoul and the meat slid right off its bones. The sinew and cartilage underneath darkened and cracked and it fell face forward across the packed dirt of the barnyard. The wizard just laughed.

"There's more where she came from, gal. And even that one ain't finished." It was true. The now legless ghoul kept coming for Ayaan, skinned hands digging into the soil with slow but total determination.

Ayaan spun around and blew the head off a tall ghoul that had been creeping up behind her. Flesh peeled off its skull in dry strips and fell away, its black tongue flopping to the ground in one piece. That one went down for good—but while she had watched it die others had flanked her, as she had known they would.

Skinless hands closed around Ayaan's flesh, pinching her mercilessly. The eyeless dead wrapped their arms around her and lifted her off her feet. She kicked and struggled and threw her center of gravity around, but every time she slipped out of their dry gray arms another would come up to grasp at her hair or her wrists. She managed to get one quick shot off that seared a ghoul to death where it stood—the naked muscles of its chest and neck withering visibly, the individual strands of fibrous tissue splitting and peeling and blowing away like dandelion fluff. But it wasn't enough.

Without a word, without a command they carried her inside the farmhouse. The front door led through a simply decorated parlor and into the back of the house, to an enormous kitchen. A wood-burning stove blazed merrily in one corner while a barn door up on trestles filled the center of the room. Dark blood stained the wood in several places.

A painted wooden door in one corner stood ajar. Something bright glinted behind it. As the corpses carried Ayaan inside, she caught a glimpse of blond hair, no higher than the doorknob, and then the door closed silently. Ayaan had no time to wonder about that—she was too busy fighting her captors.

The skinless corpses threw her down onto the table hard enough to make her head reel. While she tried to pull her brains back together, the wizard came in and secured her, spread-eagled, with stout iron chains. He'd clearly done this before. His wooden arm was no use for the job, but he worked the manacles quite adeptly with his callused hand.

"My name," he told her, as if it were a courtesy, "is Urie Polder, and I eat the dead for the magic they got. Don't you get me wrong, gal. I didn't come to this lookin' for a taste of gray meat." The ghouls moved to the corners of the room while he busied himself with pots and pans and especially knives. "It was a kinda court of last resorts arrangement, you unnerstand. The larder," he said, stabbing a butcher's knife into the wood of the table until it vibrated in place, "was bare. Now that's an old, old story and I don't need to be retellin' it. I ain't the first, I figger, but God help me, I hope to be the last." He brought a cleaver down to stick in the wood as well. "It was only when I et her heart that I felt it. That was when I feel the holy power for the first time, and I knew what God had given to me."

"Whose heart?" Ayaan demanded.

"I'm a rebuilder," Polder told her, ignoring her question. "Some folks come on through here and see all the skulls and like and say I'm some nature of demon, but it ain't true." He gestured with a steel knife. "This is where it begins once and over again, it's the Garden, right? Only this time, the Fall came first, and now we're goin' back to the good place. It's Eden in reverse."

He looked up at the ceiling and brought his hands together in prayer. The stick fingers of his artificial arm wove around the living fingers of his right hand. "Our Father," he began, "who art in Heaven, ahallowed be—"

A horrible, murderous scream interrupted him. He stopped in mid-prayer and looked down at her, though it was clear to Ayaan that the noise had come from outside.

"Hell's hinges, it'll be lunchtime afore I get somethin' to eat." He waved at them with his wooden arm and his skinless ghouls filed out of the room to the barnyard. "So you're not alone, well, I shoulda guessed so much, uh-hum." It took Ayaan a moment to realize she was being addressed. "Evil comes in threes, don't it just. The furry fellow, you, and who else? Who else is out there knockin' at my gate?"

Another scream came. Another—they made Ayaan grit her teeth. One long, extended howl that seemed to come from everywhere at once. Then one of the skinless ghouls came smashing up against the windows outside. His denuded face flattened against the glass and then he slid off, leaving a thin scum of pus against the pane.

"What's that blurrin' out there, it moves so fast, like a car used to," Polder said, staring out the window. "And there, a green fellow, now what could that be?"

"Death," Ayaan said, "for you, anyway." She lay back on the table and closed her eyes.

The wizard grabbed her leg and shook it painfully. "Now you start talkin,' gal, as I will have none of silence. Who is that, and what does he want? His boys are awful fast." He grabbed up an iron poker and laid it across the crook of his human arm. "Don't you go astray now, you mind?" he told her. His smile told her he had meant it as a joke. Throwing open the kitchen door he strode out into the barnyard to do battle with the green phantom.

Before he'd taken three steps, an accelerated ghoul leaped to his shoulders and slammed him to the ground. He cried out and tried to raise his wooden arm in self-defense, throwing the handless ghoul away like a piece of trash. Another ran at him and he tore its head free of its neck with his wooden fingers. A third ghoul already stood behind him. It raised its doctored arms and jabbed his back over and over again, the sharpened bones moving so fast they shimmered in the air. Blood leaked out of the wizard in great gouts and his energy started to flicker. He shouted and turned, both arms raised in attack.

"Da," someone said, near Ayaan's face. She turned to look and saw the interior door ajar again. A skinny little girl, maybe thirteen years old, stood there, her face pocked with acne and her hair the color of corn floss. She looked up at Ayaan with very wide eyes. "My da," she said, as if that conveyed a full message on its own.

In the barnyard the handless ghouls were taking Polder's skinless ghouls to pieces. The wizard shouted for them to press the attack, but he was outclassed. He was also bleeding profusely.

"Da!" the little girl shouted, and Polder turned to wave her back. The second his attention faltered, he had three more handless corpses on his legs and arms, their lipless mouths sinking long teeth into his skin. He staggered under their weight and then Ayaan couldn't see him anymore—he had moved out of view. She could hear him screaming, though, and she imagined the little girl could, too.

"They're killing my da!"

Ayaan nodded solemnly. "I know. But we have to think now. We have to think about what we're going to do. Are you alone?" That elicited an obedient nod. "It's just you and your da?" Another. Crap, Ayaan thought. This wasn't going to end well. "Do you know how to undo these chains? This is very important."

The girl ran to the exterior door and looked out. Her face went white and then she stepped back into the kitchen. She took an enormous iron key out from under the kitchen table and made short work of the manacles. Ayaan sat up on the barn door table. "What's your name?" she asked. She had a duty to this girl.

The girl looked at her dazedly for a while before answering. Visibly she pulled herself back together—someone had trained her in how to speak to company. "I am called Patience, if you please," the girl said, and did a little curtsy. She smiled sweetly. She would have been trained to smile sweetly. Ayaan knew that training would only get her so far. The girl was going to collapse in tears very soon. She stepped down from the table and took Patience's hand.

"Well, Patience, it's very good to meet you. Now. Come with me." She kicked the door closed so the girl wouldn't have to look at her father's body or what was being done to it. Ayaan took a momentary glance for herself. Very little of Polder's face remained.

She led the girl deeper into the house, into a room where the breaking dawn barely lit up an overstuffed couch and a few simple end tables. Ayaan studied the place looking for exits and ways to fortify the structure. It was no fortress, but it had potential. There might be a cellar and probably other places to hide. The hex signs outside would protect the house for a while—at least until the goat blood powering them dried up and flaked off.

Patience flopped down on an ottoman and studied the seam of her little black dress. She found a loose thread and started picking at it. Any second now, Ayaan thought. Any second and the girl would lose her calm.

She had to decide what to do. The battle for the farm was over and the green phantom had won. Ayaan couldn't let him find Patience. But even if she hid the girl, well, then what? Ayaan couldn't stay behind to protect her. She couldn't send anyone else to pick her up and take her to a better place. There was probably plenty of preserved food in the house, but it wouldn't last forever. Eventually Patience would have to come out of the cellar and face the big bad world. She would have no chance out there, not without her father's magic to protect her. Ayaan hadn't seen any firearms in the house. Certainly not the kind of weapons the girl would need to survive on her own.

Ayaan could turn the girl over to the green phantom. She could be raised as one of the Tsarevich's zealots, get a little education, be well fed and brainwashed and turned into one more slave of the dead. She could look forward to the day when she, too, would die and have her hands and lips surgically removed.

There was one other option, of course. Wouldn't it be better, Ayaan thought, to just put her down?

It could be done so simply, so painlessly. Ayaan could hold the girl against her breast and then just use her power, just a little, to end the girl's life. Or even better, she could just . . . just . . .

Patience was the first living human Ayaan had been alone with since the Tsarevich remade her. The girl's energy burned inside her, hotter than the stove in the kitchen—Ayaan hadn't really expected that, that it would be so warm and radiant. She felt quite cold, suddenly, quite chilled, and she longed to have a little of that heat inside her. No malice, no threat came attached to that desire. It was the simplest, most wholesome feeling in the world.

"Come here, Patience," Ayaan said. "I want to hold you in my arms and make everything better."

The girl slid off the ottoman and onto her feet. She looked down at the carpet but didn't come any closer. Tears slicked down her cheeks.

"Come here," Ayaan said. She took a step closer to the girl. "Come here." She reached out one hand and touched Patience on the elbow. The little girl's face came up, her eyes tightly shut as if she knew what came next, as if she was bracing for it.

Behind Ayaan a door opened and Erasmus stepped inside. Ayaan could feel his energy behind her, cold and unwanted. "Well, what do we have here?" he asked in a high-pitched, singsong voice, and held out his arms. The girl ran to him and embraced him like she would a giant teddy bear, her arms tight around him, her sobs buried in his fur.

A tremor of revulsion went through Ayaan's body. She had come so close, but—no. She wouldn't have done it. She told herself she never would.

She stood up slowly and brushed off her clothes. "We were just talking," she announced. It sounded false the minute she uttered the words.

"We all make mistakes," Erasmus whispered, and she glared at him. "It can be so hard."

Ayaan stormed past him and out to the barnyard. The green phantom stood there waiting for her, his ghouls standing as motionless as statues once again in a line behind him. No sign remained of the skinless horrors from the barn. The body of the dead wizard had been completely devoured. Only bloodstains remained in the barnyard.

"You did well," the phantom told her. "I guess you get to live."

14.

"DO YOU FEEL the power here?" the green phantom asked. His withered face was creased with a beaming fascination. It looked grisly on him, but Ayaan got the point. His curiosity was killing him—he really wanted to know what was inside the wizard's silo.

Ayaan felt less a burning need to know than a profound caution. Smoky, curling tendrils of purplish dark energy licked out from the metal structure. Its metal staves looked scorched, as if by a terrible fire. The six hex signs mounted around the silo's door would burn her flesh if she tried to enter.

Patience came forward, her face still wet. She hadn't collapsed yet—she was tougher than Ayaan had thought she would be. She had agreed to help them with very little encouragement. Maybe she was just glad to have something to do. The girl approached the silo with a bloody knife in her hand. She had just slaughtered a goat while they waited, something that came naturally to her from long practice, and now she made cutting motions around each hex sign with her gory blade. One by one they faded, their potent magic fizzling away. "The door is open now," she said in the hushed tones

Ayaan associated with how men spoke inside a mosque. She started to move aside to let them in, but then she looked up at Ayaan and Erasmus. "She was very nice to me," she told them. Ayaan had no idea who she was talking about. "Please don't hurt her."

Ayaan turned and looked at the green phantom. "What's going on here? What is this thing?"

He shrugged. "It's a reliquary, I suppose."

Ayaan shook her head in frustration and approached the door. If it was going to spit lightning or set her soul on fire, there was nothing she could do about it. She pulled down on a lever and a bar slid away from the door. It swung open on rusty, squealing hinges.

Inside dust filled the air—no, not dust, ash. White, flaking ash that lifted on the few beams of light that filtered in through the slatted walls. Ash covered the floor, a pile of it so deep it came halfway up Ayaan's ankles. A dry, burned log covered on one side by silver ridges like the skin of an alligator leaned against the far wall. It had a hole dug in the middle of its widest part. At first Ayaan thought someone had carved a human face into the top of the log. She knelt down by it, though, and saw actual skin, warped and turned to charcoal by incredible heat.

She knelt in the ash and tried to brush away some of the soot and dirt to see the face better, but part of the cheek fell away at the first touch. She studied the face in horror and then looked down. What she'd thought was a log was all that remained of a woman's body. She could see the rib cage sticking out through black lumps of burned flesh, she could trace where the arms and legs would be. Most horribly, she saw what must have been done to the woman before she was burned alive. Someone had opened up her sternum with a saw and pulled out her heart. The hole Ayaan had seen was the gaping cavity where the heart had been.

Erasmus came inside the silo, ash sticking to his glossy fur. The wound in his own chest took on new meaning to Ayaan. He led a goat that bleated and kicked as he dragged it inside. The animal must have understood this was a place of death. Maybe the goat had been around to see the wizard set the woman alight, years previous.

"This is going to be a little messy," Erasmus warned her. She didn't move. Whatever was about to happen, she wanted to be by the woman's side. It was a grim duty, but Ayaan knew no one else would be there to hold the dead woman's hand, even metaphorically.

Erasmus tore the goat's throat out with his claws. He held the animal tight around the neck as it thrashed and its eyes rolled, and then lifted it up so the blood, which fell out of it like water from a punctured water balloon, splashed across the burned woman's chest. A good quart of blood went right into the hole where her heart had been.

When the goat stopped bleeding, Erasmus set it down gently in the ash. Slowly it raised its head, its eyes a darker color than before. It rose on wobbly legs and started walking around the silo, looking for meat. It turned to look at Patience. Ayaan blasted its brain with dark energy and it lay down again, this time for good.

"What exactly was that supposed to accomplish?" she asked.

"We're bringing her back, of course." Erasmus sucked at the blood on his furry hand. "These old ones, the first ones, they're all super tough. You can blow them up, set them on fire—it doesn't matter, they can always come back. It isn't easy, and I'm told it's incredibly painful, but with time and blood it can be done. It shouldn't take more than a couple of months. Her cells will need to rehydrate, of course, and that's a lot of gross tissue damage to recover from, but—"

The woman's face filled out and turned pale in the space between two heartbeats. She reared up and gasped to fill her lungs, then screamed in absolute pain and rage. Her arms came up, fully formed if still black with soot, and she clutched at her cheeks, her forehead, her eyes. She stared at Ayaan, then at Erasmus, then down at her own naked body. Then she disappeared completely.

Ayaan wanted to rub her eyes, she wanted to blink back whatever was obscuring her vision. But no, it was true. The burned woman had revived and then vanished into thin air.

The green phantom stamped into the silo. "Erasmus!" he shouted. "Where is she?"

The furry lich could only raise his arms in protest. Ayaan wanted to smile to see the two of them so helpless. She closed her own eyes and listened.

There. A skittering sound, then a quick rhythm of metallic thumps. There was something wrong with the sound. It was less as if she heard it than as if she imagined it, or as if someone else in another place were hearing it, not her. Ayaan opened her eyes. A ladder, directly in front of her, led up into the upper reaches of the silo.

She looked up and saw a hatch rusted shut in the dome at the top. Sighing, Ayaan wrapped her nerveless hands around a rung of the ladder and hauled herself upward. Her undead limbs protested immediately. She felt as if she were slipping, as if she would fall back onto the hard packed earth of the silo floor, but she grabbed at the next rung anyway. One after the other after the other. Occasionally she stopped and hooked her arms through the ladder's rungs and tried to listen again, but she heard nothing more.

"What are you doing?" the green phantom demanded, only his cowled head poking into the silo. Ayaan ignored him and kept climbing.

At the top, a thin seam of metal ran around the base of the dome, perhaps four inches wide. The hatch she'd seen from the bottom stood immediately at the top of the ladder, mounted on this thin ledge. Ayaan grabbed for the lever that worked the hatch and yanked hard at it, putting all her weight into it. With a horrible groan that sounded like the silo was about to collapse around her the hatch slid open, grinding in its tracks, and bright sunlight blasted inside the metal dome.

The blond woman appeared there as if she'd come in with the light. She stood braced precariously on the thin seam, her pale skin reflecting the sunlight, her hair glowing in an unkempt halo around her face. She had a bite mark on her shoulder, the only sign of violence on her, and a black tattoo of a radiant sun on her belly. Her bright form was doubled, though, echoed by her aura—a howling void of dark energy more vibrant and at once more tenuous than any Ayaan had seen before.

"Are you a good lich or a bad lich?" the apparition asked, and Ayaan could only crouch in the silo's hatch with her mouth open, wondering what was going on. The woman leaned forward, across the dome, and grasped at Ayaan's outstretched hands.

"Who are you?" Ayaan asked, finally.

"Who aren't I?" the blond woman replied with a sad smile. "I was called Julie, once, but I don't remember much about her. I call myself Nilla now." She shrugged. "I've been called worse."

Ayaan decided to put that line of questioning aside. "What happened to you?"

Nilla looked away for a moment, as if trying to remember. "I was burned to death . . . but I guess it didn't take." She shrugged again. Ayaan thought something was wrong with her, something psychological. Though she supposed having her heart eaten by a wizard and then being burned alive gave her an excuse for carrying a little mental baggage.

"I was headed for New York, I wanted to see Mael. We were discussing the big plan. I stopped wherever I could, wherever people would have me, living or dead. I helped them, if I could, if I felt they deserved it." Her eyes went very wide. "I was never a very good judge of character. Lots of people tried to kill me, I was used to that. No one tried to eat me before, though. Do you know what it's like to see your own heart ripped out? Lucky me, being dead, it didn't matter. I didn't need my heart after all. He might as well have taken my appendix."

At the bottom of the silo Erasmus called up to them. "Miss, we don't want to hurt you," he insisted. "We want to honor you."

"He thinks that's true," Nilla told Ayaan. "I guess we should go down."

"Wait," Ayaan said and grabbed the woman's shoulder. "I have so many more questions."

Nilla smiled again, that sad, even heartbreaking, smile. "I've never been good with questions. You need to have some answers first, before you can be good with questions." She looked down at her hand and then turned it palm up. A little blob of silvery metal sat there. It looked like it could have been a piece of jewelry once, but the fire had melted it. "Take this," Nilla said in a soft whisper. "It used to be in my nose."

Ayaan nearly dropped it.

"Not like that," Nilla chided. She touched the side of her nose and showed Ayaan where it was pierced. "It was a nose ring. Sarah will want it."

Ayaan opened her mouth to speak, but Nilla was already climbing back down the ladder. She stayed visible this time. At the bottom Erasmus waited with a handmade quilt he'd probably found in the farmhouse. Nilla wrapped it around herself gratefully. When the green phantom bowed before her, she returned the gesture.

"Our master awaits," the green-robed lich said. "He is the—"

"I know all about your Tsarevich, and what he wants. Mael Mag Och and I spoke of him often. Let's go make all his dreams come true, shall we?"

Ayaan led the way back to the truck. While Erasmus danced around their new friend, blathering away like a puppy in heat, she smiled and laughed and seemed genuinely excited about what lay in store. Only when she saw the corpses with their hands and lips removed did she seem to frown, and then only for half a moment. Ayaan imagined she was the only one who saw.

20.

SARAH LEANED FORWARD and puked up her guts. The hands in her armpits held her perfectly steady as her body wracked itself over and over again, her lungs and her stomach expelling their contents all over a cobblestone curb. She stared at the mortar between the paving stones, stared with an intensity she couldn't have mustered normally, until sparkling lights appeared in her vision.

With a great braying cough she opened up her whole body and spewed out another measure of filth.

The mucus running down her face, the tears in her eyes were full of black flecks. Her nose pulsed and ran with a stale reek, an earthy, disgusting stink.

There was more of it, more foreign crap in the hollow parts of her, but she lacked the strength even to heave. She sank back against waiting arms that lifted her up into the light. Someone wiped her face with a rough cloth and someone else poured water across her forehead and her eyes.

"Come on, pumpkin, just a little more," her father said, and Sarah turned her head to the side under his bony fingers. "Just open your mouth, just a little more."

She couldn't have done it herself. Something else crept inside her, something cold, and pushed. A thick sludge of black and yellow nastiness drained out from between her lips. Then she slept.

Ptolemy stood guard, squatting on top of a brick wall. When she awoke, light the color of wine colored his bandages and bounced off his painted face. When he turned to look at her, she saw white patches in the death mask. Some of his linen was gone, too, probably devoured by fungus. He looked smaller, as if he'd lost weight. She wondered what he looked like under the bandages.

She remembered suddenly her arm—the compound fracture, the bloody mess that was all that had remained of her right arm. She lifted it now and examined it. Dark bruises wrapped around her elbow and a twinge of pain went up her shoulder when she tried to make a fist. But the skin was unbroken, and she could bend her arm just fine.

That injury should have killed her. Any of her injuries should have killed her—up to and including the time she fell and skinned open her chin. When the Epidemic came, when the bodies of the dead filled up the cities and countries of Earth, every strain of microbe and virus had gone through a population boom. The world was full of horrible infectious little things just waiting for you to get a bad scratch. She had lived most of her life deathly afraid of thorns and hornet stings and anything that could break her skin—any of them could have been her death. Now she'd been torn apart and put back together again. But here she was. She didn't feel great, not by a long shot, but she could tell she wasn't going to die.

Sitting up a little she coughed noisily but unproductively. She saw she was wrapped in thick blankets that were only a little tattered along the edges—had they been taken from one of the houses nearby? She looked around and saw she was in a kind of courtyard. Dead leaves filled its corners and a dry fountain stood at its center, a big cracked concrete bowl decorated with nymphs and cupids and dolphins. Lying on a cloth next to the fountain were a sword, a noose, and a length of fur. The relics, she remembered. The relics of the Celt, whoever that might be.

Ptolemy leaped down from his perch and offered her his hand. As she struggled up to her feet she checked her pockets and found her pistol there, its magazine completely empty. She touched the soapstone scarab.

i death thought sent you sent me thought to my death, he told her. He sounded embarrassed. **was but strategy it was but strategy**

"Yeah," she said, "well. Just don't doubt me again." Guilt bit her hard but she kept her face calm.

He bowed gallantly. Behind him Gary scuttered over the wall on his six bony legs. She could have talked to him if she'd wanted—she still had his tooth in her pocket—but she remembered what had happened before and didn't dare. Her father arrived a few moments later, forced to take the long way around. He emerged through a door in the house behind the courtyard. "Oh, sweetheart, you look so much better," he said, putting a withered hand on her cheek. She closed her eyes and smiled. It was so good to be back with him, to have him be alive. She refused to question that feeling.

"You saved me, you healed me," she said, feeling like a toddler, feeling like her dad was the strongest man on earth. "I got too close to the fungus queen. That was supposed to be fatal."

Dekalb put an arm around her shoulder and led her through the house. The furniture inside, the fixtures of the rooms meant nothing to her. They passed through the front door and into a street overrun with trees.

"I didn't know I had it in me," he said. "Your Egyptian, um, friend came and found me. He said you were dying and I was the only one who could stop it. I didn't know what he was talking about, but then I saw you looking so blue and still and I couldn't help it, I just picked you up and held onto you and suddenly you started coughing. I guess I did something. It left me so tired, though. I kind of want to just go back to my tower."

"What about her?" Sarah asked, fear suddenly blooming inside her, cold and sweaty. "What about the one I shot, the—the lich I shot?"

Ptolemy raised one arm and pointed down the street. Sarah saw the building where she had taken refuge. One whole side of its facade had crumbled down into the street. In the exposed innards of the place she saw a tangle of rebar sticking out of half of a retaining wall. A human figure had been impaled on half a dozen spars— clearly the work of someone with superhuman strength. She glanced at Ptolemy, and the mummy bowed.

The impaled woman looked nothing at all like the blight demon. She was short, almost as short as Sarah, and her skin was barely mottled with fungus. Her head was missing altogether. Sarah looked down and saw it near the woman's feet, scorched and silvered. It sat on top of the remains of a campfire.

"He burned it for six hours straight," her father told her. "That should do it. She wasn't like Gary. At least, I'm pretty sure."

Sarah felt weak and sick and feverish, but she had to see for herself. She climbed up into the ruined building, whimpering a little every time she put her foot down on a pile of broken bricks and it started to slide away from her. Eventually she reached the skull. She picked it up and slammed it against a block of concrete. It cracked open, and inside she found only ashes.

It was about as dead as you could get. It would have to be enough.

Looking at the corpse, at what had been done to sanitize the lich, a cold feeling seeped through her hands, her wrists. Up her forearms. She had something to do. A duty. She had pretended as if she was done, as if her responsibilities were discharged. She had hidden in fear. Not anymore. She knew what had to be done.

"The Tsarevich isn't going to like this," she said, scrambling back down into the street. "I think we just declared war. What happened to her soldiers?"

The soapstone buzzed under her fingers. **i scattered chased them chased they scattered**

Sarah nodded. "So they probably went back to their master. What about those relics she was after, did you figure out why he wanted them?"

no

Sarah frowned. He could speak clearly when he wanted to.

He had gathered them up while she was examining the dead lich's skull. He handed them to her and she studied them. The length of fur was matted and disgusting. The noose looked like it might fall apart at any second. She studied the sword, though, and something about it called to her. It was ancient, truly ancient, and bright green with verdigris. The blade had fused with its scabbard so thoroughly that it didn't even rattle when she shook it. A spot of bronze glinted at its tip, as if someone had used it like a walking stick and repeatedly struck it against hard ground until the patina wore off. The hilt was made of twisted cable and fashioned in the shape of a howling warrior. She grasped it with one hand, intending to wave it through the air a few times and get a feel for its balance. Before she could lift it, though—

—dare you, I've given you a command! You will do as I say, and you'll do it now, lass, because there is one fucking lot more riding on this than you think. I—

The voice in her head made her want to drop the sword, made her want to cover her ears, it was so loud. It made her teeth shake. When it stopped she felt like someone was looking right into her head, like whoever it was who belonged to the sword had noticed her intrusion, had become aware that she could hear him.

Sarah, he said. **Dearie, you're not supposed to be here. Not yet.**

She recognized the voice right away. Which was funny—always when she communicated with the dead like this she heard their voices as her own, her own inner voice as if she were just thinking to herself. This voice was no different. Yet from its anger and its condescending tone she knew exactly who it must be. Or, at least, who it had always claimed to be.

"Hi, Jack," she replied. Angry vibrations buzzed up through the metal and stung her hand. She let go of the sword. It clattered on the street. Her hand buzzed and shook—she had to grab her wrist to make it stop. It felt like she'd been polluted by bad energy, but the feeling faded once she was rid of the relic. She turned to her father. "Whose sword is this?" she demanded. "Did it belong to Jack before he became a ghost?"

Dekalb's eyes clouded over. It was a lot of memories to process at once, evidently. "Jack? No . . . no, he never had a sword. And Jack's no ghost, sweetheart."

"What?" she asked. She was still connecting the dots in her head.

"Listen, I knew Jack pretty well. We worked together, fought together. He even killed me, after all. But now he's just another ghoul. He was chained to a wall uptown from here the last I saw of him, with a broken neck, unable to move or walk or hunt. He was as brainless as any of them. Jack was never the type to become a ghost, anyway. He would have erased himself from the network before he let that happen."

"I never questioned him . . . I never doubted he was exactly who he said he was. God, I am such a moron. Listen," Sarah said. "I have the ability to talk to—to ghosts, and ghouls, and dead people who can't speak for themselves, but only if I have something really important to them. Like Gary's tooth or Ptolemy's heart scarab.

Who does this sword belong to? It was somebody the Tsarevich wanted to talk to, they called him, what was it—the Celt?" She glanced at Ptolemy, who nodded in agreement.

"There was this one guy," her father told her. "He was a ghost, sure. Gary knew him better than I did, but he was from the Orkney Islands, up in Scotland. He was a Druid." Dekalb picked up the sword and looked at it, then showed it to Gary. The scuttling little skull-bug jumped up and down on his six pointy little feet in excitement. "Gary says yes, this was his sword. His name was Mael something, I remember now. He helped me at the end, he talked to the mummies on my behalf. Mael Mag Och. Why, sweetie? What does he have to do with anything?"

"Well, he's lied to me, for a start. He's lied to me for years. He told me he was somebody else. He pretended to be Jack, in fact."

Dekalb shook his head in confusion. "You can do what?"

She was too angry to repeat herself. "This Druid brought me here—he's been playing me for a fool. Who knows what else he set up?" She frowned at the green sword in her father's hand. "Right now, I am willing to believe," she told him, "that Mael Mag Och has been playing with us all, like checkers on a board."

The skull-bug did a little dance, it was so excited.

"Yeah," Dekalb said, "Gary says that sounds exactly like Mael."

PART
THREE

L.

THE GREEN PHANTOM smiled, his withered features pulling back from his skull. "Are you comfortable? Is the refreshment to your liking?"

They had found clothes for their blond guest, a white lace dress with voluminous sleeves and a pair of flat leather shoes that looked comfortable. Nilla leaned back on her divan and lifted her snifter in silent toast. It could have been tomato juice in the glass, but Ayaan doubted it. The green phantom bowed deeply, leaning on his femur staff, and moved back to one corner of the room. On her own stool, Ayaan crossed her legs and wondered how long this was going to take.

They were all—with the exception of Amanita, who was still out on assignment—gathered inside mad-o-rama, where the Tsarevich was due to make an appearance at any moment. Erasmus stood behind her in a stiff posture, not allowed to sit down because he had nearly compromised the mission. He was going to have to apologize. Ayaan had been given a huge, overstuffed armchair, a little moldy but meant as a place of honor. Semyon Iurevich perched on a three-legged chair near the back, his eyes very wide, as if he expected to witness something monumental and didn't want to blink in case he missed it. The fiftieth mummy stood holding the brain in the jar. Nilla made a point of not looking at it. Cicatrix was with her master, the two of them hidden inside his pretzel car throne, which was still turned to the wall.

Without preamble, the Tsarevich's image appeared in the center of the room, facing them. He bowed deeply in Nilla's direction and spoke in fractured English—the only language Nilla had. "My lady. What honor you give me. I have sought you for years now, to only glory you. How kind of you is to come. May I introduce myself, I am Adrik Pavlovich Padchenko, who some too kindly call Tsarevich."

"Enchanted to meet you," Nilla replied. She looked sincere enough. "I'm nobody."

The boy lich smiled broadly, as if she'd said the most amusing thing he'd ever heard. Then he turned and faced his generals. "With this nobody and her gracious presence, we are made ready. Most of you know what means this. We have worked so long, so hard. Tomorrow we begin!" With the exception of Ayaan, the mummy and the brain, the entire room cheered.

"There is perhaps one, though, who knows not why we celebrate today." The image came to take Ayaan's chin in both of his small, pale hands. She gave him her best smile though she wanted to knock him away from her. "Why, she does not know real me at all." That elicited a few chuckles.

"My story is starting in tragedy," he told her, walking toward the throne, which hid his true body. "Is starting with being hit by car, at tender age of nine years old. Many thought I would die. I did, yet not in the right away." More laughs.

The story he told her then was either heart-wrenching or blood-curdling, Ayaan couldn't decide which. The boy who would become the lich had been a child of moderate accomplishment—good grades, a promising future of higher education, and the chance to really make something of himself. Then came the accident. Most of his tiny bones had been broken, many of his organs ruptured or crushed. He was brought immediately to a hospital where it was discovered that he could not breathe on his own and that his heart was barely moving. After dozens of surgeries over the course of two weeks, he was eventually stabilized—alive, but unable to regain consciousness.

In a country where advanced medical services were rarer than gold, his family had been wealthy enough, or at least desperate enough, to hire specialists to try every possible remedy. Mostly they ran endless tests and rated him on various scales—the DRS, the Rancho los Amigos Index, the Glasgow Coma Scale. They tried to get him to blink his eyes, to wiggle his toes. They stuck him with pins, made him smell unpleasant odors; a nurse moved his hand around on a computer keyboard and helped his fingers twitch and spell out nonsense words.

Eventually the doctors presented their findings. The boy was not in a coma, they assured his parents. Coma victims could not react to unpleasant stimuli. He was not in that darkest of closed-off places, the persistent vegetative state, because his brain was undamaged, at least physically. He was not in a stupor, nor had he suffered cataplexy, or narcolepsy, or any of a hundred other things.

He was, the doctors whispered, "locked in." For whatever reason, his brain continued to function and his body lived, but they weren't on speaking terms anymore.

"To myself," the Tsarevich explained, "is not so bad. I had dreams, nice dreams. An angel stood in my corner and showed me pictures of world. This was in actual a television set, ha ha. Every day beautiful nymphs they came and washed my body, was quite stimulating. Were nurses, of course. Prettier inside my head than out. I lived in fairy-tale land, where I am Prince Ivan, yes? You know the story of Prince Ivan? He is taken away by the gray wolf, to fabulous and magic land, and has great adventure. He even fights Koschei the Deathless, and he wins! No one ever told tale of Prince Ivan grows up to turn to Koschei. Never before."

The causes of locked-in syndrome had always eluded the medical profession. Nor was there any real treatment, the doctors told his parents, only therapies with little hope of any real amelioration of his condition. There was very little hope of his just coming out of it on his own, though here the doctors split. Some suggested it could happen, that children were resilient, that there was always room for a miracle. Most of the doctors suggested quietly removing the boy's feeding tube and ending what promised to be a short and extremely unpleasant life.

American consultants and Orthodox priests were contacted and their advice sought. Decisions were made. The machines that kept his body going were paid for. His room was kept sterile and safe and free of intruders. Everything was kept on battery power because the local electrical grid was unreliable. All of his supplies—liquid food, replacement parts for the oxygen supply, pain medication—were ordered in bulk and fed into automatic delivery systems. When the Epidemic came, the nurses deserted the hospital, but the boy's life hardly changed.

At least, until the food in the automated feeding machine ran out. For days he languished, his body quietly devouring itself. Death and life combined, tried on each other's mantles. In that bad place, the Tsarevich said, "My angel he closed his eye, yes. I saw no more."

In darkness he was blind and alone. His world collapsed to become a narrow space, between a blanket and a mattress, a softly respiring universe no larger than a bed. And then, without warning, he wasn't alone.

"Lad," someone said, calling from very far away, "lad, you've known so little of life. It's time you learned of the other thing."

In the darkness the voice spoke to him of what had happened. It pulled no punches and spared no pains explaining things in minute detail. The boy had never learned so many basic concepts—to him death had been a true abstract, to him, perhaps alone in Russia, hunger was a complete blank.

He had not known, for instance, that he was created to oversee the destruction of the entire world. He had not known that God had ordained him the angel of death.

The voice that spoke in the darkness helped him understand. And then it helped him open his eyes. In the dimly lit room, with just a little sunlight sneaking in through the closed blinds, the boy saw his benefactor for the first time. A hairy man covered in blue tattoos. Wearing a noose around his neck and a strip of fur around his arm.

Ayaan gasped a little when the Tsarevich described his mysterious benefactor. She had, of course, seen the same vision. She glanced over at the brain in the jar. Then she looked back, hurriedly, afraid someone had seen. No one had—or at least no one wanted to interrupt the Tsarevich's story.

Back in the hospital room the tattooed man smiled and held out his hand, and the boy rose out of his bed, cables and tubes and needles and wires falling from him like the leaves falling from a dead tree in autumn. He felt as if he were floating up out of the bed, as if he were raised up by pure glory.

"Look at you, lad, you've been made more than you were. You've been made noble, no, you're royalty now, one of three creatures in this world with any power or strength left. You're the very prince of death, aren't you?"

In Russian, the word was *tsarevich*.

"He teaches me then, how to control and instruct dead man. He shows me powers that are mine, and powers that are his. And why we have power at all. To wipe out all humans, he says. He begins to tell me who authorizes such a plan, and why it must be so. And then he goes."

The benefactor had disappeared in mid-sentence, in mid-instruction. The Tsarevich was supposed to go forth and kill every living human he could find, he knew that much. The benefactor had never explained what this was supposed to achieve. Without warning, without completing his instruction, the tattooed man had just vanished.

"Only later, only much later do I learn. Was eaten, yes, eaten by one like me. One like Nilla, you, too. One that was him called Gary."

Ayaan uncrossed her legs. She folded her arms across her chest.

"Yes, yes," the boy said, waving at her. Every eye in the room turned to look at her. "Now you know so much. Why I do not hate you, for one. Why I wanted our friend ghost." He pointed at the brain in its jar. Ayaan didn't look. "That is him, and I seek him for twelve years to find out rest of command. Go forth and kill so that

. . . so that what? Now he changes tune, of course. Now he tells me sacred mission is called off. I don't know what to do." The boy smiled. "Is little joke, of course. I know exactly what to do. I must heal myself. I must make myself whole again."

Ayaan frowned. She looked over and saw Nilla, whose face was a mask of perfect attention.

"You must to see this now, is not pretty, and I am sorry. But you must. I continued to grow, you see, even after car hits me. My little body keeps to growing, but lying in bed, could not grow right. I was in bed seven years before Epidemic came and started the healing process on me. Seven years I grow wrong."

The boy vanished without so much as a flicker of light. The throne, which had once been a car on the mad-o-rama dark ride, turned around on a circle of revolving floor. Cicatrix was revealed inside, her limbs tangled with those of the Tsarevich, the real Tsarevich. Cicatrix wore nothing but a slip. The Tsarevich was sucking on a cut in her thigh, sucking out her blood.

It wasn't the vampirism that made Ayaan and Nilla both shift in their seats, however. It was the boy. He had a skull shaped like an eggplant, much broader at its crown than at his chin. A single patch of hair stood off-center atop his head. His face was distorted, pulled out into a long parody of a human visage. One eye was permanently closed by a fold of flesh, the other protruded from his head so much it looked like it might fall out. His mouth contained three or four teeth growing at random angles—when he removed it from Cicatrix's thigh, a mixture of blood and saliva drooled from his lower lip, which didn't close properly.

They couldn't see too much of his body, which was hidden behind Cicatrix's curvaceous form. Ayaan could tell, however, that his arms were different lengths and that only one ended in a hand—the other was a squidlike mass of fused digits growing at abnormal angles. His chest had caved in on one side, and his pelvis seemed to attach to the wrong bones.

"He cannot take solid food," Cicatrix said, breaking the silence that had filled the room like something solid, like all the air in the room had been replaced with solid glass. "His body no longer func-tions so. Only blood can he eat. My blood. I eat all sugar and candy I like, and he takes away from me, so I stay slender. Is good arrangement."

She chuckled, and the monster on the throne smiled. His tongue wagged inside his mouth and words formed. His voice was changed, but recognizable as the same voice that had told the story. "I go now to Source. All pieces are in place. Soon, this body is no more. Soon I am real boy again!"

Ayaan's hands were grabbing at the air before she realized what she was doing. She was pulling energy toward herself, gathering power for a massive death bolt that would destroy the two of them and probably turn the throne into dust as well. She could do it, there was absolutely nothing stopping her.

It had not been her own decision, however, to gather that energy. Maybe, she told herself, her subconscious was so disgusted by the sight of the Tsarevich that she just wanted to destroy him, to put him out of his misery—and everyone else's.

Or maybe Semyon Iurevich had put that thought in her head.

Does it matter? she heard, the words blasting through her cra-nium like a chill wind off a freight train's passage. **This was the deal. From the beginning, this is the way we played the course. You put on a wonderful show, lass. You made so nice even I started to believe it. I honestly started to believe that you had come around to his side.**

She didn't turn around and look at the brain in its jar. Instead she looked at Semyon Iurevich. His eyes tracked hers perfectly.

Destroy him. Do it now. It could have been either of them saying it.

"No," she said out loud, and folded her hands in her lap.

2.

EVERYONE WAS STARING at her. She found that mildly unnerving.

"Why are you to saying 'no'?" the Tsarevich asked. His voice sounded like rotten peaches being poured out of a rusty can. Cicatrix had a look on her face of deep concern. Did she understand? Did she realize this had all been a setup?

The voice of the disembodied brain raged and railed inside Ayaan's head, but she refused to move. **How dare you, I've given you a command! You will do as I say, and you'll do it now, lass, because there is one fucking lot more riding on this than you think. I—**

Then nothing. The voice was gone from her head.

You'll what? she asked, silently. No reply was forthcoming. The voice had disappeared with as little warning as it came. She turned and stared at the brain. It didn't move at all, of course. Its energy was unchanged. Why had it stopped in mid-sentence?

Before she could even begin to wonder she was knocked off her seat. Semyon Iurevich had come at her with a spike in his hand, growling for death. She rolled across the floor and came up in a stiff-legged crouch, only to realize that he wasn't trying to kill her after all. He'd been aiming for the Tsarevich.

His plan had failed—his programmed assassin had refused to kill on cue. So he had gone with a contingency plan. He would throw away his own life to murder the Tsarevich. Unfortunately, there was one problem with his thinking. Like all liches, like all undead things, his motor skills were quite poor.

The spike in his hand was little more than a sharpened metal rod. One of the crudest weapons imaginable. He had probably meant to push it through the Tsarevich's eye, but his hand went wide and he caught the point in the skin of Cicatrix's neck. Bright red blood erupted from the wound and splattered Semyon Iurevich's bathrobe, pooled in the Tsarevich's twisted lap. The hypnotist lich tried to pull his spike free for a second attack, but the green phantom swooped into the middle of the room and held out one hand and the would-be assassin collapsed in a volitionless heap.

The lights flared on—Erasmus had switched them on. Mad-o-rama's dark corners were speared by floodlights that showed every speck of dust and curl of old black paint.

"I must have," Cicatrix said, her voice high and brittle with shock. "I must have the machines with crash cart, it is being promised to—to—to me, I live forever!" She sounded like a mewling cat as her blood ran away across the floor. Erasmus dragged Semyon Iurevich's motionless body out of the room as Ayaan lifted Cicatrix down from the throne. She tried putting pressure on the wound, but the spike had gouged out half of Cicatrix's jugular vein. It didn't hurt that the Tsarevich had already drunk enough of her blood to leave her anemic and weak as a kitten.

"Is good life, I want more," the scarred woman begged, but there was nothing Ayaan could do. Clearly she had been promised eternal life as a lich. Instead, in a few minutes she would die and rise as a ghoul.

Ayaan looked up at the Tsarevich, who was literally foaming at the mouth with excitement. "What do you want me to do?" she asked.

The single eye rolled in her direction, but the Prince of the Dead said nothing.

"Damn you," Ayaan said. Cicatrix had lost consciousness and was barely breathing. "There's no time to make her a lich, even if I thought it should be done. I can keep her from coming back, though."

The Tsarevich sucked on his lower lip and convulsed in his throne. Was it a nod, a shrug, or merely an involuntary spasm?

Ayaan frowned and pulled power into her hands. She leaned forward and closed Cicatrix's eyes. In a very perverse way the living woman had been her closest friend in the camp of liches. She kissed the shaved head and said a brief prayer for Cicatrix's salvation, begging Allah to see past the woman's decadence and her fraternization with monsters.

Then Ayaan brought up her hands and blasted Cicatrix's head until the skin and muscle and fat melted away and the skull beneath turned yellow. She kept it up until the bone scorched and steam fizzed out of Cicatrix's eye sockets.

For a long moment, while she hovered over the dead woman, Ayaan could think only of Dekalb. At the end of his life she had offered this same service. He had refused, and she had simply walked away. She'd always regretted that, leaving such a hero to become just another shambling, mindless wanderer. Perhaps this duty made up a little for her previous failure.

Eventually she rose to her feet and straightened her hair. She felt drained. She felt hungry and wondered if any of the goats from the farm in Pennsylvania were still available. A tang of disgust bit into the back of her throat—she had just boiled the brains of a friend, she had turned Cicatrix's eyes to running custard. She should hardly be thinking of food. Yet she was a dead thing and she knew the hunger would never stop.

"Be taking this one away," the Tsarevich said. Ayaan looked up, startled, expecting to be accosted by handless ghouls. The Russian lich had been talking to the green phantom, however, who grabbed up Cicatrix's pink ankles in his skeletal hands. He dragged her from the room without further ceremony.

Ayaan turned to face the mummy who held the brain, then to face Nilla, who just looked sad. She glanced back at the Tsarevich. "I will take them to a safe place," she announced. "There could be a follow-up attack. I recommend finding a hiding place for yourself."

It turned out the Tsarevich was capable of nodding after all.

Nilla led her small procession out of mad-o-rama and up the boardwalk, the silver planks of wood echoing like drums under her boots. Before they had taken a hundred steps, the brain spoke to her again.

Bollocks, he swore. **I can assure you we won't get a chance like that again. We could have killed him! Slaughtered him where he sat! From now on he'll be expecting an attack. He'll take precautions, perhaps hide himself**

away again where no one can find him. And it's all your
fault.

Ayaan looked at Nilla. The blond lich pushed her hair out of her
eyes with one pale hand, but the breeze off the sea kept fluttering
her locks down across her eyes.

The brain sputtered inside Ayaan's mind. **Don't worry about
her, she and I are friends from far back. You can speak
as you please. Now tell me, lass, did you lack courage?
When it came to the fatal moment, did you lose your
nerve? Tell me just what in the blooming bastard hell
were you thinking?**

Ayaan addressed the brain directly, leaning down toward the
mummy's hands to get closer. "I was thinking I don't trust you."

Hah! You don't trust *me*?

"I don't trust the Tsarevich, either, if that's what you're driving
at. He turned me into a monster and I will never forgive him. But
how much do my feelings matter in this? He is the only one who can
rebuild this sad empty world. He is the only one who has the
power."

**Strength should never be concentrated in the hands of
one man. It must always be tempered with the wisdom
of those who went before.** It sounded like a recitation of holy
scripture. Ayaan ignored it.

"You told me he had to be destroyed, that he had a plan of ultimate evil in mind. Now that grand secret plan is revealed—he simply wants to heal his broken body! I should kill a crippled man
because he wishes to be whole?"

**The power of the Source can do anything. It can
reshape his body, fair enough. Yet coupled with his level
of control there's not a lot he couldn't do. He could end
all life on this planet, lass, if he chose. Cause wanton
destruction, vanquish all who stood before him. He could
rule this world by fire.**

"He needs to take power into his own hands if he's to do anything valuable," Ayaan scowled. Why couldn't she make the brain

understand? Humanity needed a leader. It needed a leader who could work miracles.

She felt the brain trying to turn over in its jar. **It's an ugly stretch of road from here to there. Do you truly expect him to do his best by all the wee folk in his wake? He mutilates their corpses!**

"That's true. Who ever built a mosque, though, who didn't tear down hovels to make room? If you gave me a good enough reason, if you had given me any kind of reason at all, I would gladly have sacrificed myself, and yes, all of his followers, to destroy him. But you didn't. You decided instead to pollute my mind with posthypnotic suggestions. Why should I give you my loyalty, when you try to take it by force?"

The brain was silent for quite a while.

You've gone soft.

Ayaan roared with disgust.

Fathers before us. You've actually fallen for the codswallop that tosser spews out, haven't you? You've turned. I had our Semyon lie on your behalf but he needn't have, eh? They brainwashed you just fine.

"Be careful what you suggest," Ayaan told him. "I happen to be a specialist in laying the dead to rest. I've never killed a ghost before, but I'm willing to learn how."

If only it were that simple.

Ayaan stormed away from him, but only for a few paces. She was alone, all alone in the midst of monstrosity. She was enmeshed in secrets and lies and plans she hadn't had a hand in forming. She could not afford to give anything up. "What about you?" she demanded, staring at Nilla. "What's your part in this?"

The blond lich turned to face the sun. "I've already told you, I'm nobody. And that's what makes me special."

Ayaan shook her head and dropped to sit on the sand. She stared out at the water as it broke in white curls. The sun had moved visibly across the sky by the time she noticed something flailing in the surf, something yellow and red and black with a bit of silver on one end and white spars sticking out of the sides.

Its limbs extended and then dropped, digging deep into the sand. It reared up, water pouring from its orifices and crevices and nooks and crannies. It had been human, once. Now it looked like a portioned chicken. The silver bit had been a helmet, strapped to its head. It had slipped down to cover one of its eyes; the other eye socket was empty and raw, as if it had been gnawed on. Long strips of its skin had come off in the water while the salt had washed its exposed bones quite clean. It was the ugliest thing Ayaan had ever seen.

"What now?" she demanded.

The brain answered. **That's one of Amanita's foot soldiers. If it came here on its own that can only mean one thing. She must be dead.**

3.

BACK ON GOVERNORS Island the living came before Dekalb, one after the other. He sank lower and lower in the lawn chair they'd set up for him but the survivors didn't seem to care. One by one they came up and he put his hands on their shoulders and when they walked away they breathed easier and their skin looked clear.

It seemed to surprise no one on the island that Dekalb could heal them. It was lich magic that had infected their crops, their buildings, their bodies. Of course it was lich magic that would undo the blight. Sarah wondered if they expected her father to clean the mildew off the buildings, too. Did they want him to go around the gardens in the middle of the island and heal each individual stalk of winter wheat?

"I'm getting hungry," he said, when she stopped the line momentarily. He had slipped down so far in his chair his arms lay across the ground like discarded bones. His head rolled around on his chest.

"But don't worry, pumpkin, this will all be over in a little. Then we can find a house for you."

Sarah stood up and looked at the ones who had already been healed. They were gathered in a joking, laughing knot, their hands on their knees, their mouths open and wet as if they were practicing being healthy again. "You guys," she said. "Help me out, will you? He needs food. Meat, if you have any."

"I'm not wasting my time hunting up grub for some fucking ghoul," one bearded man shot back. "Not after years of them hunting me."

Sarah sighed, exasperated, but her father clasped at her wrist. "Honey, go easy on them. They've lost so much. They don't have what we have now."

She left him there with the living still crowding in, demanding their turn with the healer. She headed toward the warehouse buildings at the south end of the island—there had to be something there for him. On the way she touched the soapstone. "Is he behaving himself?" she asked. She had left Ptolemy in charge of Gary. The skull-crab hadn't made a threatening move since the time it had paralyzed her, but she hadn't lived to the ripe age of twenty by being stupid around the dead.

he quietly in speaks in riddles and riddles sits speaks in quietly, the mummy told her.

Sarah let it go. She crossed through the cool, shadowy interior of Liggett Hall, which bisected the island, and came out into the verdant fields beyond. The southern part of the island resembled what it had been before the Epidemic, a sprawling Coast Guard base. Three piers stood out into Buttermilk Channel, their names drawn from a naval alphabet: Lima, Tango, Yankee. The old ball fields might have been turned into farmland, but basketball hoops still stood in the middle of green pastures, listing a little in the sun and the wind.

To get to the warehouses Sarah had to pass by the strangest of the island's structures, the commercial facilities off Tango Pier. There was a hotel, a Laundromat, even a supermarket with shelves bare so long they sagged under their own emptiness. Vending machines once full of ice-cold Pepsi stood forgotten or vandalized on every corner. Weirdest of all was the burned-out shell of a Burger King restaurant, something Sarah had only heard of before in her father's bedtime tales of a decade earlier. Metal signs creaked in the evening breeze down there and old neon tubes stood lifeless and cold. The soft and rusted shapes of cars lurked in the weed-choked parking lots.

When the kerosene lamps were turned on up in Nolan Park, in the other half of the island, they looked natural, they looked normal. In the gingerbread houses a little flickering light was a welcome thing. Down on Tango Pier an open flame looked altogether different. It looked wrong in front of all those broken, unpowered lightbulbs. It was no surprise people rarely came down so far—the survivors tended to stay on the north side except to work in the fields or if they needed something from the general supplies down on Lima Pier. Even then, they usually sent a slack to do the job.

Sarah was a little surprised, then, when she saw Marisol standing in front of the main warehouse. The mayor had a shovel in her hand and a small bundle wrapped in white cloth over her shoulder. Sarah stopped in her tracks and didn't move, embarrassed for some reason to be caught in such a quiet place.

They just looked at each for a while, and it wasn't a particularly friendly look. Marisol, after all, had threatened Sarah with summary execution the last time they'd spoken. For her part, Marisol's bundle was readily discernible, from closer up, to be a dead human body.

"Did you come to help me bury my son?" Marisol asked. Her voice was rough with crying, but it lacked much in the way of emotion.

Sarah sought out her own voice. "He didn't make it?" she asked.

"He wasn't magic, like you. Dekalb's daughter lives and my Jackie dies. We're just normal people, you see. He didn't have any magic."

Sarah started to object, to say that she had no magic, but it wasn't true. Her father could have saved the boy. If he hadn't rushed to Manhattan to fix her broken arm, he could have stayed on Governors Island and saved Jackie. If he'd even known that he had that power—if Sarah had told him, if she had broken her promise to Gary and told the secret—

There were too many ways to feel guilty, and too many possible excuses, for Sarah to make any moral sense out of the boy's death. She said nothing and hoped her silence would sound like solemnity.

The two of them entered the field of winter wheat and hacked out a narrow space for a grave. The islanders always buried their dead in their fields, just as a practical measure. The bodies returned certain nutrients to the soil. If the corpses were sunk deep enough, the health risks were minimal.

Marisol dug and Sarah pulled and pushed and carried dirt out of the hole. It was horrible, draining, sweaty work, and neither of them had brought any water or food. Sarah's sweatshirt turned into a stained rag almost instantly. The dirt got into her eyes, into her nose. It coated her lips and stuck to her hair. She didn't complain once.

At first she thought she was just being polite. That she was helping Marisol because she'd been asked to do so. She figured it was the right thing to do and she was a good person. She even considered that this would get her in good with Marisol, whose help she would probably need in the future—she was earning credit at the price of her own sweat. After the first hour, though, when her arms started to burn and her hands cramped up and her back became one fused bar of glowing heat and pain from bending down and then rising up over and over and over, after all that, she stopped thinking about herself.

Burying Jackie wasn't a political maneuver or a gesture of apology. It was an ugly task that had to be done and she was there when the time came. It was just one more chore on a list of things that had to get done.

When the hole was deep enough, Marisol knew it and she put her shovel aside. She held out her arms and Sarah picked up the boy's tiny body. Jackie weighed next to nothing, but he didn't feel like a corpse in Sarah's hands. She knew what it was like to hug a skeleton like her father or a mummy, but Jackie felt different. His flesh was cold but still soft and pliant. The winding sheet didn't cover his head very well, and she got an unwelcome look inside. She saw the hole in the middle of his forehead.

Sarah knew what that hole was for. In Somalia, in her first years under Ayaan's tutelage, when she was still too young to carry a gun, Sarah had been given the task of sanitizing the dead. She had a little hammer and a chisel for the task, and she'd learned to be quick about it—the dead didn't take long to come back, not long at all. When a soldier fell you paid them the final respect. You sent them off to rest.

She couldn't imagine what it would be like to do it to your own flesh and blood. Your only child. Wouldn't you want, despite all wisdom to the contrary, to just see them move again, to see their eyelids flutter open? Wouldn't that stay your hand even just for a moment?

But of course, Marisol was tough. Ayaan had recognized it when she'd stood on the island and looked at the bleak future facing the survivors. Marisol was tough and she could make hard decisions. Sarah handed the woman her son and watched as she laid him down gently in the worm-riddled earth. Then Sarah reached down and helped Marisol climb up out of the grave. Together they pushed the dirt over the boy, concealing him forever from view.

Marisol didn't say any prayers or offer the boy a eulogy. Her obvious grief, written in the streaks of dirt on her face, was eloquence enough. Sarah sat and watched her and wondered why she didn't feel just as strongly about Ayaan. Maybe because it wasn't real to her yet. After about half an hour of just sitting and mourning, Marisol turned and looked at her. "What do you want?" she asked.

Sarah understood what she was being asked. Why had she come to Governors Island, and what would it take to get her to leave? "I won't lie to you. I'm on a dangerous journey and no good is coming of it. Originally I was on a rescue mission. Now I'm after revenge."

Marisol smiled, a quiet, overworked smile. "Jack taught me about revenge. He said it was the only form of suicide accepted by the Church."

Sarah shrugged. "OK, maybe revenge isn't the word I want. We used to call it *sanitation*. The woman who raised me is dead now. Undead. It's my last duty to her to put a bullet in her head." She looked down at the fresh grave. That had been Marisol's last duty to her son. It was the same. She wanted to say as much, but she knew the words would profane Jackie's death. "I need guns, and I need soldiers. Right now, though, I need some meat to feed my father."

Her father—wasn't it also her duty to sanitize him?

No. She would never think about that again. Anyway. Ayaan had told Sarah a hundred times what she wanted done if she ever turned into one of the walking dead. She had left explicit instructions. Ayaan wanted to be sanitized. Her father seemed to want to go on.

She refused to explore that thought any further.

Marisol helped her find what she needed in the main stores. An economy-size bag of pork rinds, guaranteed not to spoil for decades to come. They brought it north, into the half of the island where a bonfire was already being built, where lights were coming on in the houses and the sound of playful violins and acoustic guitars hung in the air as if the music had gotten caught in the tree branches. They found Dekalb slumped forward across his own knees, still sitting in his lawn chair, while all around him living people set about making a communal dinner. The lich took the pork rinds from his daughter and tried to tear open the bag, but he just didn't have the strength. Sarah did it for him. As she handed the bag to her father she looked at Marisol, and Marisol looked back. It was a lot more comfortable, the silence that passed between them, than it had been before.

"We need to find you a house," Dekalb said around a mouth of what looked to Sarah like dirty pink Styrofoam. "If you're going to stay here with me you'll need a proper house. You can't live in the ventilation shaft with us, it's not healthy."

Sarah's brow furrowed. "Daddy, I didn't plan on staying," she said. "I've got work to do. Important stuff." She felt like an infant as the words came out of her mouth.

Dekalb shook his head. "It'll wait," he told her. "We have way too much catching up to do. And there's the question of your education. Marisol, what about the officers' quarters over by the schoolhouse, what's available over there?"

"Dad!" Sarah interjected, "I—"

He pushed his hand into the bag and rustled it in his annoyance. "I will not let you be put in danger again," he told her. He drew out a handful of rinds and shoved them into his permanently stretched-out rictus. "Who's the grown-up here, after all?"

4.

THE GIANT TRUCK rocked up on one set of giant tires as it crushed an abandoned car on the interstate, a thousand tiny glass cubes exploding from the crushed windshield, rotten struts and shocks popping and collapsing and squealing, and then it was over. In the bed of the truck Ayaan held onto a roll bar until the truck stopped bouncing and then clicked on her walkie-talkie. "Bring up a wrecking crew," she said. "The flatbed won't make it past this one."

A few dozen living men in blue paper scrubs came rushing up with pry-bars and sledgehammers. They made short work of the rusted-out car, taking it to pieces and hurling the wreckage into the undergrowth on either side of the road. They had to move quickly. Behind them the Tsarevich's flatbed trailer was surging forward, its ranks of wheels turning in fits and starts as the giant vehicle moved forward one staggering step at a time. A hundred corpses heaved it forward with their shoulders, their bent backs, their straining fingers. On top, six more ghouls turned the cranks that kept it level and its ride smooth even as it rolled over broken pavement. Living gunners crewed heavy machine guns mounted in pintles at two positions on the flatbed. At its front end the green phantom sat strapped into a chair on a high superstructure from which he commanded a good view of their surroundings and everything that happened in the column of vehicles. At the back of the flatbed the Tsarevich himself reclined in his yurt, quite hidden from view. Among the liches there were rumors that claimed he was actually not in there at all, that the flatbed was a complete ruse and that he was hidden elsewhere. Ayaan wouldn't have blamed him for being a little cagey.

The attack on his person had shaken him badly, and the death of Cicatrix had left him without a familiar supply of food. Once the Tsarevich had learned of Amanita's death, something had changed. He had gone from being hurt and confused to being galvanized. He had moved quickly to get his people on the road. He'd had plenty of enthusiastic help, too. The living and the dead had worked side by side to get vehicles ready, to pack up their supplies and belongings and do whatever it took to stay near the prince of the dead. Where they were going and what they would do when they arrived was still a complete mystery. Ayaan found she had too much work to get done to be asking a lot of questions anyway.

Behind the flatbed, a fleet of hundreds of barely functional cars and buses followed, their engines blowing blue smoke across a landscape that had reverted to the primeval. Ayaan remembered a time when cars were commonplace, even in her native Somalia, but she had forgotten just how noisy they were and how much of a mess they made. Most of the vehicles hadn't seen use in over a decade, and many were so badly rusted they fell to pieces after only a day or two. It didn't matter. The Tsarevich had all the gasoline he could ever use from his refinery on Cyprus, and there was certainly no shortage of cars.

Ayaan had been on one of the missions to collect vehicles. Regardless of what she'd lived through and regardless of what she had become, it still spooked her. The cars had been waiting for them, parked in orderly rows outside shopping malls and airports and stadiums. They had been left there intentionally and their owners had fully expected to come back and reclaim them at short notice. Every vehicle had been personalized in some way—a faded bumper sticker, a graduation tassel hanging from a rearview mirror, a paint job with simulated flames. Personal effects littered the passenger seats, fast-food wrappers were stuffed into the leg wells. The doors were all locked, the windows rolled up tightly. But no one had ever come back. The cars were forgotten. Left for dead.

It had spooked her not for the presence of any real horror but for the absence of any normality. It was easy to forget, sometimes, that 99 percent of the world's population had died in the first months of the Epidemic. Surrounded by ghouls and cultists and liches, it was easy to pretend that the world hadn't been emptied out. Standing in a parking lot bigger than the village where she'd been born, however, watching the sun gleam from every piece of glass and mirror, Ayaan had been forced to accept it, to accept everything that had been lost.

The cars had been given a kind of afterlife now, she supposed. Each car held a single living person—the driver—and as many handless ghouls as could be stuffed into the rest of the interior, the backseat, the trunk. The green phantom and the Tsarevich kept them docile, but Ayaan kept wondering what the drivers must be thinking. Were they pleased with themselves, were they secure in the knowledge that they were doing a holy duty? Or did they worry every single second that one of their passengers would wake up hungry?

Ayaan looked forward and saw the road obscured ahead by the branches of a weeping willow. The tree's roots had torn up the asphalt and sent cracks running through the blacktop in every direction. "I need a lumber crew," she said, and living cultists with chainsaws came running forward. Ayaan tried not to think about the last time she'd seen a chainsaw.

Behind the ghoul-filled cars came tow trucks and fuel tankers and 18-wheelers containing mobile mechanics' shops and crates full of spare parts for the cars as well as kitchens for both the living and the undead. Behind the support vehicles came the stragglers—those living who didn't know how to drive, mostly, a tailback of them that receded into the distance. They kept up as best they could. The column of vehicles moved forward only a few miles an hour but it never stopped. The wrecking crews and chainsaw teams cleared debris while a pair of steamrollers and road graders were available if the way became truly impassible. Whatever the Tsarevich hoped to find out west, he intended to get there in a hurry.

There would be serious obstacles to come, Ayaan knew. Rivers to ford. Mountains to climb. There would be weeks of slow going ahead of them. So far not a single person had complained.

Well. There was Semyon Iurevich. Though he didn't complain so much as beg for forgiveness and for an end to his unlife. Even over the noise of the cars and the chainsaws Ayaan could hear his screams.

There had been quite a bit of debate over what should be done with the apostate lich. It had been suggested he should be fed to ghouls—the ultimate insult paid to the most vile of traitors. Yet ghouls did not eat their own kind. The dark energy repulsed them far more than the decomposing, suppurating flesh enticed them. It had been noticed that ghouls would quite happily eat dead human meat as long as it wasn't currently being animated. It would have been simple enough to smash in Semyon Iurevich's brains and then feed him to the dead, but that lacked an element of dark justice, as far as the Tsarevich was concerned. It lacked torture.

Behind her on the flatbed Ayaan could have watched, if she so chose, what the Tsarevich had finally deemed fit. Semyon Iurevich was hanging from a gibbet by his neck, his eyes turned up to the sky. Stripped of his bathrobe, his body had been revealed to be quite corpulent. Now a living man with a machete was slicing off thin strips of the lich's body, starting with the soles of his feet and working his way up. As each slice came off, he would drop it in a blender and puree it until its dark energy had completely dissipated. The resulting slurry was dribbled into the mouths of the ghouls who'd worked so hard hauling the flatbed across New Jersey.

The other liches wagered that Semyon Iurevich would be nothing more than a screaming skull long before they reached Indiana.

The bastard lich had diddled with her head, he'd gotten his rotten little fingers in her brain. Ayaan did not enjoy listening to his screams, but she found she had no sympathy for him, either.

5.

IN THE DARK Sarah lay in bed and tried not to look across the room. Not more than four feet away, sitting in a chair because he did not sleep, was a corpse. A walking corpse, a hungry, dead, ex–human being with broken nails and ruptured skin and a face stretched as tight as a mask across his skull. The feeling had started to slide over her like a cold wet blanket at dinner the night before. He had sat apart. He had put people off their food. She had realized, while she gnawed on a stalk of celery, that he disgusted her, too. That this particular corpse was her father made less difference than she might have hoped. He was dreadful in appearance. Lesions filled every crease of his skin. Fluid had pooled in one half of his body and left dark patterns of bruising down one arm, one cheek. His eyes had sunk into his skull, his nose had shrunk down to little more than a scrap of leather. Even just by moonlight it was hard to look at him and not feel her skin crawl.

Dekalb stood up against the light coming in the window. He tapped at Gary's skull with a finger no thicker than a pencil. In silhouette he looked terribly thin. More like a stick figure than a man. The terror drained out of her little by little. It was her father, she told herself, it was the man who used to hug her and feed her pieces of carrot out of a plastic bag and who would carry her canteen for her when it got too heavy.

It was also a dead thing, a withered, sad thing. Just like Jackie had been, the little boy she had helped bury.

Too many thoughts. She rolled over and pretended to be sleeping.

Sarah wondered if everyone went through this. At a certain age, did everyone look at their father, that being who had once been so tall and strong, and see just a frail old man? Of course very few people would ever see their fathers like this.

Too many thoughts. She couldn't sleep. She took Gary's tooth from her back pocket and looked across the room at the crab-legged thing on top of the dresser. The skull had a full set of teeth, both top and bottom. The tooth in her hand was an incisor, but he wasn't missing any. He must have regrown the tooth the mummy had pulled out of her head. Instead of shuddering at the thought she curled her hand around the tooth and made contact.

Why, look who's dropped by for another chat. The skull-bug didn't move or react in any way. It looked preternaturally like a sleeping cat basking in a ray of moonlight. In her head Gary sounded a lot more excited.

"Let's get one thing clear," Sarah told him, the words staying in her throat. "If you try any of that paralysis bullshit again I will personally take you out to the middle of the Atlantic Ocean and drop you in. Dad might subconsciously heal you, but I don't think he can teach you how to swim."

I can't tell you how scared I am.

Sarah glared at the skull. "I already have the boat."

And I have something you need, or we wouldn't be talking. You can threaten me all you like, Sarah, but you can't do anything about it.

He was baiting her. He wanted her to get angry. He wanted her to kick him or throw him against the wall or say something cruel. Why? She doubted it was simple masochism.

"It's about Mael Mag Och. The guy I thought was called Jack."

Ah. The old bastard. Yes, I knew him well. Did you want just general information or did you have a specific question?

"Why did he lie to me?" she demanded. She had tried to find out for herself, earlier, by going to the source. Time and again she had grasped the hilt of the green sword. Mael Mag Och never answered. When she'd asked her father about that, he'd said the old Celt must be screening his calls. Then Dekalb had been forced to explain to her what that meant. "He won't talk to me now. For years, though, he came to me. He taught me things, gave me advice. Why? Why was it so important that I think he was Jack?"

He probably chose Jack's name as someone you would have heard of, somebody you could be expected to trust, Gary told her. His voice was surprisingly soft and kindly. **He was never the kind of person who could tell you simple facts. He came on like a nice guy and frankly, I still believe he has a good heart. But he has some pretty crazy ideas about who we are and why the world had to end. If he doesn't want to talk to you then count yourself lucky.**

"I guess he fooled you, too, huh?" Sarah asked.

For a while. Then I ate his brain. Of course, that says more about me than him.

Sarah shook with horror.

He's insane. I can tell you that much for free, shortcake. He told me once his God sent him back from death so that he could oversee the extinction of the human race. Whatever he asks you, whatever he asks from you: don't give it to him.

"Thanks for the advice." Sarah put the tooth back in her pocket and rolled over again. She could hear her father moving around on the hardwood floor. He didn't sound like a human being. His footsteps weren't loud or strong enough.

Too many thoughts.

In the morning, white sunlight marched up the sheets and eventually hit her in the face. Sarah wrinkled her nose but eventually she had to give in. She sat up in bed and saw her father sitting in the chair across the room. He had a book in his hands.

"There was a time when I was too weak even to read," he told her, his mouth curved into something wistful, something approaching a smile but never quite reaching it. He was so much less horrible—less, well, disgusting when he talked. He had her father's voice and that made all the difference. Grateful, she sat up and listened attentively. "That was before I figured out I could take energy from the ghouls like some kind of vampire. I've had a hard time of it, kiddo."

"I'm . . . sorry, Dad," she said, and put her feet down on the floor. Her shoes were lined up next to the bed. Ayaan had taught her that, not her father. She slipped into them effortlessly.

"I can't tell you how proud I am of what you've accomplished. It's not easy moving around the world these days. I should know. I came to New York back when all the ghouls were still here. I'm a little peeved with Ayaan. She said she would take care of you."

Sarah looked down at the floor. Her head was too fuzzy to process much. "Actually, that's kind of something I've been meaning to talk to you about." She stood up and shivered. Her sweatshirt was in the laundry, leaving her with just a tank top. It was cold in the bedroom—no central heating anymore. Wrapping her arms around herself, she tried to look him in the eye, like an adult. "She's . . . dead. She got captured by the Tsarevich and . . . I've been following her, trying to save her, but I waited too long, I could have, I could have stopped it, somehow, if I had taken the fight to them, if I hadn't been so cautious but now she's a lich and . . . And. And. I have to sanitize her now. I have to save her from being one of those . . . things." She stopped herself. She had been about to say that she needed to save Ayaan from being a lich. He might take that the wrong way.

He stared at her unblinking. She couldn't remember if he still had eyelids or not.

She felt like an idiot when he looked at her like that. Like a child. "OK, that came out all wrong. Can I start again?" she asked.

"No need," he told her. His eyes clouded over and she wondered if he was having the ghoulish equivalent of a stroke. Then he went to the dresser and touched the green sword. "So you were trying to rescue Ayaan. I see. It didn't work out. You can't blame yourself for that. It wasn't your fault."

"It's . . . not?" Sarah asked. She wondered what he could know that she didn't.

"Ayaan was a devout Muslim. She hated the idea of ever becoming ritually unclean," Dekalb said, fiddling with the sword. He was too weak to actually pick it up. "But she was also fiercely practical. I don't think she would like the idea of anyone going out of their way to clean up after her. Especially not if it meant putting yourself in danger."

That didn't matter, Sarah thought. It wasn't a question of what anybody wanted. It was a question of duty. She started to say it out loud . . . and couldn't.

She left him, claiming she was going to eat breakfast with the survivors. The little house that Marisol had sorted out for the three of them (herself, Dekalb, and Gary) was on the north side of Nolan Park, well away from the Victorian houses where the survivors lived. It was easy to slip away with no one seeing her. She remembered the time she'd slipped away from the camp in Egypt, scurrying over the wire. Funny that after so much time she was running away for exactly the same reason.

She went to the gardens and found a slack right away. Any of them would do. This one had been a woman and she still had breasts like empty wine sacks that dangled down every time she bent over to pull up a weed. Her hair was cut with precision, perhaps right before her death—though it badly needed to be washed, Sarah could still see where it was supposed to flare out in a bob.

There was nothing in her eyes. Nothing at all. Sarah knew that look. She knew that when most people died it was their personality and their memories that went first. Everything that made them human beings. When oxygen stopped flowing in the brain the fine tracery of personhood just melted away, like frost from the underside of a leaf when the sun comes up. Now there was nobody home in this shell. It smiled at her with cracked lips, but only because it had been programmed to do so.

It was what she needed. She lifted up the noose in one hand and the fur armband in the other. There had to be a reason why the Tsarevich had sent half an army to retrieve them. "Mael Mag Och," she said, staring into the slack's eyes. "Mael Mag Och, please. Please, come forward and . . . and make yourself known." She sighed. She had no idea how to do this. In the past he'd always come to her.

"Mael Mag Och . . . Jack . . . please. I need to talk to you. I need advice so badly and there's nobody else. Please."

She kept at it for far too long before she finally had to admit defeat.

6.

CRATE AFTER CRATE of MP4s lined the metal shelves of the smallest of the island's warehouses. The small arms magazine was the best maintained of the buildings outside Nolan Park. Fresh paint inside and out, not a speck of dust. Someone had been busy, and it wasn't the slacks. "We still don't trust them in here," Marisol explained. She showed Sarah the basement, filled with collapsible cots and a gravity-fed water purifier.

"About three years after we arrived, a ship came through. People, living people were on board, and I can't tell you how excited we were." Marisol's eyes went misty with time as she remembered. "We'd just gotten through yet another terrible winter and we were all half-dead. None of us had the energy to start digging up the baseball diamonds and start planting seeds. So when we saw the newcomers we shouted and waved and set off flares. That turned out to be a bad idea."

"This must have been when I was still recovering," Dekalb said. "I don't remember any of it." Gary perched on his shoulder like a morbid species of parrot. Sarah wished she could have left him resting in the house—this errand was one she definitely needed to be in charge of—but so far she hadn't been able to deny her father anything.

"They were pirates," Marisol went on. "They traveled from one enclave of survivors to the next, killing all the men, raping all the women and then killing them, too, and stealing all the food. We figured that much out when they started shooting at us. I got everybody in here and sealed the door before they could even make landfall."

There were weapons in the small, well-lit building that were advanced beyond anything in Sarah's experience. Crazy Special Forces stuff. Experimental arms. Sniper rifles that got plugged into laptop computers and fired by remote control. Unmanned aerial vehicles little bigger than cooking pots that could fly into buildings and kill everyone inside of their own volition. Sarah picked up an enormous pistol from an open crate and checked its action. It was a .45 caliber ACP, a Heckler and Koch Mark 23 Mod 0 according to its spec sheet, and it had a tubular laser aiming module on top. Sarah pointed the weapon at the wall with the safety still on and flicked on the laser. Nothing happened. Well, sure. It had been twelve years at least since the weapon had been stowed away. The batteries would have run down or something.

Marisol came over to her, smiling, staying well clear of the pointed weapon. She slapped a pair of night-vision goggles on Sarah's head and switched them on. In the green world of the NVGs, Sarah saw a brilliant pinpoint on the far wall—exactly where the laser was pointing. *Nice,* she thought.

"We keep all the batteries charged with a little windmill on the roof. Not enough power to let us have light or heat in the houses, but it keeps the guns ready to shoot." Marisol took back the NVGs and continued her story. "Well, with us locked in here and with enough guns to last until the Second Coming, the pirates didn't have a lot of options. A couple of them got killed. We specifically didn't go for head shots. When their own people got back up and started eating them, they fell back to their boat. A couple of days later they just left. We shot the ghouls and came back out hungry but unscathed. The pirates had messed the place up a little, spray painted graffiti on the houses, burned up half our furniture for firewood. They took those few crops we'd already put in the ground, even though nothing was ripe. It didn't matter. We were alive."

"I wish I had known this was happening. I would have helped," Dekalb said.

Marisol and Sarah looked at his slight, bony frame, and then at each other. Nothing more needed to be said.

Sarah opened a crate in the middle of the room and dug through the shredded newspapers inside. Gingerly she lifted out a rifle with a bizarre blocky forearm and a curved rail running from the muzzle back to the receiver. It weighed less than the Mark 23 Mod 0 had, she thought. It wasn't made of metal at all, but some kind of lightweight resin. The only metal she could find on it was the stubby little barrel and the bullets themselves.

"Is this . . . ?" she asked, unwilling to say it out loud in case it sounded foolish.

"Objective Individual Combat Weapon," Marisol said, nodding. "The rifle that was supposed to replace the M16. It's just a prototype. We have ten of them—I think they only ever made about five hundred before Congress killed the project."

Ayaan had spoken about such weapons the way some people might talk about the houses they wanted to live in someday or what kind of food they would serve at their weddings. It fired regular NATO rounds, or, with minimal reconfiguration, airburst munitions, the so-called smart grenades. The sighting system—which included not just an optical scope but laser, infrared, and night-vision elements—had its own computer that could tell the difference between an ally and an enemy. If it detected an ally, it wouldn't shoot. The rifle was supposed to be smarter than its user. Sarah laid it back down. "So I'm sorry I interrupted. You fought off the pirates."

"No," Marisol told her. "We sat them out. From day one we've had a place like this. Someplace safe we can run to and fortify as necessary. Whenever bad things happen we're trained to come here and sit tight and wait it out. Jack taught me that." ·

"Jack." Sarah turned away so Marisol wouldn't see her face. She felt deeply, deeply embarrassed, too lame even to feel guilty. As if she had had an affair with a man she'd always been told was

Marisol's husband, only to find out he was somebody else altogether. Jack was dead, Jack was a ghoul hanging from a chain miles to the north, but he lived on Governors Island and always would as long as the survivors remembered his teachings. Sarah had never met Jack in her life.

"You remember Jack, sweetie," her father said, coming up to put a hand on her shoulder. "He was the Army Ranger who killed me."

"Yeah," Sarah said, blushing. She reached for another weapon and found a heavy plastic pipe with a slick translucent coating inside. Various bits and pieces could be clamped onto the tube. It was an "SMAW" according to its crate, but she couldn't remember what that stood for. "Marisol, that's a great story about the pirates. I guess you weren't just making conversation, though."

"No," the mayor admitted. "I need you to understand. I owe you for killing the lich in Manhattan." Sarah understood what Marisol didn't say: she would have owed Sarah a lot more if Jackie hadn't died. "You can have all the guns you can carry out of here. My people, on the other hand, are all staying here where I can keep an eye on them. OK? I'm not going to let you have so much as one soldier."

Sarah started to speak but she was forestalled by her father. "That won't be a problem," Dekalb chirped. "Since we're not going anywhere, either. Sarah's going to stay here with me." He stepped between the two women. "I have my own people to look after."

Sarah shook her head. She was going to have to confront him, and soon. It was just so hard. When he sat motionless in a chair he terrified her, he was one of the walking dead. When he got up and moved around and talked, he was her long-lost daddy. A big emotional part of her was convinced that if she said anything he would stop loving her and leave her life again.

Finding him on Governors Island, finding him still, in a certain sense, alive, meant so much. It changed her whole life. It gave her a life, where before she'd had only a past. On some level she wondered if she was expecting too much from him. If she was setting herself up for disappointment. But no, she wouldn't explore that just yet. She retreated into those corners of her mind where Ayaan's training still reigned. Connecting with her father was going to make her vulnerable. It was going to hurt. She didn't have time to resolve any of it, just yet. "Excuse me," she said, and slipped out of the warehouse.

Outside she put her hand in her pocket and touched the heart scarab. "Ptolemy," she whispered. "Have they mobilized?" Time for business.

perhaps vehicles one hundred perhaps vehicles, he told her. **west heading west**

She bit her lip. There was still time to catch the Tsarevich—and sanitize Ayaan—but she needed to get moving herself. "I only wish we knew where they were headed. We could just get there first and ambush him. If we follow in his footsteps there's no telling what will be lying in wait for us. But the only person who might know where he's headed isn't talking to me."

perhaps, the mummy told her, **i help can be i of help there**

7.

THERE WAS NO roof on top of the ventilation tower, just a lattice of metal bars designed to keep birds out. Greasy lint matted the lattice, black with soot spewed from generations of cars going by in the tunnel underneath. Sarah kept slipping, but Ptolemy was right there to grab her, his hands dry and very, very strong.

His painted face betrayed no emotion whatsoever.

In the sunlight, standing upright in the breeze and the blue sky, she studied him as she never really had before. She saw how his bandages gathered in his armpits and how they had been woven across his back. There must have been dozens of layers of cloth wrapped around him. She saw flashes of gold from the small of his back, from his kneecaps, and knew he must have amulets buried in all that swaddling. She smelled her hands where he had grasped her and smelled the spice, the cinnamon and ground-nutmeg smell of the resins that preserved his body. She smelled the millennia he had outlived and the strange worlds he had inhabited. He had died at the height of the Roman Empire, only to be reborn at the end of history. She wondered what that could do to you, what it might do to your mind, your sanity.

"What did you want to show me?" she asked. He grabbed her hand.

Hard. He grabbed her hand very hard. It started to hurt.

She started to protest, but suddenly his energy flooded through her body, dark and thick, and her arcane vision flared up, over-whelming all of her senses. She saw him, the darkness inside him burning intensely. She saw herself, full of golden fire. She saw through his eyes, though. Her own vision had never been so sharp. He saw what she did but with far greater detail.

Amazing. She wanted to study herself in the mirror of his eyes, she wanted to look at everything the way he did. There was no time for that, though. He turned her to look to the west. Her vision sped across the world until she saw what he wanted her to see.

Pure energy. It radiated from a single point well to the west, high in mountains in the middle of the continent. It should have been impossible for her to see it—it lay around the curve of the Earth— but with Ptolemy's help all was revealed to her. A broken chain of enormous rocks like an exposed spinal column cradling a fallen star. The light that flooded outward in long flickering beams from that place was colorless and perfect. Colorless, neither yellow nor pur-ple, though she knew it had to be the energy that created both. Col-orless because it wasn't light at all, but life, the very energy that made her cells divide and her hair grow.

It was awesome in its beauty. Jaw-droppingly, hypnotically beau-tiful. Sarah felt a powerful urge to get closer to it, to that source. "That's where he's headed?" she asked.

it is go where we all go want to go, he told her. **it source is the source**

The Source. She understood immediately. If the Tsarevich was headed west—well, there was nothing else out there, nothing else he would want. "We'll leave today, if we can," she told him. The Tsarevich had a long road ahead of him still, but she couldn't afford to lose a step. "Your friends are ready?"

He nodded again. This time just a simple nod, his painted face bowing up and down. She followed him back down a ladder to the ground and then across the narrow causeway to the island. Osman was waiting for her, a stack of cheaply printed technical manuals in his hands. He gave Ptolemy a nasty but brief look and then turned away, gesturing for Sarah to follow him.

"Marisol didn't want to give up any of them, and I must say I understand her logic," the pilot told her as he led them deep into the island's interior, to where the big aircraft hangars loomed over the slack-haunted gardens. "If something should happen to this place, they'll need all the vehicles they have to get away. I had to really sweet-talk her for just the one."

"Do you want a medal?" Sarah asked. "I'll make sure you get a medal when this is over."

He laughed and nodded appreciatively. "All right. What we have here," he said and grunted as he shoved open an enormous hangar door. It was counterweighted so it could be opened easily even without power, but it was still huge. "What we have here is American airpower at its finest. The HH-60 Jayhawk, which is just a United States Coast Guard version of the UH-60, I do not lie."

The aircraft in the hangar had the stubby nose and long tail that just said "helicopter." There was little to distinguish its lines except its white and safety-orange paint job.

"This is the workhorse of the U.S. Army. Medium-range, medium-lift, twin-engine, single-prop, it stands up to any kind of duty you'd care to mention: medical evac, air cavalry, troop transport, point to point, and my least favorite, direct air assault. It's the best helicopter ever built by human hands."

Sarah peered into the darkness of the hangar. "Medium-range? We're going quite a ways." She tried to remember what she had learned of American geography. "The Rocky Mountains, I think."

Osman shuffled through the tech manuals in his hands and pulled out a heavily annotated military aviator's map of the country. Sarah recognized the mountains she'd seen and pointed out the Source at once. With a ruler Osman measured the distance, his thick fingers smoothing out the paper map as he went. "A little under two thousand miles," he told her. He scratched his beard. "Fine, just fine. We'll need to stop once and refuel. There's a major air base here," he said, pointing at a star on the map labeled Omaha. "They'll have what we need."

"We can just do that? The fuel won't have evaporated or gone stale in all this time?" Sarah asked.

"No problem, boss. Gasoline goes bad over time, that is true. Jet fuel, on the other hand, is just very pure kerosene. It lasts forever if it's stored properly."

Sarah nodded and looked up at the helicopter. "OK, I'll take it."

"Wonderful," Osman said and gestured broadly with his arms. "Once again I get to fly into my certain death. It had better be a very large medal, with many ribbons."

Sarah smiled and took some of the tech manuals from him. There was no time to waste. She was about to start looking for the fuel hoses when a shadow passed across the mouth of the hangar.

"Hi, Dad," she said. Dekalb didn't look happy.

"Sarah. I thought we discussed this." Gary, on his shoulder, looked like he'd gone to sleep, though Sarah knew better. "I don't want you in harm's way. So please, just. Just step away from that helicopter."

"I won't let Ayaan down," she told him. Maybe if she could just talk him into going back to the house. Maybe if she just lied to him then he wouldn't notice when she left. "Not when I've come this far already."

"Fine," he said and stepped inside the hangar. "Then I'll do it."

It took her a second to realize he was serious. "Dad, this isn't the time," she insisted, but he was already climbing inside the helicopter.

Osman dropped what he was doing and came over to stand next to her. Slowly the pilot folded his arms across his chest. "I know you from old times, dead man," he said to Dekalb. "I respect you for what I've seen you do. So I'll ask you nicely to get out of my vehicle."

"Osman." Dekalb looked at the pilot as if trying to place him. "It's been so long. Please, take me to where Ayaan is. I have to dispatch her."

Heat filled Sarah's throat. Was she about to cry? Somebody had to teach her father a lesson about reality. Somebody needed to point out his folly.

Why did it have to be her?

"Dad," she said, very, very carefully. "It's not up to you. This isn't your responsibility. It's mine."

"I'm your only surviving parent, Sarah." He wasn't even looking at her. "*You* are my responsibility. Your safety."

Sarah glanced back at Osman, but the pilot had nothing for her. He had taught her before to finish off her own liches.

He wasn't going to give in without a fight. Clearly he'd decided that this was when he would make his big stand. "I've lost too much already," he told her. He glanced at Gary on his shoulder. The skull-bug didn't so much as twitch. "I forbid this. I mean it."

"Stop this, Dad," she tried.

"I died for you. I died so you could have some kind of life in Africa. Do you understand what that means? Do you understand what I gave up for you?"

"Please stop," she whispered.

"I died and then I locked myself away with this freak of nature," he told her, gesturing at Gary, "to make the world safer for you. Don't you dare make me throw all that away by getting yourself killed now. Not for some pointless idea of camaraderie with a dead woman. Not after all I've suffered to protect you."

"Stop," Sarah said. And surprisingly enough he did. He'd said his piece.

Her turn.

She closed her eyes and tried to remember how she'd felt earlier when she'd looked at him and seen nothing but decay. It gave her a little strength. "To protect me?" she asked. "You came here to protect me? How did you protect me, when did you protect me when I was eleven years old and hungry and the Somali government collapsed and we had to run and the ghouls were after us and some didn't make it, huh? How were you protecting me when we finally ran out of food, when for three weeks we had nothing whatsoever to eat? We made little cakes out of clay, Dad. We ate clay because it expanded in your stomach and made you feel full. Clay, Dad, I ate dirt I was so hungry."

He winced visibly, but she refused to stop there.

"Where were you, where was your protection, when the women came for me and said it was time I got circumcised? They wanted to infibulate me, do you know what that means? No, probably not, because you weren't there. You were too busy over here, trying to *protect* me. If Ayaan hadn't been there I would have been sewn up, they would have sewn up my vagina with yarn, leaving me just a little hole to pee and bleed out of. So I would be pure for my future fucking husband. You weren't there!"

"Sarah," he said, his voice completely altered.

She refused to let him speak. Instead she screamed at him. "Listen, you maggoty old wound, I guess you can come along for the ride if you want to *protect* me now. It'll be handy to have somebody who can heal bullet wounds. But I'm in charge. I'm in fucking charge! If you can't accept that I'll pick you up and carry you out of here myself."

"You have no idea what my existence is like. Don't you dare say that to me!" he howled.

"I already did." She turned around and started walking away.

"Wait a moment," Osman said. "I did not say dead things could come!"

"Yeah, well, you're not in charge, either," she told the pilot. She wondered how he was going to feel about the soldiers she'd recruited. She walked back out into the sunlight to wait for Ptolemy.

8.

"**YOU'VE BEEN HERE** before," Ayaan said. It wasn't a question.

Nilla turned around to look at her, but the pale face under all that blond hair gave away nothing. "I've been to lots of places," she replied.

Ayaan nodded and smiled to herself. Her radio crackled and spat white noise at her, but she ignored it for the time being. The two of them stood at the front of the flatbed. Ahead of them Erasmus guided the giant hot rod over a road surface that had been washed away by a dozen winters. Little but a scoured-out track in the side of the mountain remained.

They were getting close. Even Ayaan could feel it, a deep thrumming in her bones. An almost musical feeling that something big and powerful and wonderful was right over the next rise. Of course she'd been feeling that for days, since long before they'd reached the foothills of the Rocky Mountains.

It had been a long and arduous journey. The Tsarevich had given them little encouragement, but the zealots had never so much as murmured a complaint. Dozens of them had died along the road: dehydration and the meager traveling rations had taken some while others had been accidentally crushed by the drivers of the transport vehicles. A few had succumbed to violent fevers or terrible infections. It didn't matter. Moments after their eyes fluttered shut their bodies rose and they simply entered their next phase of service to their master. It was something they looked forward to.

Almost all of the vehicles had broken down eventually. The dead and the living together took to walking along after the flatbed, taking turns at the ropes when they hauled it over rises, heaving with all their strength to pull it out of muddy ditches.

After the first week they came across larger and larger breaks in the tree cover, and then the world seemed to open up wide. The sky seemed to grow bigger as the forest ended and the prairie began, but little changed. On the plains they weathered brutal sun and punishing rain. The column had never stopped. The rain gave way to days so dry and dusty Ayaan had to wear a cloth around her face and sunglasses to protect her eyes. The ghouls were oblivious to the dust that scrubbed their skin right off and burned their faces an angry red. The living made do as best they could.

In all of that empty land Ayaan had seen not a single survivor. Of course the living were hardly likely to make themselves known to the column, but she had seen no signs of them at all: no villages, not even a thread of smoke from a distant campfire. If they existed at all they were like the fallen creatures she'd seen in Pennsylvania. Hidden away in places no one ever wanted to go.

Of the dead they saw many, and all of them were headed west. Whatever it was that pulled at Ayaan's bones pulled them even more strongly. They could be spotted far to the north and south of the column sometimes, plodding along at the speed of death. Their faces didn't turn to look at the strange caravan that passed them by. Their feet didn't falter. They were being drawn onward inexplicably and inexorably. Ayaan wondered if something had happened recently to inspire them to come or whether this had been going on for years.

Prairie gave way to desert. The hills they climbed over turned silver or purple with sage, or a brilliant yellow where they were covered in millions of black-eyed susans, asters, and fleabane. In the troughs between the rises, broad swaths of grama or fescue or big bluestem grass flourished, anywhere there was a little water. They started to climb, the roads got steeper as the hills turned into mountains cloaked in loblolly pine and fir trees. They began to find pockets of snow hidden anywhere a hollow in the earth might give a little shade from the sun.

"This was all different," Nilla said. She sat down on the edge of the flatbed, dangling her legs over the track. She gestured around at the mountains green with stunted pine trees and juniper bushes. "There was less green, more brown. All of this looked like . . . I don't know. Like another planet, a dead one. I guess the ghouls ate it all, the vegetation, but then it grew back. It's funny, isn't it. The Source is for all of us, living and dead. It makes everything grow and it doesn't play favorites."

Ayaan didn't pretend to follow Nilla's train of thought. As for herself, she wasn't thinking much of anything, really, just watching the road go by beneath their wheels like the most tranquil movie in history. Here a sprig of bitterbrush would squeeze up between the broken rocks of the track. Next she would see the broad chevrons of the hot rod's wheel tread where it had spun out a little in loose dirt. She had learned over the space of weeks to fall into a trance state whenever she wanted to. She remembered Erasmus standing at the portholes of the nuclear waste ship *Pinega,* watching the waves for days on end, just watching them rise and fall. She supposed this was the one great consolation of being dead. She was removed from time— her body did not recognize the passage of hours or days or months the way it had before she was murdered. Her period, or at least the time when she should have menstruated, had come and gone without so much as an episode of spotting. She was glad enough for that.

"Oh, shit," Nilla said. It was shocking enough to make Ayaan look up. She saw nothing, really, except for a scar on the side of the mountain. A place where the trees weren't as dense. She looked closer and saw a twisted piece of metal glinting dully between two trees.

"Something has come back to you," Ayaan suggested. "A memory."

Nilla grasped her wrist. Not in an aggressive manner. Like a little girl wanting some reassurance. "Come with me," she begged, and then she leaped down to the road. Ayaan followed, of course, though not altogether happily. She understood what was happening. Nilla had come this way on her journey to the east. Now she was going to have to re-create that passage, but in reverse.

There had to be things in the past that had driven her across the country. Things no one would ever want to revisit.

Together they wove through the trees, climbing over deadfalls, picking their way through whip-thin branches that showered them in dust and organic debris and crackling snow as they pushed through. The snow underfoot had formed a thin crust and it crunched like Styrofoam under their footsteps.

Ayaan looked back at the column, which hadn't stopped moving. She hadn't been so far away from it in weeks and she felt strangely vulnerable, even with the trees arching over her. She turned again and saw Nilla getting ahead of her.

"What is it?" Ayaan called out. "What was it?" she asked, more softly. She found the piece of metal she'd seen from the track, rusted and scorched. A line of rivets, some of them burst by metal fatigue and time, bisected the shard. She moved deeper into the woods and found more pieces, some of them embedded in tree trunks. The pines had grown around the wreckage in soft, flowing contours.

"Oh, no," Nilla said from somewhere farther into the forest. Her voice was as soft as the constant sound of needles falling through the branches. The same sound, the same softness, that the snow made when it fell from the trees. Ayaan hurried on.

A long vane of metal arched up from the snow ahead of her like a pole driven into the ground. Though rust and general decay had claimed it, Ayaan recognized it as the rotor of a helicopter. In a clearing ahead, the majority of the aircraft's wreckage stood forgotten and ill used by weather, a standing circle of broken titanium and steel and Plexiglas. There had been a bad fire there once, presumably when the helicopter crashed. There were human remains in the circle. Simple bones, black with soot, white where the sun had bleached them. One set of remains was still moving.

He wore the uniform of a soldier, faded by sunlight but still draped with insignia and medallions. He had been partially eaten, most of the flesh of his legs and arms having been torn away, and he had been burned as well. Eyeless, nearly faceless, his skull stared up at the sky. The few muscles left in his arms were straining at a jagged length of metal that erupted from his rib cage. He was trying to get himself free. He'd probably been trying for twelve years.

Nilla knelt next to his head, her hands across her face. She didn't say anything.

Ayaan understood. She came forward and put her hands on the tattered skin of the dead man's head. She closed her eyes and let a pulse of dark energy trickle through her fingers into what remained of his brain. He fell back on his spike and stopped moving. Nilla nodded emphatically and rose to her feet. "He didn't want to trust me, but he had to," she said.

"Careful," Ayaan told her. "You're starting to turn into a somebody."

Nilla gave her a smile that started to melt Ayaan's dead heart. The smile dropped from her face almost instantly, however. "Am I losing my mind, or do you hear that, too?" She turned around to look at the pieces of the downed helicopter.

Ayaan stood perfectly still, more still than she ever could have in life, and made herself all one ear. She listened, and tuned out the natural sounds around her, and listened again. She definitely heard it. The sound a helicopter's rotor makes when it's moving under power. How was it possible? Was this some kind of vehicular ghost? Ayaan had seen a lot of strange things, but she wasn't ready to accept *that*.

Then a real helicopter went by over their heads, so low its shadow darkened the clearing, so fast it was gone in the time it took for Ayaan's eyes to adjust to the dimness. She glanced at Nilla, then started running back toward the road. The explosions started before she'd covered half the distance.

THERE WERE HUNDREDS of them down there. Most of them dead, but not all. She saw golden energy sprinkled throughout the column. The vast majority of them were on foot. They trailed along for a quarter of a mile as they threaded through the narrow pass in the side of the mountain. Some of them were alive.

"Am I clear?" Sarah shouted into her microphone. Someone

tapped her shoulder—that was the signal for "affirmative." They had practiced this, drilled it in Omaha, but that hadn't really counted. The fuel depot at the air base there had been swarming with ghouls. They had flown around for nearly three hours picking off the hungry dead from the air until it was safe to land. That time nobody had been able to shoot back.

The flatbed beneath them, the same one she'd seen in Egypt, had two machine gun positions on its back. Both of them were crewed by living people in light blue paper shirts. Sarah had never killed a living person before.

In any war, she told herself, somebody had to shoot first.

The SMAW, which she had learned stood for Shoulder-launched Multipurpose Assault Weapon, came with a little rifle built into the side of the tube. You weren't supposed to hurt anybody with the rifle. It was just for lining up the real shot. Sarah squeezed the trigger and a cloud of splinters jumped off the flatbed. One of the machine gunners looked down, his head turning comically fast.

"Rocket," she announced, and depressed the firing bar at the same time she touched the trigger mechanism. The magneto at the back of the SMAW clicked, and super-hot exhaust jumped out the back of the tube and through the far crew door, which she had remembered to open first. There was no recoil whatsoever, though the rocket launcher vibrated so much that her hands went numb.

When she had chosen the SMAW from the arsenal on Governors Island, she had rationalized that she was fighting liches, not just ghouls, and so she needed something bigger than just a sidearm. She hadn't considered at the time that she might be aiming her rockets at living people.

She had no choice. Those machine guns had to be taken out, and quickly. They could chew up the Jayhawk in seconds. She had no choice. She kept telling herself that.

Her rocket looked to her like a perfectly straight silver line drawn between the helicopter and the converted railroad car. When it reached the wooden surface of the flatbed it expanded in a cloud of brown and gray smoke. What looked like two hundred pounds of red jelly splattered across the flatbed and painted the side of the yurt, coated the dead men turning the flywheels near the front of the car. The dead men didn't stop at their work.

The other machine gunner, the one she hadn't aimed for, was down on the deck, clutching his ears. He was coated in red jelly, too. Sarah couldn't find any sign that her target, either the machine gun itself or the man who had been standing next to it, had ever even existed. Except for all that jelly.

She wanted to vomit, she very much intended to lean out the crew door of the Jayhawk and heave her guts out. Instead she rolled back inside and got out of the way of her replacements.

Mael Mag Och had told her to find an army, but Marisol had refused her any living soldiers. Sarah had taken the next best option and recruited the mummies who had once watched over her father. The mummies from the Metropolitan Museum of Art in New York. When Ptolemy had called them forward, they had not hesitated.

Three mummies stepped into the rectangular crew door opening and pulled open the telescoping tubes of their M72 Light Antitank Weapons. In perfect unison the mummies lifted the tubes to their cheeks, selected targets, and let fly. Their rockets popped out of their tubes with a hollow sound, *fah-wuhp, fah-wuhp, fah-wuhp,* and twisted in midair as stabilizing fins popped out of their casings. Lying on a ballistic blanket on the floor of the helicopter, Sarah couldn't see where the rockets went. Each M72 held only one 66-millimeter rocket: in chorus the mummies dropped their tubes out of the crew door and then stepped back to let the third wave move into place.

The solid fuel in the rockets combusted entirely before the rockets left their tubes. The exhaust gases thus produced could reach 1400 degrees Fahrenheit. Sarah thought Ayaan had been right. She'd told Sarah many times that if you focused on the numbers and statistics and technical details, it helped you not think about what you were doing to human bodies.

Red jelly . . . Sarah shivered and pulled the hood of her sweatshirt over her head.

She moved forward to stand in the hatch to the crew compartment where her father sat next to Osman. Gary crouched on the floor behind her father's seat. He looked different somehow, but she couldn't place it. Maybe he had grown some—yes, his legs looked longer. Maybe her father was subconsciously working on him even in that moment. "Make a wide circle but let me see what we achieved," she told Osman, who simply nodded.

Through the crew door she studied the column of people living and dead. She saw that half the flatbed looked damaged and parts of it were definitely on fire. It was still moving. It should stop at any moment as the Tsarevich gave the signal to halt the column and take cover. That was basic military tactics—the longer he stayed out in the open, the longer she could dominate the engagement from the sky.

This was exactly what Sarah wanted. She wanted him to run for cover, because the best available cover was a narrow cut in the mountain about half a mile back down the road behind him. It would be impossible to attack that defile effectively from the air— the Tsarevich would make for it at once. Sarah had spent most of a day burying remotely detonated mines in the road surface there.

She was pretty proud of her strategy. It made a lot of logical sense. There was only one flaw in it.

"He hasn't changed course at all," she said out loud when five minutes had passed. That was more than enough time for a retreat order to go down the chain of command. The flatbed still crawled forward. The dead—and the living—still clustered in its wake. They were sitting ducks. She could pick them off at her leisure.

"Did he bring them all this way just so I could kill them?" she demanded.

"He doesn't seem the type to cry over casualties," Osman replied. She was glad somebody was talking to her. She looked back to the tail end of the crew compartment where Ptolemy stood waiting with a fresh SMAW for her. She chewed on her lip.

"He must know something I don't," she announced. She leaned out of the crew door and studied the column once again. One machine gun position remained on the flatbed, but nobody stood anywhere near it, nobody with hands. The living cultists down there had assault weapons, but she could easily stay out of their range. The Tsarevich's yurt was on fire. That was something. As she watched, however, a group of cultists with fire extinguishers blasted it with white foam.

"OK," she said, uncertain of what else to do. "Let's get ready for another attack." Even as she said it, though, she heard something. The noise of the helicopter drowned out almost every sound, but she heard another engine roaring, a gasoline engine. She looked down and saw an enormous truck gunning up the side of the road, looking like it might collide with the flatbed. It had flames painted on its doors and its exposed engine chugged madly.

Standing up in its cargo bed, a gorilla or maybe just a really hairy man lifted a long tube to his shoulder. Sarah recognized the rectangular plates mounted on its business end. It was a Stinger missile, an antiaircraft weapon.

The Tsarevich must have learned about repelling airborne attacks after the time Ayaan tried the same trick on him in Egypt. A pile of Stingers lay at the gorilla's feet.

"Dive!" she shouted, and Osman spun the helicopter into a banking descent so sharp she lost her footing and fell out of the crew door, her fall cut painfully short as her safety line snapped taut. "Osman!" she screamed, dangling in midair three feet below the Jayhawk's belly. "Osman!"

"I'm busy," he shouted back.

The gorilla discharged his weapon. A silver line of smoke shot out of its muzzle. Osman dipped the helicopter over to one side, but the Stinger was a guided missile and it was already locked on to the Jayhawk. As Sarah watched, it rolled over in mid-flight and gimbaled around to track the helicopter's exhaust.

Osman dropped the helicopter again and Sarah bounced madly on the end of her line. With hands like claws she grabbed again and again, trying to grab the cord. The green pointy tops of the fir trees below came rushing up at her but—but—yes—she had one hand on the cord. She managed to pull herself up a fraction of an inch before the rolling helicopter knocked her loose again.

She could hear the Stinger coming. It cut through the air with a high-pitched screech. Sarah grabbed the line with both hands and hauled herself up, her body flailing in the wind.

A dozen linen-wrapped hands reached down and grabbed her shoulders, her arms, her neck, even her ears. The mummies hauled her up and inside the helicopter moments before the belly of the Jay-hawk started hissing and rattling, smacking aside the higher treetops. Osman dropped them another two feet, and wood and pine needles exploded against the undercarriage. Everything smelled like sap.

Fifty yards behind them, the Stinger's stabilizing fins tangled up in a mangled larch. The missile exploded in a brilliant cloud of fire and dark smoke. Osman tapped his yoke and the helicopter lifted up, out of the trees again.

"All right, girl," he said in her earphones. "What in hell comes next?"

10.

SARAH COULDN'T THINK. She could barely breathe.

"What's our destination, girl?" Osman demanded in her ear. His voice sounded tinny and stretched out. It irritated her as if an insect had flown into her ear canal. She tried pulling off her head-phones, but without their protection the noise of the helicopter's rotor was deafening. It was like a buzz saw sawing through her sinus cavities. She hurried to pull the headphones back on her head.

She didn't know what to do next. Ayaan had taught her a lot about small-unit tactics. There had been lessons in stealth and camouflage and guerrilla warfare. None of it came back to her then as she sat down on the deck plates of the Jayhawk and stared at Gary.

He had grown. There was no mistaking it. The stubby little crab legs that had once supported his skull were now as long as Sarah's forearms. With her subtle vision she could see that the process was still going on. She watched it happen. He was drawing energy out of the Earth's biological field, using it to heal himself. He was drawing on the energy supply that Ptolemy had shown her, the Source, to rebuild his form—except it wasn't his human form he was re-creating. It was something new.

This close to the Source, energy permeated the air she breathed, it filled up the sky. She could almost see the Source itself, right through the fuselage of the helicopter. It was like a projection on top of her vision, a torrent, a shower of pure light and form that constantly erupted and burst and flashed across her. Her very own light show.

"Sarah," Osman said, at the same moment Ptolemy stepped forward and touched her arm.

sarah, the mummy said.

She stared up at him with wild eyes. "Help me," she said, "give me some advice. I'm, I'm drowning here. What do we do?"

our flying only machine advantage is this flying advantage machine, Ptolemy told her.

"We can't loiter forever," Osman said. She had spoken into her microphone and he had heard her, assumed she was talking to him. "We'll eventually have to set down."

we aloft must stay must aloft, the mummy said.

They were both right. Sarah remembered perfectly well when Ayaan had ordered Osman to set down back in Egypt. When she had ventured out on foot and immediately been overwhelmed by accelerated ghouls and the green lich who commanded them. Sarah had, herself, protested against a landing. She had said it was stupid. That it was suicide.

She had no choice. "Take us down, Osman," she said, her eyes fixed on Ptolemy's face. "Get us about a mile's clearance from that column and then find a clearing we can set down in."

Ptolemy did not chastise her. She'd made a decision, which was the main thing. They would go on foot from here. They really had little choice. The gorilla in the hot rod had a whole pile of Stingers ready to go. The one advantage Sarah had possessed, air superiority, had transformed into a liability.

It took a while for Osman to find an acceptable landing site. Even then it wasn't perfect—a rough hole in the trees where a limb of unbroken rock stuck up out of the side of the mountain. It had little cover and it provided no kind of access at all to the road. Had Sarah considered the possibility earlier, they could have brought rappelling gear and hot-roped down into a better spot. But she hadn't thought of that. She hadn't thought of any possible problems. Her plan had looked so good she'd forgotten to make sure she had a backup.

Ayaan would have slapped her, she thought, and rightly so.

The mummies jumped down from the crew hatch. She tossed them their guns from the weapon rack and slung her own over her shoulder. Before she left the aircraft, she turned around to look at Osman. He was frowning and drumming his fingers on the instrument panel as if he was counting down the seconds until he could lift off again.

Her father started pulling at his crash webbing and she shot him a nasty look. "You're staying here. Guard your freaky skull thing or whatever," she told him. Her anger over his trying to forbid her to undertake this mission had yet to subside.

"Sarah. Please. Just be safe," he pleaded with her. He kept trying to unbuckle his straps.

She leaned across him and pulled his chest straps tight. With a look of total dejection on his face he let his hands fall to his sides.

"I'll be as safe as I've ever been," she told him. "Which is not very. At least I have this," she said, brandishing her Makarov at him. "Your generation made sure we had plenty of these." Rage had pooled in her stomach. It started surging up her throat and she knew she was about to say something horrible. Her insecurities, her fear and her panic and her general misery were fueling a really colossal explosion and she knew she couldn't fight it back. What came out of her mouth was going to be fiery and acidic and mostly just cruel.

"Don't go," he begged. "As your last remaining parent I'm ask-ing you, please. Stay here."

She exploded. "My parent! My guardian! You can't get enough of this power trip, can you? Can you?" She stabbed one finger in the direction of Gary, who failed to move at all. "You've been his guardian for twelve years. You must have loved that."

"It was my sacred duty," he told her. His voice was very soft.

Almost soft enough to stop her. "Yeah, well, that's one fucked-up duty you have there. Spending twelve years alternately smashing and healing a dead human brain. Wow. Way to keep the eternal flame alive, there, Dad."

His face—what was left of it—fell. He understood instantly what she was saying. He'd always been a smart guy. Smart enough to think he knew what was best for everyone else.

Something changed inside her. A chemical reaction that froze her rage and turned her volcano of anguish into a glacier of pure hate. When she actually heard her voice she sounded cool and passion-less. "Ayaan was my parent," she told him. "You're just my father."

Osman's fingers on the panel drummed faster and faster. His agi-tation filled the cockpit like a bad smell. Sarah stepped backward once, and again, and her foot hit solid rock. She ducked down and gestured for the mummies to stand back as the helicopter lifted from the ground, its rotor beating thunderously at the air.

When it was gone Sarah was alone with the mummies. Ptolemy stood near her but facing slightly away. Ready to accept orders with-out expressly demanding anything. The others studied their weapons. She'd given them shotguns, M1014 military-grade shot-guns with gas-operated actions and short, blocky buttstocks. The mummies possessed a little more manual dexterity than garden-variety ghouls but their bandaged hands and desiccated eyes just weren't enough for precision firearms. The shotguns were a perfect balance between stopping power and ease of use.

She inspected them, her squad, before moving out. Six of them, the entire contingent that had once been on display in an art museum in New York. Two of them had painted faces like Ptolemy, though the renditions were pretty crude by comparison. The rest were truly ancient mummies, their tattered wrappings stained with bodily fluids and rotten with time. Here and there a length of withered forearm or a gruesomely dried-out glimpse of cheek poked through their unkempt linen.

Sarah picked one of these relics for point man and handed him a machete. He wasted no time, but moved steadily into the trees surrounding the landing zone, his arm flashing back and forth like a pendulum, his blade clearing out undergrowth, chopping through tree roots, splattering his bandages with thrown tree sap. The others clustered up tight behind him, with Sarah and Ptolemy taking the rear. It was hard work keeping up with him. They were on the side of a mountain, a rugged side that had never been developed, which might never have been touched before by human hands. Sarah's gloves tore and snagged every time she reached for a tree root to haul herself up, and her boots skidded on the precariously balanced talus of the slope. She started to sweat, even though the snow all around her reflected a cold sunlight that made her face sting. Her nose began to run and she was instantly miserable with having to snort up the snot or wipe it away with her sleeve every ten seconds. She tried to just let it run, but that was excruciating—every nerve ending in her face was red and raw with the mountain air.

In time—she could not have said how long it had been and in fact she wasn't wearing a watch, but it was still daylight—she reached up and found a piece of stable rock and pulled and dragged and cursed her way up until she was doubled over the top of a ridgeline, her legs on one side and her face on the other. She looked up and saw the mummies standing on the rocks like mountain goats or Sherpas or something. Between oxygen deprivation and sheer exhaustion she lacked the strength to curse them.

When she had stopped wheezing and was merely panting, when she had wiped the sweat out of her hair and shaken most of the pine needles out of her underwear, she saw that Ptolemy was pointing at something. She followed his linen-wrapped finger and nodded. The Source was beneath them, now, down in the hollow of a valley below. She blinked her eyes. Her arcane vision was almost dominant so close to the energy supply—it was hard to see things in normal, visible light.

When her eyes did clear, she found herself looking down into a modest bowl in the side of the mountain, a semicircular valley about a hundred and fifty feet straight down the side. There were a couple of buildings down there and some sculptures, their forms half-erased by wind and snow. The valley itself was full of human bones.

LL.

FIRE ERUPTED ALL around her. It touched the trees and filled the air with the stink of burning pitch, it ran in liquid waves over the snow and left smoldering ground behind. Ayaan dropped to her knees with her arms over her head as a second explosion tore into the roadway, a third, fire everywhere and the noise, a fourth, the noise was hammering at her, the air was jumping with it. She could see pine needles leaping up off the ground as if the entire planet had been picked up and given a good shake.

She rolled onto her back and slid down into a hollow, into a little space of snow where a boulder had sunk into the earth. She reached out her hands and pulled Nilla in after her. Nilla started to speak, but Ayaan shook her head no. She peered up, around the side of the boulder, and saw a helicopter hanging there in the air, close enough to touch, no, that was just her poor depth perception, the inability of her dead eyes to focus properly. The helicopter stood in the air over the flatbed, white and orange, and mummies leaned out of its crew hatch, mummies in the name of the Prophet mummies— *did they want revenge? Did they seek revenge for the forty-nine mummies she had killed on Cyprus?* she wondered—and then there were more explosions, brilliant flowers spreading overhead, fire and smoke.

Her brain rattled in her skull like an animal trying to get loose.

She pulled her arms in close to her body, brought her chin down. Made herself small. Nilla's dress was stained, ruined, and they were both soaked in snowmelt and splattered with cinders, some of them still on fire. Ayaan brushed at the embers on her jacket, ran her fingers through her hair to shake them loose. The helicopter just hung there in the air. Rifles started firing back from the ground, living cultists with rifles shooting at the helicopter, but its pilot knew enough to stay out of range. Where were the machine guns? She had inspected the .50 caliber machine guns on the flatbed herself, had stripped and cleaned them on the long trek when she had been glad for anything to do, anything to break the boredom. Where were they, why weren't they firing back? They had plenty of range.

The helicopter assault must have targeted them. Smart. Nilla started climbing up, clambering up the side of the boulder, but Ayaan pulled her back down. They were only ten feet or so from the roadway, the column. Even if the mummies didn't get them the column might, it had to turn around. It was the only logical move. The column had to turn around.

Where was Erasmus? Where was the truck? She hadn't seen it in days, it had been sent on some special errand, but they needed it now. The column had to turn around. There had been a narrow defile in the side of the mountain maybe a quarter mile back, it wouldn't be easy but the column had to turn around and head for the relative safety of the rock walls. Where was Erasmus? The column could move a lot faster, could get turned around a lot faster with the truck, the straggling cultists could clamber up onto its cargo bed, they could hang on to the outside of the truck.

The Tsarevich wasn't turning the column. The column was still plodding forward, cracking maybe three miles an hour as if there had been no attack, staying its course as if nothing had happened at all.

Another explosion tore through the thin air. Debris and metal fragments like flying daggers and body parts, human body parts and it didn't matter if they'd been alive or dead or undead, human bones and flesh went flying over Ayaan's head like a horizontal rain of gore.

Where was the fucking truck? She heard it before she saw it, saw it only moments before it went roaring right over her head, its wheels barely gripping the road. Mud and cinders poured down into her defile, splashed against the boulder. The truck roared past—and then she heard the distinctive fizzle and bark of an antiaircraft missile jumping out of its launcher and she saw the rocket's exhaust, a thin banner of white wind superimposed on the blue sky. She opened her mouth wide in exultation, in excitement, and whooped with joy as the missile bent like a perfectly hit football in the air, bent right for the fleeing helicopter. Something fell out of the side of the helicopter as it banked to try to throw off the pursuit. Something fell out and dangled there on a line like a spider.

It was Sarah.

Ayaan was too far away and the helicopter was moving too fast for her to really get a good look. She didn't use her eyes, though. She sensed the energy there, as familiar as the hairs on the back of her own arm, an energy she'd lived with for years, since long before she had understood that such energy existed and could be felt with the right senses. She knew that energy.

It was Sarah.

The whoop died in her throat and she grabbed at her teeth, literally reached into her mouth and grabbed her own lower jaw in terror. At any moment the AA missile was going to collide with the helicopter's airframe, it was going to plow right through the tender aluminum skin of the helicopter, lodge itself inside and then go off, detonate, its high explosive warhead would burst apart in a million tiny jagged pieces of shrapnel, each with its own trajectory, its own ballistic intent, and there would be enough of them to cut every person in the helicopter to shreds. There would be nothing left but pieces, parcels of flesh raggedly torn apart and bleeding and unrecognizable.

"Sarah," Ayaan croaked.

"That's Sarah?" Nilla asked, her face wide with confusion.

Ayaan got her feet under her and she climbed back out of the defile, back up onto the roadway. The helicopter had dipped down into the trees and the AA missile followed. Ayaan's chest lurched and a horrible belch came out of her, stinking of dead things. The missile touched the tree line and exploded harmlessly well behind the fleeing helicopter.

OK. Sarah was safe. Ayaan didn't breathe a sigh of relief. She no longer breathed. But her body sagged. Relaxed a little. OK.

Except—if Sarah was attacking the Tsarevich, then—then—Sarah was—Sarah had chosen to become—Sarah had unwittingly aligned herself against—against Ayaan, who had—in some non-committal way—sided with the Russian lich.

She had it an instant later but it didn't help. Sarah had to know, had somehow learned that Ayaan was now a lich herself. Sarah had attacked specifically with the intent of sanitizing Ayaan. Except she had missed.

And except for the fact that Ayaan didn't want to be sanitized. She had always believed that when the moment came she would beg for the bullet in the head. Kneel in the dirt and grovel for it. Only now—now she had something to live for, something bigger than herself. The Tsarevich was going to rebuild the world. Ayaan wanted to help him.

Sarah was fighting against them.

"For Christ's sake, woman, help me," someone screeched behind her. Ayaan turned and saw the green phantom literally, physically pulling ghouls and living cultists toward the flatbed, pushing them toward the fires there. They grabbed up armfuls of snow and tossed them on the flames. A few had real fire extinguishers and were trying to save the yurt. They moved faster than the others, faster than human beings were supposed to move. The green phantom was accelerating them. Ayaan glanced forward, at the machine gun mounts. One of them was gone altogether. A crater in the side of the flatbed was all that remained. Molten metal had dripped over the side of the bed and formed long silver icicles.

The other machine gun was on fire. Its ammunition crates were right there. If they went up, if they got too hot, every round in those crates—thousands of bullets—would go off at once, firing in random directions, carving out bloody linear tracks through the living and the dead on the flatbed, all of the cultists clustered around it, everyone in range. Ayaan surged forward and was repulsed by a wave of fire that tore upward on a gust of wind. She moved forward again and saw that the crates were already on fire. She had a split second before she was shot full of random holes. Without even thinking she gathered up energy and blasted the crates with her power.

Stupid—incredibly foolish—but it worked. Fire couldn't exist without fuel. The wooden crates disintegrated under her blast, the wood darkening, turning gray, turning to dust. Long belts of ammunition slithered out and slunk away across the flatbed or over the edge. It didn't matter—the fire was out.

Ayaan adjusted her footing as the flatbed went over a dip in the road surface. It was still moving. She shook her head and then she grabbed the green phantom's arm. "We have to stop the column," she shouted at him. He didn't respond fast enough for her. "Let me in to see the Tsarevich. Let me talk to him."

"Who are you?" he demanded. "A month ago I punished you for trying to kill my master. Now you want to be his ally?"

She didn't have time for this. "I do what I think is best."

He crossed his arms across his robe. "A dangerous policy in the best of times. You can't see him. He's already given me his orders and they are that the column must keep moving, at all costs."

"There could be another attack—if it were me I would have an ambush waiting for us up ahead. Come on. I know you don't trust me. You called me a dog once, a dog that had to be kept on a short leash. But trust me now. Please. So much is at stake."

He shook his skull-like head. "I have my instructions. Why don't you go and find Nilla? Make sure she's safe."

Ayaan grunted in frustration and turned away from him. The green phantom was willing to give her something, though.

"My name is Enni Langstrom," he said.

She turned around. He was squinting at her, his sunken eyes narrow, suspicious slits.

"My name *was* Enni Langstrom. All right? I trust you enough to know my name."

She nodded, understanding. He wanted her to feel like part of the Tsarevich's inner circle. He wanted to reward her allegiance. She was in.

Now she just needed to figure out where Sarah fit in. *Please,* she thought. *Please, Sarah, just give up. Go home.* She stared out at the trees that blanketed the mountain. Sarah had to be out there somewhere. *Please, don't make me fight you.*

Ayaan had always been willing to sacrifice her life for a true cause. She had always believed that one life was a small price to pay for the common good.

If it came to that, to firing a blast of her darkness into Sarah's body. If doing that meant preserving the Tsarevich and therefore the only chance the human race had left. If it came to that.

She nodded to herself. She would do it.

12.

THE VALLEY FORMED a shallow bowl with a low ridge at the far end. There were buildings up there and the weathered statues Sarah had seen before. They looked like simplified animals from the bottom of the valley.

Dead men and women stood at the edge of the valley. Not many—only three or four. They weren't doing anything. Just standing there. The closest of the standing ghouls—a really nasty-looking guy with little skin left on his body and no arms at all—turned to glare at her with empty eye sockets, but he didn't take a step toward her. After a moment he turned his face back toward the source and his toothless jaw fell open. He wasn't doing a thing. None of the corpses in the valley were doing anything, but then most of them were truly, finally dead. One motionless body lay not three feet from where Sarah first stepped down into the valley.

A human body, half-decomposed, and it wasn't even twitching. It had been a long time since Sarah had seen that. She nudged it with the toe of her boot. She could see yellow ribs sticking out under its coat. She could see where the flesh had been torn away by teeth.

Nothing. No movement.

Squinting, she adjusted her grip on her OICW and glanced over her shoulder. The mummies waited patiently behind her, their shotgun barrels pointed at the sky. Ptolemy stood to one side of them. He shook his painted head back and forth—he had no better idea what was going on than she did.

Directly ahead, the valley was carpeted with bones and moldering bodies. None of them moved. Skulls stared up at random angles at a lifeless sky. Femurs and humeri stuck up like fence posts. Heaps of pelvises and spines and xyphoid processes and metacarpals and phalanges made narrow hummocks, obscuring the soil beneath. Thousands of people had died in this valley, or at least died somewhere else and come here to fall down. No one had buried them or done anything with their corpses. They had been allowed to just rot away.

The freshest ones formed a perimeter, a wide semicircle of stinking carrion. Toward the middle, where the ground began to rise, the bones were the oldest, broken and beige with time and neglect. No plants grew there, no birds flew overhead.

Sarah figured it had to be the Source that drew the bodies to this place. It was so bright she had to shade her eyes when she turned to face it, so close she could feel its energy like warmth on her skin. The dead had come for years, pilgrims to the place where the Epidemic began.

Sarah stepped over the corpse. It took a real act of will. For all of her life, at least all of her life that she could remember, rule one had been to never turn your back on a dead body. It was how you got killed. This one wasn't hurting anybody, though. She stepped over it and dug her boot through a pile of bones to touch the ground beyond. She took another step, careful not to put any weight on the carpet of bones. Nothing happened.

Did the dead come so far just to stand around, to wait to fall to pieces? Did they come because it felt good to be surrounded by that energy? Did it nourish them? Sarah had a lot of questions. What was that smell?

She turned and saw that one of the mummies had followed her into the bones. He stood there motionless, as still as a statue, his shotgun braced on his shoulder. She sniffed the air. He smelled like warm apple pie. Sarah tried to remember when she'd ever had the chance to smell a piece of apple pie. Maybe with her father, before the Epidemic. Her father—just thinking of him sent a jagged length of metallic guilt stabbing through her heart. What she'd said to him had been unacceptable.

Burning apple pie. Apple pie? Maybe pumpkin pie. Hot spices. Burning spices. A trickle of white smoke wafted out from the mummy's chest. With a hissing sound a piece of the wrappings on his head fluttered open and more smoke came out. The smoke smelled pungent, like incense. Like burning spice.

No way, she thought. "Back!" she shouted. The mummy didn't move. "Get back!" she said and shoved him backward. She slapped at his pectorals and at his forehead, and he rocked away from her as if there was no volition at all in his body. She grabbed the soapstone scarab in her pocket. "Ptolemy. Don't let them come any closer."

warms it the source consumes us it consumes even warms as it warms consumes us, he sputtered.

"Just stay back!" Even as she said it, though, another of the mummies—one with a poorly painted face—stepped forward. They wanted it. They wanted to be closer to the Source. It drew them just as it must have been drawing ghouls for years. And when they got close enough, when the energy in the air was thick enough, their bodies literally burned out from overexposure. The one thing they wanted more than anything in the world would kill them if they got too much of it. There was a sort of line, an invisible, fuzzy boundary beyond which no dead thing could cross without being burned to a crisp. It was like the event horizon of a black hole. The point of no return.

A flash of motion on the far side of the valley startled Sarah. She flicked off the safety of her weapon, but nothing appeared to attack her. It could have just been the sunlight bouncing off snow or a pile of bones falling over in the breeze. It could have been lots of things. She glanced back at the mummies and saw that they had all taken a step closer to the Source.

"No, listen to me," she said, and moved to push the nearest one back. "You guys don't even eat living things. How can you want this so badly?"

source . . . source, Ptolemy told her.

She shook her head. She heard a sound, like the noise a match makes when it bursts into flame. She turned around again, her weapon up and ready.

A human form made of pure flame was running right at her, faster than a cheetah. It came out of the middle of the valley. Flames licked backward from its face, its chest. Its hands were wreathed in yellow fire.

Sarah brought up her OICW and fired a three-shot burst. She caught her target in center mass but it didn't even slow down. Barreling toward her, it left a smear of light on her retinas, it was so bright. She fired again at its head, one burst, two, three, the rifle making a mechanical sound, a machine-shop sound as it pumped bullets through its mechanism. She hit the head but nothing happened. She switched her rifle to full auto in the same second it shot past her, its fiery tail whipping at her exposed face and hands.

Ptolemy brought up his shotgun and blasted the back of its knees as it ran past him. The fiery thing stumbled and fell and rolled forward for a while, sliding over the carpet of bones. It writhed horribly, the flames off its back gusting and snapping, its bodily fluids sizzling out of it. Now that it had come to something approaching a stop, Sarah saw the motorcycle helmet on its head, the bare teeth where its lips had been cut away. Its hands were nothing but sharpened ends of bone.

The Tsarevich had arrived. On the far side of the valley dead men and women were lining up to get into the bowl, to press closer to the Source. The giant truck weaved through the crowd, the gorilla perched on top of its cab.

Sarah grabbed the nearest mummy and tried to pull him away. It was like tugging at a marble column. She let go and reached for the soapstone.

"Ptolemy," she said, "we're dead if we get caught in the open like this. We have to fall back and hide."

source . . . the source

"Fuck the Source!" she shouted. "Fall back! That's an order!"

One of the mummies—one of the extremely old ones—started to move. He took a step away from the Source. Sarah nodded and shouted and jumped up and down. He took another step.

On the other end of the valley the flatbed appeared, hauled forward by a hundred ghouls. On its back stood three figures dressed in green, black, and white. Sarah stared at the one dressed in black. It was Ayaan. She was too far to see, it should have been impossible. But she knew. She lifted the OICW to her shoulder and looked through the scope. Yeah. The skin around her lower jaw looked too tight and her eyes were dark pits sunk into her face. But it was Ayaan.

In a moment, in a space of time so short she didn't breathe, the valley was full of the running dead.

13.

SARAH AND THE mummies fell back to fighting positions. They grabbed cover, braced themselves for battle. Readied their weapons, laid out their spare ammunition. Prepared themselves for a guts-and-glory firefight.

They didn't stand a chance.

The mummies were fast. Faster than any living human. The carried plenty of ammunition for their shotguns. It didn't matter. The accelerated ghouls were faster.

Sarah had watched her ambush turn into a rout without really being able to identify the turning point. She only knew she had fucked up. With the mummies crouched behind boulders, with herself on a high crest of rock trying to snipe the enemy with an assault rifle, she knew it was going to end badly.

One by one the mummies were picked off. The younger ones, the Roman-era mummies with painted faces, went first. One of them was stupid enough to run out into the denied zone, the region too close to the Source, where the undead caught fire. He was smoldering before three of the accelerated corpses piled on top of him. All four of them caught flame at once, a rolling, scrapping funeral pyre. The mummy's arms pinwheeled as he tried to throw the ghouls off of him. He was slowing down as Sarah watched, however, and in a moment he had stopped moving altogether.

The other painted mummy had a little more sense, but less luck. He moved steadily from rock to rock, picking off ghouls and then diving back into cover. In the end it wasn't a ghoul that got him at all but something else, some weird magic that turned his linen yellow. His wrappings began to tatter as if they were torn at by hurricane-level winds, and then his bones just seemed to give out and he collapsed in a heap.

Rifle fire picked off one of the older mummies. He had been smart enough to stay put and wait for the ghouls to come to him. Hunkered down between two rocks, he kept the barrel of his M1014 high, ready to take opportunistic shots. He was severely outranged, however, by a cultist with a Dragunov sniper rifle. Through the scope of her OICW Sarah saw the sniper line up the perfect bead. He took his shot before she had time to even shout out a warning. The mummy's head popped open like a bag full of meat.

The rest of the mummies died when the Tsarevich decided to stop playing games and sent his whole force into the valley, hundreds of ghouls, at least a hundred living men and women with assault rifles and pistols and machine guns. The enemy just tore her troops to pieces. What had been a battle of attrition turned into a plain old-fashioned defeat as bodies living and dead flung themselves at Sarah's positions. Ptolemy threw away his weapon and threw himself into the melee, grabbing at ghouls and hurling them into the denied zone, turning around to kick in the faces of living zealots, moving so fast Sarah saw him as an off-white blur digging into the enemy's ranks. Then he disappeared.

He was there one moment and gone the next. "*Magic,*" she breathed, but no. She would have seen magic. He had simply been tackled by so many of the Tsarevich's forces that she couldn't see him anymore.

There was no more time.

So this is it, she told herself. *The moment of truth.* The mummies had sacrificed themselves so she could get close enough to finish her mission. Seven mummies had died for this. Two liches. Marisol's son. All so she could fire a single shot. Sarah lifted the OICW to her lips and kissed it. She needed luck. She had the determination.

She looked down from her perch and saw Ayaan standing in the midst of the dead and the living. She was wearing a leather jacket with skulls on it, but she didn't have her AK-47 anymore. Sarah lifted the scope of her weapon to her eye and centered the crosshairs on Ayaan's forehead. It was a duty, a sacred duty that she carried out. The shot would give away her position. She would have only moments after she killed Ayaan to get the barrel in her own mouth and destroy her own brain. But then it would be over. A cold, almost frozen calm came over her. She slipped off the safety. Just one shot. She just needed . . . she needed something. One shot, right, she just needed one shot.

Sarah blinked, but it just made her vision blur. She licked her lips but her tongue was dry. Was she . . . was she afraid? She just needed the one . . . the one shot. Silence filled her head—she couldn't hear anything.

The OICW clattered against the slickrock at her feet. Somehow it had fallen out of her hands. She shook her head and reached for the Makarov in her pocket. It felt as heavy as a rock, as a—a boulder. Why was she so tired suddenly? Sarah sat down, hard, and closed her eyes. She couldn't open them again no matter how determined she was. What was going on?

Oh, she thought. This time, yeah. It was. *Magic.*

She felt hands grab at her, rough hands. Someone went through her pockets while someone else took the green sword away from her, tearing it off her belt. They pinched her around the thigh, around the upper arm. Someone was dragging her, she could feel the top of her head sliding along the rock. She couldn't hear anything, she was deaf. Her hands were pulled in front of her and encircled with a length of rope. She was being tied up.

Instantly her energy returned. Her eyes shot open and she could hear again—every ragged breath, every beat of her own heart. She turned her head wildly to the side to see what was behind her, what was flanking her. She was kneeling on a pile of bones. Somebody else's bones were digging into her shins, her knees. She rolled around, trying to get comfortable. She couldn't see Ayaan. The green lich—the one in the monk's robe, the one whose face looked like a skull—was standing next to her. He pointed, his arm stretched out, one bony finger stabbing at the air, and she looked.

They had beaten Ptolemy to a pulp. His legs were splayed wide open and bent at wrong angles. His arms were broken in a dozen places. Men in light blue paper shirts stood around him, sledgehammers balanced on their shoulders. A girl maybe two years younger than Sarah was bent over him with a pair of scissors. She cut right through his painted face, cut away at the plaster at his neck. She tore open his linen and exposed his head.

His skull was the brown color of a brazil nut. Papery skin covered the round back of his head while bits of withered flesh clung to his cheeks and throat. His lips had drawn so tightly over his teeth that they looked scalloped. His eyes were closed, sewn shut, two dashes sunk deep in their sockets.

Sarah could just reach the soapstone in her pocket, just touch it with the tip of her pinkie. It was enough.

one here of mine is here mine, he told her. **her save her**

Sarah shook badly, her body vibrating like a milkweed plant in the wind.

One of the blue-shirted men held Ptolemy's head down against the rock. The other brought up his hammer and brought it down hard, made it clang against the ground as Ptolemy's skull burst into fragments that spun for a moment on the slickrock and then fell down and were still.

The green phantom grabbed Sarah's collar and dragged her to her feet. "Walk," he told her. No threats, no promises. Just walk. She stumbled forward, her legs weak. She passed through a gauntlet of cut-down ghouls and wild-eyed cultists, but none of them moved toward her, none of them spat at her or shrieked names at her. Her own eyes were very wide and dry. They itched. The green lich marched her right up to the flatbed. There had been no attempt made to repair the damage she'd done to it. Sarah tried to gloat about that, to exult in how badly she'd hurt the Tsarevich. The message she was being sent, however, was to the contrary. She hadn't even slowed him down.

She swallowed convulsively. Acid was boiling in her throat but she refused to vomit. She was led up to the side of the flatbed and then she was told to stop. She did so. She shoved her hands in her pockets. The Makarov was gone.

The green lich jumped up on the flatbed and leaned his face inside the yurt. He nodded a couple of times—he must have been discussing her fate with the yurt's occupant. He jumped back down and gestured at a living woman. She came over and handed him something. A Russian pistol. Her own pistol.

No undead creature could fire a handgun—it was an axiom of Sarah's existence. They just didn't have the eye-hand coordination. Their nervous systems didn't work properly. They couldn't run and they couldn't shoot. Then again, she'd seen plenty of them run.

The green lich shoved his finger through the trigger guard, then used his free hand to mold his fingers around the grip. Then he shoved the barrel against her chest. He smiled down at her and slid the handgun a little to the left.

"Wait," Sarah said. "Just let me see Ayaan first."

He fired. At point-blank range he couldn't miss. There was a lot of noise, though Sarah's ears blocked most of it out. There was some light but she blinked as the gun went off—just a reflex action. Her body tensed and curled around the impact, her muscles and skin and sinews convulsing inward as she fell backward, flat on her back, and hit the ground. Blood splashed up across her face, fell wet across her chest, her legs. She could feel it pooling around her, soaking into her clothes and her hair. She couldn't breathe, which wasn't really a problem at first but she was dully aware that it would become important in a few seconds.

She brought her knees up, her body wanted to double up. Death was on its way, mere seconds off. The world got darker and louder, she could hear screaming but it wasn't her own, the screaming got louder. And louder. She felt something tugging in her chest. It jerked and ripped and tore at her like a bird eating her guts but higher, near her heart. She opened her eyes and looked down.

The bullet edged backward out of the wound as if it were being pushed out from inside. She could see the striations on its surface, the rifling marks. It hurt a lot more going out than it had coming in. Pain wracked her body and suddenly it was her screaming, she could hear her own screams again. The bullet fell out of her and rolled down onto the bloody slickrock. She sat up and screamed and screamed. The green lich stared at her with genuine curiosity.

Was she . . . dead? Undead? No. She was breathing. The dead didn't breathe. She was still alive. She was still, somehow, alive. Her chest was full of blood, her lungs congested with it, but she could talk, kind of. "Dad," she wheezed. "Daddy."

14.

"SHE'S GOT SOME charm against bullets," the green phantom said. Enni Langstrom. That was what he was called. Ayaan was still trying to get used to the name. "When we have a chance we'll get a bathtub and see if she can breathe underwater, too." He was dragging Sarah along behind him, literally pulling her through the dirt.

Ayaan ran a hand over her chin. "Enni," she said. "Let's give her an opportunity. Let's allow her to join us, if she will."

"She tried to kill the Tsarevich," he told her. Sarah's head rolled to one side and she vomited blood all over the hem of his robe. "Stupid bitch," he snarled. He kicked her in the ribs until she was coughing blood all over herself.

Ayaan rushed forward and knelt down by Sarah's side. "Enni," she said, "the first time you saw me, I was trying to kill you. Look how that worked out."

She had been willing to kill Sarah. She had convinced herself that if it meant saving the Tsarevich—and humanity's last hope—she would kill Sarah herself. But now it wasn't necessary. Sarah no longer had the means to hurt anyone. Surely—surely a little mercy was in order. She wiped Sarah's mouth with her hand and lifted her head a little to make it easier for the girl to breathe.

"Ayaan," Sarah said, her eyes wide, so wide. "Ayaan, you're an abomination."

Ayaan just nodded.

"If you want her so badly, take her. If she causes trouble you'll both be executed." Enni shook his skull-like head and stormed away. "I have work to oversee," he shouted back over his shoulder.

She lifted Sarah up to a sitting posture. "Listen," she said, but Sarah interrupted her.

"I was hoping I would find you were a prisoner here," the girl said. Her eyes were very hard. "I assumed you wouldn't willingly let them turn you into a lich."

"It wasn't my choice." Ayaan shook her head. "Sarah, just listen.

They'll kill you. I don't care what kind of magic you've found, they'll find a way to get around it. You only have one chance to survive."

"Ayaan never worried so much about survival," Sarah said. "I don't know who you are. I know who you serve, though."

Ayaan closed her eyes and said a brief prayer. "'He is Sublime,'" she recited, "'the Tremendous.' I thought as you did originally. Now I've come to understand. The world is in bad shape, Sarah. There are fewer living people every day, and more of the walking dead. I used to think there was one answer to that problem: shoot them all. Now I know better. Somebody has to rebuild this planet."

Sarah licked her lips. "The Tsarevich. You really want to live in the world he wants to make?"

"Yes," Ayaan said, without hesitation. "Because I've seen the alternative. Come on. You have to stand up. I can't carry you." She helped Sarah up to her feet. The girl looked pale and weak, but she didn't collapse. Was that just the result of good training? Had Ayaan taught Sarah how to be tough? Or maybe the girl's magic was just that strong.

Magic. Ayaan's world had always been predicated on the idea that magic was dangerous at best and a sure route to damnation. Now she was a magical being herself. She wouldn't admit that Sarah's anger had shaken her faith in the righteousness of her path, but she knew it, consciously.

"Just be quiet. You can achieve nothing by talking now," Ayaan said, letting Sarah lean against her.

"When they decide to kill me, will it be you who blows my brains out?" Sarah asked. "Or will you let them cut off my hands and my lips and make me one of their soldiers?"

There were worse fates. Ayaan said nothing.

She led Sarah deeper into the encampment, into the throng of cultists who were busy preparing for the Tsarevich's great moment. The living and the dead were busy unloading several crates of equipment from the back of the flatbed. Others labored at assembling strange contraptions Ayaan could not recognize. A narrow scaffolding made of aluminum poles was already rising from the carpet of bones, far closer to the Source than Ayaan thought safe. A work crew was putting together what looked like a giant metal coil as thick as her arm while others tested vacuum tubes and then fit them together in various metal cabinets. It looked as if they were preparing for a rock concert.

The crowd parted as a long wooden crate was brought forward. A cultist with a crowbar bent to open the crate and reveal a pair of metal spikes, each of them ten feet long and wickedly curved. Their tips looked sharper than ice picks.

Erasmus waved at Ayaan and walked over to stand next to her. "It won't be much longer," he said. "Wow, did you ever really think we'd make it this far?"

"Yes," Ayaan said. "I believed. This is Sarah, by the way."

"Uh. Yeah. Hi." The cheerful werewolf didn't seem to know how to talk to the girl. He looked instead at the two metal spikes. "Nice to meet you, I guess."

"It isn't mutual," Sarah spat, but Erasmus was unwilling to take the bait.

"I think I see how this works," Ayaan said as the work crew bolted one of the long spars to either side of the scaffolding. "The Tsarevich will climb up there and grasp either of these extrusions with one of his hands. The energy will then flow through him like an electrical current."

"Yeah, kinda," Erasmus said. He scratched at his face with his inch-long fingernails. "Look, Nilla's ready to go."

Ayaan looked where he pointed. The blond lich was moving steadily toward the Source. Two female cultists—living women—followed behind her. Each of them carried a spool of wire which she unwound as she walked. The loose ends of wire connected to the scaffolding.

As Nilla approached the zone of exclusion, where any undead thing would catch on fire, Ayaan wanted to rush forward and drag her back. Erasmus knew better, however. "It's OK. This is why we needed her so much. You'll see. Nilla is the only one who can actually go to the Source. As far as we know she's the only dead person ever to get close enough to touch it."

"And she will take those wires and connect them to it?" Ayaan asked. She'd never been very good with electronics.

"Yeah, although on their own they don't do anything. She needs to act as a conduit for the life force. A transformer, I guess—she can take the power of the Source and feed it to the Tsarevich out here as healing energy."

Nilla vanished without fanfare as she crossed the event horizon. She just turned invisible. The female cultists in her train looked frightened for a moment, but they must have been warned of what would happen, because they kept walking.

"He's coming," someone said in Russian. "He is ready," someone else shouted. Some of the cultists dropped to their knees as the flap of the yurt was drawn back. The ghouls kept working—they didn't even look up.

A young girl, maybe twelve years old, stepped out of the yurt. Her head had been shaved and she had a fresh cut on her cheek. She wore a silk dress stained with blood in a couple of places. Ayaan barely recognized her at first but slowly her brain worked it out. It was Patience, the girl she had taken away from the farm in Pennsylvania. By the look of things she was the new Cicatrix.

A hand appeared out of the darkness of the yurt. A length of twisted forearm. The Tsarevich hauled himself forward, pushing his misshapen skull out into the light. He couldn't walk. His legs were two different lengths—his left was nearly a foot longer than his right—but clearly he intended to emerge under his own power. Inch by inch his deformed flesh hauled itself out of the yurt.

The green phantom waited at the side of the flatbed with a shiny metal shopping cart. The Tsarevich lurched forward and slid down into it, his off-center hips jamming down into the metal basket. His shorter arm reached forward and his fingers wove through the bars while his longer arm draped over the side of the cart and nearly dragged his knuckles in the dirt. The green phantom pushed him forward with visible effort toward the scaffolding.

"What's that?" someone said, and Ayaan assumed they'd never seen the Tsarevich before. She almost laughed. She had been holding her breath—except that she had no breath to hold. Her chest had locked into rigor with anticipation. "No, seriously," the voice called again, and she turned to see who had broken the tension. "What is that?"

She looked—everyone looked—and saw someone walking toward them from the far side of the valley. A dead person, clearly, because his face was a bare skull. There were scraps of skin adhering to the bone and a pair of prominent eyes in the sockets, and a wispy lock of hair or two. The figure was perhaps six feet tall and extremely thin—except for the skull its entire body was wrapped up in a heavy olive drab blanket.

It didn't really have any feet, though. Sharp-looking ends of bone stuck out of the bottom of the blanket. Instead of walking forward it scuttled, kind of like a crab.

"Dad," Sarah breathed. But the figure wasn't Dekalb—it couldn't be.

"Get a sniper over here," Ayaan shouted, but it was too late. A female cultist in a paper smock approached the strange figure. She had a pistol in either hand and she raised them to shoulder height. She demanded that the creature stop at once. "Come on, we need a fire team!" Ayaan yelled. She half turned to relay her instructions to Erasmus, but that would mean taking her eyes off this new enemy.

The woman with the pistols opened fire, her handguns barking like angry dogs. Bullets tore into the green blanket and spun the stranger around in a circle. It fell over not like a human being falling to the ground but like a camera tripod being knocked over. And then it got back up.

The blanket whirled open and away. The creature had no body, only six enormous jointed legs of yellow bone that flashed out like the fingers of a giant hand. Two of them snapped outward and neatly impaled the living woman. They flicked in different directions and she came apart in pieces.

Screaming and shouting and general alarm rolled around the encampment. Cultists and ghouls rushed to the attack. Snipers climbed up into the rocks surrounding the valley while a team of rifles rushed forward to kneel in the dirt before the Tsarevich, protecting him.

Someone brought out a machine gun, a crew-served RPK-74, which looked like a big AK-47 with a reinforced stock. A teenage boy fed the long curving magazines into the weapon as its operator lay prone on the ground, angling the barrel up on its tripod. The operator tore through an entire magazine of forty-five rounds in a few seconds.

The monster took another step forward and fell on its face, three of its legs crumpling beneath it. Chips of bone fell from its body. One of its eyes burst and jelly dripped out of the socket like ugly tears. Ayaan closed her mouth. It had been gaping open. The thing was dead. Its skull had been punctured in a dozen places.

Somebody cheered.

Then the monster stood back up. A new eye opened in the empty socket. Its broken legs fused themselves back together. If anything the beast looked bigger—it looked like it was ten feet tall. It surged forward fast enough to impale half a dozen ghouls. Around Ayaan the living began to panic. They ran in every possible direction, some of them throwing away their weapons. Disorganized and panicked, they posed no threat to the monster. It came right toward Ayaan. It came right for her.

"Who . . ." she wondered out loud. Except she already knew. "Who is it?"

"Gary," Sarah gloated, her face parted by a broad and exultant smile. "It's fucking Gary, that's who!"

15.

GARY SWEPT THROUGH the crowd, slashing cultists, disemboweling them, stabbing them in their throats. He was vicious and completely remorseless. He seemed to have no plan, just an insatiable need to kill. Someone hit him with a grenade and he fell down on one knee—then rose again unharmed. Twelve new barbed spines emerged from under the bottom of his skull. They shot out like pistons and skewered the heads of ghouls, right through their helmets.

"He gets stronger every time you shoot him," Sarah said. She had told her father Gary's secret in an attempt to break his heart. Instead he had turned it—turned Gary—into a weapon of mass destruction. Maybe she'd been wrong about him. Maybe Dekalb had more strength than she'd thought. "It's all over, Ayaan. It's all over."

Ayaan sucked on her lower lip. Sarah watched the woman who had been her mentor. If you just glanced at her she looked the same as ever—she was still Ayaan—yet if you took a closer look it was unmistakable. She was a corpse now. You could see the way her skin was tightening in her face. You could see it in how much weight she'd lost—she was half the size she used to be. Or maybe it just seemed that way. In life Ayaan had been a towering figure to Sarah. She supposed everyone's parents were like that. In death she was just one more ghoul.

"Stay here," Ayaan told her, and started hobbling away toward the yurt. Was she going to protect the Tsarevich? Sarah could hardly believe it. They'd done it. They had broken Ayaan, broken her mind. Such a thing shouldn't have been possible. Yet Ayaan herself had frequently warned Sarah that humanity was a liability. Sarah remembered perfectly what Ayaan had said around the campfire one night when Sarah was sixteen years old. "None of us," she said, "is immune to death or madness. The time may come when you have to sanitize me. You may have to shoot me because

I've panicked so badly I threaten the squad. None of you may hesitate, when that moment comes."

Now she seemed to have changed her tune. Was she really a believer? Did she really believe in the Tsarevich, like the two liches Sarah had already killed? Or was she just afraid of death, like her father had been, and Gary before him?

Speaking of the devil—Sarah looked up to see Gary whirling through the Tsarevich's army like a top. He was under sustained gunfire and his skull had taken on a patchy and mottled appearance—he was being healed as fast as he was being injured, but the process wasn't perfect. Sarah just didn't know how long it could be kept up. She knew her father was doing it. She knew he had to be somewhere nearby. Gary's legs flexed and sharp fragments of bone jutted out of him, covered him in vicious spikes. He tore through a machine gun position and the weapon's wooden stock shivered into pieces. The gunners were thrown away like crumpled bits of paper.

Sarah suddenly realized she'd been left alone. Ayaan and the werewolf had both abandoned her. Well, they had more serious problems. Sarah's hands were tied so securely there wasn't much she could do, anyway.

Or maybe there was. She turned around in place, taking in the frenetic energy of the camp, the people running in every direction, the ghouls taking up defensive formations. She found what she wanted and headed toward it at a run. A single mummy, standing alone at the back of the valley next to a big rock formation. It—she—held a jar in her hands with something round and murky inside.

"I was sent by Ptolemaeus Canopus," she said, skidding to a stop in the dirt. "Are you all right? We need to work together if we're going to get out of here."

The mummy didn't move. The thing in the jar didn't move, either, but she could feel a haze of dark energy wafting off of it. It was desperately trying to get her attention. She looked down, through the glass, and saw a human brain there. Nasty, but hardly the worst thing she'd ever seen.

Behind her she heard a prolonged scream and she turned to look. Blood jetted high over the crowd, a fountain of it. Gary had grown an extra joint at the end of his legs, a curved, scythelike foot that looked perfect for evisceration.

She looked back down at the brain. It was trying to tell her something. She felt a strange weight in her left hand. It felt heavy, as if it were being pushed downward. She frowned. What the hell did the brain want? She could reach into the pockets of her sweatshirt, just as she had done while she watched Ptolemy's execution. She reached in and felt something soft and hairy. She drew it out of her pocket.

Oh. OK. They had taken the green sword away from her, as they had stripped her of all her weapons. They had left her the noose and the withered piece of matted fur Mael Mag Och had once worn as an armband.

Sarah, he said, as she ran the fox fur between her fingers. **I didn't really expect you to make it this far. I suppose I didn't expect you to fail, either. Though some things run in families, alas.**

"Hello," Sarah said. "You must be Mael Mag Och. I've heard all about you but I don't think we've been properly introduced."

The voice that roared its reply into Sarah's head held a trace of regret. Or maybe she was just imagining it. **If I had come to you in my own shape you would have run away from me. I pretended to be Jack because I knew it was a name to conjure with, lass. Does it really matter so much? I still gave you your gift.**

"Why?" she asked. "Why did you do that? Why did you do any of this? Did I really need another parent who was just going to disappear on me at the worst possible moment?"

It was Nilla's notion, to be honest. The blond lass you saw vanish out yonder.

"I've never heard of her."

Ah, Mael Mag Och said, **and yet she's heard all about you. The daughter of the lost hero, turned out in a foreign**

land to be raised by warriors, made strong and fierce. Her heart went out to you, lass, and where Nilla's involved, my heart goes there, too. She and I have much in the way of history, and I owe her a significant debt.

"I refuse to believe you did anything out of the goodness of your own heart. You planned this—all of this. I half believe you got Ayaan captured just so I would come chasing after her and end up right here."

All too true, he admitted. **Yet incomplete. The entire world does not revolve around you, Sarah. I had plans for the others as well. Ayaan was supposed to assassinate the Tsarevich for me. She was the perfect candidate, I thought. Once he was dead I could take over his empire, seeing that I was the only one capable of controlling his undead army. That didn't work out. You were my backup plan, and you failed as well. It is supposed to be me who triumphs today, not his Majesty the undying deformity. Didn't I tell you to bring an army? Instead you brought a handful of mummies and one twisted freak.**

"My freak seems to be doing all right for himself," Sarah said, turning around to watch Gary plow through a line of ghouls. His bony frame had grown considerably while she spoke with the brain, until he resembled nothing so much as a giant spider with a tiny human skull perched atop its carapace.

The werewolf came at him, claws on hands and feet flashing through the air. Gary stabbed downward with a bony tail like a scorpion's sting that penetrated deep into the earth. Erasmus rolled to the side and came back up to slash at one of Gary's tree-trunk legs. Gary knelt forward under the pressure, and Erasmus tried to scamper up onto his back, his clawed feet digging into Gary's bony carapace to find purchase.

A toothy mouth opened in Gary's side. Lips studded with bony spikes grabbed at Erasmus's left arm and the teeth sheared it clean off. Erasmus howled in agony as his furry body pinwheeled down to the ground while the giant mouth chewed the werewolf's limb into pulp. A dozen thin spines lanced down from Gary's body to impale the werewolf in as many places. Erasmus didn't get back up.

"See? Look at that," Sarah crowed, excited.

Ah, the druid said, **our Gary. He's a scrapper, I'll allow you that much. Yet the only thing he believes in is the integrity of his own hide. He'd never take on this fight if he was in any danger. And unless I miss my guess, your Ayaan is about ready to strike.**

"What are you talking about?" Sarah demanded. The mummy holding the brain inclined her head and Sarah pivoted around to look where she indicated. She just had time to see Ayaan crest a pile of boulders high up on the ridge wall to the south. Sarah looked closer and saw her father on the other side of the pile. He was sitting calmly, his eyes closed, his arms outstretched, the palms of his skeletal hands pointed at Gary.

"No," Sarah said, the syllable meaningless in her mouth. "No, that's not right."

It's a hard world, lass, Mael Mag Och told her. **It has been for twelve years.**

Ayaan grabbed Dekalb's head in both of her hands. He jerked and flexed and tried to escape from her, but he was caught like a fish on a line. Ayaan pressed harder and the skin on Dekalb's head darkened and split like the skin of a rotten fruit. Sarah's father kicked out with his legs but he couldn't seem to hit Ayaan.

Sarah watched in mute horror as her father's face peeled off in long dry strips of skin. The skull underneath glowed with dark energy. The skull flexed and shook and a network of fine cracks appeared over its surface. Shafts of dark energy leaked through the fissures. Darkness burst from empty eye sockets and Dekalb's skull cracked open in a hundred pieces.

Ayaan let the headless body fall forward. She was done. Down on the battlefield, Gary must have felt it right away. He must have realized instantly that he was no longer immune to the attacks of the Tsarevich's army. He made a quick slash at all the ghouls and cultists nearby and then ran for the hills.

Just like that, his attack was over. Just like that he was gone. The green lich sent cultists to chase after Gary, but everyone could see he was retreating.

Sarah had more important things to worry about, of course.

"Daddy," Sarah said. The last thing she'd said to him was that he was a bad parent. He had begged her not to get herself into this mess.

"Daddy," she said again. The brain had enough tact to keep silent.

16.

"IF," THE TSAREVICH said, his voice loud enough to roll around the rocks and bones and echo in the still, cold air, "if there are to be no more of interruptions. Then perhaps it is possible to do this thing."

Some of the cultists were still screaming. All of them had been shouting for help or succor. They fell silent at their lord's command. Those who had been busy before with assembling the machinery around the scaffold and those who had been erecting the two sharp metal spikes at its top got back to work. There were a lot of bodies to be removed from the battlefield, many of them already struggling to get back up, to begin the next glorious phase of their existence.

No one touched Dekalb's headless body. It was just so much dead meat to them. Sarah wanted to go to it, to hold her father's hands one last time, but she knew if she tried to do so the Tsarevich's troops would simply shoot her. There would be no warnings, no second chances. They would kill her. Without her father to protect and heal her she would just die. And then come back.

A sort of convulsion went through her, wracking her body. Her muscles spasmed and her eyes ached. A sob came up out of her throat and threatened to turn into a wail. She was surprised by the emotional reaction. She didn't understand it. It was grief, and she had known she would feel grief, but this just wasn't the time. It wasn't yet time for her to process everything that had happened.

It shook her and shook her until she dropped to her knees and bowed her head and hot tears fell into the dust. It made no sense. She was tougher than this. She shoved her hands in her pockets to try to keep them from trembling. She found the noose and ran it between and around her fingers as if she were making a cat's cradle.

Lass, I feel for you, I do. But I'm the last fellow you should be coming to for comfort. You failed me. You failed all of us.

Sarah shook her head, uncomprehending. "What is so important," she asked, staring into the brain's jar, wanting to reach into the liquid there and shred the gray matter inside. "What is so important that it had to bring me to my father, and then tear him away from me like this? What is so important that Ayaan had to be turned into a monster? Please, Mael Mag Och, help me. Help me understand."

The end of the world, he told her. **What could be more important than the end of the world?**

She stood up, straining her legs to get up off her knees. The mummy holding the jar stood as still as death. A perfect statue, a thing to prop up the jar and nothing more. The mummy didn't react at all when Sarah stumbled forward and grabbed at the jar with her bound hands. She had trouble grasping it so she put her chin down on its top and supported it from beneath with spread fingers. The mummy didn't try to stop her. It didn't even relax its arms—it just stood there, elbows bent, hands extended, waiting for her to put the jar back.

Instead she turned around and started walking. Toward the Source. Toward the event horizon.

What should have been won by strength of arms can still be won by guile, he told her. She ignored him, though she didn't let go of the noose, either. She stepped on a piece of pelvis and nearly fell over but managed to recover her balance.

She took another step and felt the jar grow warm in her hands. The brain inside had no muscles and couldn't spasm, but she could feel its consciousness bashing against the walls of the jar, trying to break free.

Lass! Don't quit on me now. I took a chance with your Ayaan and she quit on me too soon. That's why so many had to die. I'm telling you the full truth, now. Don't make the same mistake she did, not if you value the things I've given you.

Sarah took another step. Another one. A bubble appeared inside the jar and splattered apart against its lid. She felt Mael Mag Och kick at her hands. It was all in her mind, she knew that, but he was fighting her. He didn't want to go any farther in.

"My mother. My father. Ayaan. Jack. All of my parents, all of them dead. Undead. And then murdered. fucking again," she chanted.

I feel I really must protest. Ayaan isn't twice dead, Jack was just a false persona, and your mother—

"You know nothing about my mother! Neither do I! That's the goddamned point!"

She kept walking. The liquid in the jar grew uncomfortably hot. Her chin burned against the hot lid. Her hands ached from his attacks. She took another step and the heat was just too much. She let go and the jar fell away from her. The glass cracked as it struck the carpet of bones. The jar broke apart and half the liquid inside sloshed out. The brain sat in what remained of the jar—a kind of broken-edged cup, half-full of liquid. Steam lifted from between its two hemispheres like a ghostly crest.

Do you think this will kill me? he asked. He sounded quite calm. **There's no point to this, whatever it is you may want, lass. I have as many bodies as I like. I have as many—**

She shoved the noose back into her pocket. She didn't want to hear any more. She watched the brain turn white and shrink down as the liquid bubbled and hissed and frothed. She watched the brain boil in its own juices. That was the point. It made her feel a little better. That was the point.

A mountain of flesh that stank like an unwashed cultist grabbed her around the waist and hauled her up into the air. She didn't scream. Bodily she was carried back to the Tsarevich's camp, most likely to be killed.

Life had a little surprise still in store for her, though. Ayaan was waiting near the scaffolding. Sarah was dumped at the lich's feet. Ayaan helped her stand up.

"You're extremely lucky that the Tsarevich was done with that brain." Ayaan shook her head fiercely. "I hate to play at being the adult and telling you not to meddle in things you don't understand."

"Then don't. And I'll return the favor." Sarah refused to meet Ayaan's eyes.

The two women who had attended Nilla as she approached the Source returned. Their wires led across the valley and up the ridge on the far side. Their faces and hands were covered in a fine powdering of white and yellow dust. A boy with a bucket of water and a ladle ran up to them and let them drink and wash up.

The Tsarevich, still sitting in a wire shopping cart, was wheeled closer to the scaffolding. His head dangled over the side and his knuckles twitched against the bones as he was brought bumping and rattling to the base of the construction.

"This is the master you serve," Sarah said. She lacked the energy to really belabor the point, but she couldn't let it go without comment, either. "The monster's monster."

"He'll be transformed in a moment. If physical beauty is all you look for in a leader then I've taught you poorly." Ayaan sounded pissed. Sarah wondered how far she would have to go to make the lich attack her. If she was doomed, if she had no more chances, maybe it would be worth it. Maybe she could anger Ayaan so much that her former mentor would destroy her so completely her body, or rather her corpse, would be of no use to the Tsarevich.

Sarah's blood went cold at the thought. Not at the thought of becoming a ghoul. At the thought of dying at all. She knew it was just her biology speaking, her ingrained survival instinct, but it didn't seem to matter. Her body didn't want to die, no matter what her mind might decide. It would rebel against her if she tried to commit suicide.

The electronic boxes bolted to the scaffolding started to buzz and the exposed vacuum tubes came to life, glowing a cheerful orange. One of them flared white and then burst into darkness, then another. The cultists were ready for this and switched out the bulbs with remarkable speed. They must have been training for this for months, Sarah decided. Drilling for their one big moment, their contribution to the Tsarevich's ascendance.

Under the power of his own unequal arms, the arch-lich dragged himself up a ladder on the side of the scaffolding. Rung by torturous rung, he hauled himself upward. The air smelled of ozone and real heat was coming off the machinery by the time he reached the top. He waved at the crowd, who cheered in return. Then he threw himself forward, right onto the twin giant metal spikes.

He sank downward with a gurgling scream. The spikes transfixed him. Impaled him. Pure energy rushed through them like water down high-pressure hoses. It flooded into him. Sarah could see it crackling around him like electricity crawling over his skin. His one visible eye went wide with it, his mouth opened in a perfectly round O. A stench of burning hair rushed down off him and flowed across the spectators. Sarah raised her bound hands to her face.

"You can be part of the future, Sarah. You can come with me and build something. Wouldn't that be nice? To stop destroying, to stop killing, and build?" Ayaan was shouting in her ear. Sarah hadn't realized how noisy the little valley had become with all the popping vacuum tubes and crackling skin.

Every bone in the Tsarevich's left arm cracked with a series of pops like muffled gunshots. The skin of his deformed hand flowed and flexed like a piece of rubber under stress. His face was changing shape, its contours shifting, rebuilding themselves.

"You don't have to die today. It will be difficult," Ayaan told her, "but I can convince them. I know I can. I only need you to say yes. I need you to agree to be a part of what we are working for."

Sarah opened her mouth to reply. Then she closed it.

The Tsarevich's mouth was moving, his jaw flexing. It looked like he was trying to say something. His right leg, the short one, flapped like a sheet on a clothesline.

The fingernails on his hand curled and bent around themselves. They split the flesh of his fingertips. His hand tried to close in a fist but the fingers spat out wet, dark sparks. His body twisted and shook and pulsed with noisy explosions. Sarah could only imagine that his internal organs were exploding one by one like potatoes left too long in the coals of a campfire.

Something was wrong. So very, very wrong.

With a wet splash his good eye burst in its socket. The green phantom hobbled forward and tried to smash at the vacuum tubes with his femur staff. There was no on/off switch on the machinery. Energy slashed out at him and he staggered back. He tried again and got knocked back again. It didn't matter, after a moment.

Up on the spikes, the Tsarevich's face split open in a horrible grimace as steam built up inside his head. It shot out of his ears, his nose, his eyes. With a noise of air being sucked into a vacuum his entire body caught fire. He went up like a torch.

17.

THE TSAREVICH'S BODY burned like a log soaked in gasoline. His dry tissues, overloaded by the energy of the Source, hissed and spat and started to break down. A chunk of jagged bone flew from one spasming leg. Patience was standing just below him—it fell on her and cut open her cheek. She reeled back in horror and pain, a scream pushing out of her lungs even as she dropped to her knees to retrieve the bone fragment. She clutched it to her breast like a holy relic.

Above her the Tsarevich's head slumped to one side and fell off. It hit the ground in a splatter of sparks and flame. A lot of people screamed then, and almost all of them moved backward, away from the scaffolding.

At the back of the crowd a male cultist in a blue paper shirt screamed bloody murder, much louder than any of the other spectators at the Tsarevich's grisly demise. Ayaan grabbed Sarah's arm and yanked the girl along behind her as she rushed to see what was going on.

Through a gap in the crowd she could see the screaming cultist, his face a mask of agony. Four spikes of filed bone burst from his chest as a ghoul sank its exposed teeth deep into the back of the cultist's neck.

The dead were attacking the living.

Ayaan shook her head. No, that wasn't acceptable. The ghouls couldn't disobey their orders. Their minds were too simple—they couldn't overcome the Tsarevich's command. The Tsarevich was keeping them under control.

The Tsarevich was dead.

A new ghoul, one of Gary's victims, came stumbling through the crowd, her face and hands bright red. She grabbed at Sarah but the girl twisted away. Ayaan swiveled around on one boot heel and blasted the ghoul's face with dark energy. The undead features cracked and peeled away from smoking bone. Ayaan didn't bother to watch her die a second time. "Are you all right?" she demanded.

Sarah nodded unhappily.

Enni Langstrom, the green phantom, appeared at Ayaan's elbow. "Enough of the concern for her well-being," he shouted over the screams. "Just kill her already!"

"No," Ayaan said, "no, that's unnecessary. She's harmless."

Enni shook his head. "She came here to kill him. Now he's dead. You can call it a coincidence if you want but I want her dead. Jesus Christ, look at this! This is Armageddon. We can sort out who did what later. Just kill her. Where's Erasmus?"

Ayaan frowned. "Didn't you see? Gary ate half of him. He's dead. I'm sorry, I know you two were friends."

The skull-like face turned even paler than usual. "Then it's just you and me. We have to save as many of the believers as possible. They served him well, they don't deserve to die like this, not in this place." He stared deep into Sarah's eyes and grabbed her face in one thin hand. "Anyone we can't trust dies, now. I'll let you do it, but kill her! She's an unknown factor. She could ruin everything." He knocked Sarah into the dust with a backhand slap. Then he stomped away, his femur staff clicking on the rocky ground. As he moved through the crowd he touched each ghoul he passed and they slumped to the earth, the life force drained out of them.

Ayaan wasn't sure what to do. She had turned on Sarah and all of her past. She had found a new cause to believe in. Yet if the Tsarevich was dead, who would rebuild the world? What was she giving her allegiance to? If Enni could remake the world and save the human race, if she truly believed he had it in him, then she had no choice but to obey and kill Sarah.

Langstrom didn't have the ability. She knew it.

She grabbed Sarah's bound hands and helped her stand up. There were ghouls everywhere, their eyes dead, their lipless mouths open wide. "He's not a good man," she shouted into Sarah's face. "But I saw him show compassion once, for some people who were barely even human. I don't like betraying him, but that's what it's come to." She tore at the knots that held Sarah's hands. Her fingers were too dead and clumsy. She gasped in frustration—then realized that the rope was made of organic fibers. Careful not to damage Sarah in the process, she fed a little of her energy into the rope and it withered in place until it was so thin and insubstantial Sarah could just pull her hands apart.

Sarah rubbed at her wrists for a moment—they had chafed so much she had bled a little—then threw her arms around Ayaan and held her tight.

"I didn't expect a hug from the girl who crossed half a continent just to put a bullet in my head," Ayaan said, laughing a little.

"When I do it, when I sanitize you, it will be an act of love," Sarah muttered. "Can we not talk about it now? We have a mini-apocalypse to worry about."

It was true. There were hundreds of ghouls in the valley and perhaps half as many living cultists. The ratio was getting steeper with every second. Enni was cutting swaths of destruction through the undead forces, but he was just one lich. The cultists were fighting back and their firearms filled the air with noise but they were disorganized and as much danger to one another as they were to the ghouls—especially since the latter were all wearing bulletproof helmets.

It had all happened so quickly—the instant the Tsarevich had perished the ghouls had become their own creatures again. They had reverted to their violent, mindless selves and once again succumbed to their terrible hunger.

If someone didn't get the situation under control it was going to be a massacre. Ayaan led Sarah over to the flatbed and crawled up on top of it. "This way," she shouted, and at least a few of those still alive in the valley heard her and looked up. "Come on, retreat, out the way we came. Come on!" she shouted it again and again, as loud as her undead lungs would let her.

A teenage boy broke from the crowd and ran toward the flatbed. Ghouls chased after him but they were slow and clumsy without Enni's power behind them. The boy ran right past the flatbed and into the pass beyond, back the way they'd come. The road was down there. If he could find it, maybe he would survive long enough to find some shelter.

It was the best solution Ayaan had. "Come on," she shouted again. "Fall back!"

One by one the living broke away from the dead, their legs pumping, their eyes wet with horror and shock. They had been promised so much. Now they had to start over again, from scratch, in a country few of them had ever seen before. "This way," Ayaan screamed. It was better than being eaten alive.

A band of ghouls came at the flatbed but Sarah was ready. She brought the heavy machine gun around and cut them to pieces before they could climb aboard.

Ayaan kept shouting even when the flow of living cultists had all but stopped. When she realized she was just wasting her breath she looked and saw that the valley was full of nothing but ghouls. They faced her like a ragged army, their helmets shading their eyes, their wicked arms held at their sides. She had stolen their prey. And yet it wasn't her they wanted. Enni stood in the midst of them. He had lost his staff somewhere. His hands lifted and swung at the air as he tried to dampen the ghouls' energy, but he was clearly exhausted. He had used up everything he had, and even while the Source was radiating life energy from no more than a thousand yards away he was about to collapse.

One of the ghouls came up behind him and swiped at his back. The sharpened bone of its arm tore off a strip of green cloth. Two more ghouls flanked him, coming at him from the sides. He couldn't seem to resist them in even the most basic way. They tore his robe from him in rags.

Exposed to the air, his emaciated body was as white as bleached bone. He looked like something carved out of soap. He had big ears that had always been hidden before by his cowl, at least in Ayaan's experience. He had a few long strands of hair plastered to his otherwise bald head.

He turned, his body swooning backward, to look at Ayaan. She couldn't read his eyes. Then the ghouls fell on him and tore him to pieces. Sarah fired wildly into the seething mass of bodies but there were just too many of them.

"Why are they attacking him?" Ayaan demanded. "He's already dead!"

When it was over, the ghouls fell back out of Sarah's range and stood in an orderly formation like soldiers in a parade. It didn't make any sense. There was no one around to control them, no lich who could command them. Their attack on the living had been predicated on that simple fact. Now that the living were gone they had nothing to command their attention. Yet there was no reason for them to line up like that, either, just as there had been no possible explanation why they should attack Enni.

A voice sounded from atop the scaffolding. "The stench up

here," it intoned, its timbre watery and barely recognizable as human speech, "is bloody awful."

A single ghoul stood there above the twin spikes. It was one of the most horrifying creatures Sarah had ever seen. Its skin hung off its chest in long, tattered strips that fell across its groin like a gruesome kilt. Its face was a smudge of once-human features that had been battered and burned out of all recognition. Its legs, thick and muscular, were covered in sores and lesions. It had no arms whatsoever, just ragged ends of flayed bone that hung down like tiny, broken wings.

18.

"HELLO, LASSES," THE armless ghoul choked out. It laughed at them, a sputtering, horrible noise. "Honestly, I am glad to see you both still with us."

All that remained of the Tsarevich were a few lumps of indistinct meat skewered on the steel spikes, fuming and smoking as they smoldered away to black carbon.

"I want you to know that I never wanted anyone to suffer." He staggered closer to the edge of the scaffolding. Another step and he would fall onto the spikes.

"Mael Mag Och, I presume," she said.

The ghoul flexed the ragged nubbins of bone he possessed in place of arms. "In the flesh."

"What's going on here?" Ayaan shook Sarah's shoulder but Sarah didn't know how to answer. "What happened to the Tsarevich? The machinery was supposed to heal him! It was supposed to make him whole again. What went wrong?"

Mael Mag Och shrugged. It made the skin of his chest split and peel. "The machinery worked just fine, lass. Or at least it would have, if I'd let it."

"You? You killed him?" Ayaan was nearly shrieking. Sarah wished she would calm down. "How is that possible?"

"It helps to have friends on the inside."

"Nilla," Sarah said, getting it.

He tried to smile but the remains of his mouth merely twitched. "His plan required her to condition the energy of the Source. To step it down to a level his bodily tissues could accept. At my command she merely fed him an extra little jolt."

"But why?" Ayaan demanded. "Why did you do this? Why did you kill him?"

"Sarah knows," he told her. Sarah bit her lip. She had a feeling she did know, and it terrified her. When Gary had told her about Mael Mag Och she'd thought of him as a laughable sort of visionary. Someone stuck in the mind-set of the Dark Ages. That was, of course, before he'd gotten his hands on the ultimate power of the life force itself.

He wanted to end the world. Finish ending it, anyway.

"So I was saying that I never wanted this to be such a *difficult* transition. You should ask Gary sometime, Sarah. He would tell you, I'm sure, just how much compassion I still had in my heart, back in those all-too-brief days when I still had one to call my own. A heart, that is. How I wanted to make things easy on you. All of you survivors. Instead you chose bloodcurdling violence and pain."

"We chose nothing," Ayaan spat. "What are you talking about?" She leaped down from the flatbed and took a few steps toward the scaffolding. The ghouls moved toward her just as quickly. She had watched them tear Enni Langstrom to pieces. She took a step back.

Mael Mag Och acted as if nothing had happened. "It's a hard lot to be a raw consciousness stripped of form and left spinning in the void. If it made me a bit cranky, well, I do apologize."

Ayaan grabbed Sarah's arm tight enough to hurt. "What is it, Sarah? What does he want? What is he going to do?"

She struggled to find the best words. "His God told him to destroy the human race. Like, all of it. I think he's going to do something to the Source. He's going to collapse it—make it stop altogether somehow."

"Very good," he told her. "The Source is a hole in the side of the world. Imagine a balloon with a tiny little pinprick in it. Imagine the air coming out, just a little at a time. Enough to keep the likes of you upright, that's all. Now imagine what happens if you let all the air out of the balloon at once."

Ayaan shook her head in disbelief. She'd seen what had happened to the dead who got too close to the Source. If enough of that energy was released at once, how much damage could it do? Plenty, she decided. "You'd kill everything. Animals, plants, trees, people. Everything."

"Hmm. It is a pity about the trees. But I've been given a mission. If I'd had a bit of help from the start maybe things wouldn't have come to so drastic a pass. I asked Gary for his help and the buggering bastard ate my head. I asked the Tsarevich and instead he turned himself into the king of the blighted world. I asked you," he said, the clouded orbs of his eyes burning as he stared at Ayaan, "and you spat in my face."

Sarah put her hands over her mouth. She couldn't believe this.

"Ah, yes, I asked young Sarah as well, though I was a trifle dishonest about things. She was the only one who actually tried to help me. Too bad she was such an ineffectual little child. In the name of the father of tribes himself, lass, did you honestly expect to fight an army with a couple of mummies? I'm fond of the Egyptian folk, I truly am, but they're crap against modern weaponry. You really missed the point."

"You've been planning this all along," Sarah said, dumbfounded. "You wanted me to kill the Tsarevich. You tried to get Ayaan to kill him, too. So you could take his place. You put the idea into his head in the first place that he could come here and heal himself. Because this is where you needed to be. How long have you been playing this game?"

"Since your Gary slaughtered me, since I realized how silly it was to think I could finish humanity one at a time. Since I realized it would take cunning, not main force. You have no notion, lass, of how many snares I've laid and schemes I've hatched to get us here."

"And my gift, my special vision?" Sarah demanded. "That was all part of your plan?"

"No, no, lass, that was Nilla's idea, you've her to thank. She took pity on you, a soft wee bairn in the hands of such rough folk. So just as I had helped your father I helped you. And just like the geezer, you were a complete and utter failure. He couldn't kill Gary though he was given *years* to pull it off. You couldn't do anything right. If I ever wanted for proof that humanity is too far gone for saving, well, you've provided it in full, lass."

Sarah's cheeks burned with her blood. She had failed everyone. She had failed so many times over. And now . . . and now . . . the enormity of what was about to happen was impossible. She started to faint. She could feel herself spontaneously losing consciousness in the face of such a horrible ending to her life, to her rescue attempt.

"And you, Ayaan. I actually held out some hope for you," he said. His voice was tinny and small in Sarah's ears. She was losing it. "We're the monsters," he said to Ayaan. She could barely make out the words. "Why couldn't we please just start acting like it?"

Sarah's eyes fluttered closed and when they opened she was looking at a rocky landscape that belonged to another planet entirely. Maybe Mars. Or Pluto. She saw the mountains around her and the blue sky and the white puffy clouds. She saw the valley stripped of its carpet of bones. The mountains were naked, totally devoid of trees, of underbrush, even of the patchy lichens that mottled the highest peaks. There were no birds in the air. No fish in the sea. No bacteria. Not even a virus. The air itself had become poison to her—with no plants there could be no oxygen. She started to choke, to asphyxiate, and then she opened her eyes again.

Nothing had changed. She had just become so painfully aware of what was about to transpire that she had seen it. Call it pretraumatic stress disorder. She had literally seen the lifeless world to come. And it was all her fault.

"Good night, ladies," Mael Mag Och said. Sarah expected him to throw himself down on the spikes as the Tsarevich had done. He didn't, though. The vacuum tubes lit up of their own accord. The air hummed with power. Mael Mag Och screamed so violently the noise must have shredded his borrowed throat. Then he threw his head back and his spine went rigid. Power, raw energy, neither dark nor light, just powerful, crackled across his skin and leaked from his eyes, his mouth, the center of his chest. Laughing as his nervous system lit up with the clear fire of it he turned—and walked right past the event horizon of the Source. Flames whooshed to life on his shoulders and his back but he was not consumed, not as he should have been. He simply walked off, toward the center of the Source. Nilla, Sarah realized, must be protecting him somehow. Sheltering him at least partially from the dreadful energy at the center of the world.

Sarah turned to Ayaan. What could they do? There was nothing they could do. The scaffolding was out of machine gun range. If they tried to rush the scaffolding on foot, the remaining handless ghouls would slaughter them before they could cover half the distance. Even if they could get to Mael Mag Och, what would they do then? Shoot him, when he could just flit from body to body as often as he liked? It was over. In a moment the life force would be released, dispersed, whatever. It would be gone. That life force was the only thing that kept any human body together. It held the pattern of evolution that told her cells how to grow and kept all the pieces working with each other. When it was gone Sarah's cells would turn against themselves, cannibalizing each other for what little golden energy remained stored inside them. In a matter of minutes they would fade out of existence altogether, depleted of the raw mainstay of life. Ayaan would merely collapse. She would fall forward on her face and be truly, finally dead. Sarah would have just enough time to watch that before the cells that made up her eyes devoured each other and she went blind. Before the cells of her brain ate their own memories and thoughts and feelings.

Ayaan leaned forward and kissed Sarah on the cheek. "I've missed you," she said. She had a trembling smile on her lips.

"I've missed you, too," Sarah said. She wasn't crying. She thought she should be crying but the tears wouldn't come. Maybe she was just too scared.

Ayaan reached into a pocket of her jacket and took something out. Something small and silvery. It looked half-melted. "Here," she said, and put it in Sarah's outstretched hand. "I don't suppose it makes much difference now, but I was supposed to give this to you." Sarah closed her fingers around its sharp edges, its smooth curves.

Why, hello, someone said inside her head. Someone pleasant and female. **I've been waiting for you.**

24.

"THEY'RE OUT OF range," Ayaan said, leaning over the edge of the flatbed. She had tried, with no success, to engage the army of ghouls that waited below them. Every time they made a move to come down off the flatbed, the dead men with their sharpened arm bones and their lipless grins would take a step closer. Every time Sarah moved toward the machine gun they would take a step back. "It's a stalemate." Not that it mattered. The world was going to end any second.

Sarah clutched the half-melted nose ring in her fist.

You look scared, Nilla said. **That's the first thing we need to fix.**

"Of course I'm scared." Sarah sat down on the deck of the flatbed and watched Mael Mag Och's stolen body dwindle in the distance. "You're part of this," Sarah said, her voice very high. "Without you he couldn't be doing this."

That's true. Listen, there are better ways for us to talk. Close your eyes.

"Are you kidding?" Sarah demanded. "Now?"

Nilla wasn't kidding. **Just close your eyes. It won't make things any worse.**

That was fair enough. Sarah's blood was racing too fast to let her truly relax, but she leaned back against the machine gun's pintle and forcibly closed her eyes.

Instead of darkness she saw bright white light. It filled her head and stroked her brain. It calmed her down and slowed her breathing.

"You're inside the Source, sort of," Nilla said. She came forward out of the center of things and moved toward the edge without walking or passing through any kind of space. "Or maybe this is its shadow."

Sarah blinked and everything changed. She found herself sitting on a landscape of bones. Heaps of bones, piles of them. Unlike the bones that littered the valley of the Source, this bonescape went on forever. Or at least as far as she could see. The hills and rises of bones before her were obscured by a thin, brownish red mist. Sarah turned around and saw she was standing ankle-deep in a pool of bright red liquid. Blood. She looked down at her reflection and saw that she, herself, had been skeletonized. She could see her bones, picked clean of all her soft tissues. Her hands were bony claws, her body defleshed, her sweatshirt draped over her pelvis and rib cage. She looked up and saw Nilla come toward her. Nilla was nothing but a skeleton as well. A skeleton dressed all in white.

Sarah had no idea what was going on.

"When we die, our bodies decay. You've seen plenty of that," Nilla explained. She took Sarah by the humerus and led her around the curve of the lake of blood. "Our personalities, though, and our thoughts, our feelings, all of the electrical patterns in our brains, don't just disappear. They're stored here, in what he calls the *eididh*. It has lots of other names, too: the Book of Life, the Akashic Records, the Monobloc, the Omega Point. Gary called it the Network. He imagined it as a kind of Internet with human souls instead of packeted data."

"It's all written down and stored forever?" Sarah asked.

"Not exactly. This place is outside of time. There's no storage. Here all of your thoughts and memories and beliefs are all still happening. All of them you ever had—and all of them you ever will have. If you know how you can read them."

"What about his memories and ideas?" Sarah asked. "The Druid's, I mean."

Nilla nodded. Her skull swayed back and forth on top of her spine. It was impossible, there were no integuments or sinews holding it on, but somehow the skull didn't fall off the vertebral column. The bones made a squeaking noise as they moved, that was all. "Yes. His personality is here. It's what you're looking at. None of this," she said, and waved a bony hand at the bony world, "really exists. It's simply how he imagines the network."

"We're inside his soul, then. You've seen his soul. So you must know he's crazy," Sarah tried.

"I've seen his visions here. They're here and they're real. I've seen the father of tribes at the bottom of his bog. He's never lied about that—he really did see what he claims he saw. If you want me to stop him because he's insane, you'll have to convince me that what he saw was less true than what you're seeing right now."

Sarah's rib cage flexed in despair. "So you believe him? You believe that he should kill everyone just because some moldy old god told him to? You think that gives him a right?"

"I think he's a monster," Nilla said, and her skull turned toward the sky. There was a moon up there, directly above them. It was, of course, an enormous skull. Sarah got the idea that it was Mael Mag Och's skull. "But I don't see how else this should end. I mean, what's more important than the end of the world? I'm sorry, Sarah. I hate saying that, it just sounds mean. But it's true. The only way the dead can get any peace is if the Source is collapsed."

"Bullshit!" Sarah leaped up and down in her rage. "I refuse to accept that!"

"Relax, Sarah. Won't it be such a relief not to have to fight anymore? I can tell you from personal experience. Death is no biggie. You come here and you spend eternity with your own memories."

"And your own guilt?" Sarah demanded.

"Yeah, there's some of that, too. But I know what I'm talking about. Before Mael taught me how to access this place I was a mess. I had massive brain damage and I couldn't even remember my real name. Now I'm back in touch with my life. It was a good life, if a little short, and I'm grateful. That's what I owe him."

"And me?" Sarah said, grabbing for Nilla's ulna. "What do you owe me? Why did you bring me here?"

"You were so upset. I thought it might help if I showed you the other side. It's so calm here. Peaceful. But maybe you don't see it that way—you're still alive, so maybe this place is scary to you."

It wasn't. That was the weird thing. Standing on the edge of a lake of blood, watched over by a moon that was nothing but a giant grinning skull, Sarah did feel the peace, the tranquility. The permanence of the boneworld gave it a certain kind of security. Nothing would ever happen there—which meant nothing bad would ever happen there.

Nilla touched her jawbone with slender phalanges. "You can go back now, if you like. I won't hold you against your will. Or you can stay with me and just . . . wait it out."

Sarah thought about it. She was going to die in just a few minutes anyway. Would it be easier if she just stayed there in paradise or whatever it was? She kicked at some of the bones at her feet and a fine powdery dust blew up, the dust of bones so old they had been worn down by eternity and yet still something remained. Her own memories were in that dust, in a very real way. Everybody's were. Some of her memories concerned Ayaan. Ayaan was back in the real world. Would Ayaan think she was being abandoned? Sarah dug in the bone meal with her hallux. The dust brought up memories, random memories, but literally—as she stirred the dust her brain cast itself backward on days of her life. The day she had ridden a camel with the Bedouins. Wow, that had been a good day. The day her father had told her she was going away to boarding school in Switzerland and she cried because she was afraid of all the white girls with their straight hair. The day Ayaan had first let her hold a pistol. The first time Jack had asked her what was more important than the end of the world.

"Wait," Sarah said.

"There's not much else I can do in here but wait," Nilla told her. "And in another sense there's no such thing. What's on your mind?"

"You asked me, what's more important than the end of the world?"

Nilla nodded. "Mael says that all the time. It's like his mantra or something. I've been over it a million times and I've never come up with an answer. There is nothing more important than the end of the world. I mean, really, how could you top apocalypse?"

"Only a dead person would think that." They couldn't change, the dead. Her father couldn't understand she had grown up. Ayaan couldn't accept that she'd become an abomination. Jack—or Mael—couldn't see that his old God was dead. For a living person, of course, the answer was easier than the question. Ayaan had shown her as much, by way of example. By the example of her entire life and also by recent events.

Her father had shown her the answer the day he'd left her behind. The day he'd turned her over to the Somalis and asked them to care for her.

In their own self-serving ways, Gary and even Marisol had demonstrated the truth of the answer. Every survivor, everyone who had lived through the Epidemic, had shown her the answer. The whole living world was the answer. It had been for twelve years.

"The next day." The only thing more important than apocalypse was what you did afterward. What you chose to do when the world stopped making any kind of sense.

"The next day," Sarah repeated. "That's the answer. The one thing more important than the end of the world is the next day."

"Seriously?" Nilla asked.

"Yes. Even if the world ends. Even if everything goes to hell— you still need to keep living. You have to get up, dust yourself off, and rebuild."

"I didn't think of that," Nilla told her. "We should go back." The *eididh* itself bent and curved around her. Sarah was pulled sideways through space and time and plunked down on the flatbed, right where she'd been before. Ayaan was there, and all the ghouls. Except none of them were moving. Sarah looked down and saw that her flesh was back, though she wasn't breathing.

"I've stopped time for a few seconds, at least time as you perceive it," Nilla said. She stood beside Sarah, perfectly clean and enfleshed in her white clothes. Where she sat, Sarah was at eye level with Nilla's belly button, which was surrounded by a black sunburst tattoo. She looked up and saw Nilla looking down at her. "We have no time left to waste. You'll need the relics. The Tsarevich knew that Mael was up to something and he figured out the right spell to truly trap him in that jar. He sent his best lich to collect them—Amanita, I'm sure you remember her. She was after the three items he needed to really bind Mael. Then you beat her to them. That was a really good thing, Sarah. It's going to save us now. Go. You have to catch him and bind him before he reaches the Source!"

Nilla disappeared and time started up again. Sarah looked at Ayaan, who just looked confused. Then she jumped down from the flatbed and started running toward the event horizon of the Source.

20.

A FEW GHOULS chased her, but she was faster and she passed the boundary before they could even come close. Her feet stumbled constantly on the broken bones that littered the valley floor, but she kept running. Once she tripped and fell forward, her hands reaching out for solid ground, a jagged end of femur looming up toward her face. Somehow she managed to roll back up to a standing position.

It was not difficult to find Mael Mag Och. His body was burning, although not as quickly as it should. A thin reef of smoke hung in the air where he passed, a semivisible trail for her to follow. He was moving slowly, his undead body unable to hurry, and the way was difficult. Sarah figured she had a good chance of catching him, but then what? How was she supposed to bind him?

I'll show you, when the time comes, Nilla said inside her mind. Sarah nearly fell over—she'd forgotten the half-melted nose ring in her hand. She'd forgotten she could still talk to the blond lich.

"When he reaches the Source, what will he do?" she asked.

Hopefully it won't come to that, Nilla told her. **If it does—he'll step right into the middle of it, into its center. Even I won't be able to protect him then, but it won't matter. His body will disintegrate but his consciousness will merge with the life force itself—not just the Source, not just the rupture, but the biological field of the planet itself. At that point there's not much he _won't_ be able to do. He'll have more power than his Teuagh ever dreamed of.**

"You're right," Sarah said. "Hopefully it won't come to that."

Ahead of her, maybe a quarter mile up the slope, she could see Mael Mag Och. Flickering light touched his shoulders and his head. It was too much to hope that his brain would boil in his skull. Even if his body failed, he could merely grab another from the mob of handless ghouls back by the flatbed. She pushed ahead, pulling herself up the side of a mountain, clutching at spines and skulls and arm bones, pushing herself bodily up the hill.

The relics will allow you to bind him to this body, Nilla said. **It's why the Tsarevich wanted them so badly. Then you can destroy him, and it will be over. He'll be destroyed. Even the part of him that still resides inside of Gary will be drawn out and dissipated.**

Sarah panted and sweated and cursed as she moved higher, up into thinner air. It was hard to breathe. She could see very little, her eyes dazzled by the light of the Source. She put her arm over a knob of rock and hauled herself up and there she was, on top of the valley. She saw the eroded sculptures of dinosaurs, sunlight streaming through the chicken wire–lined gaps in their plaster. She saw the low buildings, which had collapsed over twelve hard winters.

At the center of it all, where the Source was so bright it made her head throb, an honor guard waited for Mael Mag Och. Two skeletons, held up by nothing but pure energy, stood there on either side of the singularity. They were like something from the vision of the *eididh* she had shared with Nilla, and yet perversely horrible at the same time, as she had come to expect things to be in reality. One was nearly human in appearance, or at least he looked like a human skeleton, except that the top of his skull was torn off as if he'd blown it off with a shotgun in his mouth. The serrated edges of his skull made him look like he was wearing a profane kind of crown. The other skeleton—and somehow she knew it was female—was twisted and bent, her bones deformed in some way Sarah didn't recognize. They were pitted and chipped and in places looked like melted wax. Her skull was fused into the top of her rib cage and the bones of her left shoulder. She looked as if she'd slowly melted, a candle left out in the sun.

The skeletons were undead, surely—they were animate, anyway, because they moved as she watched, shifting their weight from foot to foot, raising their hands to beckon the Druid onward—yet their energy was not dark, nor was it bright. It was pure, clear, the unadulterated energy of the planet itself.

Mael Mag Och stepped up before them and they bowed to him, welcoming him to his destiny. Sarah rushed forward as Nilla shouted instructions at her. **Throw the noose over his head.** Sarah did it. Mael didn't even turn around. He was too close to achieving his apocalypse. **Place the armband on his—on his stump.** Sarah did it.

Now. The sword.

Sarah remembered she didn't have the sword. She still searched her belt, her back, but she knew she didn't have it. "The Tsarevich's people took it from me."

You need to pierce him with the sword. It's the only

way to keep him from jumping to another body. The sword, Sarah. The sword.

"I don't have it! I don't even know what they did with it."

Nilla was very close to her, physically nearby. Sarah could feel the disappointment in the air. The fear, and the failure.

"There has to be another way," Sarah said. But of course there wasn't.

There is.

Mael Mag Och had finished with the skeletons. Whatever passed between them was not for Sarah's ears. The Druid walked past them, into the wreckage of the buildings. The skeletons closed ranks—they would not let Sarah pass.

There is a way. It's so simple. He needs me to shield him from the Source. I can't stop doing that, any more than you can stop breathing. But I can make myself visible.

"What?"

Nilla's voice was very soft. **I'm only able to perform this function because of my power, the ability I have to subtract my own aura. If I make myself visible I will be consumed by the Source, just like any other dead thing. Mael Mag Och will lose his protection and his body will be destroyed. I think his consciousness will be trapped here, since all the possible bodies he could inhabit are too far away. Does that make sense?**

Sarah's body shook. "I can't—I can't ask you to do that," she said, but she knew that if Nilla refused she could, in fact, ask, she would beg her to do it. She would threaten her, plead, beg. "But you'll die!"

I died a long time ago, Nilla said. **It's OK. I've got my memories.**

It happened so fast, then.

Nilla appeared before Sarah, beautiful, blond, dressed all in white. There was a sad smile on her face. She erupted in a column of flame, instantly. Sarah could only hope there was no pain. Even her bones burned, reduced in a second down to nothing but ash.

The skeletons didn't move. From beyond their barrier Sarah heard a single, throttled scream and saw another burst of fire. She rushed forward. The skeletons held her back but she could see Mael Mag Och's body burn as fast as Nilla's had. Perhaps even faster.

21.

BANNERS OF FLAME licked at Mael Mag Och's ashes. The skeletons waited for a moment, then parted, allowing her past if she so chose. She could have the energy of the Source if she wanted it, they were telling her. If she possessed the faculties to manipulate it. If she knew how, she could undo everything. She could lay the dead to rest and make the world green again. If she knew how.

She didn't, and there was no one left to teach her.

She turned around and headed back to the flatbed in the valley below.

"What did you do?" Ayaan demanded when she arrived.

Sarah couldn't seem to get the words out. She could only point. Her finger stabbed out toward the mass of ghouls that had been waiting patiently in perfect formation for the world to stop. Now they were moving, surging forward as a mass. They were headed for the event horizon. Sarah had an idea why. Mael Mag Och was trapped, just as Nilla had suggested. He could project his consciousness a certain distance to take another body, but all the available bodies were too far away.

"What did you do?" Ayaan asked again. She grabbed Sarah by the arms and shook her.

Sarah looked up into her mentor's face. "I answered a question," she said. "They asked me what was more important than the end of the world, and I told them."

Ayaan released her. "What could be more important . . . ?"

The ghouls marched right into their own destruction. As each of them reached the event horizon he or she was consumed, utterly.

"You stopped him, I take it," Ayaan said, very quietly. "That . . . that's good," she said. The smoke from the burning dead stained the air around them and the stink was oppressive.

Eventually there were none of them left.

"It's over," Ayaan announced. "Come on, let's get out of here." She jumped down from the flatbed and headed for the pass that led down toward the road.

"I just have a couple of things to do," Sarah said. "You stagger along. I'll catch up."

Ayaan frowned at that but she could hardly deny that Sarah could walk a lot faster. She shrugged and headed down the path.

Sarah pulled Gary's tooth out of her back pocket. "Are you watching this?" she asked. "He's out of bodies. He's trapped inside the Source. I don't know if that counts as killing him or not, but he's powerless now."

I don't think you can kill him anymore. Believe me, I've tried. As for being powerless—don't make the mistake of underestimating him. I've got part of him inside of me. He likes to taunt me and call me names. He's still there. You've stopped him, though, for now. Gary sounded very faint and very far away. Sarah imagined it had to be a trick. He would be somewhere close, holing up and licking his wounds. He didn't want her to find him.

Well. He had good reason.

"Gary," she told him, "there's no one left to heal you. You're not bulletproof any more."

I have a right to exist, he told her.

"I don't recognize that right," she replied.

He was silent for a very long time. **Let's not forget that I helped you out when you needed it**, he suggested.

"And let's not forget you kept my father a prisoner of conscience for twelve years. I'm coming for you, Gary, and I will put you down.

That's what I do. I kill liches." She didn't want to hear his reply. She threw the tooth as far away from her as she could manage. It was lost instantly in the scattered bones of the valley.

Ayaan wouldn't have approved. She would have said that the tooth represented a source of intelligence, that the more Sarah knew about Gary the easier it would be to kill him. Sarah reminded herself, though, that everyone who ever listened to Gary had reason to regret it. He could seduce with words and he could lie with the best of them. Let him fear her. Let him wonder where she was. It would do him good.

That was taken care of, then. Just one more loose end to tie up. She searched the yurt at the back of the flatbed. She found the female mummy waiting for her, her arms still outstretched to take back the jar. Sarah shook her head. "You're free now. Ptolemaeus Canopus died to make you free."

The mummy didn't move. She might as well be dead. Well, she had plenty of time to figure it out on her own. Most likely she wouldn't spend eternity there waiting for the jar to return to her arms, but if she did—it was her own choice. At least somebody had been successfully rescued. Sarah sighed and dug through the various boxes and chests in the yurt until she found what she wanted. Her Makarov PM. She shoved it in the pocket of her hooded sweatshirt and stepped back outside and down from the flatbed.

Ayaan was about two hundred yards away, her back turned to Sarah. It couldn't be that easy, though. Sarah owed Ayaan something more. She jogged to catch up and then tapped the lich on the shoulder.

Ayaan turned around painfully, as if she had a stiff neck. She didn't look at all surprised to see the pistol in Sarah's hand.

She didn't waste any time begging for her life. She had a better argument to make. "When your father was dying I was with him. I was in your position, looking down my sights at a monster. He asked me not to shoot, and I didn't. I think you're probably glad for my decision."

"You just *killed* my father, like, permanently!" Sarah said, blood rushing into her cheeks. "How dare you invoke him now?"

"You had a little more time together. Wasn't that better than nothing? Life is precious, Sarah, and death is eternal. Any reprieve from the void is a good thing," Ayaan said.

"Come on. You're a lich, Ayaan. You're an abomination. What would your God say if he saw you now?" Sarah's hand was shaking. She switched to a two-handed grip and it helped.

"Oh, He sees me just fine," Ayaan said. She closed her eyes and her mouth moved silently for a while. Sarah knew exactly what she was doing. She was praying. When she finished she opened her eyes and looked very calmly down at Sarah. "This is what you've made up your mind to do, then. I will not beg like a dog. If you truly believe you can pull that trigger, then please do so now."

Sarah gasped. She could barely think straight. "It's what you taught me to do."

"I did not," Ayaan said, very slowly, "teach you to talk. I taught you to shoot. I hope you will remember what it takes to kill a lich. I hope you remember how you will have to mutilate my corpse. You will need to smash my head to powder, are you prepared for that? My body should be burned, or crushed with heavy stones."

"You think I can't do it," Sarah said.

"I'm betting on it, actually." Ayaan considered her with a long, cool look. "I think you haven't prepared yourself psychologically for this. I think that you will be haunted by it for a very—"

Sarah squeezed the trigger. The noise of the gunshot bounced off the walls of the valley. When Osman found her, several hours later, she had burned Ayaan's body with gasoline and spread the ashes on the wind. Only the heart remained. It refused to burn. There was no magic in that—a human heart was a hard lump of dense muscle tissue and not very flammable. Sarah held it in her hand when Osman came for her. She was hoping to hear Ayaan's voice in her head. She was hoping that Ayaan had become a ghost like Mael Mag Och.

She was also hoping that nothing of the sort would happen. In that she got her wish.

Osman took one look at the charred organ in her hand and

rubbed his head with his long fingers. "You can't bring that on my helicopter," he said. "No way."

Sarah dug a little hole in the ground near the valley of the Source and buried the heart. It was the closest thing to a grave Ayaan could have. Sarah remembered what Ayaan had taught her about *baraka*, the dangerous blessedness of the Sufi saints. It was said you could invoke *baraka* when you stood by the tomb of a powerful person. Sarah wondered if in some future generation warriors would come to where the heart was buried and from it gather some strength. She left no marker, no gravestone. Those future warriors would have to find the burial place on their own.

She strapped herself into the copilot's seat of the Jayhawk and they lifted up and away. Osman carried her off over a green world, a world of trees and rock and water and no people. An emptied-out world where even the dead were in scarcity. A truly silent, truly haunted place.

It was that kind of planet. It was going to be that kind of planet for a long time to come.

ABOUT THE AUTHOR

DAVID WELLINGTON WAS born in Pittsburgh, Pennsylvania, the hometown of George Romero and therefore the birthplace of the modern zombie. He attended Syracuse University and then Penn State, where he received an MFA in creative writing. He currently resides in New York City.

For more information or to read other works by the author, please visit www.davidwellington.net.

The Internet phenomenon that became the first volume in the hit Monster trilogy

The most developed nations of the world have fallen to the shambling zombie masses. Only a few pockets of humanity survive.

In New York City, the dead walk the streets, driven by an insatiable hunger for all things living. One amongst their hordes is different: though he shares their appetites, Gary Fleck has retained his human intelligence. He is an eyewitness to the end of the world—and perhaps the evil genius behind it all.

From the other side of the planet, a small but heavily armed group of schoolgirls-turned-soldiers has come in search of desperately needed medicine. They think they are prepared for anything. On Monster Island, they will find that there is something worse even than undeath . . . while Gary learns the true price of survival.

Praise for *Monster Island: A Zombie Novel*

"Page by page, the story is inventive and exciting as Wellington exploits his familiarity with New York's nooks and crannies as settings for flesh-chomping battles and narrow escapes. . . . The novel offers some provocative thoughts about the purpose of life and death underlaid with some ultra-dark humor." —*Publishers Weekly*

"This is a zombie novel—a fantastic zombie novel. . . . The questers get ringside seats for some of the apocalypse's finest moments, and no matter how prepared they thought they were, something worse awaits in the depths of New York. . . . There are many layers to this zombie apocalypse, and this book just gets things rolling. Stay tuned." —*Booklist*

Monster Island | Thunder's Mouth Press | 288 pages | $13.95
ISBN-10: 1-56025-850-0 | ISBN-13: 978-1-56025-850-6 | 2006
Available from all chain, independent, and online booksellers

In this prequel to *Monster Island*, Wellington takes us back to where the horror began

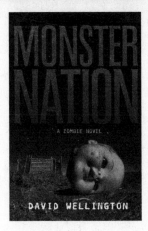

In the heart of America, in the world's most secure prison, something horrible is growing in the dark. A wave of cannibalism and fear is sweeping across the heartland, spreading carnage and infection in its wake. Captain Bannerman Clark of the National Guard has an impossible mission: discover what is happening—and then stop it before it annihilates Los Angeles.

In California, he finds a woman trapped in a hospital overrun with violent madmen. She may hold the secret to the Epidemic but she has lost everything—even her name.

David Wellington's first novel, *Monster Island*, explored a world overcome by horror and the few people strong enough to survive. Here, he takes us back in time to where it all began—to the day the dead began to rise . . .

Praise for the Monster trilogy

"Glorious and grisly. Click over and feast with the undead, you won't be left unsatiated."
                                                            —*Rue Morgue*

"Excellent. It's got all the stuff a zombie aficionado wants . . . plus a lot of welcome surprises that add a level of richness to the genre."
                                                —Mark Frauenfelder, BoingBoing.net

Monster Nation | Thunder's Mouth Press | 304 pages | $13.95
ISBN-10: 1-56025-866-7 | ISBN-13: 978-1-56025-866-7 | 2006
Available from all chain, independent, and online booksellers